The Golden Gardenia

Jan. 17, 2009

Dear Ozzie

This is book #2, a continuation of Gardenia of Love.
I do hope you enjoy it.
Best wishes + love

Leola Hamparian

ALSO BY LEOLA HAMPARIAN:

GARDENIA OF LOVE
(BOOK 1—2005)

The Golden Gardenia

A Novel

Leola Hamparian
Author of *Gardenia of Love*

iUniverse, Inc.
New York Lincoln Shanghai

The Golden Gardenia

Copyright © 2007 by Leola Hamparian

All rights reserved. No part of this book may be used or reproduced by any means, graphic, electronic, or mechanical, including photocopying, recording, taping or by any information storage retrieval system without the written permission of the publisher except in the case of brief quotations embodied in critical articles and reviews.

iUniverse books may be ordered through booksellers or by contacting:

iUniverse
2021 Pine Lake Road, Suite 100
Lincoln, NE 68512
www.iuniverse.com
1-800-Authors (1-800-288-4677)

Because of the dynamic nature of the Internet, any Web addresses or links contained in this book may have changed since publication and may no longer be valid.

This is a work of fiction. All of the characters, names, incidents, organizations, and dialogue in this novel are either the products of the author's imagination or are used fictitiously.

ISBN: 978-0-595-44906-4 (pbk)
ISBN: 978-0-595-69267-5 (cloth)
ISBN: 978-0-595-89229-7 (ebk)

Printed in the United States of America

I would like to dedicate my second book to the memory of all the men, women and precious children who throughout the years became victims of genocide, terrorism or were held hostage.

A lesson in humanity
we need

A lesson in courage
we lack

A lesson in love
only our own?

Leola Hamparian

I would also like to make a very special dedication to the memory of my dear nephew

Mark Haig Safarian

May 27, 1956—October 17, 2005

The Power and The Glory
Forever ... And Ever ... And Ever ...

Once again I would like to thank my daughter Janet for all her help and persistence in helping to complete *The Golden Gardenia*.

Also a special thank you to my daughter Diane for her support and contribution to *The Golden Gardenia*.

The Golden Gardenia

Love and passion, happiness and tears
Hate and remorse, conquering fears
The blooming gardenia, so fragile so white
In death it's just sleeping but something's not right.

Happiness is short, and death is so long
We think we are right, but really we're wrong
The petals don't fall, they just turn to gold
They don't really die, they slowly grow old.

The blooming gardenia, so fragile so white
In death we're just sleeping
Good-bye love—good night.

Leola Hamparian

Chapter One

The sun was just beginning to set as Roberto sat on his horse looking out over the horizon. A ruggedly handsome man with the dark eyes and dark hair so typical of his Spanish ancestry, he sat with a straight and proud bearing that left no doubt of his military background. His ancestry could also be easily traced back to royal nobility. He was a direct descendent of Charles IV, King of Spain.

Now 38 years old and Chief of all the Armed Forces in the Dominican Republic, he was also a very humble person. The many medals he won during the Civil War lay in a drawer back at the Villa instead of decorating his uniform. When asked why he would insist the real heroes were the guerrillas who had lost their lives in the war and that the glory belonged to them. That was ten years ago when he was the young charismatic leader of a band of guerrillas fighting a Civil War in the northern mountains of the Dominican Republic. They were able to free the Country of the corruption that had plagued them and Roberto Enrique Castaneda was hailed as the savior of the people and the Country. He was faithful and he risked his life over and over again proving his dedication to the Dominicanos. They trusted him, his was the voice of freedom and he gave them the strength to believe in themselves and live with pride in there beloved Country. He was there when they needed him and he was their long-awaited liberator. It was because of him the war-torn Country had made a successful transition to normal life.

Dusk was beginning to fall and as Roberto looked out across the ocean towards the horizon, he stood in awe of the vastness surrounding him and he could feel the strong presence of God. He bowed his head and asked forgiveness for the killings he had committed and knew he would have to kill again. "Dear Lord, what kind of world do we live in when we are compelled to kill to survive? We are like animals."

So much had happened in the last ten years. A few changes had been made at the Villa. The manservant Seville who had been hired to replace Raphael seemed perfect for his job. He had excellent references and after a background check, which was a necessity on anyone near or in the Villa, had turned out to be clear, he was hired. Two weeks later he had been dismissed by Ramon while Roberto was away. When Roberto questioned Ramon on his return all he would say was "I just send him away—he not stop staring at Senora Shane."

Roberto was deeply concerned for the future and for his family. He had a premonition that something was about to occur and it left an uneasy feeling inside him. He was now the new leader of all the armed forces in the Dominican Republic but he knew this was no guarantee that his loved ones would be protected. His concern for his children, eight year old Frederik and Enrique, the twins as everyone referred to them and seven year old Camille, was always there. Shane of course was always on his mind. She was still his vision, the love of his life, his soul mate, and he adored her to the point of finding it almost unbearable if she were away from his side for more than 24 hours. If anything happened to her he could not even imagine such a thought.

As he thought of Shane, a smile would light up his face. Just thinking of her had quickly brought him back to the present and he felt blessed. How fortunate for him that Shane had decided to vacation in the Dominican Republic with two of her friends. The first time he saw her was when she arrived at the airport and he had acquired information on who she was before kidnapping her the day before her departure. He knew it wasn't right but he also knew he could not live without this woman who had captivated him.

Now ten years and three children later he had no regrets. Shane was the love of his life and he would do it all over again if he had to. Whenever she would look at him, her green eyes would mesmerize him. He seemed to lose himself and as if this wasn't enough she had the most remarkable porcelain-like skin that never seemed to darken from the sun. In contrast to her jet-black hair, Shane's beauty was truly amazing. She had a wonderful way about her when meeting someone as she portrayed her warmth and sincerity. She was not only admired but also highly respected and Roberto was extremely proud of her.

Carlos Martinez, now that was good reason for concern.

The forty year old had chosen Bolivia to rule as a drug lord taking advantage of the poverty of the Country to become extremely powerful and wealthy. He was also very dangerous. Roberto was fully aware of him and was determined not to let him infiltrate into the Dominican. He would not tolerate the unspeakable terror that Carlos Martinez was capable of and Roberto had seen to it that his men were exceptionally well trained along the border. "Come on Allegro," he said speaking to his horse, "let's get back before they send someone out looking for us."

Roberto turned back towards the Villa. There was no need for anyone to search for him as the beach was patrolled day and night and he passed Damien, one of the bodyguards and waved to him.

"Senora," said the man approaching Shane and removing his hat, "forgive me for being so bold, you are very beautiful …" His words were cut short as Ramon suddenly appeared and shoved his machine gun into the ribs of the startled man.

"Ramon, no!" exclaimed a frightened Shane putting her hand on his arm, "no, please."

The few people standing nearby started to scatter and the man backed up against the counter, sweat breaking out on his forehead. Ramon stared into the man's eyes for a moment, then said in a low voice "desaparecer." The man disappeared like magic.

Shane and Ramon left the store and entered the waiting car. Ramon always sat next to the driver but now he sat in the back with Shane. He knew she was upset but he wanted to make himself very clear.

"Senora, I do not like what happened but I do not apologize. Roberto says Ramon must protect Shane but stand back and I not agree. This is what happens. If I stand closer, this not happen; I tell him when we get back."

"No Ramon, you must not tell Roberto. You know how he is, he will find out who the man is. He will do something, I know he will."

Ramon was right, Shane was very upset.

"Senora, do not worry, the man not do anything. I must tell Roberto, he trusts Ramon with your safety. I not risk losing his trust."

They arrived at the Villa and Shane went up to her room. The twins were away at boarding school in Switzerland and Camille was visiting with her aunt Maria and uncle Skye. She still had an hour before dinner so she changed her clothes and feeling tired, lay on the bed. Would she always have to live this way she wondered. Would there always be a machine gun accompanying her wherever she went? Would the fear of death be in their lives every day? Maybe she was getting paranoid she thought because of the children, and with these thoughts drifted off to sleep.

Shane awakened when she felt something touch her face and she opened her eyes. Roberto had returned from his meeting and lay on the bed beside her, his face against hers. Her arm went around his neck and he held her tightly. For a moment they did not talk then Roberto broke the silence.

"I want to take you away Shane, a holiday. Now would be a good time and I can reschedule anything coming up for the next few weeks. What do you say my little one?"

"I say Ramon has been talking to you, Roberto."

"Yes he did," admitted Roberto, "and I found the incident very disturbing. However, it has been a while since we have gone away together, just the two of us. I know of a place here in the Dominican, very remote, very beautiful, that you would love. It would do us both a lot of good. What do you think Shane, wouldn't this be an ideal time for us?"

Shane turned to look at him. She loved to look into his eyes and remembered a time when she was too frightened to return his gaze, a time when he was a stranger to her. And still, there seemed to be a part of himself that he always kept hidden, something that bothered her and she couldn't quite perceive what it was but every so often it would resurface.

As if reading her thoughts his lips touched hers ever so lightly as he whispered "you'll never know the depth of my love for you, Shane. Just looking at you makes my heart beat faster. I'm so glad that you married me my little one, so happy."

Shane laughed. "As I recall Roberto, I had no choice."

"You had a choice Shane, you could have left. I would however just have to go after you again, you know, kidnapping, locking you in that room, having Raphael serve you your meals and ..." He stopped short not realizing until it was too late, that Raphael's name had come out.

Shane looked startled and Roberto took her hand. He could never forget Raphael. How do you forget your best friend, someone you had grown up with, someone who stayed with you, and faced the horrible atrocities of the war.

Raphael was a good and kind man. His only misfortune was falling in love with Shane and the unfortunate incident that happened in the stable where she had gone looking for him. He had held a weeping Shane in his arms and she would never forget his words, "you are Senora Castaneda and I cannot do this to Roberto, I will not dishonour his wife." His last words to her were, "why did God make you so beautiful? Adios Shane, I will never ever stop loving you."

After Raphael left, life continued on at the Villa as usual as the years went by. Roberto and Shane were kept busy with their three children and the demand on Roberto's time as Chief Commander (Comandante En Jefe) of the armed forces kept them occupied.

They went downstairs together. Both Roberto and Shane knew that it would be a painful period for both of them once they realized that Raphael was gone and would never again live at the Villa.

It was Friday and Rosita had made a very special dinner.

"What's the occasion Rosita or is it just your way of saying you love us?" said Roberto, winking at Shane.

"You don't know what day this is Roberto?" said Rosita, putting another dish on the table covered with pastries.

Roberto thought for a moment and shook his head. "I'm afraid I will be embarrassed, Rosita. I cannot remember, you must tell me."

Rosita smiled, and kissed Shane on the cheek. "It was exactly ten years today that you brought your beautiful bride here to the Villa."

Shane looked surprised, "you remembered, Rosita? How amazing—I was not aware of the date."

"Roberto smiled sheepishly. "A good reason to celebrate, Rosita, let us bring out the champagne and drink a toast."

"What an amazing surprise you did for me that day Roberto. Seeing my parents and brothers meant the world to me."

"And it was my pleasure just to see how your face lit up, my little one." Then with a thoughtful look on his face he continued, "Shane, your friends that were vacationing with you, do you ever hear from them? Did they ever express a desire to come back and visit with us?"

Shane laughed. "They were probably too frightened to come back. Actually, Mary got married a few years ago and last I heard Jodi-Anne, well Jodi we call her, went back to school to become a vet."

"A vet?" said Roberto with raised eyebrows.

"A veterinarian, an animal doctor."

"How interesting," said Roberto. "Invite her to visit us. Would she come? I'm sure you would like to see her."

"I would love to see her Roberto but …"

"What is it Shane, why do you hesitate?" asked Roberto looking at her closely. "Don't tell me I frighten her. Everyone seems to be afraid of me, except for my children, and you of course, my little one—I hope."

Shane laughed and looked at her husband. How could a woman, thought Roberto, as lovely as Shane, possibly become more beautiful after a ten year period. Emerald green eyes fringed with long black eyelashes and a face like an angel was too much for Roberto to bear. He stood up and lifted a surprised Shane in his arms and walked to one of the large windows.

Shane was stunned. She knew that Roberto could be impulsive on occasion but did not expect this right now.

"Roberto, we were discussing Jodi coming here to visit us. What brought this on?"

Roberto just stood there for a moment, then spoke, "Shane, do you remember the day we got married and I called you to the window to see the horizon? Look my little one, it's almost the same. I could see it before us as we sat at the table just now. Jodi-Anne can come whenever she wants but this moment is ours, my love, this gift from the heavens."

Shane smiled, yes the scene was breathtaking, but suddenly she couldn't help but laugh.

Roberto, still holding her in his arms looked at Shane and frowned. "You are laughing at me, my little one, and what is so funny?"

"You, Roberto, you are so funny" she said. "You are an incurable romantic. We were talking about Jodi and you suddenly lifted me from the chair." Shane stopped and laughed again, "and carried me to the window, oh Roberto," she laughed, "please don't be upset with me, but sometimes you are a bit comical."

"Comical?" said Roberto, "comical? I've been called many things but—comical?" he said in bewilderment. "Shane, I am the Chief Commander of an entire army and you find me comical?"

"Roberto, please" laughed Shane, "you are making it worse. I don't intend to make fun, but" and she looked at Roberto who was starting to glare like he would at a disobedient child or a soldier, and she was suddenly hysterical with laughter. Roberto tightened his grip and she felt the pain but this made the situation all the more hilarious and then, she totally underestimated Roberto. It was meant to be a kiss but his anger turned it into a violent kiss as his mouth came down hard on hers, and Shane panicked. He was very strong and she was completely helpless. Was he punishing her? Was this the part of Roberto she did not know? It was like two different men and now this was the stranger holding her.

Suddenly, he pulled away and looked at her.

"You are not laughing at me now, my little one" and there was a pause. "I'm sorry if I hurt you, I did not mean to, it just happened." He sat her down at the table again and poured two glasses of Champagne as if nothing had happened. "Here my love, let's drink a toast to us, and our future."

Shane looked at Roberto with disbelief. She was frightened more than angry and stood up slowly. She started to sway and Roberto caught her arm and she pulled away and looked at him.

"No Roberto, I will not drink to that." Then she stopped and slowly measured her words. "Who are you? I really believe now that I did marry a stranger." She walked out of the room and Roberto sat alone in a state of disbelief.

It was their first real argument since they had been married.

He knew that inevitably his obsession for Shane would some day cause this to happen, but he couldn't help himself. His adoration for this woman was so intense that it was going to ruin his life if he didn't change his ways. Who could he go to for advice? Raphael was out of the question but he would have been the one who understood. Maybe he could talk to Skye. He liked Skye, he was a good brother-in-law but what would he say to him? Skye, I am having a problem with my marriage, I love my wife too much, I adore and worship her, I'll do anything in this world for her. Give me some advice.

Roberto shook his head, Shane was right, he was becoming what was that word, oh yes, comical, that was it, and he had to smile in spite of himself; after all, he was Roberto Enrique Castaneda, Commander-in-Chief of the Armed Forces. Once again, he smiled to himself. Yes, it was comical.

He went upstairs but she wasn't in their room. He quickly went back down and asked Rosita but she hadn't seen Shane.

Outside one of the guards had seen her riding towards the beach—alone. Roberto ran to the stable and quickly saddled and mounted Allegro and was galloping down the beach in search of Shane. Why was she alone? Where was Damien or Ramon? How did he let things get this far? He would order a full investigation in the morning and there would be strict changes made.

Off in the distance a lone figure could be seen. Shane's long dark hair blowing in the wind was unmistakable and Roberto quickly caught up with her and shouted for her to stop. It was like a command but Shane had no intention of doing so. He grabbed the reins of her horse and pulled it to a halt.

"I'm sorry Shane, really I am," he said.

Shane looked at him. She knew he would never plead but there was a look in his eyes that seemed to say forgive me. Her dark hair fell past her waist and her eyes sparkled.

He dismounted and his first instinct was to pull her off the horse and hold her tightly in his arms but he held back. He wanted her to know that he was trying to change. She looked at him for just a moment, then slowly dismounted and took his outstretched hand.

They walked along the beach and talked under the hot sun. A gentle breeze blew around them as the waves hummed endlessly. Finally, they mounted their horses and turned back.

Shane had become an excellent horsewoman through the years and Roberto was proud of her as she sat with confidence in the saddle. They rode back silently aware of the magnetism that always existed between them. When they reached the Villa, Shane went inside while Roberto talked to the guards as they returned the horses back to the stable.

Several calls had come for him and while he returned them, Rosita and Shane planned the menu for the weekend, a time when they did most of their entertaining. The day went by quickly and by the time Roberto went upstairs to retire, Shane was already in bed but awake. He lay down beside her not knowing what to say but she spoke first.

"I should not have laughed at you Roberto, it's my fault and I'm sorry. It was really rude of me."

That was all Roberto needed to hear. He held her in his arms and promised her he would change. "You know better than anyone that I am not perfect, my little one" he said touching her lips gently with his fingers. "How could I hurt someone that I love so much. But you too must promise me something Shane. No matter what happens," and he paused and looked at her in that strange way that he had. "Don't ever, ever—ever leave me like that again. Promise me Shane, promise me, I have to know."

Shane looked at her husband, his voice was stern but there was love and passion in his eyes and she embraced him. "I was not leaving you Roberto; I just had to get away. I'll never leave you, no matter what; I love you too much to do that."

Roberto felt like he had conquered the world. She gave him the strength he needed; she was truly a part of him. Outside a full moon glowed in the sky and far in the distance the cry of a night bird filled the air.

Chapter Two

Shane awoke the next morning to the delicate fragrance of gardenias. Roberto was not there and she sat up and stretched, then suddenly stopped. Bouquets of gardenias were everywhere, on the table, the window ledges, in vases on the floor. It was then she noticed the note pinned to her pillow with a single gardenia attached. She smiled to herself as she opened the letter and read:

My beloved Shane

Words do not exist in Spanish or English that could possibly describe what is in my heart. By dawn tomorrow, this beautiful flower will bow its head and concede defeat to your beauty. It will become a golden gardenia. I too have become the golden gardenia. I will always concede defeat to you Shane because I hold you in my heart forever.

Roberto.

Shane held the gardenia against her cheek as tears rolled down her face. Life was never dull with Roberto and their love had grown more beautiful through the years. Quickly she dressed, brushed her hair and pinned it back with two gardenias. She descended the stairs and found Roberto in the kitchen deep in conversation with Rosita. He quickly got up and went towards her.

"Shane, did you sleep well my little one?" he said with a smile.

"I did Roberto. The flowers are beautiful, thank you, but where, what, how did you do that?"

By now Rosita was getting curious. "Roberto gave you flowers Shane? It was something different? He always brings flowers to you."

"Yes Rosita, you could say different. When you get a moment you must go up to our room and see for yourself. They are really beautiful."

Roberto and Shane sat in the dining room and had breakfast together. They talked about the children and how they missed them. Roberto assured Shane that they would visit the boys in Switzerland and they knew they would see Camille when Skye and Maria brought her back. Camille felt very comfortable with her aunt Maria and uncle Skye and now that her cousin Beatriz was home for a holiday from the private school she was attending, she enjoyed it more. Although Beatriz would soon be sixteen and Camille only seven, the girls were very close and Camille looked up to her older cousin like a sister.

"Where did you find so many gardenias in such a short time?" asked Shane while Roberto poured their coffee, "I didn't hear a sound last night."

Roberto smiled, "I cannot divulge certain secrets to you, my little one. Let's just say I have contacts in very high places. And speaking of high places, I received a call from President Gomez early this morning. A rather serious situation has occurred and he has called a meeting. Nothing for you to be concerned about" he added quickly as Shane looked alarmed. "It is just something that has to be stabilized as soon as possible—actually certain measures are being put into effect at this very moment, but do not worry," and he put his hand over hers. "I have to leave soon, but I will return tonight and we will make our plans for a holiday, very soon."

"Roberto, is it the situation at the Haiti border?" asked Shane with concern in her voice.

Roberto looked up quickly. "How did you know that?" he asked looking at her.

"I do read the newspaper, Roberto. Something in yesterday's paper made mention of an uprising of an organized group and two border guards had been shot."

Roberto frowned. "That should not have appeared in the paper; they are becoming too powerful and influential. I will have to contact them. In the meantime my little one, you read too much of the wrong thing. Is there a shortage of good reading material in our library? I shall have to see about bringing in more interesting material for you."

"Roberto," remarked Shane, "you know how I like to keep up with things. I have always shown an interest in current events. Maybe Terry might contact us about this."

"I don't think this is big enough for your brother to look into Shane. He is a foreign correspondent, am I not right?"

"Yes—hmm, I wonder" she said with a far-away look in her eyes.

"Stop wondering my little one" said Roberto getting up from the table and going to her side. "I should be leaving now."

Shane stood up and they embraced and Roberto looked into her eyes.

"How I despise having to leave your side, how I hate to say goodbye, how I—I'd better go." They kissed and he left with three gendarmes and his bodyguard, Garcia.

The meeting was serious enough to be attended by President Gomez and it lasted past midnight.

"Why don't you stay the night, Roberto?" said the President, "it might not be a good idea to travel so late. You could have breakfast with Isabella and myself and leave afterwards. We would love to have the pleasure of your company at breakfast."

"Gracias for your kind hospitality Juan but Shane would worry. I told her I would be back in the late evening."

"You could give her a call but then, I do not blame you at all my friend, a beautiful woman like Shane should not be alone. However, you must come back and bring Shane with you and spend some time with us. Isabella and I would be delighted to have you both as our guests. You know you are more than a friend; you are like a son to us Roberto. Oh, by the way, were the flowers to her liking? Was everything as it should be?"

Roberto took his hand, "How can I ever thank you, always you come through for me."

"We will never forget what you have done for this Country Roberto, it is I who am grateful to you. The Dominicanos owe you a great deal. However, be careful, we still have enemies around us and we must still look over our shoulder, but things have improved vastly. It is late and I will have two of my guards accompany you back—no, don't resist" he said as Roberto started to protest, "I insist. You have an hours' ride and it is late." They bid their farewells and embraced and Roberto left with the two presidential guards, his three gendarmes and Garcia.

It was quite late by the time they arrived at the Villa and Roberto was feeling the strain of the day and the intensity of the meeting. He immediately retired being careful not to awaken Shane but stayed awake thinking of the changes that would be taking place in the next few days and knew it would be impossible to get away with Shane as he had hoped.

"You should contact your friend Jodi-Anne," said Roberto in the morning as he sat across from Shane at breakfast. "Have her come and stay for a while. It would do you good."

"I'd like that," said Shane, "I haven't talked to her since the time we went to Canada just after we got married, do you remember?"

"I certainly do," said Roberto. "If she is hesitant about traveling alone I can send one or two of our men to accompany her."

Shane started to choke on her coffee. "Are you all right?" said Roberto with concern as he got up quickly and went to her side. Shane put her coffee down and coughed as tears ran down her cheeks. "I'm fine Roberto, the coffee just went down too quickly," she said hoarsely and dabbing at her eyes with a tissue, "I don't think Jodi will mind traveling alone."

"Well, find out Shane, we want her to feel welcomed. Are you sure you're all right my little one, can I get you something?"

"No, no," insisted Shane, "I'm just fine. Roberto, you didn't tell me, how did your meeting go? I didn't get to see you last night. It must have been late when you got back."

"The meeting went over very well and yes, I did not get back until after 1:00 in the morning. Juan made me promise that we would visit them and I told him soon. Shane, would you come riding with me this morning? I have some time before getting into this border situation. Actually, by the time you change I'll have the men bring the horses around. I'm already dressed for riding and I was going to go alone, but I decided it would be a good time for us to talk, away from here."

Shane looked up quickly at Roberto. Was there something he wasn't telling her? She could sense something in the air. "Roberto, I ..."

"It's okay Shane, don't worry and let's not waste any more time. I'll have the horses brought out front."

Shane's mind was racing, something had come up but she would wait until they were out on the beach.

It was another beautiful morning as they set out together on their favorite run. Many times they had ridden on the white silky sands and past the palm trees.

It was a stunning sight as Allegro, the shiny black stallion that Roberto always rode and Galaxy, the white horse that he had chosen for Shane trotted side by side along the beach. Behind them in the distance four gendarmes armed with machine guns watched closely.

Security had relaxed after President Gomez became elected but recently an obvious change in the number of bodyguards had become evident. Shane wondered how Jodi would react to their way of living.

After a long ride they stopped at a hill overlooking the ocean and Roberto spread out a blanket under a tree. Rosita had packed one of her famous lunches and the morning jaunt had given them an appetite and as they ate Roberto told Shane the latest news. A band of men, about twelve, had been caught trying to cross the border from Haiti into the Dominican Republic with drugs. This was not the biggest concern but what was most disturbing and had alerted the Elite Police Force was the quality of the drugs; methamphetamine, unmixed, pure, so in demand and so deadly. It was an obvious sign that they came from an area that was directly connected to Carlos Martinez, the notorious drug lord from Bolivia.

"Shane, this drug is so highly addictive that we would have a gigantic problem in this Country if we did not put a stop to it right now." The name of Carlos Martinez would bring a shock to the island. No one wanted to have any involvement with this man and something drastic had to be done to stop him.

Shane looked at Roberto, fear and concern in her eyes.

"Roberto, wasn't he the one that threatened you when he found out how successful you were in ridding most of the cocaine from being imported into the Country? I remember him appearing on television and making threats. He said 'someday Comandante Castaneda we will meet face to face' or something like that."

"Si, something like that" said Roberto. "The snake has resurfaced but I am not afraid and I do not want you to be afraid either." He put his hand under her chin and turned her face toward him. "Look at me Shane, look into my eyes. You know how much you mean to me, I don't have to tell you. I would never let anything happen to you or the children, trust me."

Shane's eyes filled with tears. "I do trust you Roberto, it's not me I'm thinking of, it's you. You know this man will not stop at anything."

"Neither will I, my little one. Come here, closer to me" and Shane moved towards him. His arms went around her and he talked. "Do you remember Shane when we got married and I made a vow to protect you always? Then later, we danced under the stars, the music in the background and the way you looked, indescribable. It felt like a dream, unreal, you were everything I'd ever wanted, and later that night in my arms, I will never forget my beautiful, beautiful Shane, again it was impossible for me to actually realize that you were really mine. The moments we shared are inscribed in my heart forever. With God watching over us and you by my side do you think Carlos has a chance of destroying my kingdom, my euphoria? I have already demolished him in my mind. No one—no one except God knows my power."

Shane looked up at Roberto. There it was again, something that made him seem different than anyone else. He was staring off into space, his eyes had a faraway look and on his face was something she hadn't seen before. It was almost as if he was eager for the bloodshed to begin and it sent a shiver up her spine. Suddenly, he seemed to come out of the trance and looked at her.

"You are cold, my little one, let me put my jacket around you" and he draped it around her shoulders. Shane did not protest, she had suddenly felt very cold indeed although the sun pouring down on them was hot and he put his arms around her and held her close to him as he often did.

"I swear to you Shane, before God, I will always protect you, have no fear my beloved, always."

A gentle breeze swayed the palm leaves and a cloudless blue sky looked down on them as they sat on the hill by the ocean under the trees.

Roberto took Shane back to the Villa, said his goodbyes and left. He wasn't sure how long he would be gone but there were drastic measures that had to be put into place. Once again Shane was left alone but she kept herself busy. She spoke to Jodi on the 'phone and was pleasantly surprised to hear that she did not have to coax her for a visit. The timing for Jodi was good; she had just finished her last year of school as a veterinarian and was contemplating on taking a holiday before starting up her career. She could travel on the coming weekend and was actually looking forward to seeing her friend. Shane was very excited and told her she would meet her at the airport. She made no mention of the bodyguards that would also be waiting with her.

Saturday night Shane, Ramon and Damien waited at the airport for Jodi's arrival. The plane touched down at 9:00 p.m. and Shane immediately recognized her long-time friend. Blonde and very slim she ran towards her friend just as both Ramon and Damien stepped in front of Shane. Jodi looked up shocked and Shane quickly put out her hand and grabbed the startled girl's arm.

"Jodi it's wonderful to see you," said Shane trying to squeeze past the two men.

"It's okay, this is Jodi, Jodi I'd like you to meet Ramon and Damien—they follow me everywhere." The two men stood back and Shane clasped a surprised Jodi to her as they hugged each other with Jodi looking warily around her.

"Where did they come from?" she whispered to Shane as they picked up her luggage.

"Don't worry Jodi, you'll get used to them. They are my bodyguards."

"Bodyguards!" exclaimed Jodi, "is this how you live?"

"It's okay," said Shane, "you get used to it. Come, our car is just over there. It's so good to see you." The girls walked arm in arm towards the parked vehicle. Two gendarmes with machine guns stood beside it and as the girls approached, the driver looked out and smiled and Jodi hesitated.

"Come," said Shane tugging at her arm, "this is our car. I'll get in first, just follow me."

Jodi stopped and tried not to show her fear but actually she was terrified.

"Shane, they're all holding machine guns."

"You'll love Rosita," said Shane ignoring Jodi's remark and pulling her arm. "She's a fabulous cook and she'll have dinner waiting for us."

"Do you actually think we'll ever arrive there to eat it?" asked Jodi as Damien sat with the driver and Ramon squeezed in back next to her.

Shane laughed, "I see you never lost your sense of humor Jodi, I'm so glad you're here. We could use some of that humor around here."

"Can they talk?" whispered Jodi.

"They not only talk" laughed Shane, "they can hear also."

Jodi turned to look at Ramon sitting next to her. His face was inches away from hers and he was staring at her, both hands on the machine gun resting across his knees, no expression showing on his face. Jodi gave a half-smile and turned away. How was she going to stay the full two weeks as she had planned. She had already been scared out of her wits and hadn't even met Roberto yet. She asked herself why she came. Was she that bored back home? Home, it sounded so good. She would have to think of a reason why she'd have to leave earlier, without offending Shane.

In the meantime, Shane was delighted to have Jodi visit her and she chatted all the way to the Villa. They arrived during the night and the grounds were very dark. Floodlights suddenly lit up the area as they stepped out of the car and went inside. Jodi was shown to her room where she freshened up then joined Shane for a late dinner. She took an immediate liking to Rosita and they sat around the table and talked until after midnight.

"You must be tired," said Shane looking at her friend, "but you look great considering the long trip."

Jodi agreed that she was really tired and thought she would turn in. Tomorrow they could talk some more.

Chapter Three

The next morning Jodi awoke to the sound of singing birds and sunlight pouring into the room. The wonderful aroma of coffee was like a lure and she quickly dressed and glanced out the window before going downstairs. Several gendarmes were standing around talking and all around were beautiful blooming flowers and bushes. This is such a lovely place she thought but what a strange background against the gendarmes armed with machine guns on horseback scattered around the Villa.

As she descended the stairs she could hear voices and she recognized Shane's voice, the other voice was a man's. She reached the dining room and stood hesitantly in the doorway. Shane was sitting at the table facing her and a man with his back to her was sitting across from Shane.

"Good morning Jodi" said Shane looking up, "please come in and join us." The man immediately stood up and turned towards her. "Jodi, I would like you to meet my husband Roberto, Roberto, this is Jodi." Roberto took Jodi's hand and bowed.

"Jodi-Anne, this is indeed a pleasure," he said. "I hope you enjoy your stay here with us." He pulled out a chair and waited for her to be seated before sitting next to her. After pouring her coffee Roberto asked Jodi what she preferred for breakfast. Rosita had made a variety as usual and Jodi settled for pancakes. Roberto filled her dish while Jodi sat very still.

"Roberto," commented Shane, "you remembered Jodi's full name, very impressive indeed. We've always called you Jodi. Do you prefer Jodi-Anne?"

Jodi sat quietly for a moment. "That's quite all right Roberto, I don't mind if you want to call me Jodi-Anne, not at all."

"I understand you are a veterinarian," said Roberto looking at Jodi over his coffee cup. Jodi felt uncomfortable. This was the notorious Roberto that she was having breakfast with that she'd heard and read so much about. She was actually sitting next to him. How was she, hungry as she felt, going to down those pancakes while sitting next to this man.

"Uh, yes," said Jodi answering his question, "that's right." She knew she sounded nervous and looked helplessly at Shane.

Roberto stood up, "I just remember I have to see Rosita about something, will you excuse me please, Shane, Jodi-Anne. It was so nice to meet you at last. Maybe the three of us could go riding later. Have you ever ridden horseback Jodi-Anne?" Jodi nodded. "Good" said Roberto, "then it's settled. I'll meet up with the two of you later."

After Roberto left Shane shook her head. "Poor Roberto, so many people feel intimidated by him, and really, he is very sweet."

Jodi was quiet for a moment. "He is very charming and sort of fascinating. I guess I can see why you married him, but he frightens me a little."

"Frightens you!" exclaimed Shane, "you can't be serious Jodi. What makes you say that?"

"I guess frighten isn't the right word, but there's just something that I can't seem to put my finger on, like—an air of mystery."

Shane laughed, "To be honest with you Jodi, I used to feel that way at one time. However, he has a very kind heart and once you get to know him, you will see what I mean."

"I know this is going back ten years Shane," said Jodi, "but weren't you frightened and shocked when he kidnapped you and right before our very eyes? Mary and I were so upset we cried for days afterwards every time your name was mentioned."

"I know, Jodi, I know" said Shane looking serious. "I can't deny the fear I felt at the time, not knowing what would happen to me. But, I learned so much about the people here, the situation with the ongoing Civil War and the tremendous part Roberto played in all of this. He's done so much for the people you will see for yourself how the Dominicans look up to him."

"Yes, I read the big write-up your brother Terry wrote in the Toronto paper at that time. Your family thinks the world of him. By the way, how is your other brother the doctor doing? I heard he married a girl from here and is running a pretty classy hospital by the ocean."

"That's right; Skye is doing very well, married to a lovely girl, Maria. They have a daughter Beatriz whom they adopted ten years ago from the orphanage here. She was only six at the time and now she's almost sixteen. I can't believe how time has flown. Beatriz is a very bright and pretty girl; you will meet them on Saturday. They will be here around lunchtime and our daughter Camille will be returning with them. It's too bad that you won't get to see our boys. The twins are away at boarding school in Europe."

"Yes, that is too bad but I'm looking forward to seeing the others on Saturday," said Jodi. "Really Shane, I'm so happy for you, you seem to have settled down nicely despite everything. But Shane," and Jodi looked at her curiously, "may I ask you something?"

"Of course" said Shane, "anything."

"What made you actually marry Roberto so soon after you were kidnapped? Did you fall in love with him or … did he somehow force you to … or …"

Shane laughed and interrupted Jodi. "No Jodi, not at all, Roberto did not force me into marrying him. It was my own free will but he set out these terms and …"

"Oh Shane, how awful that he would set out terms. That's like a forced marriage."

Shane smiled and took Jodi's hand. "Jodi, you are my close friend and I want to share with you something very intimate that not too many people know."

Jodi's eyes widened. "I'm all ears Shane."

"Just days after I had been kidnapped Roberto told me he had to leave in two days to engage in some heavy fighting in the mountains because of the Civil War that was raging in the Country. He said if I married him the day before he had to leave and if he should die, I would be free. He would leave a one way ticket to Canada with his trusted friend Raphael so I could go back home if I wished. I remember his exact words, Jodi. I'll never forget them. He said 'I will send to you a gardenia each day, my love, until I return. If the day comes when you do not receive the flower, then you will know that I shall not be returning and it is the will of God.'" Tears had suddenly sprung into Shane's eyes and rolled down her cheeks.

"Shane, that is so beautiful, so romantic. Please don't cry, I didn't mean for you to cry."

"There's more," said Shane, wiping away her tears. "One day, the gardenia did not arrive and it hit me badly. Jodi, I was heartbroken, I had fallen in love with Roberto but it was too late so I thought. As it happened, he had been seriously wounded and he was secretly brought back to us. We later found the blood-stained gardenia in the pocket of his jacket."

Jodi shook her head. "Oh Shane, this is an amazing story, I had no idea."

"There was some adjusting in the beginning" admitted Shane, "and a few frightening moments which I will tell you sometime but I have no regrets, Jodi, I'm so happy."

Jodi stirred her coffee and smiled at her friend. "I can see that in your face, Shane. I guess that's what life is all about, being happy. How I envy you. By the way, will Eenie and Meenie follow us wherever we go? I don't know if I can get used to that."

"You mean Damien and Ramon?" laughed Shane, "really they're harmless as long as they don't get nervous. They've been with me for years. They're boys just doing their job."

"They're a little scary-looking, maybe it's the machine guns. You have to admit Shane, we're not used to that kind of thing back home. We come from a different world."

"Yes," agreed Shane, "a different world" and her eyes seemed to go back to a different time. "Let's finish here," she said suddenly "and I'll take you around and show you the area, then we'll have more time for ourselves before we go riding. I'm so glad you were able to come" she said reaching across the table and squeezing Jodi's hand.

The girls chatted and laughed as they caught up on each other's lives. In the meantime, Roberto had stepped outside and was speaking with the guards. He wanted to make doubly sure that the grounds were patrolled to his satisfaction. Complete safety was imperative if it had to mean his home would be turned into a fortress until the border situation was brought under control but he did not want to alarm Shane or Jodi-Anne. He smiled as he tried to picture Ramon and Damien at the airport with Shane when they met Jodi-Anne and regretted not being able to be there.

It was another perfect day for riding. The sun was bright and warm as the three of them set out together followed a short distance behind by the ever faithful Damien, Ramon and Garcia.

It was already mid-afternoon and the sky was a haze of topaz gleaming like a big jewel and giving a fairy-tale background to the turquoise ocean. Jodi was really impressed and they stopped at an area shaded by the palm trees and sat down.

"I have never experienced anything like this in my life," said Jodi, "the scenery leaves you breathless" she said with a deep sigh. "How fortunate you are to live amongst all of this," she said with a wave of her hand.

"We love it here," said Shane, "I wouldn't trade it for anything."

Roberto was standing looking out towards the ocean and turned to look at Jodi. "Would this kind of life appeal to you Jodi-Anne?" he said. "I could arrange for you to stay if you wish."

The girl was caught off-guard. She still did not feel comfortable in the presence of Roberto, why, she did not know. She quickly looked at Shane.

"No, no, I didn't mean to sound that way. I … I …" and her hand went up nervously to the chain around her neck. "I would miss my family and home too much, but thank you, Roberto, that's very nice of you to say that."

"Oh Jodi!" exclaimed Shane, "I never thought in my wildest dreams that this could happen. Roberto, can you do this for Jodi?"

"I have no doubt, but that is up to Jodi-Anne," he said. "We haven't recruited anyone since Skye came up to visit and look what happened to him."

"Well yes," said Shane, "he got married. Jodi, if you stay you too would probably marry down here. There is an abundance of attractive single men on the island that would love to meet a pretty blond, blue-eyed girl like yourself."

Jodi laughed, "An abundance! You make it sound like a food market. No thank you, I don't intend to marry. I will be completely devoted to my career and I don't need a husband or anyone looking after me. I'm quite independent you know."

"Yes you are, Jodi," said Shane. "I remember you were the one that always said you didn't want to get married. However, you never know whom you might meet. I never thought I would get married here when I came on vacation; marriage was the farthest thing from my mind at the time."

"Yes, but what happened to you was scary," said Jodi.

"We promise not to do anything scary," laughed Roberto. "Tell me Jodi-Anne, where did you learn to ride so well?"

Jodi was relieved that the subject had changed. She eagerly talked about her uncle's farm and the many horses. It was there she developed her love for animals and knew that she would some day become a veterinarian. She had been riding since the age of eight.

"I too grew up with horses, Jodi-Anne," said Roberto. "I was about the same age as yourself when you started, maybe a bit younger. My two brothers and sister and I rode every day." His face suddenly looked sad and he was quiet. Jodi looked at Shane with questioning eyes. "Roberto lost his entire family during the Civil War" said Shane "like so many others during that time."

Jodi looked troubled. She glanced at Roberto and immediately the fear she had was replaced with sorrow. "I'm sorry Roberto, I had no idea."

Roberto quickly composed himself. "It's all right Jodi-Anne, I always hold in my heart the memory of my parents, my sister Charro and my brothers Marc and Andre. This is a great comfort to me. Shouldn't we get back?" he said glancing at his watch. "It's almost dinnertime and I'm expecting some visitors later this evening."

"You didn't mention anything about visitors coming to the Villa tonight," said Shane. "I hope everything is all right."

"Nothing to worry about my little one," said Roberto kissing Shane on the forehead. "Actually, they are army personnel and they have some news about this border situation that's causing a bit of a commotion. If my informants are correct, it is very good news indeed," but Shane looked doubtful as they mounted their horses.

"I see we have Eenie, Meenie and Mynee with us today," said Jodi noticing the three bodyguards following them.

"We will be adding Moe tomorrow," said Roberto with a smile, "just for you, Jodi-Anne." Jodi looked quickly at Roberto in surprise but he had moved up ahead.

"I didn't think they had those nursery rhymes here," she said. "Is Roberto serious about Moe?"

Shane laughed, "well he did mention the other day that we should have another guard with us. There's a lot you don't know about the people here Jodi. They are warm, wonderful and hospitable, you will see."

They rode back as dusk was beginning to set in and on arrival were met with the wonderful aroma of Rosita's cooking. After dinner Roberto excused himself and went to the library to await his military guests. Their meeting ended late and after they left Roberto sat for a while looking over some documents. He did not look too happy. The news was not good but he had no intention of upsetting Shane and Jodi-Anne.

Why should they know about Carlos Martinez? Why ruin Jodi-Anne's vacation and alarm Shane? Putting the man behind bars was not good enough. He would just have to get rid of him for good. It would be dangerous but he knew he had to do it himself, there was no other choice, he had to make sure. Now he felt guilty trying to convince Jodi-Anne to stay when he knew there might be a great deal of danger involved but he knew Shane wanted her friend with her. How could he allow that especially when they lived not too far from the Haitian border?

Saturday came and the Villa was getting ready for Skye, Maria, Beatriz and Camille. Rosita bustled about the kitchen happily preparing her delectable dishes. She enjoyed cooking and took great pleasure in making favourites for certain people.

In the meantime Jodi had arisen early and wanted to stroll down to the beach before breakfast. Such a luxury being so close to the beach she thought as she left the Villa and wandered down the path to the ocean. Different shades of blue were in the sky against the dark blue of the ocean in contrast to the white sand. She sat on the ground and took a deep breath. I could get used to this she thought and closed her eyes. The sound coming from the ocean was unbelievably soothing and she felt her body relax.

"Hola Senorita," came a voice over her head and her eyes flew open. Standing over her was Ramon. "I not want to frighten you so I say hola" he said looking down at her.

"You did frighten me Ramon; I didn't think anyone would be in this area this early."

Ramon sat down, "Roberto tells me I must watch you, so I watch you."

Jodi looked at the machine gun on Ramon's shoulder and cringed. "Er, isn't that gun awfully heavy to carry around all the time?"

Ramon looked at her very suspiciously. "I get used to it."

Why does everyone here say that wondered Jodi. "So, I guess you have to put it down somewhere when you sleep, right?"
"Wrong, gun stays with Ramon, I take it to bed."

"You must be kidding," said Jodi, "I can think of better things to sleep with."

Ramon looked at Jodi up and down, no expression showing on his face. "Senorita too skinny" he said.

"Well excuse me," said Jodi, "I was not referring to myself, don't flatter yourself." Really, she thought, what nerve.

"Gun does what I tell it to do, woman not that easy," he said looking her straight in the eye.

"Oh, there you are," said Shane coming up to them. "I was looking for you Jodi. I'm so glad you are both having a conversation at last, how nice."

"Right," said Jodi dryly, "very nice" and wondering if she'd really had that conversation with Ramon or did she imagine it.

"Gun very reliable Senora," said Ramon patting the machine gun. Shane thought she detected a glint of humor in his eyes. Just my imagination she thought. No one had ever seen Ramon smile or with humor in his eyes, not ever. Jodi took Shane's arm. "Let's go down to the beach for a walk before breakfast, Shane. Do you mind?"

"Not at all," said Shane still looking puzzled as they walked arm in arm towards the beach, trailed by Ramon and his machine gun.

Chapter Four

Seven-year-old Camille was the first to leave the car when it stopped in front of the Villa. Quickly she ran inside into the arms of her mother. She looked so much like Shane, black hair, bright green eyes and porcelain-like skin. She was a beautiful child and her sweet personality won over everyone who met her.

"I missed you maman, I love you so much," she said.

"I missed you too Camille, so much my little girl."

"Where is papa?" said the girl looking about her. "I thought he'd be here."

"He'll be here soon—this is Jodi my friend from Canada. She will be staying with us for a while."

"Hello Camille," said Jodi taking Camille's hand. The little girl reached up to her and gave her a hug, much to Jodi's surprise. "Shane, your daughter is enchanting, so lovely. She looks so much like you, what a darling," she said bending down and clasping the child to her. "I love you already."

Camille smiled back, "I love you too. May I call you Tia Jodi? Will you stay here with us? You can sleep with me." Jodi smiled, something about the little girl touched her heart. Was it her beauty, her loving nature? She didn't know. At that moment Skye came in with Maria and Beatriz. Shane introduced Jodi to them and Skye remembered Jodi well and was eager to hear all the news from Toronto. While Jodi sat with Maria and Skye in the library, Beatriz and Camille went outside to wait for Roberto. They found him returning from the beach with Allegro and he immediately dismounted upon seeing them.

"And how are my favorite girls?" he said holding open his arms and embracing them both.

"Papa, I was looking for you," said Camille, her arms around Roberto's neck. "I was frightened; I thought I would not see you."

"I will always be here for you my little Camille, you know that," he said brushing her hair back from her forehead and kissing her. "And you, Beatriz, my little flower, how you have grown. Each time I see you there is something different. You are quite a beauty. Barra de labios? You are much too young and pretty for lipstick."

"I will be sixteen next month Roberto, have you forgotten? My friends are all wearing lipstick. I am now grown up."

"Don't grow up too fast Beatriz, you will always be my little flower, don't you know that?" But her look of dismay was noticed by Roberto.

"Here, give me your hand and let's go inside and see what is happening," said Roberto taking the hands of both girls and entering the Villa.

Rosita had set the table and everything was ready. After lunch everyone went into the library and got caught up on local and out of town news.

"Roberto, there's a rumor that there have been some problems at the border," said Skye. "Can you fill us in on what is happening?"

"It is not a problem anymore," said Roberto hoping he could downplay the incident without arousing suspicion. "We have some men in custody. Actually I was in a meeting the other day and our Deputy in Charge of border security has assured me that everything is under control. He has been reporting to me once a day and my last contact was an hour ago and everything is fine. So tell me Beatriz, how do you like your new school?" he said quickly changing the subject.

"I am making new friends but I do miss some from the other school. I still don't understand why I had to change."

Roberto was concerned for the girl's safety. His first priority was to have his family protected at all times and he knew that his high-profile position made them a target. He was planning on discussing with Shane about the possibility of sending Camille also to a private school in Toronto near her grandparents. He knew it would break his heart to have to do that. He adored his daughter; she was so much like Shane. He would also have to speak to the Canadian Council to obtain permission for two of his bodyguards to accompany his daughter. She must be protected twenty-four hours a day.

He missed his sons terribly. It was like years wasted, years they couldn't get back. He wanted so much to see them grow up into young men before his eyes; eight years old and they were attending a military academy. He shook his head; one day this would all change but this was the price he had to pay until it was safe to bring them back.

Jodi, Maria and Shane were in a deep discussion about a new boutique that had just opened nearby. They were excited about new fashions that had been imported from France and Italy to the store and planned to go together to look them over.

"How are things at the hospital?" asked Roberto. "It's getting to be a very famous place."

"I'm glad you asked," said Skye. We've hired two more doctors and five nurses. Also, we're getting an MRI machine at the end of the month and oh, do you remember Madam Bouchard, the elderly French lady who entered the hospital the week we opened? She stayed a few months, went back home and returned a few months later?"

"Yes, I do recall her," said Roberto, a very elegant lady and a little, how do you say excentrico. Is she here now?"

I'm sorry to say that she passed away recently but she must have liked us Roberto. She bequeathed to the hospital a very large sum of money. We were quite surprised at her generosity."

"How very nice of her to do that," said Shane.

"I'm very impressed," said Roberto. "It clearly says something about the quality of care that is given. Your hospital is becoming famous world-wide and is living up to its name. I am so glad Madam Bouchard had such excellent care. She was a very elegant lady. Both you and Maria knew what you wanted—it was a dream come true and I want you to know that I am so proud of the two of you."

"All kinds of people from different walks of life end up at The Hospital of the Holy Angels," said Skye. "A little boy was brought to us yesterday, his father is a Saudi Arabian Prince."

"Skye, tell them about the man that came in last week," said Maria, "the one that can't remember anything. What was it that Dr. Valdez said, amor ... no, amesa ... no, Skye?"

"Amnesia, he has amnesia and he is under the care of Dr. Valdez. He says his name is Antonio Montesano but other than that he cannot remember anything. He seems to be well educated, good manners, a nice guy, maybe around 30. It's odd but Camille took a liking to him and ..."

Roberto had swung around so quickly that his hand knocked over the drink on the table and the glass shattered. "Camille what?" he exclaimed, "When did she see him?"

"Relax Roberto," said Skye as every eye in the room turned to Roberto who by now had stood up. "She just happened to be in the lobby at the same time."

"What was that man doing in the lobby, was he leaving?" demanded Roberto, "and where was Camille's bodyguard?"

"The man was in a wheelchair Roberto, he cannot stand too long for any period of time because of a head injury. In fact, his X-rays show a bullet lodged near his brain. He's harmless Roberto and Camille's bodyguard never left her side."

By now everyone in the room could feel the tension and Jodi spoke up for the first time.

"Do you think he's involved in something, you know, because of the bullet wound?"

"I'll have to look into this," said Roberto, "we'll have to question him. Why was it not reported to the police?"

Camille came towards her father and Roberto put out his hand to her. "Papa, he is very nice, I feel sorry for him, he has no one."

Roberto lifted the girl holding her to him and sat down. "You know my little Camille, how precious you are to us. You must not talk to anyone who is a stranger."

The girl nodded, "Papa I know, but I could not help it, he looks like you."

"Come to think of it, Roberto" said Skye, "there is a strong resemblance and that is what probably drew her to him. We will be more careful in future, that is a promise. By the way, we didn't know about the bullet until we took the X-ray and that was only yesterday."

"When can I question him? Do we know where he is from? Any papers or identification on him? Was he brought in by someone or …?"

"Whoa, hold on a minute Comandante," said Skye with a laugh, "I feel like I'm the one being interrogated. Dr. Valdez is deciding if the bullet can be removed safely. There's a possibility it might kill him."

"I want to talk to Dr. Valdez, when can I see him?"

"You don't waste any time, do you Roberto," said Skye. "Aren't you glad you came Jodi? You've been here two days and you've probably seen more excitement than you have in the past five years."

Jodi laughed, "actually, I don't mind one bit. Shane said I'd get used to it and she was right."

"Let me give Dr. Valdez a call Roberto and see when he'll be able to talk to you," said Skye getting up. "I'll be right back."

Roberto had bought gifts for Camille and Beatriz. He kissed his daughter and told her to take Beatriz up to her room and to look under the bed and in the closet. After the girls had left the room Roberto spoke to Shane about sending Camille to Toronto to a private school. He thought it advisable for Beatriz also but Beatriz had stubbornly refused the last time he had mentioned it. "I don't want to be away from here" she had said defiantly and threatened to run away if they forced her to.

"Roberto, couldn't we have a tutor come here? Camille is so young," said Shane. "I would hardly ever see her if we sent her out of the Country."

"I know Shane, I thought about it a great deal. I've been going through my own hell since we sent the twins to Switzerland but I really believe it was necessary. This will change one day soon I hope. But I have to think about the present and right now this is not a good time for them to be here. I am also very concerned over Beatriz—I just cannot convince her."

"She is a strong-willed girl," said Maria. "Skye has tried talking to her also."
"Skye will have to talk to her again," said Skye entering the room and hearing Maria's last remark. "Dr. Valdez said that you could see him tomorrow evening at 6:00. Come to my office and I'll take you to him."

Roberto was satisfied with this information and they spent the rest of the day catching up on current events and future programs. The following day Roberto arrived at the hospital and met with Skye. Together they went to Dr. Valdez's office where they briefly discussed the new mystery patient. He had arrived alone at the hospital, disoriented and confused speaking only in Spanish. Very reluctant to be admitted he was convinced to stay after a fainting spell in the Emergency. An X-ray confirmed a bullet near the brain and they decided to operate some time in the next few days, if the patient gave his permission.

"Would you like to see him?" said Dr. Valdez.

"Very much so," said Roberto and the three of them went to the room on the top floor.

As they entered Roberto saw the young man lying on the bed, a cloth over his eyes. The man immediately removed it when he heard them enter and Roberto felt a sudden twinge in his heart. The stranger had very dark eyes and a week's growth of beard but there was a familiarity about him and Roberto felt his knees weaken. He knew what he was thinking had to be preposterous.

Dr. Valdez spoke in Spanish and introduced Roberto and said he wanted to ask him a few questions. The man's eyes darted to Roberto and he stared for a moment, then nodded. Roberto looked at the man, the twinge did not go away and he had to swallow hard.

"Como se llama usted?"

"Antonio Montesano," said the man without taking his eyes off Roberto.

"Cual es su direccion?"

The man shook his head.

Roberto continued, "Quien es su pariente mas proximo?"

The man looked at Dr. Valdez.

"Cuanto tiempo tender que quedarme aqui?"

Skye spoke up, "What did he say?"

Before Roberto or Dr. Valdez could answer, the stranger spoke again. "I speak English. I do not know my address, I have no relatives, no one."
The others looked astonished; Dr. Valdez was the first to talk. "We assumed you did not understand English. Why, I am curious, do you speak it now?"

The man looked at Roberto again, and then said "I do not know."

Then Roberto made a very strange request, "we would like to see your face; will you shave off your beard?"

"I do not want to do that," said the stranger simply.

"Then we will give you an injection and do it ourselves," said Roberto to their astonishment.

The man looked at Skye and Dr. Valdez. "Can he do that? Do I not have any rights? I have done no wrong."

"Yes, you do have rights," said Dr. Valdez and he turned to Roberto. "Is he under arrest Roberto? If so, I shall turn him over to you but he should still, under my way of thinking, have the operation. It could save his life."

Roberto could feel the tension building up inside him and the blood pounded against his temples. He touched Dr. Valdez's arm secretly and said to the man, "The doctor tells me you have bruises on the left side of your chest. Have you been in an altercation with someone?"

The man lifted his top, "See for yourself, I have a large birthmark, it is not a bruise. Are you satisfied?"

Roberto's breath caught in his throat. He could not speak for a moment and the others stared at him. He turned slowly to Skye and Dr. Valdez and spoke in a low, unsteady voice.

"Could I have a few moments alone with this person? I won't be long, it is very important." His voice had suddenly sounded strange and his heart pounded inside him. Skye and Dr. Valdez glanced at each other and agreed. They stepped out of the room leaving Roberto alone with the stranger. Roberto pulled up a chair and sat beside the bed. He was shaking inside but tried not to show it. "Look at me, look at me closely. Do you not recognize me?" he said in a shaky voice.

The man looked at him and shook his head. "I do not know who you think I am. I have never seen you before."

"My name is Roberto, Roberto Enrique Castaneda and your name is Andre Castaneda."

The man looked at Roberto for a long moment then once again shook his head. "I don't know anyone named Roberto, and my name is Antonio not Andre. You are mistaking me for someone else."

"No I am not," insisted Roberto, "your real name is Andre, Andre Cristian Castaneda. Good Lord Andre, you are my brother." Roberto wanted to embrace him but knew the timing was bad. With tremendous force and willpower he held himself back. He could feel the emotion welling up inside him but it was impossible for him to shed tears. He just sat there and stared trying to come to grips with what was unfolding before him then finally the man spoke.

"You are wrong, I don't know who you are and what you are telling me about myself. I am very sorry but you are wrong. I want to speak to Dr. Valdez."

Roberto gave a sigh but it did not matter. The exhilaration he felt was spreading through his body. He had found his brother. He got up and went to the door and all around him there seemed to be a thousand coloured lights flashing. A miracle had just taken place, a dead memory had been brought back to life. He stopped and turned around.

"Andre, I am putting you under twenty-four hours surveillance. You will not be allowed to leave this room until I come back. Anything you might need will be brought to you." He opened the door and told Dr. Valdez what he planned to do. He then took Damien and Ramon into the room and introduced them. "They have orders not to leave you alone until I return." Under no condition was anyone to leave the room and all meals would be served there until further notice. He then motioned to Skye to go with him out to the car and they left followed by Garcia.

"Can you come back to the Villa with me Skye? It is important." Skye nodded and they got into the waiting car.

"What's up Roberto?" said Skye curiously. Roberto turned to Skye, "I don't know how, where or why, but that man that we just saw is my brother Andre."

"Your brother!" exclaimed Skye, "I thought your entire family had been killed during the Civil War. Are you sure?"

"I'm sure Skye, there is no doubt." Roberto shook his head in disbelief. "I don't know the details, or where he has been for the last fifteen years but" and he stopped and shook his head again, "can this be real?"

"Just a minute Roberto" said Skye, "it's possible that he could have escaped. You won't get the full story however unless his memory returns. Then there's this operation, and it's pretty risky."

Roberto thought for a moment before answering, then said, "that operation, hmm, I don't know if he should be having it."

"You don't know all of this for sure Roberto, what makes you so positive he's your brother, is it the resemblance?"

"No no, I didn't tell you, it's the birthmark. My brother had a birthmark on his side, the left side near his ribs, exactly the same shape. There's absolutely no doubt, I know that's him, that's Andre."

"Wow! Okay Roberto, let's say it's him, but getting back to the operation, from what I understand the risk is pretty high. X-rays showed bleeding in the brain. If we do not operate—well, Dr. Valdez thinks the bullet could move and possibly kill him at any time. With the operation there is a big risk involved but it gives him a chance."

"A chance for what?" asked Roberto.

"To live" said Skye, "it might be a success."

"Might?" said Roberto, "you say there is a big risk?"

Skye was not too happy but he had to say it. "Look Roberto, it means with the operation Andre has a chance for a normal life, without it, about two months at the most."

Roberto's newfound joy was now mixed with sadness and fear. He could not stand the thought of losing his brother again and immediately agreed to Andre having the surgery.

Shane's reaction was disbelief, then happiness followed by shock when Skye went into detail about the impending operation. Roberto excused himself and went inside.

"He must be going through something terrible" said Jodi. Shane agreed, "His new-found happiness is being shattered. Oh Skye, I must go to him" she said getting up quickly.

After Shane left, Skye sat with Jodi and they talked. "My heart goes out to Roberto," said Skye, "actually him and his brother, if he is really his brother."

"But the operation could be successful, is that not so?" said Jodi. "Let's be optimistic Skye, how wonderful it would be for both of them, and all who know them. Skye, this is absolutely amazing."

"Unbelievable, it's a miracle." Skye let out a sigh. It had been a stressful day and he knew that he had to get back to the hospital. After he left, Jodi went inside and found Rosita setting the table.

"Rosita, did you hear the news? Roberto thinks he has found his brother Andre. It is a miracle. Did he tell you?"

Rosita clasped her hands and looked up as if in prayer, "I only hope this is true, Jodi. Yes, he has told me. Did you know he is planning on bringing him here?" Jodi was helping Rosita set the table and suddenly looked up.

"He is going to visit us Rosita? He is coming here?"

"No no my dear, I think he wants the young man to live here. Roberto is very kind-hearted and protective of his family. He would do anything for them."

Jodi stopped what she was doing and was deep in thought for a moment, a serious expression on her face. "But supposing, Rosita, that this young man is not his brother. He might actually be bringing a stranger into his home. I don't like the sound of that."

"He seems pretty sure, my dear. I guess we will just have to wait and see."

"Did he say when?" asked Jodi arranging the gardenias on the table. "Mm, these are lovely," she said burying her face in the bouquet.

"From what I understand," said Rosita, "the young man might have to have an operation first. The gardenias? Yes, Shane loves the flower and Roberto is always bringing them to her."

"Well," said Jodi," I hope everything turns out okay and this person turns out to be his brother without a doubt."

Shane found Robert going through the mail on his desk. She quickly went to his side and they embraced.

"Roberto, I am so happy for you, I don't know what to say," she said. "Is he able to provide you with any information about what happened?"

Roberto shook his head. "He denies everything I say about him but he's really not in a position to make a statement because he does not remember. He refuses to have the operation but Dr. Valdez is doing a DNA test that will prove we are brothers. I know we are, Shane, without any doubt but I want Andre to know also. He will also undergo neurological tests and I will then sign the papers and take full responsibility for the operation and leave the rest to God. What do you think Shane, am I doing the right thing? Would you feel comfortable with him living here? Tell me my little one, am I doing the right thing?"

"Of course you are," said Shane, "he would be family—oh my goodness!"

"What is it Shane, what are you thinking of?" asked Roberto with concern.
"I just realized, he could be my brother-in-law."

"That's right," laughed Roberto, "and it would mean another uncle for Camille and the twins."

"Don't forget Beatriz," said Shane, "an uncle for Beatriz."

Roberto suddenly looked solemn. "I can never forget Beatriz," he said. How those words were going to come back some day to haunt him. "Of course, an uncle for Beatriz, but I worry about her Shane. I pick up something from that little girl, a sadness. Do you not see it?"

"She's not a little girl Roberto, she's almost sixteen. She might be experiencing growing pains."

"Growing pains?" said Roberto, "I don't know Shane, it's something else. I think we should spend more time with her. Who are her friends? Does she have any? She should be with youngsters her own age. I must talk to her, maybe tomorrow."

"That might be a good idea, Roberto. Actually," said Shane thoughtfully, "she will be turning sixteen soon. Why don't we give her a surprise birthday party?"

"That would be a good start," said Roberto. "Let us contact her school and find out who her friends are and we can go on from there. Maybe that's all she needs. In the meantime, my muchachita," he said putting his arm around her waist and drawing her close to him, there is something that I want you to have." He took a box out of his pocket and handed it to a surprised Shane. She opened it and a beautiful diamond bracelet lay nestled against a velvet cushion.

Shane gasped, "Roberto, what ... why ... what is the occasion?" Roberto took out the bracelet and clasped it on her wrist. It was stunning—the entire bracelet was covered in diamonds and looked amazing on Shane's slender wrist.

"Roberto, it is unbelievable," said Shane. Roberto smiled at her, "it is more unbelievable than you might think my little one."

"How does it come off?" asked Shane turning the bracelet around her wrist.

"It doesn't," he said and when Shane quickly looked up at him in surprise, he brought her hand up to his lips and kissed it. "Trust me my darling, just trust me."

Shane tried to hide her alarm, she wasn't sure what had just happened and wondered once again if she really knew Roberto. She did not see him place a gold band around his wrist and click it shut. It also would not come off.

Chapter Five

Jodi sat on the sand listening to the sound coming from the ocean. It was so relaxing and the sun beating down was strong. This place grows on a person she thought as her body relaxed and her mind entered a state of semi-consciousness. She was rudely awakened when she became aware of someone close to her and opened her eyes to find Ramon staring at her.

"Is something wrong?" she asked nervously picking up her sunglasses that had slipped off when she moved quickly.

"Nothing wrong Senorita, "said Ramon handing her a kerchief. "Put this on head, sun too strong."

Jodi was surprised then touched by this act of kindness. Shane was right, these people were very friendly and hospitable. She smiled and took the kerchief tying it around her head.

"Ramon" she said, a thoughtful look on her face, "can you tell me how to say in Spanish 'It is nice to meet you.' I want to say this to the young man who will be coming here, you know, the gentleman who Roberto thinks might be his brother. I think his name is Andre."

Ramon nodded. "That is very nice Senorita. Si, I teach you that, very easy. You say 'guaperos Senor.'"

"Guaperos Senor," said Jodi, "that's all?"

"Si, that is all" said Ramon. "Do not tell anyone, make it a surprise."

"Oh yes," said Jodi, "you are right Ramon. They will really be impressed when I say that. Thank you so much."

"Si Senorita, everybody will be surprised."

The next two days were exciting and fulfilling ones for Roberto. The DNA tests proved without a doubt that Andre was indeed Roberto's brother and Roberto's joy was evident as he started to make plans for a large welcome party but first they had to pass another hurdle. Andre had to have the operation and everyone knew of the risk involved. Roberto, however, believed in his faith deep within himself. He felt that there was a reason Andre had been spared and that he would not be taken from them now.

The operation was performed and the bullet removed successfully but Andre's memory did not return. When Andre awoke in the Recovery Room, Roberto was by his side.

"Hola de sangre," said Roberto. Andre smiled. "Como esta usted?" continued Roberto.
"Good, very good Roberto," said Andre.

During his ten days in the hospital, Andre had a few visitors and Shane was one of the first and felt an immediate bond with Andre. Camille, who already knew Andre was overjoyed that she was the one who had "found" Tio Andre. Shane had tried to coax Jodi to meet Andre at the hospital but Jodi insisted that it was a family time for them and she would wait until he was discharged.

It was a bright and sunny day when Andre came to live at the Villa and Rosita had taken great pride in showing off her culinary skills. Andre was very quiet and overwhelmed by all the attention. They were all strangers to him except for Camille who he felt close to.
He called her "Mantecado," which meant shortcake. Like Roberto he had a habit of giving nick-names to people he liked.

When introduced to Jodi he commented on how much she looked like Skye referring to the blue eyes and blonde hair. Jodi smiled and said, "guaperos Senor Andre," and Andre's eyebrows flew up and Roberto immediately interceded.

"I think," he said trying not to laugh, "someone has given Jodi-Anne the wrong lesson in Spanish." Camille giggled as her hand went up to her mouth and Shane, not understanding, looked surprised.

"I knew I should not have trusted Ramon," said Jodi, her face turning a bright red. "I'm afraid to ask what I just said."

"It wasn't too bad," said Roberto laughing, "You just told Andre that you thought he was attractive."

"No papa," said Camille, Tia Jodi said he is a pretty boy."

By now Andre was beginning to blush also but Jodi was angry and embarrassed. She stormed out of the Villa and looked around outside. Ramon was nowhere to be seen. She ran out towards the beach and kept running. She knew he would appear from somewhere—he always did. Soon she heard footsteps behind her and someone calling but by now she was in tears and out of breath as she fell to her knees on the sand, angry and very upset.

"Senorita," called out the familiar voice, "Senorita, que le ocurre?"

Jodi looked up, tears were streaming down her face but the anger showed in her eyes.

"For heavens sake," she blurted out, "talk in English so that I can at least defend myself. That was a mean thing to do."

"I just asked what is wrong," said Ramon sitting on the sand beside her.

"You know what's wrong, how could you humiliate me like that. I trusted you Ramon," said Jodi wiping her face on her sleeve.

"Oh," said Ramon, "you met Roberto's brother." He paused then continued, "I guess not too funny—I am sorry, Ramon make—disculpa."

"I don't understand what you are making or saying Ramon, but it doesn't matter. You never liked me from the first day I came here, I could feel it."

"I just made apology, you know, disculpa. Senorita, I am sorry, not a good idea," said Ramon handing Jodi an old handkerchief. She took it and blew her nose, then handed it back.

"I was embarrassed," she continued, "but I guess you wouldn't care about that," she said starting to sob again.

"Women always cry," he said sounding impatient, "I said sorry, and I not say I not like you." He paused then said, "You not know my life, what I have seen, your life easy. You have nice face, look at my face—ugly."

Jodi looked up quickly. The last statement had caught her by surprise. She looked at him, his machine gun lying across his knees, his dark eyes shining, the scar on the side of his face very obvious. It was true, she knew nothing about him, whether he had family or anyone for that matter. She stopped crying and thought for a moment.

"Okay," she said finally, "let's call a truce."

Ramon looked puzzled, "what is troos?" he said looking at her closely.

"It's when people are fighting and they decide to not fight anymore and make peace," she explained. "There's too much fighting in this world."

"Si, too much fighting," echoed Ramon.

"You will not play any more tricks on me Ramon?" asked Jodi.

"No more tricks," he said. "What is tricks?"

"You know, like what you just did. It embarrassed me Ramon. I have feelings believe it or not."

"Si Senorita, I believe you, no more trucks."

"Tricks Ramon, tricks."

"Okay, okay, my English not like yours." He gave a long sigh and patted the machine gun. "This my best friend. It understands what Ramon says, never argue, never cry like woman, never give me headache."

"Now you're telling me that I give you a headache," said Jodi desperately. "Is that all you need in life, your … your crazy old machine gun?"

"This is not crazy old machine gun," said Ramon raising his voice, "it saved my life many times." He lifted the gun and kissed it. "It is my best friend but you not understand this. You do not like gun, I know this. Why?"

Jodi looked at Ramon. She was suddenly seeing him as a person, not as a gun-toting fighter. She looked away from his piercing eyes. The sand was warm and silky and she ran her hands through it while searching for an answer to his question. The bright sun cast coloured lights across the ocean and the lull coming from the waves was the only sound to be heard. Jodi finally spoke, hesitant at first, then strongly.

"Because it is so final, so final Ramon, it just kills."

"There are bad people in this world, Senorita. Gun kills bad people so good ones can live."

"But the good ones die too," said Jodi, "because of the gun."

Ramon spoke softly, "Senorita is afraid of gun?" he said. It was more of a statement than a question.

Jodi nodded, "I always have been, Ramon, they make me nervous."

"You are nervous," agreed Ramon. "You not eat enough, too skinny."

Jodi quickly looked at Ramon. "There you go again, saying things to me." She stood up and so did Ramon. "I can't see how we can ever become friends. You just don't understand," she said walking away. Ramon shook his head muttering under his breath something about "woman not like gun, gun much better" and followed behind her.

Roberto had gone looking for Jodi but when he saw her and Ramon sitting together and talking on the beach, he stepped back. He decided to leave them alone and work out things on their own. He went back into the Villa and told the concerned group that the situation was under control. He couldn't help but wonder about Ramon and Jodi-Anne. They were two very different people, from two very different worlds, very opposite, yet, there seemed to be something that ... he couldn't quite figure it out, but something.

Things were beginning to quiet down at the Villa. Andre was settling in nicely and Jodi had overcome her embarrassment from the other day. The border situation was keeping Roberto busy and he was away often. He was glad that Shane would not be alone at the Villa and hoped that Jodi would stay awhile. Shane went a step further and was hoping that Andre and Jodi would become more than just friends. When Shane mentioned to Jodi if she found Andre to be a rather handsome young man and they would make a nice couple, Jodi blushed and reminded Shane that she did not want to marry anyone and enjoyed her freedom to do as she pleased with no responsibilities whatsoever. The three of them spent a lot of time together and it was evident that Andre was actually a very remarkable young man.

As they were getting to know him, they discovered that he had the ability to carry on a conversation in such a manner that whoever was with him would be completely relaxed and at ease. His manners were meticulous and he had characteristics similar to Roberto. Andre was thirty-four, four years younger than Roberto but seemed much older.

Chapter Six

The weekends came and went quickly and Jodi extended her stay much to the delight of Shane and Roberto. Beatriz was back at school and Camille also started a different school that Roberto had insisted upon. Shane had mentioned to Jodi that Damien and Ramon would be accompanying Camille to her school and returning at 5:00 PM on weekdays.

"We won't be seeing too much of Damien and Ramon except in the evenings and on weekends," Shane had told Jodi. "Roberto preferred them to be with his daughter more than anyone else. I think he's still worried though and is still thinking of having her sent to Canada to stay with my parents. He's concerned about this border situation, I can tell. Lorenzo, you haven't met him yet, will be with us when we go shopping or riding. I'll introduce you to him later, Jodi."

"Lorenzo? What happened to Moe? That's what Roberto said, remember?"

Shane laughed, "That's just a bit of Roberto's humour, Jodi. He's not usually very humourous, believe me."

"This kind of life must be hard for you Shane," said Jodi. "Will things ever change for the better?"

"Actually, things are much better compared to a few years ago, but the problem now is Carlos Martinez."

"Who is that?" asked Jodi.

"He's a drug lord from Bolivia. Roberto says he's trying to enter into our area and if not apprehended he could cause a lot of trouble here in the Dominican."

"What makes Roberto think they're trying to enter the Country?" asked Jodi. "Have there been signs of anything suspicious?"

"Well, actually yes," said Shane. "He's a terrorist and will stop at nothing if he really sets his mind to it. But just between you and me, I know why Roberto has been concerned lately. This man does not like Roberto because Roberto has built a very strong defense to keep him out of the Country. This was his first mission years ago when he became Chief of all the Allied Forces here in the Dominican and he formed such an elite army trained for this one purpose that other countries are following his exact style. I didn't know until recently that he had special agents come here from Israel and Algeria to train our soldiers."

"Oh my goodness!" exclaimed Jodi, "there's been a great deal going on here; I wasn't aware of all this."

"As I was saying, Roberto's real concern is for the children and myself. Carlos has often gone after family members of top-ranking officials who have tried to fight him and this is why Frederik and Enrique are out of the country. Now he wants to send Camille to stay with my parents in Toronto and attend a private school there, unless he can find a way to stop him."

"Do you think he can?" asked Jodi with concern. "This is such a beautiful Country it would be a shame to see it overrun by such a person."

"He's very powerful Jodi, he's made so much money from drugs but I have faith in Roberto. He's worked too hard to let that happen and he is so dedicated. He loves the Dominican and the people, it's in his blood and the people here love him."

"I've noticed that," said Jodi, "he is highly respected by the men here and I've also noticed how dedicated he is to you"

"We're very happy Jodi. Have you noticed how much Andre seems to be like Roberto? He is such a nice young man."

Jodi laughed, "I know what you're hinting at Shane. Yes, Andre is a very nice person, I agree. However, I do not intend to marry and how do you know if he does? Maybe he also likes the single life."

Shane smiled, "come Jodi, let's sit out in the back. It's so beautiful outside and maybe Andre or Rosita will join us."

They left the Villa and were immediately joined by a gendarme who Shane introduced as Lorenzo. Lorenzo was not at all like Ramon. He was shy and smiled a lot. He also was specially chosen by Roberto to guard his family because he knew very well how to use his gun during a crisis.

They sat at one of the tables and made plans for a surprise birthday party for Beatriz. Maria had gotten names from the school and they decided to have the party at the Villa.

It seemed like a happy time and no one was aware of how tragically the party was to end. As it was her sixteenth birthday, fifteen young people were invited which included Camille, and Beatriz made up the sixteenth. Each one would hold a candle and give their wish for Beatriz as she blew each one out. Her candle would be on the cake and she would make her own wish.

The party was held on a Saturday and Roberto had made a point of being available that day—he knew that Beatriz would be disappointed if he wasn't there and all the preparations went as planned when the big day arrived. Beatriz looked very pretty when she arrived wearing a white satin dress with a blue sash and blue flowers in her hair. She knew that it was a party but thought it would be for family only. When they stepped inside and everyone shouted "surprise" Beatriz was not only surprised but there was a look of disappointment on her face. She did not want to share her "family time" with friends.

"Maybe she was frightened," said Shane as she helped Rosita and Maria hand out the candles to her friends.

"I'm not sure," said Skye. "She seems depressed lately but when we told her we were coming here she suddenly changed and seemed very happy."

"Let's light the candles," said Roberto "then let everyone give their wish. After that we'll leave them alone. There's music and games and she'll be fine I'm sure."

The lights were lowered, the candles lit, and each person gave their wish for Beatriz as she blew out the candles one by one. When she reached the last candle that was on the cake, she made her wish so everyone could hear.

"I wish … I wish … that at twelve midnight I will turn into a princess and be in the arms of my prince. That is my wish." Everyone was silent then Maria spoke out.

"You already are a princess Beatriz, our princess."

"Beatriz shook her head, "his princess" she said, "I want to be his princess."

There was suddenly a loud bang outside and everyone ran out to see the fireworks.

They were being set off in honour of Beatriz's birthday and the amazing colours were exploding in the sky. Aside from the few awkward moments in the beginning, the evening progressed beautifully.

Roberto and Skye sat outside in the back and Maria and Shane along with Jodi and Andre joined them. The music coming from the Villa was soft and most of the birthday guests were dancing.

"Beatriz is such a lovely girl," commented Jodi, "and her friends seem to be a very nice group of teenagers. She seems to be really enjoying her birthday. Please tell me something about her."

Maria gave a sigh. "Beatriz was only six when she was brought to the orphanage. She would look forward to Roberto's weekly visits when he would come by and spend time with the children. Some of them showed signs of distress and Beatriz was one of them and he would take extra time just to sit and talk with each one. Roberto is a very kind person and they all craved attention and Beatriz bonded to him immediately. She would follow Roberto to the door when he was leaving and the following week wait for him with excitement."

"That's right," said Skye, "Maria and I had visited the orphanage with Roberto on several occasions and we were enchanted with Beatriz, so we decided to adopt her. She seemed so much a part of our family right from the beginning.

"She was upset about something earlier but seems to be all right now," said Maria.

"I think so too," said Skye. "You can never tell nowadays with youngsters, they seem to be on a high one day and on a low the next. What do you think Roberto?"

Roberto looked thoughtful as a serious expression crossed his face. When he spoke, he seemed to slowly measure his words. "Is there at all a possibility that she has obtained drugs from somewhere?" Everyone looked at him with shocked expressions and Andre was the first to speak.

"Would it not show in her eyes Roberto? You don't think she's in any danger?"

"I should not have said that," Roberto said quickly. "I apologize profusely to all of you.
It's just that something is bothering Beatriz. I will talk to her tonight after her friends leave."

"Oh Roberto," said Maria, "I would feel so much better if you did. She seems to listen to you more than anyone else."

"Isn't it always the way," said Andre.

The evening continued with the music in the background and the sound of laughter coming from the Villa. Just before midnight the party started to break up and by midnight everyone had left.

"I can't seem to find Beatriz," said a worried Maria coming out of the Villa. "Has anyone seen her?"

"Did you try Camille's room?" said Shane. "Come, we'll look together."

"And we'll take a look around the grounds" said Skye. "Maybe she took a walk."

"I'll have more men patrol the beach to look for her," said Roberto and quickly gave out the orders. He could not help but feel a deep uneasiness welling up inside him. He went back inside the Villa and instinct told him to check his guns locked up in the library. They always left the library lights on but they were off when he opened the door. He turned them on and saw Beatriz sitting at the far end by the window.

"Here you are my little flower" he said, "why are you here alone in the dark? Everyone is looking for you."

She did not move and on her face was such a look of sadness that Roberto quickly went towards her. It was then he saw the gun in her hand, almost hidden on her lap, her dress billowed around her. He stopped short as his heart pounded. He wanted to prevent any sudden movement on her part and his first instinct was to stay very calm.

"Beatriz, just give me the gun, no questions asked and we'll talk."

She sat very still then spoke calmly. "This is your gun, Roberto, I broke the glass cabinet and took it."

"Just hand it to me Beatriz and we'll talk, just you and me, please."

"Yes, Roberto, just you and me, just you and me," she repeated. She spoke quietly with amazing calm. "It's loaded Roberto, watch," and his heart jumped as she raised the gun to her head.

"No Beatriz, tell me why, I am listening, please talk to me."

She stood up. "Come closer Roberto, do not try to take the gun," and as Roberto moved towards her she suddenly reached out and took his arm pulling him to her while still holding the gun to her head.

"Look at me Roberto, look closely. My heart is breaking." Her dark eyes were filled with tears that ran down her face. "I'm not afraid of dying, I'm afraid of living.... without you."

It was like an electric bolt going through his body and first he felt the pain and then the numbness. This must be a nightmare he thought, it can't be real. All his years of experience did not come to his rescue and it took him a few moments to try and compose himself. He knew he could take the gun, he had done it many times before but it was always the enemy and not a young girl close to his heart.

"Beatriz my little flower, my heart is breaking also. I've always cared for you, you know that. But there are different kinds of love Beatriz, the love I have for you is not the same as my love for Shane."

"Shane," she said disdainfully, "don't tell me about Shane. She cannot possibly give you what I can. She loves you with her beauty Roberto, that's all. I will love you with all the passion inside me that I have carried for so long."

"Beatriz, you are only sixteen, you are so young, so much to live for. Please, just give me the gun and I promise we will talk," said Roberto trying to keep himself under control. He was so close and he tried to calculate. What would be faster, him taking the gun or her pulling the trigger? It was a life and death gamble which he was reluctant to take.

"I don't want to talk Roberto, I am a woman, not a child and I want you to love me as a woman." By now her hand was starting to shake and Roberto knew the gun could go off prematurely. It was a powerful gun and he took a deep breath and prayed for forgiveness for what he was about to say and do.

"Put down the gun Beatriz, come into my arms my little flower and I will love you."

She looked at Roberto, her eyes were glassy, the pupils dilated and Roberto knew she had taken drugs but she did not put down the gun.

"Hold me Roberto, hold me quick," and her voice was shaking. He took her in his arms and he could feel her body trembling against him. "I love you so much," she said, her voice barely audible, "kiss me."

Roberto bent his head towards her and once again he prayed for forgiveness as his lips came down gently on hers. It was five seconds of ecstasy for Beatriz before the powerful blast of the gun knocked them both over and blood splattered over Roberto's face as he lay unconscious. Suddenly there was the sound of running footsteps and people shouting. It was there that they found them, Roberto still holding the body of the girl, the top of her head was gone and they were both covered in blood. Beatriz was in the arms of her prince—she had gotten her midnight wish.

Chapter Seven

Beatriz was buried in a private funeral after a Catholic ceremony. Against his doctor's orders, Roberto attended the funeral and Shane held his arm tightly as they stood with Skye and Maria beside the white coffin surrounded with flowers. There were gunpowder burns on the side of his face, the skin under his eyes was blackened and his hearing was temporarily gone.

He placed a single white orchid on the casket, bowed his head in prayer and whispered, "sleep well, my little flower, in the arms of the Almighty, sleep well." He bent and kissed the coffin and Skye had to gently pull him away. The full impact had not hit him yet and he felt responsible for what had happened. He was unable to mourn and it was like a monster within him that taunted him and kept bringing back the painful guilt that he would carry within himself.

President Juan Gomez and his wife Isabella offered to take Camille to stay with them until some of the excitement died down and Roberto's appearance improved. It was going to be difficult explaining to Camille why she would never see her cousin Beatriz again.

Skye and Maria stayed at the Villa for a week hoping they could comfort each other by being close. Roberto had changed; he was obviously devastated and living in a world of his own. He would spend most of his time in the library or on the beach. Once he went riding and asked Ramon and Damien to ride with him, not behind him as they always did.

He had never acted like this before and everyone went out of their way to try to help him but the hurt he felt was too severe and unforgiving. The report that he handed in simply stated that the gun had accidentally discharged when she had picked it up and was about to hand it to Roberto. Of course he knew he would have to explain why a loaded gun was easily accessible to anyone and he would accept the blame and take full responsibility to protect Beatriz. He made a vow that her secret would never be revealed.

President Gomez had suggested to Roberto a leave of absence would be good for him but Roberto did not want to go away. A few weeks went by and Roberto's hearing started to return. It was then that Andre stepped in and took over. He and Roberto would sit on the beach and Andre would talk while Roberto listened. Maybe it was the calmness of the ocean, the tranquility surrounding them, the peaceful azure skies maybe it was the comforting words that came from Andre and the fact that it was just he and his brother sharing precious moments together.

Roberto kept blaming himself over and over again for not being capable of taking the gun from Beatriz. He felt he had made the wrong decisions during those crucial moments and should have trusted in himself.

"Did you not think," said Andre "that if you had done so and the gun had gone off, then she would have died by your hand—it would have been like pulling the trigger yourself. What a tremendous burden you would have to bear. Could you live with that Roberto? She wanted to die, you said so yourself, God rest her soul."

Roberto looked out across the ocean. "She was only sixteen Andre, sixteen, just a child."

"Yes, a child Roberto, but also a woman. We all have the child within us, it never leaves. But she wanted you to see her as a woman, and she loved you, I believe, wholeheartedly. Roberto, love is the strongest emotion in the world, it holds no bonds. It can give life, it can destroy it. Don't let it destroy de sangre, don't let it."

Roberto quickly looked at Andre, "de sangre?" he said surprise showing in his voice, "you remember? You call me blood brother?"

Andre shook his head. "No Roberto, I do not remember anything, I am really sorry but right now the important thing to remember is that you are not to blame, just remember that, you are not to blame. Remember also that you will become a stronger person because of this tragedy, you will see."

Roberto looked sad, "When did she grow up Andre, when did that little girl become a woman?"

Andre spoke with sorrow in his voice, "Skye knew, Maria knew and so did Shane."

Roberto's eyes widened, they knew what?"

"Beatriz never belonged to Skye and Maria, Roberto, she was never their little girl, she was your little girl. She adored you Roberto and that adoration turned to love when she grew older. It's just one of those tragic things no one could do anything about."

"How was it possible for everyone to know except myself, Andre? Tell me, how is this possible?"

"I'll tell you how," said Andre, "it was because you adored her too but all you could see was that little girl. You never saw the woman she had become until it was too late."

Roberto stared hard at Andre and almost a minute passed before he spoke. "How do you know all this Andre, you haven't even been here that long. How could you possibly know this much?"

Andre just shook his head, "I don't know, Roberto, I honestly really do not know."

An investigation had begun to find out where Beatriz had gotten the drugs. Did other teenagers from the school have access to them like Beatriz? Were they in any danger? The school was ordered shut down temporarily but Roberto was not allowed to head the investigation. His feelings were too involved.

Slowly and painfully Roberto's healing process began and it was not easy at first. He would lie awake at night and see Beatriz's smiling face and her gentle laugh and then the way she would look at him. What a fool he was not to have known. The most difficult moment was the kiss, but he would remember what Andre had told him. "Roberto, she knew she was going to die and it was a goodbye kiss. There was nothing you could do to prevent it."

The pain was starting to dull and he would turn towards Shane and hold her in his arms. She was so precious to him, his jewel, his whole life, his power. He made a mental note to spend more time with her.

Chapter Eight

Jodi was staying longer in the Dominican than she had planned. She was beginning to enjoy her stay and as Shane had predicted, she was getting used to their way of life. She would spend many hours with Shane riding or lying on the beach and chatting to her heart's content.

It was a Saturday morning when Shane and Roberto left to visit President Gomez and his wife Isabella and Jodi went alone to the beach for a few hours. She was never really alone as Ramon would always be there for both her and Shane on the weekends. She lay on the blanket wearing a large sunhat and glasses and a blue outfit that matched her eyes. It was the early morning and the sun was not too hot. Jodi put down her book and looked at Ramon. He stood a short distance away throwing pebbles into the water, his face looking very solemn. What is the matter with him she thought, why does he have to look so glum all the time? She decided to ask him.

"Ramon?"

"What?"

"Don't you ever smile?"

"Nothing to smile about."

"I've never seen your teeth."

Ramon slowly turned and stared at Jodi before answering. "Why you want to see my teeth?"

"Oh, I don't know."

There was silence for a few minutes. The only sound came from the ocean, and then Ramon spoke. "You not need bodyguard. Nobody kills you, too much trouble, not worth it."

"So why do you protect me?" said Jodi taunting him.

"Because Roberto tells me."

"So do you do everything Roberto tells you to do?"

Ramon stares again at Jodi then says "Si."

"If Roberto tells you to jump in the ocean will you do it?"

Ramon looked at Jodi again. "Ramon changes mind, you need bodyguard." "That's not a very complimentary thing to say Ramon."

The ocean was beginning to gleam like a giant jewel and the pale soft blue of the sky lay like a velvet cushion behind her.

"Ramon?"

"What?"

"Are you married?"

"Do I look married?"

Jodi looked surprised. "Oh, so how does someone look if they're married?"

"Worried."

"Worried! Roberto is married."

"Roberto married to Shane."

"So what is that supposed to mean?"

"Senora is good woman."

"You mean she is very beautiful!"

Silence, then "Si, very beautiful."

"So Ramon, what are you trying to say?"

Ramon gave a big sigh and turned around, "you talk too much, and you give Ramon bad headache."

"Ramon?"

"No more questions."

"Just one, please Ramon, I promise, just one."

"Make it fast, I'm getting nervous, you don't want to see Ramon nervous."

"Okay, okay, Ramon, have you ever loved anyone?"

Ramon looked quickly at Jodi. The dark eyes had narrowed, the scar looked vivid on his face, his long hair blew in the breeze. Jodi sat very still, afraid to move. Ramon continued to stare at her and she wished she had not asked the question. In fact, she wished at that moment she was anywhere but there. Finally, he walked over to his horse and mounted. Jodi looked at him. He did not speak. He pointed to her horse and she obediently got up and walked over to it. She turned to look at him. His face showed no emotion but the eyes spoke volumes. She mounted her horse and followed Ramon back to the Villa. She would not admit that he had frightened her.

The next day Shane and Jodi had lunch together. Roberto would be gone for several hours and Jodi took the opportunity to speak to Shane alone.

"What do you know about Ramon, Shane? I think he's a little strange."

"Not really," said Shane, "he's actually quite a sweet person."

"I'll bet you didn't think that when you first met him," said Jodi.

"You're right, I didn't. But we've gotten to know him through the years and we get along fine. Just don't make him nervous."

"Oh," said Jodi, "well it's too late. I think I did just that yesterday."

Shane looked up quickly. "Well the fact that you are sitting here at this table right now is like a miracle. He must be changing."

"Aren't you just exaggerating a little Shane?"

"Not at all. Ask Roberto what he has seen Ramon do. But we don't know anything about him, or what has happened to him. Just be a little careful Jodi. That's all I can say."

Serious meetings were being held at the Presidential Palace. President Juan Gomez agreed with Roberto to tighten the laws in regards to drugs that were filtering into the Country. Both Roberto and the President were aware that Carlos Martinez was behind this and their first reaction was to protect the schools. Roberto had sent in Special Forces to inspect the schools and a frightening discovery had surfaced. A large cache of mortars and assault rifles had been found in the basement of one of the schools. Why was ammunition being brought into the schools? What did it have to do with the drug problem? Was there someone inside working with Carlos Martinez? What was the connection? Every student would have to undergo questioning.

Another fight had broken out at the border and two men with suspected links to Carlos Martinez had been killed and Roberto immediately made plans to send Camille out of the Country. His anger was evident when he addressed the situation to the President. Then there was the big question … how was Beatriz able to obtain drugs?

"How dare he attack our young people, said Roberto. They are so vulnerable. I know this man better than anyone and I want to confront him with your permission. I have something I want to tell him, a message, and if he disagrees, I want him to know that he will have to answer to me."

Juan Gomez was quite aware that Roberto had not fully recovered from the shocking experience with Beatriz and that he held Carlos Martinez responsible for what had happened. "Keep in mind Roberto that we know what he has done and what he is capable of doing. His reputation alone poses a potential security risk and remember also that his citizenship was never revoked."

Roberto was quiet for a moment, deep in thought as he stood by the window looking out. "I am going to see him, I must see him."

The silence in the room was deafening. The President and Roberto were alone and Roberto turned away from the window and faced Juan Gomez. "I am going to see him" he repeated and the President immediately stood up.

"No Roberto, I will not allow you to do that. The man is a monster and he would be only too happy to have you walk into his lair. No, it is out of the question, besides, what makes you think he will listen to anything you have to say?"

"He will listen or risk losing everything. I know what to say, I must see him," repeated Roberto.

The President stood adamant. "I forbid it," he said. "I never thought I would have to say this, Roberto, if I have to put you under surveillance, so be it. Your actions are suicidal; I will not allow you to do so."

Roberto had no intention of giving up. "Please try to understand, it might be the only way."

"The only way to do what, Roberto? I have always agreed with your decisions, I always stood behind you but in this instance, I don't want a person of your caliber to die at the hands of that viper. You are too valuable to this Country. The answer is no and that's final."

After a long pause, Roberto spoke. "Okay, I can see this is going nowhere. Hmm, let me see, I have another plan. Let me make out a report and outline it for you and I'll present it at another meeting sometime in the next few days. Let me know what day you have time to schedule in a meeting and we will go on from there."

"Sounds great Roberto. Please do not be offended by what I have said. I am very fond of you. Besides being a very close personal friend, we would never be able to replace you. You understand I'm sure."

Roberto nodded and answered, "As you wish sir."

Ramon was far the best fighter that Roberto had ever come across. He moved like lightening and his senses were extremely sharp. He did not know the meaning of fear. Every move that Carlos made was watched by Roberto's elite specially trained commandos and Roberto knew he had to move quickly once given his location.

Two days later, unknown to anyone, he left in the middle of the night, Ramon by his side. He took a chance and was relieved to discover that President Gomez had not put him under surveillance and soon they had passed the border into Haiti. This surprised Roberto—he did not realize that Carlos Martinez was that close to the Dominican border.

Carlos was very unpredictable but Roberto knew that he and Ramon had backup with the commandos in the area and they brought their horses to a halt in front of an inconspicuous brown building and boldly walked in the front door. Two men playing cards by the door looked up quickly and their hands went towards their guns. They immediately froze when they saw Ramon.

"I am here to see Carlos, he is expecting me," said Roberto and he and Ramon were taken upstairs and told to wait in a room.

"This is too easy," said Ramon looking around the room suspiciously, "something not right Roberto."

"We'll find out soon," said Roberto looking out the window. There was no one to be seen and he wondered why the two men had taken a 'for granted' attitude when confronted suddenly by Roberto and Ramon carrying the machine gun.

Suddenly the door opened and Carlos Martinez walked in followed by four men. He wore a white suit and had black greased-back hair that fell to his shoulders. His face was clean-shaven, tanned and smooth, and his eyes were incredibly dark and restless. Gold rings adorned his fingers and a heavy gold chain hung from his neck.

"Please sit down gentlemen and make yourselves comfortable," he said pointing to the chairs and sitting down. "What can I bring you, tea perhaps or maybe something stronger?" He put a cigar in his mouth and one of the men lit it. He took a puff and looked at Roberto. "So you must be the famous Roberto Castaneda, si, pretty boy, I recognize you." He took another puff. "Well, should I be honoured?" he said with a snarl. Roberto sat down and Ramon stood beside him, both hands holding the machine gun and the other four men stood behind Carlos.

"So is your bodyguard as good as they say he is," sneered Carlos looking at Ramon.

"Did you want to find out?" said Roberto. "I personally would not advise it, if you know what I mean."

"I have a feeling this is not a social visit," said Carlos. You obviously came here for a reason Castaneda," he said puffing nervously on the cigar, his eyes growing shifty.

Roberto detested the man and there was so much he wanted to say but it was not the right time. "I'll get right to the point," he said not taking his eyes off him. "As long as you stay on this side of the border, we won't have a problem. Actually I would rather you not even come this close because I don't trust you. Unfortunately, this area is outside my jurisdiction otherwise there is no way you would be here right now. This includes your men also. I am warning you, stay away from the Dominican Republic, the Dominicanos and anything else to do with us. I will not tolerate anything, comprender? If you do not heed this warning," Roberto paused, "if you do not heed this warning," he repeated, "I give you my word you will discover a new meaning to the word 'destruction'. That is all I have to say. No wait," Roberto paused, a puzzled expression on his face. "I really do not understand you Carlos. Why would you go to so much trouble with a Country the size of the Dominican? You are known to work in bigger areas, Columbia, Venezuela, Argentina, is it because of your hatred for me? It does not make sense."

Carlos was silent and Roberto stood up, no one had moved except Ramon who stepped closer to Roberto still holding the machine gun as if it were glued to his hands. The look on his face spoke louder than the gun, as if it was unbearably painful for him to hold back. His eyes seemed to say give me a reason, please, and the scar on his face stood out vividly. The others got the message. Roberto started walking towards the door.

"Let me congratulate you Roberto," called out Carlos.

Roberto stopped but did not turn around. "Congratulate me?" he said.

"Si Roberto, congratulations. Your taste in women is magnificento."

Roberto slowly turned around. His eyes had narrowed into slits, his face deeply flushed under the tan as Ramon tried to push him aside with the machine gun. Roberto's voice was barely a whisper. "What are you talking about?" The next words that Roberto heard would haunt him for the rest of his life.

"Pa guapa, very, very beautiful" said Carlos in a low voice, then he paused and said "I desire your wife, Roberto, I want Shane."

The words hit Roberto like an electrical current. So that was it, now he understood—it was Shane, Carlos wanted Shane. Ramon immediately stepped in front of Roberto screaming "da chiflado" but Roberto held tightly to his arm. Carlos had stood up and his men surrounded him but amazingly no one produced a firearm.

"You see Roberto," continued Carlos, "I have changed. No violence, no fighting, I am clean. No one can arrest me, my name is clear, but ... it is known to happen ... I always get what I want."

Roberto knew why none of them had reached for their guns. Ramon was too well known to them and he held his machine gun high, his eye twitching nervously. The look on his face clearly portrayed how difficult it was for him to restrain himself from shooting and he stood there like a statue; and everyone in the room was familiar with Ramon's uncommon reflexes. This was the reason Roberto had chosen Ramon to accompany him. Roberto looked at Carlos. He knew exactly what he was going to do to this man who dared to utter Shane's name, let alone even think of her, to desire her. He shuddered inwardly as he spoke in a low voice.

"You just dug your own grave Carlos," and walked out of the room followed closely by Ramon.

Carlos stood still for a moment. He did not want to admit it to himself the impact Roberto's presence had made. Finally, one of his men spoke out.

"He's bluffing Carlos, who does he think he is?"

Carlos spoke slowly, weighing his words. "Pain, Alfredo, I want him to feel real pain. Let me see—what would hurt him the most? Si, we will take from him his beautiful wife and maybe also the little girl, no?"

Roberto and Ramon rode back quietly. For almost an hour neither one spoke and Ramon knew that Roberto was suffering. Finally he spoke.

"I will protect Senora Shane with my life, you know that Roberto, but you should have let me kill him. Very easy for me, no more trouble for you."

Roberto was still reeling from Carlos' words. He shook his head.

"No Ramon, we need information from him, valuable information that could save lives. We will get that first."

"Then can I kill him?" asked Ramon eagerly.

"I promise you, Ramon, you can do the honours."

Ramon smiled. "Gracias Roberto, that is a big honour you give to me. Ramon is happy. He is a coward, Roberto, he brings with him four men."

Roberto shook his head, "he had three of his men with him Ramon, not four."

"I counted four" insisted Ramon, "why you say three?"

"Remember the man who lit Carlos' cigar? His name is Diego Sanchez—he is one of our Elite Commandos."

"I am very embraced Roberto, that is good work."

"Gracias," said Roberto, "and the word is impressed, not embraced. Si, actually I am too. These commandos work fast."

They rode the rest of the way silently. Part of Roberto was still in shock; he kept hearing Carlos' words, "so precioso, I want Shane," and it caused him to cringe. How dare he say such a thing? Drastic safety measures would have to be made immediately. When they reached the Villa, Ramon told Roberto that he would look after the horses.

"You go to Senora, I take horses to stable. Do not worry, I protect her, Senora will not be hurt, Ramon here."

Roberto smiled and squeezed Ramon's arm and went inside eagerly looking for Shane. He knew the heaviness in his heart would not be lifted until he saw her and he also knew that his beloved Shane was now in great danger.

"Hola Rosita," he said entering the kitchen, "where is Shane?"

"Oh Roberto, there you are," she said. "Shane? She is not here."

Roberto froze, "Where … where is she?"

"She went to that new boutique. What is the matter?" she said taking his arm, "are you ill?"

Roberto felt ill indeed. An awful expression had crossed his face and nausea swept over him. He could handle anything, even Beatriz's death that took time and he was still healing, however, Shane, that was something else. If something happened to her he knew it would destroy him. He also knew that Carlos would move fast and he had to move faster. But wait, why was he so worried? It would be impossible for Carlos or his men to cross the border as it was too well guarded.

"What boutique Rosita, which one?" he asked.

"It's the new one Roberto, the one that just opened in Fort Liberte. What is it Roberto, what is happening to you?" she said her eyes wide. Roberto felt like someone had thrown hot water on his face.

"Fort Liberte? Good God, that's in Haiti, Rosita, they've crossed the border into Haiti!" It meant that Carlos might have already kidnapped Shane.

"Rosita," he said, his voice shaky, "when did Shane leave?"

"This morning Roberto at about 9:00."

Roberto did not recognize his own voice that seemed to be coming from far away.

"Who was with her?"

"Jodi her friend. Is something wrong?" she said beginning to be very worried also.

Roberto grasped both her arms. "Who were their bodyguards?"

Rosita by now was becoming alarmed. "Damien went with them. Roberto, what is the matter, what is wrong?"

"Only Damien?" said Roberto, "only Damien?" he repeated, "no one else?" Suddenly he rushed out of the Villa towards the stables just as Ramon was coming out.

Roberto was breathless, "Ramon, come with me. Shane has crossed the border; she and Jodi-Anne are in Haiti." Ramon was not alarmed; he was incapable of being alarmed but his eyes glared fiercely. He quickly brought the horses and Garcia and Lorenzo joined them as the four of them galloped off towards Forte Liberte. Roberto prayed that they would not be too late.

Chapter Nine

Shane held up the dress and looked in the mirror. "Jodi, what do you think about this one, do you like it?" she asked.

Jodi came over and looked. "That, Shane, is gorgeous, I really like it but then again everything looks good on you. Your eyes are amazing."

Shane laughed, "you always make me feel better when I am sad. I miss Roberto, he didn't come home last night and I am always worried when that happens. I know there are things he cannot tell me with so much happening right now but I do worry over him Jodi and hope he's okay."

"He knows how to take care of himself Shane, no need to worry. By the way, I haven't seen Ramon around the last few days either. Do you suppose they've gone somewhere together?"

"Probably," said Shane, "but I'm going to take your advice and not worry. I'll probably see Roberto by the time we get back. Look at this blouse Jodi. I think it would look great on you." Shane had reached for a blue top embroidered with beads and just at that moment a horrendous explosion shattered the windows of the boutique and Damien, who was standing near the door hollered out to Shane and Jodi to lie on the floor. He stood just inside the open doorway and aimed his machine gun as he looked out from one corner. Another blast was heard and Damien was thrown backwards and lay on the ground shot and dying. Then everything happened fast. Four men, their faces covered rushed into the boutique and Shane was half lifted and dragged out to a waiting car. Jodi had tried to go to Shane's aid but one of the masked men had roughly hit her with the edge of the gun knocking her against one of the tables and cutting the side of her mouth.

The whole area outside suddenly became quiet and the street was empty. The explosion had smashed their car to smithereens in front of the boutique and killed the driver.

When Roberto arrived ten minutes later this was the scene that greeted him and his heart sank. He knew exactly what had happened and he was too late. They rushed into the boutique and found Jodi on her knees crying beside Damien's body and the two terrified saleswomen hiding behind the counter. Roberto knelt beside Jodi and put his arm around her. He could see that the side of her mouth was bleeding but otherwise seemed unhurt but hysterical.

"Jodi-Anne," he said in a trembling voice, "what happened to Shane? Talk to me Jodi-Anne, what happened to her?"

Jodi continued to cry and Roberto shook her gently, "Jodi-Anne, tell me, what happened to Shane?" Ramon bent down and lifted Jodi to her feet. "Roberto, we must leave, we will look for Senora."

Roberto's brain was not functioning properly and all he could think of was that his beloved Shane was gone—they had taken her away. "They've taken Shane," he said suddenly turning to Ramon, "good Lord Ramon, they've taken Shane."

Ramon lifted Jodi and carried her out, following Roberto. People were starting to come back out slowly on the streets and Garcia and Lorenzo were getting the full story from a few witnesses that had bravely come forward. The car that had brought them to the boutique had been blown up and the driver was one of Roberto's gendarmes.

They had seen a woman, Melena, yes, very long dark hair dragged from the store by four men and taken away in a car. In all the commotion no one saw Roberto slip away. He knew this was something that he had to do alone. He had overpowered the shock that had hit him when he entered the boutique and Shane was not there. His mind was clear, there was no anger, no frustration and no feeling whatsoever. He knew exactly what had to be done. He had put himself into a trance and he was going to find his Shane no matter what and he also knew that he would break his promise to Ramon. He was going to kill Carlos Martinez himself.

Roberto touched the gold band on his wrist. It contained a tiny FM transmitter that pulsed every second and would give him Shane's location. He knew that he would find Shane but he did not know what was happening to her. He rode in the direction shown to him on the gold band. It gave him the signals that he needed and the signals came louder as he neared his destination. It was working beautifully. It had guided him to a large house in a deserted area. Roberto turned off the sound on the band and set the small dial. Next, he synchronized his watch and counted to five before moving towards the house. He had exactly ten minutes to do what he planned.

He felt cool and level-headed as he opened the door, machine gun held high. Two men stood in the hallway and Roberto fired at them. Immediately two more men came running but Roberto had not stopped firing and they also fell. He waited, no one else appeared. Maybe those were the four men that dragged Shane out of the boutique. He knew there might be more and he waited.

It was quiet, and there was no sound. He kicked open the doors but could not find Shane. There are no more, he thought or they would have appeared when the shots were fired. Quickly he went up the staircase still holding the gun high and kicked open the first door he came to. Carlos stood at the far end of the room, and his hand held a knife against Shane's neck as she sat bound and gagged in a chair. Roberto could feel his heart pounding inside him but his head was cool. He averted his eyes from his beloved Shane, as he could not bear to see her like that.

Carlos smiled, he looked sinister and evil and not at all disturbed that Roberto had found him so soon.

"Roberto, I was expecting you but not so quickly. I commend you on your brilliant work. Ah, Shane, si, you came for Shane. I cannot blame you; she really is something, very smooth skin.

"Roberto felt the pain again and at that moment he knew he was capable of tearing the man apart.

"It is too bad you cannot have her back," said Carlos. "I know you want to kill me but I will have the satisfaction of taking her with me." "You see," he continued, "when you shoot me, the explosive device in this knife will go off and it is very powerful. Your beautiful lady will be blown to pieces. Do you have any suggestions Comandante?"

Roberto's voice was barely a whisper, "you're dead Carlos, you're as good as dead."

Carlos laughed, "very dramatic Roberto, but you are not standing on a stage. You sound like a fool. Do I look dead to you? I am still standing, look."

Roberto carefully placed the machine gun on the ground. "Take it Carlos, it is yours, take it and go," he said stepping back a good distance. Carlos looked suspiciously at Roberto. He thought to himself that it must be a trick but then, if he picked up the gun he could kill Roberto and Shane would be his. It all seemed so simple. Maybe Roberto thought he would take the gun and leave. Yes, that was it and besides, what could he do unarmed?

Carlos moved towards the machine gun and picked it up. It worked, Roberto did not move. Carlos snickered under his breath; this was easier than he thought. Roberto was not as tough as everyone made him out to be. He held the gun and pointed it at Roberto.

"You really are a fool Roberto, not as clever as they say. I am disappointed. Now all I have to do is get rid of you and then," he glanced at Shane, "this beauty will belong to me. But do not worry Comandante, I shall take very good care of her, this I promise you. Now, do I look dead to you?"

The explosion that followed was deafening and the impact threw the machine gun across the room. Roberto walked calmly towards it and picked it up. He looked at Carlos lying on the ground, eyes protruding, gasping for air. He stood over him and said "no" and shot him in the face. "Now you look dead," he said. Then he called out to Shane, "close your eyes Shane, now." He then continued shooting at the dead body as if he was trying to finish the round. When he finally stopped he stood very still and did not move. His eyes were cold, he had no feeling of remorse or anger, he felt nothing. Then he turned towards Shane, suddenly realizing that she was there and rushed to her side.

He gently removed the tape off her mouth and kissed her, a long kiss filled with love and emotion. Shane was trembling, she was extremely frightened, she had seen what had happened and she tried to pull back from Roberto. He smoothed back her hair and held her. "Shane," he whispered, "you must not be afraid of me, I had to do it, I had to." He thanked God for sparing her life and kissed her again so happy that she was alive and completely unaware that she was still tied.

"Roberto you are forgetting something," she said with tears in her eyes.

"Forgetting what my little one," he said not wanting to stop.

"Roberto, please untie me," said a tearful Shane. He quickly untied her, apologizing and massaging her wrists and kissing her hands. He held her again and did not want to let her go. He knew he was obsessed but he didn't care, Shane was alive.

"Shane, are you okay, did that monster hurt you?" he said brushing away the tears from her face.

"I'm okay Roberto," she managed to say, still shocked and frightened from what she had witnessed. "How did you know where to find me?

"I will tell you later, but first let's get out of here. Are you sure you're all right or shall I carry you?"

"I'm fine, really," she said, "but Jodi, what happened to Jodi?"

"Jodi is okay, she's probably back at the Villa by now," he said putting his arm around her and steering her away from where Carlos lay on the ground.

"We just have to get down the stairs, Allegro is by the door." They went out and Roberto mounted the horse and pulled Shane up behind him.

Shane wrapped both arms around his waist and rested her cheek against his back. She closed her eyes and felt safe, but she could not get out of her mind Roberto's actions.

"I love you Shane," said Roberto as they started out.

"I love you too Roberto," said Shane in a shaky voice but she couldn't help wondering who this man was. She had never before witnessed such brutal force. How was it possible for her to feel safe and frightened at the same time?

"Roberto, Damien, what happened to Damien? I saw him lying on the ground."

"He's dead Shane, those murderers killed him. Don't cry Shane, there was nothing we could do. Just hold on tightly and close your eyes, don't think of anything right now, you're with me."

President Gomez had sent out troops to search for Roberto and Shane and they had caught up with them. By the time Roberto and Shane had arrived back to the Villa they had an escort of ten gendarmes. A great deal of excitement followed and the whole Villa seemed to light up. Not only did Roberto and Shane arrive safe and sound, but also news of Carlos' death had spread. Large amounts of drugs and cash were already being confiscated and a few men had already been rounded up. Diego Sanchez was safe. He had probably saved Shane from a horrible experience when she was brought to the hideaway. He had told Carlos that Roberto was on his way and would be arriving any minute. They decided to just tie Shane up and wait. Shane had no idea that the man who tied her to the chair was a member of the Elite Commando group. Roberto was deeply grateful and would make plans to see if it was at all possible to add Diego to the security in force there at the Villa if President Gomez would be willing.

Aside from some scrapes and bruises that Shane received when dragged from the boutique, she came through her ordeal miraculously well. Jodi was not as lucky and reacted later.

Damien was buried with full honours and Roberto expressed his sorrow to Ramon. He knew that they had fought together in his rebel army years ago as guerrillas but he did not know that they were cousins.

"He gave his life for us Ramon," said Roberto embracing him. He was one of the bravest young men I have ever seen. I am so sorry. I feel your pain … I share your sorrow."

There were no tears on Ramon's face. Like Roberto, he was incapable of breaking down.

"Si," he said calmly, "we live today and we die tomorrow."

"We are having a dinner in Damien's honour," said Roberto. "You must sit down with us."

Ramon hesitated.

"Please," said Shane taking his arm, "we would be so happy if you came."

Jodi stood beside Shane. She looked very pale; her blue eyes were filled with tears as she was obviously still going through her ordeal. There was a small cut beside her mouth and he looked at her for a moment then said, "si, gracias, I will come." This did not go unnoticed by Roberto.

Ramon sat at the large table between Roberto and Andre. Roberto had asked Andre to talk to Ramon and help him through this difficult period. By now, everyone knew that Andre had that special way of helping people cope through an emotional difficulty and by the time the dinner was over, Ramon seemed to lose much of the tenseness that he carried. No one had ever seen Ramon smile but he seemed to open up and talk as he and Andre carried on a lengthy conversation in Spanish.

Surprisingly Andre discovered that Ramon's background was so interesting that after dinner they continued their conversation in the library. What a remarkable and odd combination they made thought Roberto. The elegant, fine-mannered Andre and the tough, rough, long-haired Ramon with the machine gun always slung over his shoulder.

Another thing that Andre discovered about Ramon which no one was aware of was that along with the Spanish that he spoke, he was also fluent in Hebrew. Ramon's mother was Spanish and his father was a Jew. Andre and Ramon seemed to bond and a close friendship sprang up between them.

The guests had all left by five o'clock and Roberto and Shane joined Andre and Ramon in the library. Rosita served more coffee followed by dessert brought in by Jodi. Shane moved over on the couch and beckoned to Jodi to sit next to her. Jodi shook her head and asked to be excused. Ramon stopped talking and his eyes followed her as she left the room and went up the stairs.

"I don't think she's feeling too well," remarked Shane looking worried.

"I think the recent episode was too much for her," said Roberto "and I can't say that I blame her. She witnessed a tragedy and she refuses to see a doctor.

"Do you think if I talk to her it would help?" offered Andre.

"Let me go up and see how she is first," said Shane "and maybe we'll know what to do. Poor thing, she came here for a holiday and look what happens." Shane got up and left the room that had suddenly become very quiet. Ramon put down his cup and just stared ahead as if deep in thought.

"What are you thinking Ramon?" asked Andre gently.

Ramon did not answer immediately, and then he spoke. "Maybe … maybe, the Senorita will ride on the beach. Maybe Senorita will feel better beside the ocean. I will stay with her if she wishes."

"That is very nice of you Ramon," said Roberto. "I'm sure this would be good for Jodi-Anne right now. Let me go up and tell them what you have suggested."

Roberto left and Andre and Ramon waited. Then suddenly Ramon got up and said he had to see Rosita in the kitchen. He emerged five minutes later holding a paper bag and stood at the foot of the stairs. In a few minutes Roberto appeared followed by Shane and Jodi. As they came down Roberto looked at Ramon and whispered, "how did you know she would come down?" and Ramon said simply, "I just know."

They went towards the stable and Ramon brought out Jodi's horse then went back for his. In a few minutes they were riding off towards the beach, the brown bag tied over Ramon's left shoulder, his gun on the right. The sun was still in view sitting in the middle of the ocean, fiery and bold above the ebony waters. They rode together quietly and after traveling quite a distance, Ramon motioned to Jodi to slow down and stop.

They were a long way from the Villa and all around them it was peaceful and quiet except for the sound of the ocean. They brought the horses to a halt and dismounted to sit under one of the palm trees. Ramon took out two coffees that

Rosita had poured in paper cups. Jodi took the cup and put it on the ground beside her, sitting very still.

"Are you hungry?" asked Ramon reaching in the bag and taking out two sandwiches. Jodi thanked Ramon and put the sandwich beside the coffee. She sat quietly gazing out over the ocean, her eyes bright and shiny. Ramon drank his coffee and wondered what he could say to Jodi to make her feel better. Five minutes passed then Ramon knew he had to do something.

He moved behind Jodi and put his arms around her and they both sat facing the ocean watching the sun slowly sink into the depths of the dark waters. Finally, after a long silence Jodi spoke.

"Thank you Ramon, thank you for understanding." She gave a long sigh and said "Maybe I'll have that coffee now."

Ramon reached for the cup and handed it to her—Jodi drank but did not move.

"You have sandwich too," said Ramon but Jodi shook her head. "I can't eat, Ramon, I'm not hungry but thanks." She sipped the coffee and said "I ... I ... he died Ramon, right in front of me, he died."

"Senorita, no more talking, you finish coffee and we go back. You sleep tonight and feel better and tomorrow we talk."

They stood up and Ramon took off his machine gun, placing it on the ground. The breeze from the ocean had brought a chill to the air suddenly turning the night quite cool. He removed his leather jacket and put it on Jodi buttoning it up as she stood there like a child. He took the empty cup from her hand and slung his gun back over his shoulder and said, "we go back now; everyone will be worried over you."

Jodi looked at Ramon, she knew nothing about him, who he was, his past, his thoughts, nothing, but what she did know was that when she looked into his eyes she saw kindness, bravery and passion. It was at that precise moment that Jodi knew she wanted to marry Ramon. They rode back and it was very dark by the time they reached the Villa. Jodi was calm and relaxed and Ramon took her inside. He looked at her and put his arms around her and just held her tightly for a moment and just as suddenly he was gone.

"Jodi, you're back," said Shane coming out of the library. "Sit with us, we're just talking." Roberto and Andre stood up as Jodi entered and sat down. Her hair was wind-blown, her face flushed and her eyes sparkled with life.

"You look much better Jodi-Anne," remarked Roberto. "I am so glad."

"Yes, thank you, I do feel a great deal better," she said smoothing back her hair.

"Well Jodi," said Andre, "it's surprising what a little bit of fresh air and a lot of understanding will do."

Jodi looked at Andre for a moment. There was something almost saintly about the man. She smiled at him and lowered her eyes. "You are also very understanding, Andre."

"Well," said Roberto, "I'm glad we are all so understanding and—Jodi-Anne, isn't that Ramon's jacket you are wearing? I've never seen him let anyone wear his jacket in all the years I've known him. His gun and his jacket are sacred to him. I've never seen him without either one."

Jodi blushed and Shane spoke quickly. "Isn't that just like Ramon, to lend Jodi his jacket on a cool night, how very gallant. Jodi, are you hungry? Let's go in the kitchen and see what's there. Would you excuse us" she said and took Jodi's arm and marched out of the room.

"Actually, Shane, I am feeling kind of hungry," said Jodi as they looked in the fridge.

"Mm look," she said, "here are those delicious stuffed grape leaves that Rosita makes. What are they called?"

"Sarma," said Shane, "she showed me how to make them. So Jodi, how come you're wearing Ramon's jacket?"

"It's like you said Shane, it got very cool," she said not looking at Shane.

"Jodi, Ramon never lets anyone wear his jacket."

Jodi shrugged her shoulders; she was busy eating a large piece of cake. "Ramon would be proud of me right now, Shane. He says I'm too skinny and I should eat more. Actually, I'm full now. Do you mind, Shane, I think I'd better go to bed. I'm really tired." She gave Shane a hug and walked out of the kitchen leaving Shane to just stand there and wonder.

The next morning at breakfast Roberto told Shane that they would be leaving for Switzerland in the next day or two.

"I miss our sons Shane, and I want to take you away from all of this for a while. You, I and Camille will be spending some time with the twins and for a while we'll be a family," he said. "On the way back we can also spend some time with your parents and see Terry too."

Tears came to Shane's eyes, she couldn't believe what she was hearing. They hadn't seen Frederik and Enrique for over a year and she missed them terribly. How wonderful that they would see her parents and Terry also. She put her arms around Roberto gratefully and kissed him as the tears ran down her face.

"You have made me so happy Roberto, so very happy."

"I asked Andre to come with us but he said this special time should be for you, me and the children. He is their uncle and the boys have never seen him, but he insisted."

"He is a very special person, isn't he Roberto?" Shane looked thoughtful for a moment, "I had wanted so much for Jodi and Andre to be a couple but I don't think that's happening."

"If I am not mistaken," said Roberto, "I think there's something happening between Ramon and Jodi-Anne. Have you not noticed Shane?"

"Come to think of it," she said, "I wondered the same thing when I saw Jodi wearing Ramon's jacket, but then, he might have just been a gentleman, you know, it was a chilly evening."

"That's possible," said Roberto, "however I've seen how they sometimes look at each other, Shane. As a matter of fact," and he paused with a smile on his face, "it is a thing of beauty."

Shane looked at Roberto with surprise, "you are becoming something of a poet, Roberto, 'a thing of beauty?'"

Roberto drew Shane towards him and gazed into her eyes. "You have forgotten my muchachita, I am somewhat of an expert on beauty. Have I told you today that I love you?" he said stroking back her hair.

"Today? No Roberto and I think you have been neglecting me lately, my husband. I guess this is the price women pay after ten years of marriage."

"Neglecting you!" exclaimed Roberto, his eyebrows darting up then he stared at her. Suddenly, he picked her up and at that precise moment Jodi walked into the dining room and stopped short.

"Oh, I'm sorry," she said apologetically, "I think I'm invading your privacy."

"It's quite all right Jodi-Anne," said Roberto putting Shane down, "my wife was just letting me know that she was being neglected. However, I intend to prove to her that this is not the case."

"Shane," said Jodi, and it was almost like a reprimand, "I don't know how you can say that. I have never seen anyone showered with so much love and affection as yourself. Roberto is such a warm and loving person and you are so lucky to be married to him."

Both Shane and Roberto looked at Jodi dumbfounded. She had never mentioned Roberto in such glowing terms and they exchanged surprised glances.

"Actually," continued Jodi pouring her coffee, "I'm glad you're both here. I will be leaving tomorrow to go back home. I've stayed longer than I had intended and—I have some thinking to do." Her voice suddenly choked.

"We were hoping you might stay here," said Roberto. "Oh, and by the way, gracias for those complimentary words."

"Yes, Jodi, would you not consider living here?" said Shane feeling a sudden sadness at the thought of her friend leaving.

"Thank you, thank you so much to the both of you for being so nice to me. As I mentioned, I have some thinking to do. I really … don't…. know…. what…. to…. do,"and she suddenly burst into tears.

"Jodi, what is it?" said Shane going to her side, "has something happened?"

Roberto sat beside her and took her hand, "Jodi-Anne, we are like family; is there something we can do, has someone annoyed you? Just tell us."

Jodi would not talk, but she continued crying. Shane looked at Roberto helplessly and Roberto stood up.

"Where are you going," she asked.

"I have to see Ramon," he said. "Maybe he can tell me."

"No please," begged Jodi through her tears, "do not say anything to Ramon, he doesn't know."

"He doesn't know what?" said Roberto.

"He doesn't know that I'm going home," sobbed Jodi, "please don't say anything to him."

Roberto looked at Shane, she too was at a loss as to what to do. They helped Jodi dry her tears and sat with her while she ate breakfast. Roberto and Shane knew that somehow this was all connected to Ramon and Roberto knew that he would have to find out what was happening. They had grown fond of Jodi and enjoyed her presence around them. They decided to delay their trip until things were settled and they did not mind at all doing this.

Shane went into the kitchen to get more coffee and Roberto excused himself and followed her. "You are right Roberto," she said, "there is something beautiful happening between them. Oh Roberto, it's just like us."

He took the coffee pot from her and put it back on the stove. "No Shane," he said pulling her to him, "you are wrong, no one, no one in this whole world have what we have, no one." Then he kissed her exactly the same way he had kissed her on their wedding day. "Do you really know how much I love you Shane?" he said not wanting to let her go.

Shane smiled, "I have a pretty good idea by now Comandante and I think our guest will be wondering what happened to her coffee." Roberto reluctantly released her and they went back to the dining room to sit with Jodi.

Roberto and Shane took Jodi to the airport the next day. She did not want Ramon to know when she was leaving but to tell him afterwards. Roberto would never forget the look on Ramon's face when he told him; it was a mixture of great loss and anger. Then his expression suddenly changed and turned to hurt. He almost looked like a little boy.

"Why," he said, "Senorita not say goodbye to me?"

"Ramon, I don't know" said Roberto, "but I believe she will return."

Ramon said no more. He turned around and walked away and Roberto could not help but feel sorry for him. He knew Ramon was tough but something seemed to be gone from him now.

The next few days that followed, Shane and Roberto prepared to leave. They left Rosita and Andre in charge of the Villa and Ramon in charge of security. Skye and Maria moved in temporarily to keep them company for the two weeks that Roberto, Shane and Camille would be gone.

Chapter Ten

They left on a Saturday morning accompanied by Garcia who sat with Roberto on the plane. Roberto was unaware that President Gomez had also placed two of his own personal bodyguards on the plane and they would follow them to Switzerland and then to Canada before flying back to the Dominican. Frederik and Enrique were also unaware of the family visit, which had been intended as a surprise, and as a result Roberto and Shane had to wait in the school's office until their credentials were cleared.

Camille saw them first as they came down the hallway and her shrieks of delight brought Garcia running.

"They're here, mama, papa, they're here," she cried out and ran down the hallway with Garcia close behind and landed in their arms. Shane and Roberto stood in the doorway as Shane's eyes filled with tears.

"Roberto, they have grown so tall, so fast," she said clutching his arm. Roberto watched proudly as the boys advanced towards them in their royal blue and white uniforms.

"They certainly have Shane," and he felt something tug at his heart. There were embraces all around and after obtaining permission to leave the grounds, they entered a limousine and left for their hotel.

Frederik and Enrique, although twins, were two very different individuals. Enrique resembled Roberto, dark eyes, dark hair, but sensitive and soft-spoken like Andre but there was also something about him that seemed so much like Shane. Frederik looked like Skye with the blond hair and the blue eyes but exactly like Roberto with his mannerisms. He would quite often use the nickname "Gemelo", twin brother, when referring to his brother. He excelled at riding and target practice, was the class president and always the leader when forming groups or for decision-making.

Many dignitaries had extended invitations to the Castanedas to their homes and dinners in their honour but Roberto wanted to keep their stay in Luzern Switzerland very low-key.

The week passed quickly, too quickly, and soon it was time to leave. Roberto promised Frederik and Enrique that they would return in the Fall and he would bring with him their uncle Andre.

"You will love him," said Shane. "He is such a fine young man and he's looking forward to seeing the two of you so much. How lucky you are to have him."

They arrived in Toronto at night and although the Dalingers knew when they were arriving, Roberto did not want to be met at Pearson International airport by anyone, especially reporters, hoping to keep their visit as quiet as possible. Garcia, of course, was unable to carry a firearm due to the laws of the Country but stayed close to Roberto until they cleared the Customs.

It was 2:00 A.M. by the time they drove out to the Dalingers who were eagerly waiting up for them and their joyful reunion lasted well into the night as they caught up with each other. Everyone slept in until after lunch time and Roberto and Terry caught up on current events. Terry begged Roberto for a story for his newspaper but Roberto told him the timing was bad.

"I promise you, Terry, that in a month I will call you and give you a very important interview for your paper regarding Carlos Martinez."

In the meantime there are some very confidential things happening right now concerning Martinez which I am not at liberty to divulge at the moment, but I promise you, I will give you your story. By the way, when are you going to visit us again Terry? The Country is much more relaxed than when you were there on your last visit."

"Turmoil, Roberto, the people want to read about fighting and chaos and over-running the government, you know, stuff like that. I must say though, you've done a pretty good job in clearing out the undesirables. How are my friends Damien and Ramon doing? It's been a while since I've seen them. Are they still toting machine guns and patrolling the beach? I sure miss those guys."

Roberto was quiet for a moment. He had taken his sunglasses out of his pocket and was polishing the lens. Finally he spoke quietly without looking up.

"Damien was killed a few weeks ago Terry. He died protecting Shane and Jodi-Anne. We did not want to tell the family, as we knew you'd be worried not knowing the details. Shane and Jodi-Anne are okay but we lost Damien, Terry, we lost a fine young man who didn't have a chance to live his life to its fullest. A tremendous loss to all of us."

"Good grief, Roberto, I am so sorry," said Terry, shock showing on his face. He did not speak for a moment, then said "I am really very sorry. How is Ramon taking it? I know they were buddies."

Roberto nodded, "actually, they were cousins. Ramon really felt it, I know, but he doesn't show his feelings easily. He keeps a lot inside. Did you know that Ramon speaks fluent Hebrew? His mother is Spanish and his father is a Jew. His bravery does not surprise me."

"Really?" said Terry, "that is very interesting. Maybe there's a story there. I wonder who his father is—or was. Is he still living?"

Roberto shook his head. "His whole family was massacred during the Civil War. We don't know anything else about his background. Andre discovered all this."

"Andre—now there's a story right there," said Terry. "That is pretty amazing Roberto, you actually found your brother after all these years and more amazing, not knowing that he was alive."

"Si," said Roberto with a sigh, "I did find my brother but I didn't."

"What do you mean?" said Terry eyeing him with a suspicious look. "Is there something you are not telling us Roberto?"

Roberto gave another sigh. "Andre had been shot and the bullet had lodged somewhere near his brain. When he came to the hospital he was suffering from severe headaches and amnesia. A very risky operation was performed and the bullet removed successfully thanks to the brilliant work of a surgeon named Dr. Valdez. The doctor said that he might never regain his original memory but it was hard to tell. He does not recognize me as his brother, Terry. I am a complete stranger to him."

Terry listened quietly as Roberto talked, then shook his head. "Wow, I had no idea, I am so sorry Roberto. How difficult it must be for you. But you know what they say, we must not lose hope or else we lose the battle. So you have no idea where he's been or what he has been doing for the last … how many years?"

"Fifteen years, Terry. He might have married, had children, we just don't know."

"Hmm, maybe I'll take a trip down there soon, what do you think Roberto?"

"It would be my greatest pleasure to have you back with us again, Terry. Maybe we could get the twins to visit at the same time, like a reunion."

"I miss those little guys, Roberto. I guess they're not so little anymore."

Roberto's eyes shone. "You would be proud of your nephews, Terry, Frederik calls his brother Gemelo. Who does that remind you of?"

"You Roberto, exactly you," laughed Terry.

"And he looks exactly like Skye, that's the funny thing. I love those boys, Terry, and I love my little Camille and of course, I love and adore my Shane."

"You are a very loving and adorable man, Roberto, no, that did not come out right. What I meant was …"

Roberto laughed loudly and tousled Terry's hair, "I know what you meant Terry, just don't put any of this in print. I have a name to uphold."

"Well, what am I missing?" said Shane coming into the room, "I could hear the two of you laughing loudly."

"Just man-talk my dowdy little sister, and by the way, you shouldn't let yourself go like that, Roberto might lose interest, you know."

Shane was wearing an off the shoulder emerald green blouse and a matching fitted skirt that showed off her amazing figure. Her porcelain-like skin glowed radiantly, the blue-black hair hung past her shoulders and her eyes, those magnificent eyes that were fringed with long jet black lashes made it seem unfair that one person should be bestowed with that much beauty.

"Si Terry, you are right, that explains my loss of interest," said Roberto. "However, I must live up to my vows, no matter how difficult, to love, honor and …"

Shane looked around for something to throw and Roberto grabbed her arms and shouted to Terry to leave while he could. He held the struggling Shane and said, "as I was saying my little one, to love, honour and obey," and he kissed her passionately. "You are the best looking dowdy little woman I have ever seen and no matter what Terry says I will not lose interest, I promise you that."

"Thank you Roberto, you are so kind," she said with humour in her eyes. "I came in to ask you if you had seen Camille. I haven't seen her around lately. Do you know where she is or should we be concerned?"

"Not at all," said Roberto. "There's a playground down the street and Garcia told me he was taking her there but I'll take a look."

Roberto smiled to himself as he entered the playground. This was a far cry from his usual duties in the Dominican but his daughter was very precious to him. He sat beside Garcia on the bench as they watched Camille on the swing.

"This does not feel right Roberto," said Garcia, arms folded.

"What doesn't feel right, what do you mean?" asked Roberto.

"Gun, no gun," he said not looking too happy.

"It can't be helped Garcia, it is the law here."

"I know, but I still don't like it. Back home, I carry a big gun, no one says anything."

Roberto was quiet for a moment. Camille saw him and waved. She was smiling, dark hair flying in the wind, eyes sparkling like emeralds, a beautiful little girl who looked so much like Shane.

"I trust you Garcia, even without the gun," said Roberto waving to his daughter.

Garcia looked around the playground. "I trust nobody here Roberto, nobody. Camille is like a flower, look at your daughter Roberto, look good."

"Are you trying to tell me something Garcia? Say it."

"Si, I try to tell you that Camille should not have come here. Back home is better for her. I protect her with machine gun, here—nothing."

Roberto looked at Garcia. "You are getting soft Garcia. You worry more than Shane or myself," and shook his head. "Garcia, I would never have guessed."

Garcia watched Camille then spoke. "When she is a bebe I hold her and now I must protect her with no gun." He did not look happy at all.

The week went by too quickly. Shane had contacted Jodi and twice they had lunch together while Shane tried to understand what had happened.

"We will be returning on Monday Jodi. Why don't you come back with us? That way you won't have to travel alone. I never told you but the first time that you were going to come visit us, Roberto wanted to send two of his men here to travel with you, you know, to keep you company. I thought that was pretty funny."

Jodi smiled. "How is Ramon, Shane? Is he angry that I did not say goodbye to him?"

Shane shook her head, "not angry Jodi, just hurt. I think he was getting close to you. He's very quiet, always was, but since you left he seems to be … more like how he was when I first met him ten years ago, yes, that's it, back to how he was. I honestly think, Jodi, that you were starting to change him."

"Change him?" said Jodi, "I wouldn't want anything about him to change." She suddenly stopped, "what I mean ..." and she looked embarrassed.

"Do you love him Jodi?" asked Shane looking into her eyes, "is that what all this is about?"

Jodi turned away, she did not want Shane to see her face. "I don't know Shane, I just don't know." She paused, "I think I'm afraid."

"Afraid of what, Jodi? What are you afraid of?"

"I'm afraid of falling in love, of letting myself fall in love," said Jodi looking sad.

They were sitting by the window. It was the beautiful Fall season in Toronto, the most beautiful time of year and the trees were adorned with leaves, crimson, gold, bright red. It was a time when lovers discovered love, it was a time when poets did their best writing, and it was a time of sadness and memories that seemed to be enhanced by the beauty of the season. Toronto was all of this and more, much more. She was the promise of new life, smiles and tears and anything else that made up her ethereal innocence, and she was the dream that was sought by so many and found by those fortunate enough to open their hearts to her. Shane looked at her friend, she looked winsome and fragile and so attractive. She had those blue eyes that always seemed to sparkle and the blonde hair that fell in curls around her face, yet she looked so forlorn.

"Jodi, look at me," said Shane, "look at me," and she turned her face towards her. "You cannot stop yourself from falling in love. If you honestly feel you are and you think you can stop it, you are only fooling yourself. It will stay inside you and come back later and haunt you, believe me, I know what I'm talking about. Don't fight it, come back with us Jodi, please come back and you will see."

Jodi shook her head, "not now Shane, maybe later, maybe."

It was a Monday morning when Shane and Roberto along with Camille and Garcia arrived back in the Dominican. Jodi also returned but it was the following week. Roberto and Garcia met her at the airport and two gendarmes waited by the car for them. Jodi tried not to show her disappointment as she looked around for Ramon, but did not say anything.

Shane was thrilled that her friend had returned and a dinner had been planned for them—an invitation from Skye and Maria. They had taken over several rooms in the back area of the hospital and had turned it into a charming living area. Maria had become an excellent cook and had learnt many things from Rosita and together they had prepared an amazing feast.

It was a Saturday evening when they arrived, Roberto, Shane, Camille and Andre. Garcia and Lorenzo accompanied them and Maria and Skye had insisted they all sit down together to dinner with them. How much Maria had changed, completely at ease with everyone. Slowly, Skye and Maria were getting back to normal life. The agony of losing Beatriz was not as painful as before, something was taken away that they could never get back, but they were getting strong enough to accept it, and as always, placed their faith and trust with God. Both Skye and Maria were "strong" Catholics and attended church regularly and this is what gave them the support they needed to lean on. Ramon's absence was obvious but no one said anything. After dinner everyone sat and relaxed over coffee, liqueurs and dessert, or sobre mesa as Maria called it. Each person had a story to tell, an anecdote, a funny tale. Once more they were able to smile, once more they were able to laugh and once more the heaviness and the sadness was being lifted from the hearts of these good people … temporarily.

"Tomorrow morning," remarked Roberto, "I must meet with President Gomez about some new by-laws that will be put in place regarding the border security. Garcia and Lorenzo will accompany me and we'll probably be gone all day."

"This will be a good chance for Jodi and me to go riding on the beach," said Shane. "There is a beautiful area that Jodi hasn't seen yet. It's about twenty minutes away from where we are right now."

"That's quite a distance past the Villa Shane but I am not concerned. Ramon will be here to keep an eye on both of you. It's the Area of the Giant Trees, or we refer to it as Arbol Gigante." Jodi had looked up quickly at the mention of Ramon's name.

"Is that what it's called?" asked Skye.

"Actually, yes" said Roberto. "It's worth the ride just to see them."

The evening had come to an end, and as the guests parted, a blazing sun sat waiting for them in the middle of the ocean before disappearing into the dark waters.

Shane and Jodi had started out the next morning after breakfast with Ramon. After a lengthy ride they had reached the area and Shane and Jodi dismounted from their horses to walk amongst the leaves. They were truly giant trees and the girls chatted noisily.

Jodi suddenly stopped. She had come across a tiny bird that had obviously fallen from its nest and she picked it up carefully with trained hands.

"Shane, I must put this little guy back in its nest," she said looking up.

"Jodi, that's impossible," said Shane. "How would you ever climb this tree? Leave it on the ground and I'm sure the mother bird will come back for it."

But Jodi had already started to climb up the tree with the bird safely tucked in her pocket. It was not too difficult to climb and Jodi reached the nest and placed the bird in the nest not realizing how high she had climbed. When she turned and looked down Shane appeared very far away and as she started to descend, she discovered it was much more difficult than she had thought. She panicked as she realized it was not going to be easy and looked down again and saw Ramon riding up quickly and getting off his horse.

He was still upset that Jodi had not told him when she was leaving and did not have much to say when he saw her in the morning.

"Jodi, be careful," called Shane as Jodi tried to steady herself among the branches.

"Ramon, I don't think she can get down. Should I go for help?"

"Don't worry," called down Jodi, "I've climbed trees before," and she started to move again and slid, just catching another branch in time. "These Dominican trees are different than the ones back home," she called down trying to sound brave. "I think you have to know how to speak Spanish to be able to do this."

Shane looked up, "Jodi, this is not funny."

Ramon muttered something under his breath that sounded like "da chiflado woman," which Shane recognized as "crazy woman". "I will bring Senorita down," he said with a sigh and started to climb the tree.

"Please be careful, I'm going for help," called out Shane and mounting her horse she rode off.

Ramon continued to climb, being hindered by the machine gun that dangled over one shoulder and kept hitting the branches. Jodi could hear him talking to himself and she called out, "you don't have to do this Ramon, I am perfectly capable of looking after myself."

"Ha," was the response that came from Ramon, "you look after yourself? Ha, bird not happy, Ramon not happy and tree not happy, women, ha."

"Okay, okay, I didn't ask you to rescue me ... uh, Ramon?"

"What?"

"I think I hurt my arm when I slid."

Ramon looked up quickly. "Don't move, I'm almost there." His tone had changed dramatically.

"You should have left that crazy old machine gun on the ground, Ramon; it's not letting you move freely."

"It is not crazy old gun, I tell you that before, and I not move without it," he said impatiently.

"Well I was only ..."

"Is possible for Senorita to please close mouth so that Ramon can climb tree without headache?"

"Huh," was the only sound that came from over his head and Ramon continued to climb, stopping every few seconds to shake his head and say something under his breath.

Gradually, he worked his way up getting close enough to call out to Jodi.

"I reach out, take my hand while you hold big branch with other hand. Do not worry."

"I'm reaching out with my sore arm Ramon. I don't trust it to hold the branch."

"Okay, now let go."

Jodi's heart was beating fast. She was really frightened but did not want to admit it to Ramon. She held her breath and reached out and felt Ramon's hand grasp hers tightly. It felt hard and calloused but she knew he wouldn't let go and she suddenly felt comforted although her shoulder was aching.

"Let go," yelled Ramon, "now." Jodi let go and was suddenly gravitated so quickly against Ramon that she lost her breath as her body hit his chest. Ramon held her against him to steady himself and for a moment they just looked at each other. She could feel his breath on her face, his dark eyes holding her spellbound, his arms like steel.

A few moments passed and neither one spoke or moved. Jodi had never been held so tightly by a man and certainly not dangling from a tree. Ramon did not move, he just kept looking at Jodi, her blue eyes wide and innocent.

"You not say goodbye," he said, his face almost touching hers.

"For heaven's sake Ramon," said a terrified Jodi, "you are frightening me."

"Do not be afraid," he said softly, "I not let you go," and he slowly and dexterously made his way down, holding Jodi with one arm around her waist. When they finally reached the bottom, he gently laid her on the ground and sat beside her. Neither one spoke.

Jodi knew something had happened—she had never felt like this ever. She looked up at the sky. The sun had begun to sink and darkness was setting in. She could not describe the comfort she felt as she lay there with Ramon by her side. She did not want it to end and she closed her eyes not knowing what was happening. Suddenly she felt Ramon take her hand.

"Are you okay Senorita, something wrong?"

She shook her head, "no Ramon, nothing is wrong, everything is right." It was then she noticed his hands were bleeding. "It is nothing," he said, "do not worry." He looked down at her and again their eyes met. Ramon took the gun off his shoulder and put it on the ground, looking at her. Suddenly they heard the sound of galloping horses coming towards them. Shane had brought help and Jodi and Ramon were whisked off to the hospital. Jodi had a sprained shoulder and Ramon's hands were treated and bandaged. Afterwards Jodi was given a small reprimand and a promise from her not to climb any more Dominican trees.

Shane picked up the two coffees and went into the library. It was a chance to spend some time alone with Roberto and she looked forward to this special time.

"Shane, come here, beside me. She sat down beside him and he put his arms around her and pulled her closer to him. He pushed back her hair from her forehead and put his face against hers.

"Shane, I'm crazy about you, you know that," he said his lips on her cheek.

"That's not hard to figure out, Roberto," she said smiling.

"No, Shane, it's more than that, it's … it's …"

"It's what Roberto?" she said looking at him.

Roberto's arms tightened around her. "Do you remember Shane the day that Carlos Martinez had you kidnapped?"

Shane nodded. "How could I forget," she said heaving a sigh, "it was horrible."

"Shane, when I found out you were gone, I knew that I was on the brink of completely losing my self-control. When I think about it now, it's frightening. Do you know what that means?"

Shane looked at him wide-eyed. "What are you saying Roberto?"

Roberto held her face against his as he talked. "I was ready to destroy anyone and anything that stood in my way. Shane, I turned into a monster, just like him, I was no better than Martinez."

"You mean when you shot Carlos?"

"Si, and it didn't bother me and I couldn't stop." He looked away for a moment. "Did you know that I am capable of killing in the most blood-thirsty manner imaginable without feeling anything? I felt nothing Shane. No, I should not say that, I did feel something, I felt enjoyment." He looked down at her and shook his head. "What kind of a human being have I become Shane? I enjoy killing another human being."

Shane looked at him, she adored this man and it hurt her to see him like this. "Roberto, now you look at me and listen," she said turning his face towards her, "I'll tell you what kind of a person you are. You have done more to help the people of this Country than anyone in the entire history of the Dominican Republic. You're the kind of man who makes sure the orphans at the village are well fed and taken care of. You have fought to bring peace and freedom to the nine million people who live here on this island. Any of these men around the Villa would give their lives for you without question. Roberto, I could go on and on. You are a truly wonderful father who loves his children and wants only the best for them and their safety. You have a brother who, although he does not have any recollection of his life as a brother to you, has the highest and utmost respect for you as a human being. Even the President thinks of you as his son, and, of course, there's me." Roberto looked at her as her arms went around his neck.

"I fell in love with you the day you found me in tears, looking at pictures of my family but I kept denying it to myself. Do you remember that Roberto? It was the day after you kidnapped me almost twelve years ago. You kissed me and it was like nothing else on earth mattered and I will never, ever, forget that moment, ever. You are kind, loving, and honest, you have integrity and a heart that is soft and also full of passion, and I could go on and on."

"No, Senora Castaneda" said Roberto, "do not go any further," and he stood up and lifted her in his arms. "We would only be wasting precious time" and he carried her up the stairs.

Chapter Eleven

Jodi sat on the beach watching Ramon. He stood a short distance away throwing pebbles into the ocean and she wondered how he felt about her. Why did she find him so hard to figure out, she thought, did he like her or didn't he? She thought she would try to find out.

"Ramon?"

"What?"

"Why are you afraid to kiss me?"

Ramon turned slowly and looked at her. There was anger in his eyes but he spoke softly. "Ramon not afraid of anything Senorita, everybody know this, only you not know." His eyes had narrowed. "You make fun of me because you want kiss. Roberto says Ramon, you are bodyguard. Did not say bodyguard have to kiss."

"You are the most insulting person I have ever met Ramon. You are telling me it is not in your job description? Ha, you're acting like a *smart alec*."

"Si, that is good, I like that—job deescreepshun, big word but very good. I remember that. My name is Ramon not *alec*, and you are very bad—no, uh—spoilt, very spoilt."

"Well excuse me. Forget the kiss Ramon."

"Ramon forgot kiss long time ago."

"You are infuriating," said Jodi walking towards the water.

"I not understand that word," said Ramon sitting on the sand and watching her. Jodi took off her sandals and stepped into the cool water. She was angry with herself. Why did she throw herself at him like that, where was her pride? She decided to stay quiet and not make any more remarks to Ramon that would give him the opportunity to make her feel cheap. She also decided not to talk as openly and freely with him. She would change and show him. She stepped out of the water, dried her feet and put on her sandals.

Ramon had put on his sunglasses and she couldn't tell if he was watching her or not. Holding the reins of her horse, she walked on the sand followed by Ramon on his horse. All kinds of thoughts raced through her mind. How could such a person like Ramon appeal to her? She started to mentally count, one, he was rough, two, bad-tempered, three, sarcastic, four, had no manners, five, ignorant, and she could go on and on. How did Roberto know him? Where did he find such a person? She stopped and felt the hot rays of the sun beating down upon her. Her face and arms felt hot and she knew she was starting to burn.

"We go back Senorita," came Ramon's voice and it was like a command. She turned and looked at him. "Now" he said coming closer.

"Don't tell me when to go back Ramon," she said in an impatient tone. "Go back if you want to but don't tell me what to do."

Ramon got off his horse so quickly that Jodi didn't have time to think. He picked her up and unceremoniously almost threw her on her horse, adjusting her feet in the stirrups and handing her the reins, while a shocked Jodi just sat there.

"I tell you what to do," he said mounting his horse, "and you have to listen. Now, follow me."

He started on a trot and looked behind once as a stunned Jodi followed. They got back to the Villa and Ramon waited until Jodi went inside, then he took the horses back to the stable.

Jodi stomped into the kitchen and sat down. She was angry, frustrated and hot and her skin burned. Rosita turned away from the stove and looked at her.

"Jodi my dear, what is wrong? You look very upset and your face is so red."

Jodi just shrugged her shoulders. "Rosita, could you please give me a glass of water, I am so hot."

Rosita quickly brought her the water and looked at her. "I think you have sunburn on your face Jodi. I will bring you something for it."

When the woman left Jodi drank the water and thought. Ramon must have seen how red her face was becoming from the sun and so he brought her back. But it didn't give him the right to talk to her the way he did and the way he threw her on the horse. What an awful way to treat a woman. Just wait, she thought, I'll show him.

Rosita returned with a lotion and Jodi applied it to her face and arms.

"You are very fair-skinned my dear," she said with concern, "and you should be careful and not get too much sun at once. Such nice blonde hair and blue eyes you have, just like Skye. Did you know that he too got burnt once by the sun and he's a doctor? My goodness your eyes are very blue when you have so much colour in your face. You are such a pretty girl Jodi."

"Thank you Rosita and you make me feel so much better," said Jodi hugging the older woman. "Do you know where Shane is?"
"She is sitting outside in back with Andre. Here, I give you a hat to put on," and she produced a large brimmed hat and set it on Jodi's head. "I will bring lunch there soon; you go and sit in the shade."

Jodi tied the hat under her chin and went outside to look for the others. She found Shane and Andre sitting under a large umbrella and Andre immediately stood up as Jodi approached the table.

"How are you?" he said pulling out a chair for her. "You look good with all that colour."

"You certainly do," said Shane. "I can never seem to get a healthy glow like that but I think you are burnt a little. Be careful Jodi, you are very fair like Skye."

"Yes, I know, Rosita said the same thing. Actually Shane, I wanted to ask you about something, it's about Ramon."

"Oh," said Shane, glancing at Andre, "what has he done now?"

"Granted, I know he meant well and wanted me to get out of the sun, but he is so rough. I hate to talk behind his back but do you know what he had the nerve to do? He almost threw me on my horse. Has he always been like that?"

"Here comes Roberto and he's just the person to ask. He knows Ramon better than anyone," said Shane as Roberto approached.

"Who knows Ramon better than anyone?" said Roberto picking up the last sentence as he sat down and greeted everyone.

"Jodi was just commenting on something Ramon had done," said Shane, "tell him Jodi."

"Well," said Jodi, "he got impatient with me and almost threw me on my horse."

Roberto looked at Jodi carefully. "It looks like you have gotten a burn on your face Jodi-Anne. Were you refusing to get out of the sun?"

"That's beside the point, Roberto, did he have to be so rough?" said Jodi firmly.

"Jodi-Anne, listen to me," said Roberto gently, "let me tell you something about Ramon. I've known him since the time he was in my army over ten years ago. He was one of the first to join, barely twenty years old at the time. I have seen his bravery.

I am aware that he is absolutely fearless and tough. He is also very loyal. He's the one that I choose to take with me on my most dangerous missions. I chose him to protect Shane, I trust him to take my daughter to school and bring her back safely. Ramon is well known for his very uncommon sharp reflexes. His nerves within him cause him to make his move before his brain tells him to and I have seen this happen. It is an amazing feat. That is why, when he stood beside me pointing his machine gun on Carlos and his men, not one of them moved.

Do you have any idea how notorious those men were? He moves like lightening, Jodi. You are lucky you landed on the horse. And by the way, ask him some time how he got that scar on his face, or what happened to his missing finger, or maybe you shouldn't. The story is scary."

Everyone was quiet for a moment. The only sound heard was coming from the ocean and the shrill cry of a bird. Roberto continued: "He is one of the finest men I have ever come across, but first you have to get to know him to see this. Watch him if you get a chance and look at his face when he lifts Camille on her horse. He gives her riding lessons and he taught both of my sons to ride. He can be so gentle that it is almost unbelievable. I've seen him gently mend the broken wing of a butterfly with tape. I know this sounds ridiculous but with my own eyes I have seen it fly off. But no one has seen him smile and you might be able to make that happen."

Jodi sat very still. She felt emotional and two large tears rolled down her cheeks and her hand went nervously to the chain around her neck.

"I don't think I could do anything to make someone like him smile. All we do is fight."

"Jodi," said Andre, his eyes looking thoughtful, "there is something you could do to please the young man."

All eyes turned to Andre, and he continued. "Ramon is part Jewish on his father's side and his mother is Spanish. Why don't you surprise him one day and say something in Hebrew? He wouldn't be expecting this at all and I'm sure we can pick up an English/Hebrew dictionary from somewhere."

"That's a wonderful idea!" exclaimed Shane. "Andre, you are so clever."

"He's part Jewish?" said Jodi, "I really didn't know that. Could that explain the fearlessness, the intelligence, the …"

"Wait a minute," said Roberto, "I'm not doubting you, but the Spanish are cited through history for the same thing, but there you have it. The man comes from a very special breed, thus, we have the creation of a magnificent human being."

"Hey Roberto, you have put that very well indeed," said Andre, "I certainly hope you write my epitaph when I pass on."

"Don't talk like that my brother, we just found you, don't say things like that." Roberto looked very disturbed for a moment.

"Wait," said Jodi, "let's get back to 'the magnificent human being'. I like Andre's idea and I'm going to go into town to find that dictionary."

"I'll go with you," said Shane quickly, "how about tomorrow morning after breakfast?"

"Just a moment ladies," said Roberto sternly, "do you think I will let the two of you go off again so soon after what happened? Not a chance."

"But Roberto," said Jodi, "I must get that book as soon as possible. I want to do this now."

"I'll get the book, Jodi, and I will go into town tomorrow. What do you think Andre?"

"Sounds good to me, tomorrow is fine," said Andre, I'm looking forward to it."

Roberto stood up. "Good, then it's all settled. I have to leave, excuse me. I have an appointment in exactly one hour."

"Roberto," said Shane, "you haven't had lunch yet."

"I'll get something there at the Courthouse, I'll be fine."

After he left, Shane looked concerned. "Did he say at the Courthouse? Why would he be going there?"

"I'm not exactly sure, Shane," said Andre, "he mentioned something about an interrogation."

"I don't like the sound of that," said Jodi. "Who do you suppose he's going to interrogate?"

"I don't know," said Shane. "I worry so much over him sometimes. There's always something coming up with the army or the government."

"He has a very big responsibility on his shoulders," said Andre. "Don't worry Shane, my prayers are always with him, and all of you. You are well protected."

"Thank you Andre," said Shane, "you always say something to make me feel better."

"And I agree," said Jodi. "I can hardly wait to start learning some Hebrew. Wait a minute" she said thoughtfully, "did he say he taped the broken wing on a butterfly?"

Andre smiled, "In this world, anything is possible, Jodi, anything."

Chapter Twelve

Roberto arrived at the Courthouse. A fugitive had been caught and they had reason to believe that he had knowledge of important information regarding Carlos Martinez's drug connection. The man sat at a table with his hands handcuffed. Garcia had accompanied Roberto and stood beside him when he entered the room. One of the officers had told Roberto that the man refused to divulge any information and said he was ready to die if necessary.

"Leave him with me," said Roberto, "and we'll see how eager he is to die."

Roberto sat at the table across from the man. When the fugitive looked up, his face was tired, and he was young perhaps twenty. He gave Roberto a half-smile.

"Ah, enter the handsome Comandante, bandana around the head, your bodyguard with machine gun at your side. The brave handsome Comandante, who will kill me, si, and become idolo of the people; bravo."

"That is not my style," said Roberto removing the bandana from his head. "Garcia, you can wait outside." Garcia hesitated.

"Ahora Garcia," said Roberto, "movimiento."

Garcia reluctantly left the room and Roberto turned to the man in front of him. "You refuse to give us your name." He paused. The man continued to smile looking down, not meeting Roberto's eyes. "Are you afraid to look at me?" asked Roberto.

He looked up and shook his head. "I know my life is in your hands, but I am not afraid."

Roberto continued, "I recognize you—they call you Pajarraco, si?"

The man looked at Roberto, the smile was gone. "I have nothing to say," he said as Roberto continued staring at him. Finally the man spoke again. "Cigarrillo?" he asked.

Roberto called the guard and got the cigarette which he lit and put in the man's mouth. Then, on second thought, he called the guard back and asked for the keys removing the handcuffs as the man watched Roberto suspiciously and continued puffing nervously on the cigarette. Roberto then sat down, placed his gun on the ground and kicked it away.

"Si, they call me Pajarraco, my real name is Leandro Perreiro. That is all I have to say."

The guard returned with two coffees that Roberto had asked for and left. Leandro gave a half smile again. "You are trying to make me talk with kindness. It will not work, you are wasting your time."
Roberto took the picture out of his wallet and put it on the table in front of Leandro. "Tell me what you see Leandro, take a good look."

Leandro looked at the picture as he picked up the coffee. "So? It is a woman, so?"

"Look closely Leandro, take a good look. I want her image to stay with you, look closely."

Leandro put down the cup. He looked curiously at Roberto for a moment, and then looked again at the picture.

"Si, she is beautiful, is that what you want me to say? She is perhaps your sister, your sweetheart, or maybe someone's daughter? What does it matter? You want to tell me she is dead? So what, I have seen dead people before, so many. You think I look at this picture and then I talk? This means nothing to me, just another face, nothing."

Roberto was very quiet. The sound of someone walking down the corridor in heavy boots made an echo that gradually faded away. Leandro puffed on the cigarette nervously and stared at Roberto and waited. Finally, Roberto spoke.

"Her name is Beatriz. She was orphaned at the age of six and adopted into my family. This picture was taken on her sixteenth birthday—she is making a wish Leandro and is blowing out the candle. She is wearing her special birthday dress, it is white satin."

Roberto paused, took a deep breath and continued. "They cleaned the blood off the dress so that she could be buried in it, but they could not put back the beautiful face, it was blown away. You pulled the trigger Leandro. She was taking drugs that you helped bring into the Country—it was your hand not hers that pulled the trigger."

Leandro looked at the picture then back at Roberto. When he spoke it was almost a sneer. "You talk big and brave Comandante; you know nothing about poverty and hunger. You probably live in a nice house with lots of money, nice and comfortable. Si, and probably a pretty wife who doesn't have to work or sell her body, and nice little children, perfect little children that are clean and never hungry and you go home and play with them. You do not know the other kind of life. Well, I do, I have lived it and when I get a chance to make fast easy money, I take it."

Roberto's eyes narrowed. "Fast easy money? You mean fast easy dirty money covered with Beatriz's blood and the blood of thousands of others like her, thanks to you. You think I don't know poverty and hunger? You are wrong. You think I go home and bounce my children on my knee? You are wrong. I cannot see them grow up because they are living out of the Country because of the danger that is always around us. No one in my family, no one, can make a move without a bodyguard. The last time they walked into a store your people bombed their car and killed an innocent driver. They also killed a bodyguard, one of the finest men I'd ever had the privilege to train and who fought by my side during the Civil War to free this Country. My parents were murdered, my sister and one of my brothers were murdered and by the grace of God, another brother was found alive but shot in the head. He doesn't even know who I am.

You are so wrong Leandro. I live with pain, it never leaves me and let me tell you something else, you don't have to talk, you don't have to tell us anything. We won't interrogate you, we won't torture you. But you will go to jail and while you are there the rest of your life, you will have plenty of time to think about how many more Beatriz's will die, how many more innocent men, women and children, oh God, those precious little children will die because of you. Your hand will continue to pull the trigger while you are behind bars. But you have the ability—no—the power, to stop most of it. I don't know what is in your heart Leandro, only you know."

Roberto stood up. He looked into Leandro's eyes for a long moment, then said "may God have mercy on your soul." He picked up his gun, tied the bandana around his head and turned to leave.

"Comandante," called out Leandro and Roberto slowly turned around. "They did not tell me your name."

Roberto looked deeply into his eyes, "Castaneda, Roberto Castaneda."

Leandro gave that half-smile. "Comandante Castaneda, you can tell your men that I will give them whatever information they want. This is what my heart tells me."

Roberto smiled back, "your heart has goodness in it Leandro, gracias. We will meet again soon," and he left the room.

Roberto and Garcia drove back silently. Roberto broke the silence. "I am sorry I spoke to you the way I did, Garcia," he said. "I was not angry with you." Garcia looked at Roberto—"Roberto, it is a great honour for me to protect you. I do not feel bad, do not say sorry. You are too humble, si, too humble."

"I am glad you understand me Garcia, it makes my life easier," said Roberto and closed his eyes for the remainder of the trip back while Beatriz's memory lay heavily upon his heart.

The next day as promised, Roberto and Andre left together accompanied by Garcia and Lorenzo and the driver. They entered the bookstore and looked through the books on the shelves in the "Languages" area.

"Here" said Andre, "this looks like what we are looking for." As Roberto took the book a woman walked over to Andre and stared. Garcia moved quickly between her and Roberto.

"Father Montessano," called out the woman trying to get closer to Andre. By now Lorenzo had stepped in front of the woman but Roberto put his hand on Lorenzo's arm.

"It is okay Lorenzo, let her through" he said curiosity in his voice. Andre had suddenly stood very still. He put his hand out to the woman and she kissed it. Something was happening and Roberto was not exactly sure what it was.

"We have missed you during Sunday Mass Father," the woman continued. "So many people have been asking for you, you left without a word."

Andre still did not speak and his eyes had a far-away look. The sales clerks had approached as soon as they heard the commotion and Roberto showed his credentials and asked if they could use an office.

All five were ushered into a room and Roberto assured the woman that she would not be harmed. Then, the amazing story about Andre's last fifteen years began to unfold and Roberto was dumbfounded. It turned out that Andre had entered a Seminary and had become an ordained Catholic priest. That would explain the way he talked, this gift of understanding, his deeply religious belief. The woman gave the name of the church, Roberto thanked her profusely, and then they left after purchasing Jodi's book.

Numbly, Roberto and Andre got into the car and were quietly driven back to the Villa. Once inside, Roberto took Andre by the arm and marched him into the library closing the door behind them.

Andre sat down and turned to Roberto, "You are going to interrogate your own brother?" he asked with a smile.

"I am going to find out who my brother is," said Roberto pulling up a chair and facing him. "Now tell me Andre, what do you remember?"

It turned out that Andre was as shocked as Roberto but some of his memory was actually returning regarding this time of his priesthood. Unfortunately, however, so much before that period was still a blank. Roberto was proud and impressed that Andre had become a priest but nevertheless was also disappointed that he could not remember anything else. Roberto still did not have back his brother, and he must now face the fact that he might never have him back again.

"I'm sorry Andre," said Roberto standing up, "please don't misunderstand me; I am so proud of you but ... but." Roberto could not talk; he turned around and left the room and Andre knew and understood his sadness. He would pray for Roberto, special prayers every day.

That night Roberto told Shane everything that happened. "Can you just imagine my amazement, Shane, when that woman referred to Andre as Father Montessano. He is a priest, my little brother is a priest," and Roberto shook his head in amazement.

Shane put her arm around his neck. They were sitting on the edge of their bed facing the window and outside the foliage from the tree was brushing against the windowpane. Pink blossoms could be seen on the branches that swayed gently in the breeze.

"I am not surprised, Roberto, there was something saintly about Andre, I could feel it, couldn't you?"

Roberto looked at her and smiled, "I remember, Shane, when we were young boys, very young. My papa would say The Lord's Prayer in English once a year during Thanksgiving. My papa was educated in the United States and he kept this tradition and every year in November just before our Thanksgiving dinner he would recite the Lord's Prayer and as far back as I could remember Andre would stand up during the end, and this was difficult because he had to slide down his chair because he was so small, maybe around two years old. And he would say "forever ... and ever ... and ever ... and my papa would end by saying 'Amen', every year Shane. Andre was very little when he started doing this and even then he seemed to have the Holy Spirit inside him, even then."

"That is so beautiful," said Shane putting her face against his. "He is really a very special person Roberto, just like yourself. The Castanedas are amazing people."

"That they are, Senora Castaneda," smiled Roberto turning her face towards him and kissing her. "Have I told you today how much I love you?"

"I don't think so and I'm starting to feel neglected," she said as his arms tightened around her.

Chapter Thirteen

A few weeks had passed and the police had made several successful raids because of Leandro's information. However, Roberto knew it was crucial that Leandro be given full protection as they made arrangements to transfer him to a 'safe' prison. Roberto also had plans to see if he could possibly reduce Leandro's sentence. The transfer itself was simple, it was only a matter of leaving the Courthouse under heavy guard and step into the waiting unmarked police car. There was no reason to believe that anything would happen, it was most unlikely, and Roberto accompanied Leandro to make sure everything would go as planned.

No one was prepared for what happened next. The shots fired came from inside the Courthouse as the group had almost reached the car. Two police officers along with Leandro had been shot including Garcia when he quickly raised his gun with one arm in front of Roberto's head to protect him. The assailant was killed in the gunfire as chaos erupted around them. Roberto had not been hit but Garcia's arm was badly injured when he raised it to protect Roberto.

The two police officers were dead and Leandro lay on the ground, gravely injured. Roberto helped lift Garcia then turned to Leandro. He knelt down beside him and cradled his head in his arms.

"Stay with me Leandro, don't talk, the doctor is on his way." Leandro was having difficulty breathing and Roberto loosened his clothing.

"Comandante," it was barely a whisper and Roberto bent his head down towards him. "I … will … tell … Beatriz … I … am … sorry." His eyes closed and his head went limp and Roberto sat motionless still holding him.

Once again the drugs had won another war and once again Roberto shed no tears, it was impossible for this man to cry. So many things were running through his mind. First there was Beatriz, then Damien and now Leandro. The information they had received from Leandro had been crucially important to them but at what cost? It was impossible to put a price on it. Somehow, Roberto had formed an attachment to the young man and had made plans to help him, and it hurt, it hurt badly to see him die. When would it end? When would the pain go away? He could feel a hand on his shoulder, but he did not move. Could this happen to one of his sons one day? Would it go on and on slowly destroying them all?

"Comandante," the voice seemed to come from far away. He did not realize how tightly he was holding Leandro's body in his arms. Once again someone else's blood was covering his hands and staining his uniform. By now there were people around him, trying to lift him, to disengage him from Leandro's body. Roberto seemed to drift into a semi-conscious state. Suddenly his mind went to Andre. He could see his smiling face before him and it gave him the strength to slowly and unsteadily stand up.
"Comandante Castaneda, are you all right?" Someone handed him a glass of water and he drank it slowly and tried to pull himself together with force. He had to be strong and he was successful. Once again he was in control.

"Si, gracias, where is Garcia? I want to see him." Garcia's arm was very seriously injured and he had been given first-aid until the ambulance arrived. Roberto went straight to the hospital where they had taken him and waited while he was being operated on. The bone in Garcia's arm had been shattered and the doctor told Roberto that they had been able to save it and hold it together with the insertion of surgical pins.

Garcia had saved Roberto's life by using himself as a shield rather than taking the time to turn and shoot.

Roberto stayed at the hospital for several hours. He refused coffee or food and news of what had happened reached President Gomez. He quickly dispatched three of his guards to drive immediately to the hospital and get Roberto home. It was also decided not to tell Shane until she saw Roberto. It would be easier if she heard from him and could see for herself that he was all right.

When Roberto got back to the Villa it was very late, well past midnight and he was glad everyone at the Villa was asleep with the exception of the guards patrolling the grounds.

He knew his appearance was shocking and he immediately removed the bloodied uniform and stepped into the shower. As he stood under the steamy water it felt good on his face and body and once again the past events raced through his mind but he felt stronger for some reason and much better. He could feel the tough exterior once again a part of him but now he would pay the price. A delayed reaction was beginning to set inside him like a seizure and he had a desire to crush something with his bare hands.

He put on a robe and lay down on the bed beside a sleeping Shane and looked at her—always so beautiful, always so precious. He was afraid to hold her in his arms, afraid he would crush her and yet he needed her strength. He had to get away and quietly he got up, dressed for riding and went out to the stable. Ramon appeared out of nowhere and took out his horse also.

"Don't you ever sleep Ramon?" said Roberto as he mounted Allegro.

"I knew you not back. I don't sleep until I see you. You don't look good," he said peering closely at his face.

"Si, I know Ramon, but I'm okay. Do you want to ride with me down the beach?"

"We ride," said Ramon, "now is good time, everyone asleep, no noise, no shooting, just ocean, stars, no headache."

Roberto smiled as they trotted together on the sand. Ramon's philosophy on life was just what he needed. "Do you get headaches often Ramon?"

"Only when Senorita Jodi talk too much. She always talk too much."

Roberto was starting to feel much better. "You think Jodi-Anne talks too much?"

"Si, sometime, when with me," said Ramon.

"And not with anyone else Ramon? Did it occur to you that maybe she is a little nervous?" asked Roberto.

"Nervous of what?" said Ramon with surprise.

"Nervous of you, Ramon."

"Why? She not like me?" he asked.

"No Ramon, because she does like you, I think she likes you very much," said Roberto smiling.

Ramon suddenly pulled on the reins and stopped. Roberto stopped also and turned back to Ramon. "What's the matter bodyguard, did I hit a nerve?"

"Did you hit what?" said Ramon eyeing Roberto curiously.
Roberto laughed. He couldn't believe the conversation he was having with Ramon at 2:00 A.M. in the morning on a beautiful night on the beach under the stars. "Ramon, you are so good for me."

"You said Jodi, er Senorita likes me?"

"That's what I said my friend. Did you not know?"

"Why does she fight with me if she likes me?" he insisted.

"That's just the way it is with women, Ramon. Just a second," he said getting off his horse and picking up a large branch from the ground. He held it in both hands trying to bend it with force. Suddenly it gave way and cracked and Roberto gave a sigh of relief. The tension that had built up inside him was gone—the "crushing" feeling in his hands had disappeared and he felt good. Ramon watched curiously as Roberto got back on his horse.

"Something bothering you Roberto?" he asked.

"Not anymore," said Roberto, "come Ramon, I am famished. Let's get something to eat."
They rode back together, Roberto tall and straight and proud in the saddle, Ramon riding alongside, feeling happy and invigorated, machine gun hanging from his shoulder, head held high, long hair blowing in the breeze and the scar vivid on the side of his face.

They entered the kitchen careful not to awaken anyone. Like young boys they raided the fridge and took out chicken, roast beef and paklava.

"I make coffee," said Ramon and as he stood up a voice behind him said, "I'll make the coffee Ramon," and Andre stood there in his robe.

"I'm sorry we woke you up," said Roberto holding a drumstick, "coffee would be great."

The three men sat around the kitchen table and ate and drank coffee talking in low voices so as not to awaken anyone else. Twelve hours ago Roberto had been in shock, now he was ready to face the world and anything else it might bring.

It was 4:00 in the morning when the three of them left the kitchen. They had cleaned up so as not to leave any work behind for Rosita and each one departed to his own quarter.

Roberto lay down beside Shane, not wanting to awaken her but could not help himself. He gently took her in his arms holding her close to him. The coffee did not interfere with his sleep which suddenly hit him when his body felt the exhaustion of the day. Shane was in his arms and all was well with the world, nothing else seemed to matter. Little did he know what lay ahead.

Chapter Fourteen

The sky had darkened quickly and it was evident that a large storm was about to break loose on the beach. The wind had picked up speed and was beginning to blow around them and Ramon called out to Jodi to turn around. At that precise moment large drops of rain suddenly began to fall and Ramon called out to Jodi.

"Too late, we cannot turn back now," and he pointed ahead. Jodi looked at Ramon, the rain was now coming down in torrents and Ramon shouted to her to follow. Up ahead was one of the caves that Roberto had told them about and in a few moments it had come into sight. Jodi was frightened and did not want to enter a cave with or without Ramon.

"Get off horse," shouted Ramon, "we can't stay out here." By now both Jodi and Ramon were drenched but Jodi refused.

"Don't tell me what to do," she called out and Ramon glared at her. "Don't make me mad" he said, "just do what I say."

Unwillingly Jodi entered the cave with Ramon and Ramon put the horses to one side. He sat down across from Jodi who was shivering and he looked around. "I hope there aren't any bats in this cave, Ramon. I can't stay here if there are."

"You have to stay," said Ramon gathering twigs. "Sit down, don't talk, Ramon is thinking."

"What do you mean don't talk," said Jodi, "I'm very upset. I'm sitting in a cave, soaking wet and you have to think? Let's just leave. Aren't you afraid of bats?"

Ramon had gathered a few twigs and leaves and had produced a lighter from his pocket. Soon a small fire was burning giving some warmth to the dampness around them.

"I told you before I am not afraid of anything," said Ramon starting to sound impatient. Then Jodi made the big mistake of asking Ramon about his personal life.

"Do you have family Ramon? I mean brothers and sisters, or parents? You never talk about them—is there any reason?"

Ramon turned to look at her. He was holding a twig in his hand, his long hair drenched, his eyes dark and shining. His voice was low and he spoke slowly.

"Do not talk about my family, you go too far. Ramon getting nervous."

Jodi's first reaction was anger. "I only asked you a simple question. We're sitting in a cave, for heavens sake. Can't we have a decent conversation? You're weird."

"Not simple question," said Ramon trying to stay calm.

"And then," continued Jodi, "you say Ramon is getting nervous. Well it's too bad, because I am nervous too, so there."

Ramon continued to stare at Jodi who was beginning to get flustered. Her hair was flattened and wet against her head, her eyes a very bright blue.

"And another thing," she continued, "stop staring at me. Haven't you seen a soaking wet woman before? I don't think you know anything about a woman anyway. You don't know how to treat one, you have no feelings, you can't smile, you can't converse, you … you …" she stopped, but was not finished.

Ramon sat still, his right eye starting to twitch and the scar on the side of his face became vivid.

"And another thing," she said, "you probably got that cut on your face because you made someone angry. Well, it would not surprise me one bit. You probably deserved it." Jodi suddenly realized she'd gone too far.

Her wet clothes clung to her body and she could feel the dampness and gloom around her as the cave seemed to suddenly darken ominously. Ramon sat very still, his eye would not stop twitching, the anger he felt was making his heart pound inside him. Slowly, he removed the machine gun and placed it carefully on the ground and stood up, not taking his eyes off her. Jodi looked at him and their eyes met. Fear and panic hit her as she watched him slowly advance towards her.

Outside the storm was getting worse and the gigantic waves were smashing angrily against the rocks.

"That's an awful storm out there," said Shane peering out the window. "Should we be worried about Jodi?"

"Not at all," said Roberto. "I am not concerned, Ramon is with her and I am sure he is taking very good care of her. If they rode out too far, they're probably waiting in one of the caves along the beach until the storm passes."

"I hope so," said Shane moving away and sitting beside Roberto. "I'm so pleased that she has decided to stay longer."

"She might want to stay on here in the Dominican. Wouldn't that be nice for you? I like her Shane, she sort of grows on you doesn't she? I think also she and Ramon seem to be understanding each other much better, don't you think so?"

"Yes I do," said Shane. "I wish she'd stay. Maria is so busy that I don't get to see her as often as I'd like to but Jodi is such good company. I guess with Jodi staying right here it is like a live-in companion. I must sound rather selfish Roberto."

"No you don't my little one," said Roberto kissing her forehead. Jodi can stay here with us as long as she wants. I thought at one time there was something happening between her and Ramon but I guess I was wrong."

"I might stay up and wait for Jodi, Roberto. What do you think?"

"No Shane, if you are tired why don't you go to bed. I will wait and if they're not back soon, I'll go out with Lorenzo and meet them."

The storm had passed and a full moon shone down on the two lone figures riding along the beach. The ocean once again was tame having lost its passion to the strong winds that had suddenly left with the storm. Ramon glanced at Jodi—her hair was not pinned back as usual but hung down around her face. Her eyes were swollen and she was very quiet. They rode silently, neither one speaking and just following the rays cast down from the moon. All the way back they rode in silence with Ramon glancing at Jodi a few more times but she said nothing.

When they finally reached the Villa Ramon took the horses back to the stable as Jodi went quietly inside. As she started to ascend the stairs Roberto stepped out of the library and called out her name but Jodi just continued up the stairs ignoring Roberto. He stood there for a moment thinking. It was obvious she'd been caught in the storm but there was something else about her that disturbed him. He threw on his jacket and marched out of the Villa. Ramon was unsaddling the horses when Roberto stepped inside the stable and stood beside him.

"What happened Ramon, what happened tonight?" Ramon turned and looked at Roberto. He had the utmost respect for him. Anyone else would have gotten the silent treatment.

"We got caught in storm and stayed in cave." Ramon did not say anything else. Roberto looked at him and he knew something was not right. Ramon was avoiding Roberto's eyes.

"Did you have an argument Ramon? Did Jodi-Anne say something that made you angry?"

Ramon picked up a brush and started wiping down the horse, still not looking at Roberto.

"Si, we have argument, si, Ramon got angry."
"Ramon got angry," repeated Roberto, "then what happened. Ramon, look at me, what happened?" Roberto did not realize it but he was shouting. He grabbed Ramon's arm jerking him towards him and repeated; "look at me Ramon, what happened?"

Ramon turned quickly. If it had been anyone else's hand holding his arm like that he would have broken it. He looked at Roberto, his eyes blazing and he was breathing hard.

"I rape her, Roberto, I rape Jodi."

Roberto glared at Ramon. His face showed the shock that he felt. "You got angry and you raped her?" he said incredulously.

"It was what she said, I could not help it, but now...." He averted his eyes again and looked down, "I am sorry, was not right."

"Sorry? You are sorry?" said Roberto. "Do you realize you have probably traumatized Jodi-Anne? She is a guest in my home Ramon, and I could not even protect her! Have you no self-control?"

"I could not stop myself Roberto," said Ramon meeting his eyes.

Roberto's anger was evident. "This is a crime Ramon, you committed a criminal act and you could go to jail. Do you realize this?"

Ramon did not answer. He nodded his head and looked at Roberto. Roberto gave a deep sigh. "You'd better get out of those wet clothes Ramon before you get sick. I want to see you at 9:00 in the morning in the library. Do you understand?"

Ramon nodded and Roberto left the stable. He went into the Villa and took off his jacket throwing it angrily on the chair. He went upstairs and stopped in front of Jodi's door. He hesitated and decided against knocking and continued down the hall to his room. He moved around the room quietly so as not to awaken Shane but when he climbed into bed, he realized she was awake.

"I heard Jodi come upstairs, Roberto. I guess they waited for the storm to pass."

"Si, that's right," said Roberto. "Shane, would you please knock on Jodi-Anne's door and see if she's all right?"

Shane looked at him suddenly.

"What I mean is see if she needs anything; she got caught in the storm. Just ask her please," said Roberto trying not to show his concern. Shane looked at Roberto for a moment, then quickly put on a robe and left.

Roberto got up and stood by the window. A full moon was shining in the sky, the rain had completely stopped and a few gendarmes were walking around, talking in low voices. Roberto looked out for a few moments deep in thought. Suddenly his fist came down hard on the side of the pane cracking the glass and badly cutting his hand. He closed the curtain quickly and went into the bathroom washing off the blood and wrapping a towel around the cut. He then quickly wiped the blood off the windowsill and got back into bed just as Shane returned and quietly closed the door behind her.

"Roberto, I knocked on her door and spoke to her. She said she was okay but tired and wanted to sleep. I think she's all right, they probably had an argument or something. We'll talk over breakfast I'm sure. Roberto?" Shane bent towards him kissing his cheek, "you're so quiet. Is something wrong?"

"I love you Shane, go to sleep my love," he said putting his arm around her and drawing her close and wearily with a sigh he closed his eyes.

"Rosita, can you teach me how to cook?" said Andre the next morning putting another gatta on his plate. "You are amazing you know."

"Now why would you want to learn Andre? I will always cook for you."

"We are so lucky to have you Rosita," said Shane. "Andre is right, you are amazing."

Roberto descended the stairs and entered the dining room.

"Buenos dias," he said solemnly and looked around the room. "Has Jodi-Anne not come down yet?" he asked pouring his coffee.

"I haven't seen her this morning," said Shane. "Seems like we had quite a storm last night."

"What happened to your hand Roberto?" asked Andre. Roberto had covered the cut with three band-aids, trying to make it look as inconspicuous as possible, but the cut was long.

"I just hit my hand against something Andre, it is nothing."

"You might be wise to drop in at the hospital, Roberto. It looks like you might need some stitches."

"When did that happen?" asked Shane, a worried expression crossing her face. "I didn't notice it last night."

"It's nothing really," said Roberto looking at his watch. There was still an hour before he was to see Ramon in the library. He ate breakfast quietly while Andre and Shane chatted about the storm.
"I think I'll take a stroll along the beach this morning," said Andre. "There are probably all kinds of shells and ocean creatures scattered on the sands. Care to join me Shane?"

"I would love to," she said. "Roberto, if you see Jodi tell her to join us if she wants to. We won't be too far."

Roberto nodded and sat quietly drinking his coffee after they left. Decisions, he had many decisions to deal with that morning. He had to see Ramon at 9:00. Then he had another meeting with General Escobar at noon. The General would be leaving to go back to Argentina and Roberto wanted this meeting badly. It was very important to him and for the future of the Dominican. He loved this Country and he was going to see to it that everything possible would be done to make it even greater and her people to be able to enjoy all the benefits the Country could give them. It would probably mean that he and Shane would be visiting Argentina soon and he must prepare himself for this. Little did he know that tragedy was about to strike in Argentina in the most unexpected and unbelievable way imaginable.

Roberto went into the library and waited for Ramon who arrived exactly at 9:00. He sat at the desk opposite Roberto and placed his machine gun across his knees.

"I called you here," said Roberto, "because there's something I have to know."

Ramon met his eyes, "Si?"

Roberto did not talk immediately; he waited then spoke. "Exactly what did Jodi-Anne say to you to provoke such a criminal act?"

Ramon did not talk. The silence in the room was so strong it seemed to engulf the two men. Then his eye started to twitch and Roberto could see that he was beginning to experience something that might have been buried in the past. Finally he spoke and his voice was like a monotone.

"She ask about my brothers and sisters. She ask about my parents, if I had any. She said I deserved this," and he pointed to the scar. "Then," and he paused, "she said I must have made someone angry and … and … deserved it."

Roberto was aghast. He knew about Ramon's family, he knew the story behind the scar and he also knew how his finger had been amputated. He bowed his head for a moment then looked at Ramon. Ramon just sat there, no expression on his face, but there was sadness in his eyes that Roberto had not seen before.

"I understand Ramon, what you went through emotionally when Jodi-Anne said those things. I understand because I knew what had happened to you, but she did not know. She was not aware, Ramon, of the situation. I am not excusing you from what you did, it should not have happened, do you understand? Part of the blame lies on my shoulders. I should have noticed something between the two of you and had Lorenzo look out for her instead of you."

Roberto stopped talking. He didn't know what else to say. He liked Ramon and did not want to lose him. He knew of no one that could replace him and he didn't want anyone else to replace him. Finally, he spoke again.

"Ramon, do you have anything else to say before I decide what to do?"

Ramon did not hesitate. He looked squarely at Roberto and said, "I love her."

Roberto was taken aback. He did not at all expect to hear Ramon say that.

"You love her?" said Roberto, his eyes wide with surprise.

"Si, I love Jodi," said Ramon.

"Have you told her that?" said Roberto wondering if Ramon really meant what he was saying.

Ramon shook his head, "no".

"Are you sure Ramon, or are you just saying that because you feel sorry for what you did?"

Ramon shook his head again. "I am not sorry for what I did because I love her. When we went to airport, Senora and I and Lorenzo, we meet Jodi when plane comes, remember? We get in car and I sit next to Jodi and … and…."

"And what Ramon," said Roberto.

"And when she looks at me, I am finished."

"You are finished?" said Roberto.

"Si, finished. She looks at me and Ramon knows, he is finished."

"Ramon knows what?" asked Roberto impatiently.

"I know she talks too much, I know she gives me headache, but I love her and … I know I want to marry her."

Roberto stared at Ramon. He was amazed at the conversation that they just had. Then again, most conversations with Ramon were amazing.

"Ramon, have you had breakfast this morning?"
Ramon shook his head, "not hungry Roberto. Where is Senorita?" This was the first reference he had made towards seeing Jodi.

"I haven't seen her yet this morning Ramon. Come, you are going to have breakfast and maybe we'll see her in the dining room."

Jodi had still not appeared and Roberto finished his coffee and got up. "It's okay Ramon, don't get up. I have an appointment with General Escobar at noon. You finish your breakfast and I will see you when I get back. I'll take Lorenzo with me."

Ramon put down his cup with a bang almost breaking it and stood up quickly as his eye started to twitch again.

"No, I go with you, you do not go without Ramon." It was like a statement and he knew Ramon would not stay back.

Roberto stood for a moment. Ramon had picked up his machine gun and slung it over his shoulder waiting for Roberto. Roberto sighed. Having Ramon around was like having a watchdog.

"Okay Ramon," he looked at his watch, "be ready to leave in an hour."

"Gracias," said Ramon, "we go but …"

"But what Ramon?"

"I must see Senorita Jodi first. I must see her before we go."

"It's better I talk to her first, Ramon. I have something very important to tell her. I will tell Shane to keep her company until we return, okay?"

Ramon thought for a moment, then nodded. "Okay Roberto, okay."

Roberto and Ramon did not get back until 7:00 p.m. that evening. Roberto entered the Villa and looked for Shane.

"Rosita, have you seen Shane or Jodi-Anne lately?" he said entering the kitchen.

"They're in the library Roberto. Have you eaten any dinner today?"

"Si Rosita, we dined with the General. I am fine, I will see you later." Roberto entered the library and greeted them both.

"Shane, I must talk with Jodi-Anne alone, do you mind?"

Shane immediately stood up. "Of course not Roberto, I'll be inside with Rosita."
Shane closed the door behind her and Roberto sat down facing Jodi. Her eyes were red, her face looked sad and pale and she looked away from Roberto's gaze.

"Jodi-Anne, Ramon told me everything," and immediately she looked at him. "I am truly sorry," he continued "but now you should know something also."

Jodi kept looking at Roberto as he continued. "Ramon's entire family was murdered in front of him. Si, he had brothers and sisters, I don't know how many, I never had the heart to ask. He witnessed his parents being tortured before his eyes and he tried to help them, but there were too many soldiers. They threw him to the ground and held him there as they tried to carve his face with a knife." Roberto paused and Jodi's eyes had widened and her mouth had dropped open. "They wanted to cut off his fingers one by one," he continued. "They held him down and cut off his small finger. Then, I guess this is where Ramon must have gotten pretty nervous and he doesn't know to this day exactly what happened or where the strength came from. All he remembers he says is bodies flying around the room."

Roberto bowed his head, then looked at Jodi again.

"He must have gone half crazy because only he came out of that room alive. Since that day he has the strength of ten men and the reflexes of an animal. He is completely fearless and I know of no other man like him. This is why I choose him to go with me on dangerous assignments, all my assignments, and why you should not have said those things, Jodi-Anne, and this is why Ramon is who he is. I just wanted you to know this. One other thing, I should have protected you Jodi-Anne and I failed, and for this I apologize to you with all my heart."

Jodi sat very still, tears came to her eyes and her hand went nervously to the chain around her neck.

"Oh my God, Roberto, what have I done?" and she burst into tears. Roberto got up and looked for a tissue. He pulled the bandana off his head and handed it to her. He was starting to wonder if this was why these bandanas were being worn. Jodi wiped her eyes and looked at Roberto.

"What is the matter with me, Roberto, why did I talk that way with him?"

Roberto was glad and relieved to see Jodi's reaction. Maybe things could be straightened out after all. Maybe the relationship could be saved.

"Listen to me Jodi-Anne," he said, "I would like the two of you to have a long talk together. Meet Ramon halfway. He is pretty upset and I think there is something he wants to tell you. Are you willing?"

Jodi nodded and wiped her eyes again. "Is he still angry with me, Roberto?"
"I don't think so Jodi-Anne," he said. She looked so pathetic that he put his arms around her. "We're not terrible people Jodi-Anne, please don't think badly of us."

Jodi smiled through her tears and nodded. "Thank you Roberto, you and Shane are wonderful wonderful people. How can I possibly think badly of you?"

"Are you okay Jodi-Anne?" asked Roberto.

Jodi nodded and blew her nose in the bandana. "Shane is so lucky to have you Roberto, you such an incredible person." She reached up and kissed him on the cheek.

"It is I who is lucky Jodi-Anne, Shane just puts up with me. Come, let's see what she's up to."

The next morning gave the promise of the beginning of a beautiful day and Ramon had brought his and Jodi's horses to the front of the Villa. Shane and Roberto watched from their window as they mounted and rode down the path to the beach.

"They seem to be riding together more often, don't you think so?" said Shane turning to Roberto.

"Hmm, si, it certainly looks that way my little one," he said kissing the top of her head.

Shane looked at her husband, "you look tired Roberto, has something been on your mind lately? I think you are working too hard, too many responsibilities."

"You are on my mind Shane, always," he said holding her close. "Actually, there's more going on here inside this Villa than my work away from here."

"What do you mean?" said Shane looking at him curiously.

"Oh, you know, Shane, this situation with Jodi-Anne. It really bothered me."

"What situation with Jodi?" said Shane, "what are you talking about?"

Roberto looked at Shane with surprise, "you don't know? She didn't tell you?"

"Tell me what Roberto? Did something happen?" Shane had grabbed his arm and was looking at him.

Roberto gave a big sigh. Here we go again he thought and turned to Shane with a serious look on his face.

"Where shall I start my little gatito, what shall I tell you?"

"Roberto, you're teasing me again," said Shane trying to get out of his grasp. Roberto would tell her eventually, but right at that moment he was thoroughly enjoying his wife's curiosity and he held her tightly covering her face with kisses. There was plenty of time to tell her about Jodi-Anne and Ramon later.

Jodi and Ramon rode along the beach at a slow pace. The sun was warm, the sky a cloudless blue and the ocean was that incredible turquoise.

Ramon glanced at Jodi, she was wearing a blue hat that matched the colour of her eyes and her blouse. Her blonde hair fell loosely around her face in soft curls.

"You do not talk?" said Ramon.

Jodi did not say anything.

"I am sorry Jodi, about what happened," he said quietly. There was silence then Jodi said "I am sorry too."

Ramon looked at her. "Why you sorry?"

Jodi shrugged her shoulders, "I am sorry for what I said, and I'm sorry for what happened."

Ramon stopped suddenly grabbing the reins of her horse and bringing it to a halt.

"Jodi," he said looking at her, "Roberto very angry with me, he yell at me and say many things. I tell him I am sorry for what happened but," he stopped, still looking at her, "I am not sorry for what happened Jodi, I am not sorry."

Jodi looked at Ramon not knowing or understanding where he was coming from. Ramon dismounted and lifted her off the horse. It reminded her of the time when she got stuck in the tree and how he had lifted her down. He took her hand and they walked towards the palm trees and sat down. Ramon talked mostly and Jodi listened. She did not say too much and Ramon missed her chatter.

"Is okay to talk," he said, "I not mind headache, it is good headache, talk please."

Ramon never thought he would be saying this to Jodi.

"Maybe tomorrow Ramon. Can we go back now?" Jodi looked at him and Ramon felt sadness come over him.

"Okay Senorita Jodi," he said standing up and taking her hand, "we go back."

They rode back slowly under the hot sun, the gentle breeze coming in across the ocean flirting with the sand dunes and playing with the soft waves washing up against the shore. It was Mother Nature creating her own magic and once again, her magic was surrounding the two riders as they made their way back to the Villa.

Chapter Fifteen

Maria and Shane had joined Andre under the large umbrella near the beach. It was such a beautiful morning but nevertheless Jodi had decided to sleep in and have a late breakfast. Rosita insisted on serving the coffee outside. Rain during the night had left dew drops on the flowers and leaves, leaving the foliage lush and exotic with the morning freshness in the air.

It was Saturday morning and Roberto and Shane had asked Skye and Maria to come to the Villa early for breakfast and to spend the day with them.

"We don't see enough of them," said Roberto a few days ago. "I know they're busy with their lives but we have to find time to see them more often. Find out if they can come early on Saturday."

Camille came towards them and embraced her mother and Maria. She then went to Andre and sat on his knee.

"Tio Andre," she said putting her arms around his neck, "will you go riding with me this morning?" Andre held Camille to him. How much he loved the little girl, he did not want to resist her request.

"My little Mantecado, I did not see you at the breakfast table, you must eat something first."

"And then we can go riding Tio Andre?"

"Si, my little Mantecado, and then we can go riding," he said smiling at Camille. The child kissed him on the cheek and ran joyfully inside the Villa to eat her breakfast.

"What a joy that child is to all of us," said Andre, "I don't remember the last time I had ridden a horse but I promised her and I will."

"Roberto says you rode when you were a youngster," said Shane, hoping Andre might remember some of his past.

"Ramon will be with you," said Maria. "He always stays with Camille when she's riding. Roberto says Ramon taught her."

"That's right," said Shane. "Such a beautiful morning; I'm sure it will be a wonderful experience. I wonder what is keeping Roberto?"

"He said he had to make some phone calls," said Andre. "Maria, can I pour you another coffee?" he said; "your cup is empty."

"I can get it Andre," she said getting up. "Those flowers at the side are beautiful. I must look at them closely," she said going towards a flowering bush. Suddenly, she started to sway and clutched at the table for support. Shane jumped up and Andre reached her first. He caught her just as she was starting to fall and lifted her, putting her on the recliner.

"Quick Shane, see if you can find Skye, he might be with Roberto," said Andre pouring ice water from the water jug onto a towel and putting it on Maria's forehead as Shane ran into the Villa. All the color had drained from Maria's face and she wasn't moving. He checked her pulse just as Skye came running towards them with Roberto and Shane close behind.

"Her pulse is weak," said Andre, "and she seems to have lost consciousness." Skye quickly and professionally examined Maria. He was able to revive her but her colour did not return. Pillows were propped up behind her helping Maria to sit up as Skye gave her a drink.

"Stay here tonight Skye," said Roberto, "maybe we shouldn't move Maria around. We can give her anything she might need."

"Yes Skye," said Shane, "there are a number of us that can watch over her here. We will be able to look after her."

"I know you will," said Skye, "but I want to take Maria to the hospital to get some tests done. Two people have been admitted recently with similar symptoms and they've both been diagnosed with a rare strain of the flu that could be dangerous if not treated with antibiotics immediately; I just want to make sure." Skye looked very concerned when he spoke to the others but did not let on to Maria as he smiled at her while holding her hand.

"We'll have to take a rain check on spending more time together another day," Skye promised and said he would call and let them know the results of Maria's tests.

After they left, Ramon brought out Camille's pony and he and Camille, along with Andre set out down the path towards the beach. Roberto had bought a beautiful stallion for Andre the day after he had arrived at the Villa. It was white like Shane's only much larger, and it was named Su Majestad or His Majesty.

Andre rode like Roberto and it was obvious that he was an expert and could handle a horse of that size with no effort. He too preferred to wear a headband while riding, like Roberto, and the similarity to his brother was uncanny. As Roberto watched the three of them ride off, he had a choked feeling in his throat. His brother Marc and his sister Charro should have been there with them and that's when he felt the pain, the pain that never left him, that was usually dull but always there and now it came on stronger. He felt it when he thought of Beatriz, he felt it with Damien and Leandro, and now he watched his brother Andre ride off and it brought back memories of the others in happier days, when they rode together. Roberto vowed again that he would do everything in his power to rebuild the dynasty that was brutally taken away from him years ago and nothing, nothing on the face of the earth would stop him or ever take it away again. And he knew that if he had to resort to unorthodox methods to protect his family and loved ones, so be it.

As he stood there watching them ride off, Shane had come out and she put one arm around his waist and looked up at him. She knew what he was thinking, that look was on his face and he looked down at her and smiled. The moment before had passed and now it was their moment, his and Shane's.

"Did you not want to ride with them Roberto? she asked putting her other hand up to shade her eyes.

"I have to leave Shane, I have to see Juan Gomez about traveling. I have a little time before leaving and I'd rather spend it with you."

He turned her towards him and as she looked up at him he drew her closer and gently kissed her. "You make all my dreams come true Shane," he whispered. "I don't know why, and I do not understand this, and I know I have said it before, but when I look at you or kiss you, it is like the first time, the first day, like the beginning of my life, when I saw you the very first time. What you are doing to me, I do not understand, all I do know is that you are mine, God made you mine my little one, and I thank him every day for this." He held her to him and Shane began to cry, quietly at first then more obviously and Roberto felt her body shaking and looked at her. "What happened Shane, why are you crying?" he asked with sudden concern, wiping away her tears with his hands.

"I am so overwhelmed with what you say Roberto and I love you too, so much that I feel it pouring out of my heart," she said now sobbing.

Roberto took off his headband and wiped away her tears. "You see, my little one," he said with a smile as he tilted her chin up, "when I tell you no one else has what we have, just believe me my darling, just believe me" and he kissed her again this time passionately.

Ramon was very happy as he rode with Andre and Camille past the palm trees along the beach. Because Ramon never smiled, his happiness was not evident but he felt content within himself and that was enough for him. It was a good chance to converse with Andre; Ramon was not fond of too many people but Andre was one of his favourites.

Camille rode in front of them, the breeze lifting her jet-black hair gently, her delightful child-like laughter drifting back to them.

"So Ramon," said Andre, "how is life treating you my friend?"

"Life does not treat Ramon, Ramon treats life," came the strange reply.

"Well," said Andre, "that's different, I never heard that one before." Andre did not realize it but he was about to enter into the special world of Ramon's philosophy on life in general.

"Do you enjoy what you do, Ramon? People should enjoy what they do for a living."

"I do this for living ... and dying. Si, I enjoy the living ... and I enjoy the dying."

Andre looked quickly at Ramon. He was trying to grasp what Ramon had just said.

"What do you mean Ramon, 'you enjoy the living and enjoy ... the dying'?"

Ramon was silent for a moment, then spoke.

"I enjoy protecting people I love and if someone does something bad, is not good, I enjoy killing them."

Andre did not give a response immediately. He was shocked at how brutal Ramon sounded and was at a loss for words. He was totally against Ramon's last statement. How could anyone enjoy killing a person, how could he talk that way and how much hatred Ramon must have inside him. Andre knew he must be careful.

Ramon was calling out to Camille to slow down and he had moved up closer to her pony and grasped the reins, pulling the pony to a halt.

"When Ramon says go slow, you go slow," he said sternly to Camille. She looked at him and he kept holding the reins. "Promise Ramon," he said looking at her. Camille nodded and smiled,

"I promise Ramon," she said obediently. Ramon handed the reins back to her and lightly touched her cheek. "Good girl" he said softly, "go" and she continued while he stayed with Andre behind her.

Andre was impressed. "I like the way you handled that Ramon," he said. "I can see that she loves you."

"I protect the people I love," he said simply.

They rode on for a few minutes quietly, enjoying the beauty around them, and the humming of the ocean that seemed to follow them everywhere. It was Ramon who broke the silence, who wanted to talk.

"Why you not carry gun?" he asked looking at Andre.

Andre had no problem with that. "I think guns are too violent, Ramon."

"Si, gun is violent, it can also be friend. I can teach you," was Ramon's response.

"I know how to use one," said Andre, "my papa taught me." Suddenly he stopped, his eyes opened wide, and he didn't move, it had come out naturally. Ramon called out to Camille to stop. He turned to Andre, knowing exactly what had happened. Andre had suddenly come in contact with something from his past life that had been lost. It was like a miracle. He just sat there not moving. He could feel something in his head that seemed to come alive and he closed his eyes trying to handle it. Ramon put his hand on Andre's arm and gently shook him. He did not open his eyes and Ramon turned to Camille.

"Come closer," he said to her, motioning her towards them. She moved in closer, a little frightened when she looked at Andre.

"It is okay Camille," said Ramon, "talk to your uncle, very gently." She moved closer and leaned towards Andre.

"Tio Andre, Tio Andre," she said taking his hand and squeezing it, as the tears came down her face, "it's Camille, look at me Tio Andre."

Andre opened his eyes and looked at Camille, and suddenly his eyes focused on her and he brought himself back to reality lifting her hand and kissing it.

"My little Mantecado, do not cry, I am fine, do not cry bebe." Ramon produced a flask and poured something in a cup. "Drink this," he said to Andre and Andre hesitated.

"What is it?" he asked.

"Medicine," said Ramon still holding the cup.

"What medicine?" asked Andre hesitantly.

"Don't ask, just drink, trust me," said Ramon moving the cup up to his mouth and Andre took the cup and drank while Ramon held it.

"RAMON, THIS IS WHISKY!" he shouted.

"Si, I told you, medicine," said Ramon, "finish it, now." He did not let go of the cup forcing Andre to drink.

"Next time Andre we drink together, more fun."

The sky above, a pale azure was a contrast to the ocean, dark azure and the sands were sparkling white beneath the bright sun. It was an amazing day in more ways than one and Andre had just been introduced to one of Ramon's rare and delightful philosophies on life.

Roberto returned just before dinner. He was tired but anxious to know how Maria was. He showered and changed before going out towards the back to look for Shane. He found her sitting with Andre and Jodi at the table near the beach.

"So what has been happening here?" he asked kissing Shane and sitting beside her. "What are my favourite people up to?"

"We haven't heard anything about Maria yet," said Shane, "but Skye said he'd let us know as soon as he got the results."

Roberto nodded. "I hope she's okay; they've been through enough. Andre" he said turning to his brother, "how was your ride this morning with Ramon and Camille?"

Andre was quiet, he still had not recovered from what had happened and was trying to cope with images that were going through his head.

"Andre," said Roberto looking at him, "are you all right, is something wrong?" and he quickly looked at Shane, a worried expression on his face. "Did Ramon do something to you?"

"Andre," said Shane, "tell Roberto what happened to you this morning."

By now Roberto was looking from one to the other, many things racing through his mind, not knowing what had happened. Knowing Ramon, anything was possible.

"It's okay Roberto, relax" said Andre, "it's not anything to worry about. Ramon said he would teach me how to shoot a gun and I told him … I told him I knew how." He paused then continued, "I said … my papa taught me."

Roberto bolted out of his chair. "You remember, Andre, your memory has returned," he said excitedly and he rushed to Andre's side and embraced him.

"No Roberto, no, let me finish," said Andre feeling both emotional and sad. "Roberto, that is all I can remember, my papa, our papa, but nothing else. I have no recollection of you, our maman or anyone else. I cannot explain it."

Roberto stood back and looked at Andre. "How could that happen" he asked, "that you only remember papa?"

Andre nodded, "I can see his face and there are other faces but they are not clear." He bowed his head and sighed. "It is a form of torture."

Roberto looked over at Shane and Jodi and both were very quiet. He turned back to Andre. "How would you feel Andre if we took a drive down to the hospital and let them check you over. Maybe Dr. Valdez can tell us what is happening. Come Andre, I will be with you."

Andre looked up, his face looked very tired and his dark eyes were listless as he stood up. It was evident the wear and tear on him was starting to show.

"Would you like me to go with you also?" said Shane starting to get up.

"No need Shane," said Roberto, "we won't be gone long. You and Jodi-Anne and Camille have dinner—don't wait for us. Come Andre, the sooner we go the better." He kissed Shane and they left.

"Don't worry Shane," said Jodi, "I'm sure Andre will be all right."

"I hope so," said Shane, "he is obviously going through something."

"All the signs are good Shane. Parts of his memory are returning, it sounds so positive."

Dr. Valdez had very hopeful news for Andre and Roberto. He felt that everything seemed to point to Andre having a full recovery. The fact that he was getting flashbacks and something had resurfaced was exactly what they had been hoping for. However, he called Roberto aside to tell him the emotional impact of this happening might be so great that there was the possibility that it could cause some damage to Andre psychologically.

"The slower this comes about, the better for Andre to be able to handle," said Dr. Valdez putting his hand on Roberto's arm. "We must always live with hope Roberto and believe in the power of prayer. Andre has come this far, I believe he will recover fully."

Roberto nodded but again he felt the pain. He would fight it for Andre's sake and for his own.

They left Dr. Valdez's office and Roberto suggested they find Skye and see if Maria's test results had come through. They saw Skye coming down the hall towards them and before they had a chance to enquire, Skye ushered them into his office, closed the door and turned facing them, his face beaming.

"Gentlemen, do I have news for you, you will never guess," he said pointing to the chairs. "Sit down please."

Andre smiled, "I know," he said.

"You know?" said Skye surprise showing on his face.

"Know what?" said Roberto, "will somebody say something?"

"Go ahead Skye," said Andre, "this is your special news."

"Maria is pregnant, we are going to have a baby, God willing," blurted out Skye, his eyes starting to shine.

"That is wonderful!" exclaimed Roberto getting out of the chair quickly followed by Andre. They both congratulated Skye and there was a great deal of handshaking and embracing. Doctors had thought that Maria could not become pregnant but now they were going to be blessed with a miracle baby. Skye had grasped Roberto's hand and Roberto winced. "What do we have here?" said Skye looking at the cut on Roberto's hand.

"I told him that he might need stitches—that was a week ago. My brother is brave when he brings me to the doctor," said Andre smiling, "but is not too brave for himself."

"I promise you, this won't hurt," said Skye chuckling under his breath as he lead Roberto towards the sink. "Andre, I might need you to hold the Comandante down while I dress the wound" he said winking at him.

"Okay, okay, have a good laugh both of you," said Roberto. "Have you and Maria picked any names for the baby?"

"Don't change the subject," laughed Skye, "this is too good to let go. Hmm, actually, the cut has started to infect. Tsk tsk, this looks very serious."

Twelve stitches and one injection later, Roberto left the hospital with Andre, his hand bandaged but feeling very elated about the new baby.

Chapter Sixteen

Jodi sat with Shane under the large umbrella. The sun was bright and very hot but the gentle breeze coming in from the ocean gifted them with a feeling of paradise.

"Ramon has asked me to marry him Shane," she said suddenly. Shane looked at her with surprise and immediately went to Jodi and hugged her with tears in her eyes.

"Jodi, I'm so happy for you, when did all this happen?"

"Actually, only yesterday said Jodi with a smile. "I'm happy Shane, really happy."

"Well, I should hope so," said Shane, "we are all very fond of Ramon. Wait till Roberto hears about this. We're getting good news one after another. Maria's pregnancy is fabulous. You know something Jodi, life is good to us."

"I agree," said Jodi, "this new baby is something special to all of us." She looked around her and gave a deep sigh. "I hope my wedding day will be like this. What do you think my chances are Shane?"

Shane took off the wide-brimmed hat she was wearing. She did not like wearing hats but knew she sometimes had to.

"I think your chances are excellent, Jodi, and really does it matter that much? You are marrying the man you love and that's what really matters."

"I know," said Jodi in a dreamy voice, "you're so right." She was thoughtful for a moment, then said; "Shane, I've been wondering about something and I don't know how to go about asking."

"Go about asking what?" said Shane looking at her friend.

"Well," said Jodi, "it's about my sister Lorena. She's coming here for the wedding you know."

"Yes, of course," said Shane. "I'm sorry I didn't meet her when we were in Toronto. She's younger than you I believe."

"Yes, Lorena is sixteen and she will be arriving this Friday. But Shane," and Jodi hesitated, "what I was wondering is if maybe Roberto will talk to her."

Shane looked up. "Talk to her? What do you mean?"

"Well, let me put it this way; Lorena is really a good kid, she's just a little too grown up for her age Shane. I guess what I mean is she tries to be grown up. She dresses a little improperly, you know, too short, too tight, and there's this guy she works for. She's been seeing him and he's so much older than her."

"Maybe they love each other," said Shane, "and maybe she likes older men."

"Shane, he's married," blurted out Jodi, "he has a wife and two children."

Shane looked at her suddenly. "Oh, that's not too good is it. Why don't you get Ramon to speak to her? He has more right to do so than Roberto. He's going to be her brother-in-law."

Jodi laughed, "Shane, can you just see Ramon arguing with Lorena? He'll probably spank her. That would be an awful start for a family relationship. No, I think Roberto would handle a situation like this much better. He has more patience than Ramon; Ramon is too impulsive. I hate to think what he might do."

"Do you know something Jodi, I agree with you one hundred percent on that, but I think you should be the one to speak to Roberto."

"I'm glad you agree Shane. I don't know what she sees in this guy, but I am concerned. Is Roberto around today?"

"Actually, no. He's gone to the village and then he's going over to see Skye and Maria to see about getting more security at the hospital. I'm not exactly sure what's happening there. I know that he will be getting back late tonight and tomorrow at 10:00 in the morning he has to get to the airport to meet with a General coming in from Argentina. Try between 8:00 and 9:00 tomorrow morning; I'm sure he'll be glad to talk with you."

"Wow, you almost need an appointment to see him. I thought of Andre too, but I think she needs to talk with someone who is more stern."

Shane laughed. "So now we have a cross between Andre and Ramon and we get Roberto."

"You put that very well Shane," said Jodi, "actually, that's kind of funny," and she suddenly became very serious. "I'm really worried about her, she's my little sister and I want to look out for her until she's able to handle things herself."

Shane nodded. "Of course Jodi, I never had a sister, wish I did but my brothers are great and you and Maria are like sisters to me."

Jodi was quiet. "What is it Jodi," said Shane, "what is wrong?"

"I'm afraid, Shane, afraid of the future. Here I am getting married in a foreign Country, I'm worried over my sister, my dad is an invalid and mom is taking care of him. Am I getting paranoid? Am I worrying for nothing?"

Shane got up and put her arm around Jodi. "Yes you are Jodi, stop worrying. If I see Roberto tonight I will speak to him, okay? Let's go down to the beach, do you feel like a swim? I haven't seen Ramon today, I wonder where he is?"

Jodi tried to pull herself together. A sudden feeling of doom had swept over her and she was frightened and sad at the same time and she felt a shudder. Shane looked at her.

"Jodi, are you all right? I just wondered where Ramon was."

Jodi suddenly looked up. "Oh, I'm sorry Shane, he's probably with Roberto. Garcia is still undergoing treatment for his arm." She had recovered quickly and stepped back into the picture.

"Oh, that's right," said Shane, "the physiotherapist comes here to see him. He seems to be doing much better."

Shane had not gone swimming for months. She lay on the beach and her thoughts went back to over a decade, when she had done the same thing only then Mary was with her and Jodi. So much had happened over the years and Shane wondered what else was in store for them. Jodi came out of the water and plunked herself on the sand beside Shane.

"Thanks Shane," she said drying her hair, "I really appreciate what you are doing for me."

Roberto returned in the late evening. Shane was sitting in bed reading a book when he arrived and he looked surprised.

"I thought you would be asleep by now," he said looking at his watch. "You waited up for me or just couldn't sleep?" he said sitting on the bed beside her.

"Actually, it was both," she said putting down the book and smiling at him. Roberto took both her hands and kissed them.

"Roberto, I want to talk to you about Jodi's sister, Lorena," said Shane quickly. She didn't know why but she suddenly felt nervous to have to ask him.

"And what about Jodi-Anne's sister Lorena," he said kissing her on the forehead and the neck.

"Jodi wants you to talk to her about this relationship that Lorena has with a married man." Shane did not mean to blurt it out so suddenly but it just happened. Roberto stopped kissing her and looked up.

"She wants me to what?" he said incredulously.

Shane swallowed hard. "Roberto, wait, it's a big favour for Jodi. She thinks that maybe you can get through to her."

Roberto looked glum. "Well what about Ramon? He's going to be family and she might resent my intruding into her personal affairs."

"Now Roberto, you know what Ramon is like. Can you just imagine him talking to this girl about this?"

Roberto could not help but smile. "How old is Lorena? he asked. Shane hesitated, "she's sixteen."

Roberto's smile froze on his face. He stared at Shane for a moment then shook his head. "I'm sorry Shane, there is no way that I can get involved in this," and he got up and went to the shower. Shane knew what was bothering him. Lorena was Beatriz's age and it brought back painful memories. Nothing else was said that evening and Shane knew that Jodi would have to speak to Roberto about it herself.

The next day at breakfast Shane told Jodi what had happened before Roberto came down and Jodi said she would think of something. As it turned out, Roberto did not have time for breakfast and left immediately in the morning for the airport. He was in meetings most of the day and later he and the General went out to inspect some newly trained recruits in the Elite Tactical Emergency Response Units. Lorena would be arriving in two days and Jodi knew that Roberto might not have a chance to talk to her.

On the morning of Lorena's arrival, Shane, Jodi, Ramon and Lorenzo waited at the airport for her. None of them had met Jodi's sister but when she got off the plane, it was easy to spot her. She was blonde like Jodi and that's where the similarity ended. Her skirt was very short, her walk was sassy, her expression very defiant. Jodi ran towards her and grasped her in her arms. She loved her sister dearly and wanted to look after her.

"Lorena, I'm so glad you're here," said Jodi hugging her sister. Lorena looked over Jodi's shoulder, "and you must be Shane," she said. "I heard you were beautiful but I guess you already know that." Shane hugged the girl and thought, poor Jodi, she's going to have her hands full.

"Meet Ramon, Lorena, he will be your brother-in-law, Ramon, my little sister Lorena."

Lorena stared at Ramon and said, "hello Ramon, I hope you're not going to act like my big brother and tell me what to do, and maybe we'll get along. You look silly with that big gun, like a kid playing a game."

Ramon did not say anything but just looked at her. Jodi tugged at Lorena's arm, "and this is Lorenzo," and he will …" Jodi's voice trailed off. She was embarrassed at her sister's behavior and did not know what to say about Lorenzo. Shane came to her rescue.

"Lorenzo is a bodyguard Lorena and bodyguards are hired to look out for our safety." She hadn't realized how her words would sound and Lorena quickly looked at Shane. She did not say anything and they went over to their car and set off for the Villa. When they arrived Jodi took Lorena to her room then went downstairs to sit with Shane.

"Now you see what I'm up against," said Jodi. "Poor Ramon, I must talk to him, do you know where he is?"

"He's just bringing in Lorena's suitcases, oh here he comes," said Shane, "call him over and let's have some coffee until Lorena comes down." She put out the cups while Jodi called Ramon into the kitchen. "Don't feel bad Ramon," said Jodi taking his arm, "she's tired from the trip, usually she's not this sarcastic."

Ramon sat down. "I do not feel bad for me, I feel bad for her. Something is wrong."

"She's had her own way for a long time," said Jodi. "I guess my parents could not control her. Maybe she'll change while she's here."

"If you let me, I control her," said Ramon stirring his coffee.

"No Ramon, I don't want her to hate you and she will," exclaimed Jodi. "Let's wait and maybe Roberto can help." They could hear Lorena coming down the stairs and Ramon said he had to do something and left.

"Did I scare the cowboy off?" said Lorena joining them at the table.

"Lorena," said Jodi, "I don't want you to talk that way about Ramon. These are all very nice people here and the men holding machine guns are all specially trained. Everyone here is extending their hospitality to us and while we are in their home I hope you will show some respect. Do I make myself clear?"

Lorena just shrugged her shoulders and Shane thought there was something pathetic about the girl. She was attractive, like Jodi and her thick blonde hair hung past her shoulders. She was not quite as slim as her sister, her figure was voluptuous and she wore her clothes very fitted.

"I wish you would button up your blouse," said Jodi not looking too happy at Lorena's appearance.

"It is buttoned," said Lorena, "are you afraid Ramon is going to look at me?"

Jodi gasped and Shane put down her cup and looked at Lorena.

"What do you think, Shane," said Lorena, "do you think this does not look proper?"

"Lorena, listen to me," said Shane trying to make her voice sound friendly. "We all like you and no one wants to criticize or say things to you. However, there is no need for you to talk that way. We all want to be nice but you get off the plane and immediately insult Ramon. Now you've insulted your sister and yes, because you ask, I think what you are wearing is not proper." Shane did not want to mention to Lorena that there were a number of men in the area and she could not walk around dressed the way she was. Roberto would definitely have to have a word with her.

"How would you like to go horse-back riding this afternoon?" suggested Shane. "It might be fun."

Lorena shrugged her shoulders. "Is that all you people do for entertainment?" she asked in a bored tone. "I can see where this is going to be a long summer." She got up to leave.

"Where are you going?" asked Jodi standing up.

"I thought I'd look at the horses, where are they kept?"

"That's a good idea, come on Lorena, I'll take you there," said Jodi, "but first change your clothes. Do you have a pair of jeans and another top?"

The girl gave a big sigh and went upstairs. Shane looked at Jodi with surprise, "good for you," she said, "at least she's doing what you tell her."

"That surprised me too," said Jodi.

Lorena came down and passed the inspection test and the three of them went outside.

She loved horses and she had ridden before and wanted to ride immediately.

"This one is absolutely beautiful," she said putting her face against the black horse.

"He should be called Black Velvet. Can I ride him?"
"His name is Allegro," said Jodi, "and no you cannot ride this one. There are other horses to pick from."

"I like this one," insisted Lorena, "I can tell this horse is different and I want to ride this one."

"This is Roberto's horse, Lorena and it's a very big stallion," said Jodi. "It might not be easy to handle if he's not familiar with you."

"Who is Roberto, I'll ask him, he won't mind," insisted Lorena. "Is he here?"

"No Lorena, he isn't," said Shane. "Here is a very nice horse that Lorenzo is bringing over. I'll get him to saddle it for you."

Lorena looked at Shane angrily, "No, I don't want that horse, and I don't know who this Roberto is but I would like to have a talk with him. Tell him that when you see him," she said and angrily stomped out of the stable.

Jodi looked at Shane and put her hand up to her mouth to stop the laugh. Shane was already laughing and shaking her head. Even Lorenzo had a big smile on his face as he led the horse back to its stall. As they came out, Lorenzo commented, "Senorita has sense of humor, si?"

"Yes Lorenzo," said Jodi, "I have a feeling that life is not going to be dull on the island."

"Good," said Shane, "we need the excitement."

Lorena had taken the path towards the beach and sat down at the table with the big umbrella. Andre was sitting there reading a book and looked up and smiled at the girl.

"Would you be Roberto?" she asked impatiently looking about her.

"No, I am not," he said still smiling. "My name is Andre and who do I have the pleasure of talking to?"

"Hmm, I don't know if it's a pleasure or not … my name is Lorena."

"How do you do Lorena. What a pretty name."

Lorena was looking out over the ocean and turned to look at Andre. "Do you work here?"

"No, I don't" he said taking off his sunglasses. "I don't believe I've seen you around here before."

"And I don't believe I've seen you before either," she said sarcastically.

Just then Shane and Jodi appeared. "Am I to be followed wherever I go?" asked Lorena in a tired voice.

"Not by us" said Jodi, "Lorenzo probably will."

"Well I don't like that and I wish I had never come here," she said.

Shane looked helplessly at Andre and he put down his book and looked thoughtful before he spoke.

"Why do you say that Lorena, this is a beautiful place. You should love to be here, the ocean, the sun and beach …"

Lorena looked at him. "You don't know how I feel, so don't tell me what I should think or what I should love. You look lost anyway."

"Lorena," shouted Jodi loudly and suddenly standing up, "you apologize to Andre immediately."

Lorena looked surprised. She did not expect Jodi to react the way she did.

"That's quite all right," said Andre calmly, "I am sure Lorena did not mean anything by that."

Shane glared at Lorena and the girl started to wonder what all the fuss was about.

"Lorena," said Andre, "maybe we could spend some time together and you and I could get to know each other. Maybe we could give each other some advice—or companionship. Would you like that?"

Lorena looked at Andre suspiciously. Andre was very soft-spoken and he seemed to have a calming effect on her and yet, she did not trust him. No man had talked to her that way without something on his mind. She continued to look at him suspiciously.

"I assure you Lorena," said Andre continuing to smile at her, "I am completely harmless."

A light breeze from the ocean billowed around them and Lorena pushed back wisps of hair that blew around her face. Shane and Jodi sat quietly; they knew that Andre could handle the situation.

"I don't need advice or companionship," said Lorena. She got up to leave and turned to Shane. "Just tell this Roberto, whoever he is, that I would like to have a word with him. You won't forget will you?"

"Oh, I won't forget," said Shane, "believe me, as soon as I see him."

Lorena walked back up the path and Andre looked at Shane. "What was that all about?" he asked as Shane looked at Jodi and they both grinned. "Nothing to be concerned about Andre," said Shane. "Lorena just wants to ask Roberto something about borrowing his horse."

Andre's eyebrows shot up. "Let me know how it turns out," he said. "I'd really like to know."

Roberto arrived late during the night. He had no appointments scheduled for the morning and rather than sleeping in, he decided he would arise early and take a run on the beach with Allegro. He was up before Shane, put on his riding outfit and left without breakfast hoping to have it later with Shane. As he started out, he could see Ramon riding towards him from the other end.

"Hola Ramon, you are up early," said Roberto bringing his horse to a halt.

"Si Roberto, I just patrol the beach. Beach does not sleep, mystery at night, Ramon likes mystery."

"You are an interesting person my friend," said Roberto. "Did Jodi-Anne's sister arrive?"

"Oh si," said Ramon, "she arrive all right, live rope."

"Live rope? I do not understand Ramon," said Roberto looking at him.

"You know," said Ramon, "talk too much, yak, yak, live rope."

Roberto laughed, "Do you mean live wire? She's a live wire?"

"Si Roberto, very spoilt."

"She's young, she will change."

"I not think so Roberto, she's ... different."

"Let's have breakfast, have you eaten yet Ramon?"

Ramon shook his head, "too tired, I sleep now, breakfast later."

Ramon accompanied Roberto for a short ride on the beach and as the sun rose they both turned back and Ramon took back the horses to the stable.

The sky was a soft blue without a cloud in sight as Roberto entered the Villa to say good morning to Rosita in the kitchen.

"We missed you Roberto," said Rosita taking a tray out of the oven. "I don't think you had your breakfast this morning."

"No my Rosita," he said sniffing at the aroma. "Is this gatta, my favourite?"

"Just for you, my son. Now you go ahead inside and sit, I'll bring these in."

Roberto washed up and went into the dining room not bothering to change out of his riding outfit as he adjusted his headband. The morning ride had given him an appetite and he decided to change later. Shane was seated at the table with Jodi and Lorena and Roberto walked over to Shane and kissed her on the forehead.

"Roberto, I'm so glad you're back," said Shane, "this is Lorena, Jodi's sister."

Roberto took Lorena's hand and bowed, "welcome to our home Lorena. It is a pleasure to meet you."

Lorena looked at Roberto and opened her mouth to say something but nothing came out.

"Lorena wants to talk to you about something after breakfast, Roberto," said Shane.

Roberto looked at Lorena and said "Oh?" and Lorena's arm hit her water glass spilling it across the table. Shane quickly got up and started to blot it with a paper towel and Roberto refilled her glass handing it to her. Lorena was acting strangely and Jodi looked at her sternly.

"Lorena, did you not sleep well?" she asked. Lorena mumbled something about jet lag but she remained very quiet during the remainder of the breakfast. Shane asked Roberto how the meetings went and where the General was staying. "He could have come here and stayed with us Roberto, we have plenty of room."

Roberto nodded. "I offered our place but apparently there is a high risk involved in regards to security. There had been two assassination attempts on his life recently and they thought he could be guarded more easily with less complication, whatever that means, at the hotel."

"Do be careful Roberto," said Shane, "the last incident involving Leandro is so recent. I think we're all still reeling from it."

Roberto shook his head. Leandro's untimely death still bothered him and he knew it always would. He turned his attention to Lorena. "So Lorena, you wanted to talk to me," he said. "We can go in the library if you wish but finish your coffee first."

Lorena quickly stood up and said, "no, it is okay, I'm finished." Roberto ushered Lorena into the library and Jodi looked nervously at Shane.

"What happened to her Shane, I've never seen Lorena act that way before."

"I don't know," said Shane. "Do you suppose maybe she became intimidated by Roberto? He tends to do that to some people."

"Perhaps," said Jodi, "but I wish I knew what they were saying."

Roberto closed the library door and pulled a chair out for Lorena. She sat down slowly and Roberto sat down facing her and folding his arms.

"What can I do for you Lorena?"

Lorena hesitated; she just kept staring at Roberto.

"Shane said you wanted to talk to me about something," said Roberto unaware of the effect he was making on the girl. A few seconds went by before she spoke.

"We ... we were looking at the horses ... I wanted to go riding."

"That's wonderful," said Roberto, "and did you?"

Lorena shook her head.

"And why not?" he asked.

Lorena was quiet for a moment then said, "I wanted to ride your horse."

"You wanted to ride Allegro?" said Roberto looking surprised. "He's a very powerful horse; he might be difficult to handle by someone unfamiliar to him."

"I can handle anything," said the girl looking at Roberto. He stared back trying to analyze her. "There are several other horses available which you could have ridden."

Lorena was quiet for a moment. "Are you married to Shane?" she said suddenly.

"Shane is my wife, si, we are married," he said.

Lorena was very quiet. "Do you want to go riding today?" asked Roberto, "Lorenzo will accompany you."

"I'd love to go riding," she said, her eyes lighting up, "can you take me?"

"Not today, I can't Lorena, I have to see someone, I'm sorry."
"Tomorrow? I can wait until tomorrow," she said eagerly.

"We'll see," said Roberto, "I can't promise, but if I can, I will."

"Okay," said Lorena confidently, "I can wait, tomorrow."

"So was that all Lorena? said Roberto unfolding his arms.

"Uh, I guess so," she said.

Roberto stood up. "If that's everything, then if you will excuse me, I have to be somewhere. I'll see you later today when I get back. Feel free to browse around here in the library, we have several excellent books Lorena and you have a nice day." Roberto left the library and Lorena just stood there.

Shane and Jodi were still sitting in the dining room when Roberto went over to them.

"Shane, I have a few phone calls to make then I'm going to change and meet with General Escobar for an inspection tour and then lunch. I'll try not to be too late, maybe around dinner time."

"Is everything okay with Lorena?" asked Jodi.

"Seems to be," said Roberto. "She wants to go riding."

"She must have changed her mind, Roberto," said Shane, "Lorenzo was ready to take her out but she wanted to ride Allegro."

"She wanted me to take her but I'm busy today. I told her I might be able to tomorrow."

"No Roberto, don't," said Jodi. "Please be careful, I know she's my sister but I don't think that's a good idea. I have my reasons."

"No Jodi, you're wrong," said Shane, "it's an excellent idea. That would give Roberto time to talk to her. Roberto, she really needs someone to talk to. You should hear her when you're not around. You haven't seen that side of her. It breaks your heart, believe me."

"Where is she now? asked Jodi, "didn't she come out with you?"

"No, she might have stepped outside. Anyway, I have to get going and I'll see you both later. Roberto kissed Shane and left. He could not help but get an uneasy feeling about Lorena.

"It must be difficult for you Shane, to live this kind of life. You barely get to see your husband," said Jodi.

"It's not always like this," said Shane. "I feel bad for him though. He hardly sees Camille and then Enrique and Frederik only a few times a year. Our children are growing up and we're missing it all. Maybe one day it will all change."

"I hope so Shane," said Jodi. "I'm going to look for Lorena; do you want to come along with me? It's such a gorgeous day." Shane agreed and the girls took the path down to the beach.

Lorena had gone back to her room. She lay on the bed, her mind racing. She had never met anyone like Roberto. There was an air of excitement about him. He had a very self-assured body movement when he walked and he was devastatingly handsome. Her boyfriend Eric could not even compare to this man and Lorena decided that she would stay as long as she could … or as long as she had to. But there was Shane and she was really beautiful which Lorena found very upsetting. The more she thought about Shane, the more upset she became. A knock at the door interrupted her thoughts.

"Who is it?" she called out.

"It's me Lorena, its Jodi. May I come in?"

Lorena gave a sigh, "the door is open," she said.

Jodi stepped in and closed the door behind her. She sat on the bed and looked at her sister. Lorena was young, quite attractive and had an amazing figure and Jodi was really worried.

"Lorena," she said firmly, "please listen to what I have to say." Lorena turned her face away because she did not want to look at her sister and did not want to hear what she had to say.

"You're upset with me because I am going riding tomorrow with Roberto."

"Lorena, look at me," said Jodi sternly, "I'm very serious. I don't want you to try anything that will embarrass me or cause trouble in this family. These are not ordinary people and they do not live ordinary lives. Roberto is a very high-ranking official in this Country, actually the highest in his field and they are also very close friends of the President. He is responsible for thousands of men who are under his command so I hope you get the picture. I want you to behave yourself, be very, very careful of your actions."

Lorena looked at Jodi, "You're right Jodi, he is not ordinary." She turned her face the other way and ignored her sister. Jodi got up and went towards the door, then turned.

"Lorena, I'm getting married in a few weeks and don't spoil things for me, don't walk in dangerous waters. I don't want to have to send you back home before my wedding." She opened the door and left.

Lorena lay on the bed with a smile on her face and her heart beating wildly. She would be patient and wait for tomorrow.

Tomorrow came and it was a glorious day. Roberto did not get back until very late during the night and encountered no one except the usual guards patrolling the area. By the time he went downstairs for breakfast everyone was already at the table.

"Buenos dias," he said sitting next to Shane. "How nice to see everyone together this morning."

"You're usually the first one up Roberto," said Andre, "you must have arrived late last night."

"I did but I slept in and I feel wonderful. Thank you Shane," said Roberto taking the coffee from her. "So Jodi-Anne, the big day is drawing near. Have you completed plans for your wedding?"

"Almost Roberto, but I sometimes think is this real? I was determined to stay single, remember?"

"Si, I remember," said Roberto. "However, Ramon is a fine young man and I am very happy for the two of you."

"Thank you," said Jodi blushing.

"You are very quiet this morning," said Andre addressing Lorena. "I hope you slept well."

"Yes, thanks," said Lorena stirring her coffee.

"You wanted to go riding today I believe," said Roberto. "I have some time this morning if you're still interested."

"I'm still interested," said Lorena eagerly. "Let's go, I'm ready."

"Lorena," said Jodi eyeing her sister sternly, "let Roberto have his breakfast."

"It's okay Jodi-Anne, I'm not that hungry this morning," said Roberto. "You go ahead Lorena, I'll be out in a few minutes. Lorenzo will bring out the horses."

Jodi looked sternly at her sister. The blouse she wore was too revealing and before she had a chance to say anything Lorena rushed out leaving Jodi in a very upset state.
"I hate to say this, she is my sister and I love her, but Lorena is so selfish and stubborn. You're going to have your hands full Roberto, don't say I didn't warn you."

"I think the young lady lacks companionship and needs to talk with someone," said Andre.

"That's right Andre," said Shane, "that's why I think this would be a good chance for Roberto to talk to her. The atmosphere, the scenery, the ocean …"

"Roberto, just be careful," interrupted Jodi.

Roberto laughed, "you make the girl out to be … what is that name … Mata Hari; she's just a kid." He gulped down his coffee and stood up. "If we're not back in six hours, send out six of my men, or better still, just Ramon."

"Roberto, don't make fun of this," said Jodi, "you don't know my sister."

"And your sister does not know me Jodi-Anne." He bent over and kissed Shane.

"Don't wait up for me Shane," he whispered giving her a wink and was gone.

Lorena was already seated and waiting for Roberto and Lorenzo stood nearby holding the reins of Roberto's horse.

"Does he have to come with us?" said Lorena glaring at Lorenzo.

"It's the rules," said Roberto mounting his horse, "you won't even see him, he's protecting you."

"Why do I need him to protect me when I have you?" she said coyly.

"Come on Lorena," he said ignoring her last remark, "let's go."

They followed the path down to the beach and rode at a slow trot along the shoreline. The high tide had left an assortment of shells scattered along the sand in the early morning and the sky was an incredible blue without a cloud in sight. Lorena, like Jodi knew how to ride and her blonde hair blew around her and her face was relaxed and smiling. She glanced at Roberto. He was so handsome, why hadn't she met him first.

After a while Roberto pointed to an area where the palm trees were abundant and they stopped and dismounted.

"This is a favourite spot of mine Lorena, it's a little high and it allows you to look far out onto the ocean. The view is amazing."

Lorena sat down and took in a deep breath. "I could sit out here forever Roberto. Do you have a busy schedule today?"

"I'm afraid so," said Roberto sitting beside her, "but the morning is yours."

Lorena turned and looked at him. "Roberto?"

"Hmm?"

"How did you meet Shane?"

"How?"

"Yes, I mean, where did you meet?"

"Oh, in a night club."

"A night club!" exclaimed Lorena.

"Si, a night club."

"You mean you picked her up?"

Roberto smiled, "you could say that," he said.

"So how long did you know her before you got married?"

Roberto looked at Lorena. She reminded him of Beatriz. She was not dark-haired but the age was the same and she was trying so hard to act older but with the same child-like eyes that betrayed her.

"Lorena, I don't think we came here to talk about Shane, did we. Let's talk about you instead."

"Me? What do you want to know about me Roberto? I'll tell you anything you want to know."

"Well, for starters Jodi-Anne tells me you have a boyfriend and he's much older than you."

"Really," she said with a huff, "well maybe I like older men."

"And I understand he's married," said Roberto, "and that should tell you something."

She turned to face him and her eyes were angry. "And who are you to tell me what I should and shouldn't do? Eric says he loves me, he is very handsome and dresses better than any man I have ever met."

"Dresses better?" repeated Roberto. "Take away the fancy clothes and what do you have?" He immediately regretted what he had said but it was too late.

"A naked man," blurted out Lorena.

"I'm not telling you what to do Lorena, I'm only giving you advice. I'm trying to help you."

"Well, I don't need any help, not from you or … or … Andre. Who does he think he is anyway? I told him off the other day and I will again if I have to. He sounds a little fresh to me and …"

"Just a minute," said Roberto, feeling his blood pressure rising, "you told Andre off?"

"I sure did. I told him not to tell me what to do and I also told him that he looked lost anyway, so who is he to give advice."

Roberto looked at her, there was anger in his eyes and Lorena was glad that she could do that to him.

"What is he to you? She asked, and added sarcastically, "someone important?"

"Si Lorena, he is someone very important to me and you are a spoilt kid."

Lorena laughed, then stopped suddenly looking very serious and threw the shocker at him. "I dare you to kiss me Roberto, now," she said in a taunting manner.

Good God he thought, almost the exact words that he had heard once before, and he felt the pain that he thought had been put to rest coming back again to haunt him. All of a sudden and very unexpectedly she threw herself at him, digging her fingers into his shoulders, her mouth coming down hard on his. Roberto grabbed her arms and held them behind her back throwing her backwards to the ground. She screamed when she landed and Roberto held her there. She was strong but he was stronger and he wanted to hit her, hard. If she were a man, he would have beaten her. She started to cry and he knew she was in pain and released her. He watched her as she sat up and cried like a child, rubbing her arms, her hair disheveled, the tears coursing down her cheeks.

Roberto sat there feeling badly. How did he get into these situations? Why did life have to be so complicated? All he wanted at that moment was to take Shane and go far away from everything, somewhere where no one would disturb them and no one would be near them, just him and Shane.

"Stop crying Lorena, that's enough," he said angrily but the girl seemed almost hysterical. He looked at her, starting to feel sorry for her and being Roberto, put his arms around her. He did not like to see a woman cry and cry she did for almost five minutes without stopping and he let her. It was as if she had been holding back feelings of frustration and love and hate were the only emotions that she knew. He took the bandana off his head and wiped her eyes. She was suddenly a little girl as she let Roberto dry her tears.

"Lorena, look at me," he said lifting her chin, "listen to me. I don't think you mean what you did and I really believe that you are a good girl."

She looked at him through her tears, "I am?" No one had ever said that to her before.

"Si, a very good girl, and you know something else?"

She shook her head, sniffling.

"Although I can see the child in your eyes, some day soon you will be an amazing woman, si, amazing, and you will make a very lucky young man so happy. Believe me, just be patient Lorena and he will come to you."

"An amazing woman," she repeated wide-eyed, "really?"

"Si Senorita, amazing. Now I want you to start thinking more highly of yourself and please, please, do not try to grow up too fast. Promise me that?"

Lorena looked out towards the ocean and smiled. "An amazing woman," she said and Roberto nodded.

"Roberto, let's go back," she said eagerly, "I have to apologize to some people." She grimaced in pain as she stood up and Roberto helped her.

"I'm sorry Lorena, I know I hurt you, I am sorry, are you okay? It was not my intention."

"I am surprised you didn't hit me," Roberto. I'm okay, I deserved it. Oh, I can't believe what I just did to you. I am so embarrassed, ouch!"

Roberto smiled, "good, you see, you have changed already and I am so proud of you Lorena. Would you like to ride Allegro back to the Villa? I'll help you get seated."

Lorena looked at Roberto and her eyes filled again. "Shane is so lucky."

Roberto laughed as he lifted her onto the horse.

"Do me a favour Lorena, will you tell her that?"

As they started back Roberto glanced at the girl and she looked happy and serene.

"Lorena?"
"Yes, Roberto?"

"Did you know that Andre is my brother?"

She turned suddenly, "no Roberto, I didn't know that.

"He is also a priest."

She stopped and looked at him, her expression aghast. "Oh my God, what have I done?

Roberto I am so stupid. I want you to hit me hard when we get back. Oh my goodness, I didn't know that."

"How would you know?" he said but his face wore a smile the rest of the way back. It was turning out to be a very good day after all.

Ramon was sitting on the verandah with Jodi and Shane and stood up as they approached. They watched dumfounded as Roberto lifted Lorena from Allegro and set her down. They went up the steps together and Lorena went to Ramon and put her arms around his waist and laid her head on his chest.

"Ramon, I'm sorry, please forgive me."

Then she went to Jodi and did exactly the same thing. When she stood before Shane, she looked at her for a moment then said, "Shane, you're so lucky," and embraced her and said, "I am sorry for all the trouble I have caused."

Ramon, Jodi and Shane just stood there, no one was talking or moving. They stared at Roberto and he just shrugged his shoulders and went inside. Then they turned and looked at Lorena.

"I'm a mess," she said. "I think I will take a shower. I have to see Andre but not like this." She went inside leaving a speechless group standing outside.

Shane's curious nature got the better of her. "I'm going inside; Roberto will tell me what happened," she said and left.

Jodi looked at Ramon. "What do you think happened, is that the same girl?"

Ramon shook his head, "This one much better."

Shane waited impatiently for Roberto to come out of the shower.

"Hola my little one," he said emerging in a bath robe. "Did you miss me?"

"Yes, yes," said Shane, "what happened Roberto?"
"Nothing much Shane," he said starting to dress.

"Well tell me Roberto, look at me."

He turned to look at her and started to laugh.

"What are you laughing at," she said, "what is it that you find so funny?"

"I've always loved that curious nature that you have Shane, you are like a … a … gato, no, a gatito."

"And just what is that?"

"You are like a cat or a kitten, you know, curious."

"Roberto, for heaven's sake, please be serious and tell me what happened to Lorena?"

"We had a little talk Shane. She cried a lot, she's just a mixed up kid but I think she has a bit more self-esteem now."

"Poor thing," said Shane, "whatever you said seemed to make a big difference, Roberto. I think that is just wonderful how you brought about the change in her."

"Yes Shane, I too am glad. I hope she's okay, she had a nasty fall."

"She fell off the horse?"

"No, nothing like that, I had to throw her off me," he said going towards the door."

"Roberto, you come back here, what do you mean you had to throw her off you, what happened?" Shane had grabbed his arm.

Roberto turned around. "Oh, you really don't want to hear about it."

"I do want to hear about it Roberto, what happened?"

Roberto heaved a sigh. "I guess I just seem to attract women, Shane."

"Roberto, be serious, tell me what happened," said Shane, "why are you skipping the issue?"

"Skipping the what?" he said still laughing and grasping her wrist. "I love it when you get angry my little gatito."

"I am not angry," said a furious Shane trying to shake him but to no avail, "why are you teasing me?"

Roberto pulled her to him and kissed her—it was a long kiss. "Because I love you Shane, so very much." Shane looked at him, then snuggled in his arms. "I guess I'll never know what happened," she said.

"Nothing much happened my little one. She tried to kiss me and when I pushed her away, well, I guess I used too much force and she fell backwards. Anyway, I think she's all right but she cried a lot. I let her cry, it was good for her but hard on me and we talked. She seems to feel much better Shane, she is just a kid, doesn't even seem like sixteen." Roberto shook his head and looked sad, "and I guess that's about it."

"Do you have to go somewhere now?" she asked, "I was hoping we could spend some time together."

Roberto looked at his watch, "I have to pick up General Escobar at the hotel in an hour and we will be discussing over lunch some political issues that are affecting both our Countries. We might come back here later, I'm not sure, but I'll let you know if we do."

He kissed her and just held her in his arms. "Shane, let's get away next week, just the two of us, somewhere, anywhere."

"Are you forgetting the wedding Roberto?" she said ruffling his hair.

"How could I, don't tell that to Jodi-Anne and Ramon. Anyway, I have to get going and we will make plans after the wedding. Let's go downstairs and see what's happening."

Roberto did bring General Escobar back with him and he and the General along with his five bodyguards spent an idyllic evening on the beach. Shane, Camille, Andre, Jodi and Lorena had joined them for dinner but left right afterwards and went into the library to have their coffee. They knew that Roberto and the General had confidential issues that had to be discussed and their timing was limited.

Rosita had made several delicious dishes and everything was served outside. Torch lights lit up the area and large platters of fruit and paklava were served after the dinner.

The General, a handsome heavy-set man in his late fifties enjoyed the outside atmosphere. He was resplendent in his white uniform, the medals displayed across his chest and he talked proudly about his children. Edouard, his eldest, was twenty-three, his daughter Christine was nineteen, another daughter Carmen, sixteen and the youngest, Ricardo, was nine.

"Where does Ricardo go to school?" asked Roberto.

"It is a private school in Buenos Aires," said the General. I am concerned for his safety though. You heard of the two attempts on my life?"
"Si, I did and we were shocked when we heard about it. I also find it very disturbing that these rebels have such a stronghold on the government. I understand they control the gas-exportation of your Country. This means in exchange they are probably being equipped with assault rifles. Not AK-47's I hope."

The General shook his head, "Roberto, we have tried but it is out of control."

"How did it get out of control? asked Roberto, is it possible the police ranks have become infiltrated?"

"That is a point well put," said the General, "and it is something we have been suspecting for a long time. There will be an investigation but it will be dangerous."

Roberto was thoughtful for a moment then said, "my two sons attend a wonderful Academy in Switzerland. We are very happy and satisfied with the high standards and privacy of this particular school. If you send Ricardo there he would not be alone, Frederik and Enrique would be like brothers to him I'm sure. They will all look out for each other."

"I really like the sound of that Roberto, I am very interested. Please send me the details and I will look into it. The security is very strict you say?"

"Well Shane and I wanted to make a surprise visit a couple of months ago and because we had not contacted the school ahead, we had to be completely cleared before they let us see our sons. We had to wait a few hours before they were satisfied we were who we said. I was quite impressed."

"I like the sound of that. By the way, Roberto, I would be honoured if you and the Senora would pay us a visit soon. Mahala and I would really be delighted to show you our hospitality. You would stay with us of course."

"Gracias General Escobar, let me see how things go here with our new recruits. I look forward to having strong ties with your Country and bring about a more secure future to all concerned, gracias."

"Good, let us work together and in the meantime, you must call me Miguel por favor."

"Muy bien, gracias," and Roberto held up his wine glass. "To Argentina and the Dominican Republic, to the future of our Countries, may God give us the wisdom to guide them into safety and prosperity in the future."

General Escobar lifted his glass, "and long live our friendship." Roberto had no knowledge whatsoever of the bizarre and unbelievable danger awaiting him in Argentina.

Rosita had joined the group in the library at their insistence. This was something she seldom did but today she felt different. There was a feeling of closeness and family in the group and everyone chatted and laughed as they talked about current events, shopping, traveling and even Ramon had dropped in to make sure everything was going well. Ramon was also coaxed into staying and he did, resting the ever-present machine gun across his knees.

"Where is Camille?" he asked Shane glancing around the room.

"She went to bed almost an hour ago," said Shane with a smile. "Are you concerned Ramon?"

"May I check on her?" he asked.

"I'm sure she's all right, but go ahead Ramon, if it would make you feel better."

Ramon nodded, went upstairs and entered her room. Camille was asleep and Ramon turned to leave, hesitated and went back to the sleeping child. He looked at her and she looked so much like Shane. He bent down and kissed her forehead, looked at her again for a moment then left, softly closing the door behind him. He could not explain the strong attachment he held for the child and then again, deep inside him, he really knew.

"Sound asleep," he said to Shane when he went back down. "Looks like angel."

"Thank you Ramon, I know. Roberto and I feel very protective towards her."

Ramon touched the gun on his shoulder. "Do not worry Senora, Ramon will always protect Camille." He turned around and went outside.

Chapter Seventeen

In the next few days Roberto made plans to visit Argentina. General Escobar had contacted President Juan Gomez and they had both agreed that it would be beneficial to both Countries with Roberto's visit. Roberto planned to take Shane with him although he had debated within himself if he was doing the right thing. The two attempts on the life of General Escobar were recent and Roberto knew there was the possibility of danger. Nevertheless, he wanted Shane with him and he would take Ramon and Lorenzo also.

It was to be a short visit, only four days, and they would be back in plenty of time for the wedding. There was one other thing that Roberto wanted to look after before leaving. He wanted to help Leandro's family and arranged for his younger brother and two sisters to attend a high-ranking private school that he himself would fund personally. He also made arrangements to have a voucher sent to them for groceries every month. He did not want anyone to know that he was the donor, and the amount would be generous.

He would never forget the funeral. Leandro's mother, two sisters and brother stood by his coffin in the church and as Roberto walked up to them followed by Ramon and Lorenzo, every eye in the church turned to him and watched as Roberto took Senora Pereira's hand and spoke to her. His voice was low but very clear.

"Senora Pereira, my name is Roberto Castaneda," and he kissed her hand. "Your son was a fine young man, very brave with a good heart. He was also very special. Hold your head high Senora, my heart is breaking also. He saved many lives—May God rest his soul and give you and your children peace of mind."

"I know who you are," said the woman looking at Roberto. There was a pause and the church was quiet. Suddenly the woman put her arms around Roberto crying and embracing him. Roberto held her, consoling her, and Ramon and

Lorenzo automatically moved in very close to them. The woman finally drew back and smiled. "Gracias," she said and squeezed Roberto's arm.

Roberto moved over to the son, then the two daughters, embracing each one. He had given them each a gold crucifix with Leandro's name, date of birth and the date on which he had died. He stood by the coffin and prayed for Leandro's soul and looked at him as he lay with a peaceful expression on his young face as if he were asleep. He then made the sign of the cross and went towards the altar followed by Ramon and Lorenzo and knelt in prayer just as the choir began to sing the Ave Maria and once again he made the sign of the cross.

The priest blessed the Holy bread and wine and Roberto received the Holy Communion with Ramon standing beside him holding his machine gun. Lorenzo faced the congregation, also holding his machine gun but lowered it in respect to the people praying before him as the strains of the Ave Maria continued to float through the church.

Roberto received the Communion but continued to kneel as he softly recited:

> "Hail Mary, full of grace, the Lord is with thee
> Blessed are thou amongst women and blessed is the fruit of thy womb Jesus
> Holy Mary, mother of God, pray for us sinners now
> and at the hour of our death. Amen

Ramon had also received the blessing from the priest but did not take the Holy Communion. He kissed the hand of the priest and went to the front of the congregation and Lorenzo moved back to where Roberto was. He knelt beside him and being Catholic like Roberto he also received the Holy Communion. They both made the sign of the cross, got to their feet and kissed the priest's hand. They joined Ramon and descended the three steps from the stage and Roberto suddenly stood still and put out his left hand stopping Lorenzo as he turned towards the Pereira family and bowed with his hand over his heart. Ramon stood beside him, machine gun raised as Roberto straightened and turned and he left the church following Ramon with Lorenzo close behind. His heart felt heavy and the pain seemed to mock him. Once outside the church he turned to Ramon and Lorenzo.

"This is not right," he said, "why must we enter the house of God, a place of worship, a sanctuary, with machine guns?"

"It is okay," said Ramon, "I ask God forgive us and he said, "it is okay Ramon, I forgive you."

When they returned to the Villa, a phone message from President Gomez was awaiting Roberto. When Roberto called back Juan Gomez told Roberto that he had just received news of an uprising in an area that was very familiar to Roberto. There had been a street riot and four police officers killed and several citizens injured. It was the same street where a small boutique carried French and Italian wedding gowns and Jodi had chosen her gown from that particular store. It was still at the boutique and ready to be picked up as the alterations had been completed.

Roberto called together everyone and told them under no circumstances was anyone to venture out into that area. It was considered a danger zone and he would see to it that the gown would be picked up on his return from Argentina. They were not to take any more risks and in the meantime, hopefully, some arrests would be made.

Roberto and Shane left the next day with Ramon and Lorenzo while Andre promised to keep his eye on things. There was some very good and unexpected news, however. Juan Gomez was arranging to have Diego Sanchez transferred to Roberto's area and it couldn't have happened at a better time. Roberto was grateful for this as Diego would be responsible in taking Camille to school and bringing her back home for the next four days.

Roberto and Shane were met at the airport in Buenos Aires by General Escobar and his entourage. The General's home was on a large sprawling estate. A very high iron fence enclosed the area, and the grounds were patrolled by soldiers with trained dogs.

"Do not let this bother you," said the General. "It is the way of life for myself and my family and we have gradually become accustomed to this sort of thing."

"I know what you mean," said Roberto making a note about the guard dogs. He liked the idea.

Mahala Escobar was an attractive woman who seemed to possess the Argentinian charm that seemed to be a trademark of the women of that Country. Also in her fifties like her husband, she warmly greeted her guests and kissed Shane.

"You both are such an attractive couple, how fateful it was to find each other," she said taking Shane's arm and going into the sitting room. The furnishings were ornate and there were several servants seen in the adjoining dining room setting a magnificent table.

"My wife would make anyone look good," said Roberto proudly looking at Shane as she blushed.

"Let me show you to your room before dinner," said Mahala Escobar, "and also we have two rooms for these two young policemen directly across the hall from your room. We wanted to make sure they would be nearby."

"Actually Ramon and Lorenzo are bodyguards but si, I guess they would be considered policemen," said Roberto. "Gracias for your hospitality."

"Our suitcases are here already," said Shane with surprise when they were alone. The room was on an upper level and completely furnished in white and gold baroque furniture. Roberto stood by the glass balcony door and looked out. All around them were trees and flowering bushes, similar to their Villa back home except the grounds were patrolled by soldiers with dogs.

"This should turn out to be quite interesting," said Roberto. "I think General Escobar and I will benefit a great deal from this vacation. Let's unpack later Shane and not keep our hosts waiting."

Shane was about to open her suitcase but Roberto took her hand and drew her to him. "Come here Shane, let me hold you for a moment my beloved Shane," and he kissed her gently. "I would rather just hold you like this than go down but I guess we must."

"I think so Roberto," she said touching his face. "We'd better go or Ramon and Lorenzo will be knocking at our door."

Roberto smiled, "the illustrious Castaneda bodyguards, I almost forgot they were with us. Did you know that they are trained to break down the door if we didn't answer it?"

"Well, let's not let that happen Roberto. I hope they would check to see if it's locked before doing that," said Shane, her eyes twinkling.

"I hope so too," said Roberto kissing her. "Come on Shane, stop holding me prisoner, let's go down."

The dinner was like a banquet. The four Escobar children had joined them at the table and there was a great deal of laughing and talking while several servants served the food. They had insisted that Ramon and Lorenzo join them at the table and for this, later, Ramon never forgave himself.

"Let us have our coffee outside," said Mahala, "and we can show you the grounds at the same time. Shane and Roberto were looking forward to getting a taste of the Escobar way of life.

"The evenings tend to be a little cool," said Mahala, "maybe Shane should wear a chompa, a sweater."

Shane stood up, "I'll just run upstairs and get one," she said but Roberto took her arm.

"I'll get it Shane, in your suitcase?" Shane nodded, "the key is in my purse Roberto, on the bed." Ramon stood up, "I go with you."

"No," said Roberto, "you and Lorenzo stay with Shane, I'll be right back."

Ramon did not sit down. "It's okay Ramon," insisted Roberto, "stay with Shane."

He quickly went upstairs and entered the room. The suitcase was sitting on the bed beside Shane's purse. Roberto took out the key and unlocked the suitcase lifting the lid. The explosion threw him across the bed, face down. Barely conscious, he could feel something trickling down his face and it felt as if a hot iron was searing his arms and across his chest.

He was aware that someone was gently turning him over and he gasped as incredible pain shot through him. Someone was bending over him and kissing him.

"Shane, Shane," his voice was hoarse and he couldn't open his eyes. She was frantically touching his face and calling out his name. "Shane," he whispered again, how he wanted to hold her but he couldn't move his arms. He couldn't see her but he could feel her lips on his. He couldn't breath and started to choke and she loosened his collar. His eardrums had been damaged and he did not hear the sounds in the hallway or her desperate words.

"You cannot die Roberto, I love you so much. I won't let you die; this was not supposed to happen to us." Just before losing consciousness he forced his eyes to open—it was not Shane.

Roberto did not hear someone trying to break down the door. It had been locked on the inside and that person was in the room before Roberto had entered.

Someone had escaped through the balcony by the time Ramon and Lorenzo had crashed down the door. They were greeted by smoke and could see Roberto lying across the bed. Ramon had reached him first and had screamed out "ambulancia! Mande buscar una ambulancia," and ran to the balcony window and opened the door. Lorenzo immediately tried resuscitating Roberto as Shane knelt beside her husband, her arms trying to hold him and the General and his wife standing beside Shane helplessly. Servants were running around in a panic and someone had called for an ambulance and there was utter confusion and pandemonium everywhere.

Edouard, the eldest son of General Escobar had also run out to the balcony but was ordered back inside by Ramon. Roberto did not move, he lay very still and Shane could not hold back the tears.

Roberto was quickly transported to the hospital accompanied by Shane, Ramon and Lorenzo. The General also went in a separate limousine and told his wife to stay as the police were on their way and someone had to speak to them. Everyone seemed to be in shock, Roberto and Shane had only been in Argentina for a few hours and it seemed unbelievable that this could happen.

Shane sat beside Roberto in the ambulance holding his hand. An oxygen mask had been placed over his face and she moved numbly to one side as they prepared to take his blood pressure. Ramon sat with Shane and a doctor while Lorenzo sat up front with the driver.

"Do not worry Senora, he will be okay," said Ramon trying to sound hopeful. Shane just shook her head, the tears starting up again. "Ramon, I don't understand, who would want to do this to Roberto. He had no enemies here."

"Very strange Senora, somebody in room, somebody in house. Guards, dogs, guns, who gets through? How someone gets in I not understand, something not right but Ramon find out." He turned towards Shane and put his hand on her arm. His eyes looked wild, his right eye was twitching and he clenched his other hand and made a fist.

"Ramon will find out who did this and I will make them into pieces, I promise you, pieces."

Ramon and Lorenzo stayed by Roberto's side throughout the examination. Both of Roberto's arms were broken, he had burns across his chest, there was a welt on his forehead and his hair was singed. Miraculously, there was not a mark on the rest of his face. He was taken to Intensive Care and Ramon and Lorenzo stayed nearby, refusing to leave.

Police had been called in, the media got hold of the incident and General Escobar was not too pleased. He wanted to avoid an International crisis as Roberto was a well-known and very important political figure and God help them if he died in his Country.

News traveled fast and Andre and Skye flew down to Argentina immediately. After two days Roberto was put in a private room and listed in serious but stable condition. They wanted to take Roberto back to the Dominican and were told that it would be a week before he could be moved to a plane on a stretcher. Shane did not want to leave Roberto's side and Skye and Andre convinced her to take a room nearby in the hospital.

Ramon refused to let her return to the Escobar residence and they all took turns watching over her. No one wanted to leave Roberto alone and the Buenos Aires police were extremely helpful. Roberto was very well-known internationally and admired throughout the Latin Countries and they did everything in their power to give Roberto and his family the protection and any comfort they needed. As news spread throughout the City and Country, the number of people that came to the hospital with flowers and gifts was remarkable and heartwarming.

Lorenzo slept on a cot in Shane's room and only opened the door if given a secret signal by Skye or Andre. Ramon refused to leave Roberto's side and the anger inside him was building up dangerously. They would all be leaving in a few days.

Back in the Dominican everyone knew what had happened. Rosita cried a great deal and Lorena tried to assure her that everything would be all right and they would all be back soon. She seemed to have matured immensely and seemed proud of herself that she could stay calm and was actually helping others.

Jodi was extremely upset but very quiet. She knew that Ramon was okay but if something happened to Roberto and he didn't make it? She did not want to think of that. It was Roberto who held them all together and without him … there would not be anything. She had to think positive, she had to keep thinking that life in the Dominican would continue just as planned and she knew what she must do.

Jodi looked out the window and saw the gendarmes patrolling the area. Some were on horses and as she strained her eyes to the far right side of the Villa she saw three Jeeps parked side by side and no one in that area. She quickly tied a kerchief over her head and put on her sunglasses. Lorena was nowhere in sight and Rosita was busy in the kitchen. She stepped outside on the verandah and waited until the gendarmes had passed the front of the Villa. So far so good she thought and quickly ran towards the Jeeps. One of them still had the keys in the ignition and Jodi's heart started beating wildly. She knew that it was possible that she might be seen but she was going to chance it. She quickly zoomed out of the area and did not look back. It was possible she had been seen, but she wasn't going to look around to find out. She did not realize that she had made the biggest mistake ever. On the side of the Jeep, in bold black print was the word 'POLITZIA' and it was this that would cost Jodi her life.

She drove past the speed limit and knew that she was taking chances but didn't care. How she got past the guards at the gate was questionable and would be investigated. She reached the boutique and ran inside. No one had followed her—it was perfect. Her wedding gown was ready and she waited impatiently, glancing nervously at the door as they wrapped and boxed it. It was already paid for and she thanked them, took the box and ran out to the Jeep. This was so easy she thought putting the keys in the ignition and starting the car. The explosion could be heard blocks away, then suddenly, everything was quiet, so quiet, and the Jeep lay scattered in pieces across the street.

The doctors looking after Roberto had finally agreed that he was stable enough to withstand the trip back to the Dominican. Although heavily sedated the police wanted to question him and were allowed only a very short period of time which got them nowhere.

After they had left Roberto whispered to Ramon that he wanted to say something. Ramon sat beside him, pulling his chair closer and bending towards him to hear. His voice was barely audible and he talked with a great deal of difficulty.

"Ramon, in the room ... someone in room ..."

Ramon was looking at Roberto, eyes wide, fists clenched, and he started to shake.

"Someone you know?"

Roberto's eyes were starting to close, "Francesca" he said, trying to stay awake, fighting off unconsciousness, "Contessa Francesca," he said before closing his eyes.

Ramon sat still for a moment, then shook his head. "How this possible?" he asked keeping his voice low.

"It is true," whispered Roberto just before drifting off into unconsciousness. Shane stood beside him and looked first at him then at Roberto.

"What did he say Ramon, said Shane, I did not hear what he said."

Ramon looked at Shane, his eyes looked wild and he was breathing heavily. He turned to Skye then looked at Andre.

"What's wrong," said Andre, "what did he say?"

Ramon got up slowly and went over to Lorenzo who was sitting near the door. "Stay with them Lorenzo, I be back."

Ramon left quickly and arrived at General Escobar's house and spoke with him privately. He enquired if they had hired anyone recently. The General assured Ramon that his staff was made up of very reliable and dedicated people who had been with them at least ten years.

"Ask the Senora, maybe she hire someone," said Ramon.

They brought Mahala into the room and Ramon asked her also.
"No Ramon," she said, "our staff has been with us for many years, there is no one new here."

Ramon persisted, "think hard Senora, it is important. Anyone different here, in this building? Someone tall, dark skin, eyes narrow, long. You remember someone like this?"

"Wait," said Mahala, "si, I now remember there is someone like that but she is not with our regular staff. She came in for a couple of days to help. It seems that one of our servants had an accident and did not show up. Si, I remember now, she worked upstairs on the second floor."

Ramon immediately stood up. "She has room?"

The General stood up also, "what is happening, is this person responsible? Should I call the police?"

Ramon put his hand on the General's shoulder. "Please sit down Senor, also Senora, please sit, do not worry, do not call police. Where is her room?"

"It is on the second floor also, but she is probably not here," said the General. "Let me call the police."

"No," said Ramon, "I am the police, you come with me Senor and Senora, please, just sit and wait, no police."

"Where can I get machine gun?" asked Ramon as he and the General left the room.

"I cannot do that," said the General.

"We can take blame off your Country if we act fast. It will be better for you, quick, no time."

Take the blame off the Country? Would it be possible thought the General. He looked at Ramon then motioned for him to follow. They went to his room and the General opened a large drawer and handed an Uzi machine gun to Ramon.

"This is my own personal gun. I keep it here in my room for protection."

Ramon took the machine gun and examined it. "It will do" he said, "where is her room?"

They went down the hall and around the corner and the General pointed to a door. Ramon motioned for him to go back downstairs and he could hear the sound of water running. He waited until the General was gone then kicked open the door. The sound of the water continued and he hoped it was the right person. He quickly went towards the bathroom and tried the door. It was unlocked and he stepped inside. Someone was taking a shower behind the curtain. He held his breath, pulled back the shower curtain and came face to face with The Dragon Lady, Contessa Francesca. Their eyes met and she smiled.

"Hola Ramon, you thought all these years that I was dead. I wasn't in the car that blew up my men ten years ago. I wanted Roberto for one night and I almost got him. The bomb was meant for Shane but it doesn't matter any more. You are here now and I give myself to you as a gift."

Ramon screamed out the words—"PROSTITUTA, TERRORISMO, I give you gift, this one from Roberto," and he fired the gun point-blank into her face, "and this one from Ramon," and he finished the round. "Da chiflado," he said throwing down the machine gun and left the room.

No one had run upstairs, no one stopped him from leaving and as a matter of fact, he encountered no one. He calmly walked out of the building and went back to the hospital.

It was exactly one hour and one shower later since he'd been gone and a very calm Ramon took his place by Roberto's side and no one asked any questions.

The whole story came out later, of course, and the General was very relieved. It completely exonerated them taking away the blame and pressure and proving that their government had no involvement in what had happened to Roberto.

They left Buenos Aires and flew back to the Dominican Republic. It was a long trip and Roberto was taken on the plane on a stretcher and had to lie flat on his back across three seats that were adjusted. Skye and Shane did not leave his side along with Andre and Ramon and Lorenzo hovered over them. Roberto was taken to the Angels of Mercy hospital and put under the care of Dr. Valdez and Skye and also a specialist who flew in from England at the request of President Gomez.

Chapter Eighteen

Jodi was buried the very next day. No one told Roberto, it would have to wait. His hearing was slowly returning and it would be months before they would know if there was any permanent damage. Ramon did not talk to anyone for weeks. Always one to hide his feelings, he would go off alone to ride along the beach.

Lorena left right after the funeral. She wanted to go home and look after her parents and seemed to have matured overnight. Ramon and Lorenzo took her to the airport and just before boarding the airplane, she clung to Ramon and cried. He held her but did not say anything. He was still hurting so badly he couldn't talk. She hugged Lorenzo and he kissed her on the cheek shyly and she boarded the plane. Ramon watched it leave and just stood still for several minutes. Finally, Lorenzo touched his arm and they both left.

Eventually, Roberto was finally discharged from the hospital, and able to continue convalescing at the Villa. Camille would often stay at his side, talking about her day at the school and how she hoped he'd get better fast so they could go riding together. Ramon would continue to take Camille riding and he would try to answer her questions about what had happened to her papa. Ramon was always there to wipe away her tears and hold her and Shane was forever grateful to him for just being there when needed.

Shane spent all her time with Roberto. She would wash his face and feed him breakfast as he lay in bed with both arms in casts. Sometimes, Roberto would feel her tears on his face and he yearned to hold her.

"Shane," he would whisper, "when I get better I will make it up to you," and she would kiss his forehead.

"Just get better Roberto, we have our whole life ahead of us. I love you so much." She had suddenly stopped and looked at him. "You were right Roberto, do you remember a while back when you said to me, and I quote, 'Shane, I will make you love me,' remember? Well, you were right."

Roberto looked at her, his singed eyebrows shot up, "a while back? That must have been um, let's see, about fourteen years ago, and you are just feeling it now?"

"No, Roberto, please do not misunderstand what I am saying, I've loved you all these years, I'm only bringing back something you said and …"

"No more," said Roberto, "do not say any more, just come nearer, my Shane. You are taking advantage of my helplessness. I cannot move my arms and now I am your prisoner. But I am healing and one day soon I shall escape and hunt you down, and you, my beautiful captor will pay for every moment of torture that you are putting me through that is a promise."
"Well in that case," said Shane kissing his cheek, "I might as well take advantage of your helplessness, as you have very well put it," and she kissed Roberto's face avoiding his lips.

"Stop that Shane," he said feeling frustrated, "don't do this, you'll be sorry, I promise you."

"So what does it feel like Comandante, to be on the other end?" she said as she continued to kiss him but still avoiding his lips. She was delighted with the sudden control of power that she had over him and continued to tease Roberto.

"Shane, I command you to stop," he cried out as she ran her hands through his hair and lightly bit his earlobe. "Oh goodness, you command me, Roberto?" she said putting her arms around his neck, her face against his.

"Shane, you are going to be very sorry," he said loudly just as Skye entered the room, "I promise you this."

"Shane, you'll be sorry?" repeated Skye very surprised. "What in the world is happening here? Roberto, is Shane harassing you?"

"Tell your sister to leave the room, Skye, now," said Roberto. His face was red and a cold sweat had broken out across his forehead.

Skye turned to Shane looking at her sternly. "I can't allow you to annoy my patient Shane, out. I need some private time with Roberto, and just try to behave yourself."

Shane had a big smile on her face. For the first time she had Roberto at her mercy and it felt good. Let him know what it was like to be on the other end. She felt very happy and a feeling of complete satisfaction engulfed her. She was not fooling herself, she knew very well that she would pay the price but it didn't matter. It was worth it and she triumphantly left the room.

During the following weeks Roberto made a slow but steady recovery. His hearing was quickly coming back to normal and the burns on his chest were healing. He had now graduated to sitting outside under the large umbrella, on the recliner. Still unable to feed himself, Shane, Andre and Rosita would take turns.

One morning Ramon took over and it turned out to be another one of Ramon's delightful philosophies on life. It was a typically beautiful Dominican morning as Ramon held the cup to Roberto's mouth while he drank.

"Roberto very quiet today," he said.

"Just thinking Ramon."

"Thinking what?"

Roberto gave a sigh. "It is strange, very strange."

"What is strange?"

"Two women, Ramon, two women who have said they love me, have both died violently. What do you say to that my friend?"

Ramon was cutting up toast. "Ramon glad he is not woman," was his response as he put the toast in Roberto's mouth. Roberto looked at him. "Why?"

"Because I love you too," said Ramon.

Roberto swallowed the toast and stared at Ramon. "Perdon?"

"I love you," repeated Ramon.

Roberto stared at Ramon; somehow what he was hearing did not at all fit the description of the man sitting next to him. He had known Ramon for over twenty years and had never had reason to believe that he was different. The sun was beginning to feel hot and the lull from the ocean was beginning to annoy him but he had to know.

"How do you love me Ramon?"

"What you mean how?" said Ramon putting the cup to Roberto's lips.

Roberto moved his face to the side impatiently. "Not now Ramon, I don't want any more, just answer me."

"What did you say?" said Ramon wiping Roberto's mouth.

"Just explain what you just said," said Roberto. He was becoming very annoyed by now.

"Oh, about how I love you? You worried?" He looked at Roberto.

Roberto was almost glaring at him. "I'm not worried, just talk."

"I mean like brother, you know, I love you like brother."

"I am so relieved to hear you say that Ramon."

"You think I was guy?" he said popping more toast into Roberto's mouth.

"Gay Ramon, gay, not guy," said Roberto chewing the toast.
"What is difference, gay, guy? Did you really think I'm like that?"

"No Ramon, not at all, that is just a choice that someone makes with their life.

Everyone deserves happiness, different people, different lifestyles, who are we to judge; but there is a difference, believe me."

"If you say so," said Ramon holding the cup to Roberto's lips then wiping his mouth with a napkin.

"I never would have thought you would be doing this for me," said Roberto. "I have never felt so helpless. I don't want any more coffee Ramon, gracias."

"It is okay," said Ramon, "I did this before but different. He was gendarme, dying, and mouth was bloody, blood all over. This not bad, I see worse."

The man sitting beside him never failed to amaze Roberto. He knew very well how tough Ramon was with a strength and ability of being able to destroy anyone or anything with his hands if he so desired. He also showed his gentle side and tenderness when with Camille and it reminded him of a tiger looking out for her cub. He had proven his loyalty through the years and had a heart like steel on the outside and soft on the inside and Roberto knew this and Andre also knew. He was capable of anything except he couldn't or wouldn't smile.

Whenever Roberto needed a lift all he had to do was have a conversation with Ramon and all the big issues of the day would become secondary and so unimportant for a few hours. Usually they would have these talks at midnight while patrolling the beach, under a million stars.

"Ramon?" said Roberto.

"Hmm?" answered Ramon holding the cup to Roberto's mouth. Roberto took a gulp and swallowed. "It is because of you I keep my sanity in this crazy world."

"Gracias Roberto, I think this is compliment, si?"

"Si, I'm going to pray for you tonight my friend. I'm going to thank God for sending you to me and ask him to send someone special to you; you are so good for me."

"You are happy, Ramon is happy."

"In that case smile Ramon, come on, let's see you smile."

"Nothing to smile about," said Ramon putting another piece of toast into Roberto's mouth.

A breeze from the ocean blew around them promising the start of another incredible Dominican day.

President Gomez had made several visits to the Villa to see how Roberto was progressing. He also wanted Ramon to be recognized for his quick thinking and fast work. What no one understood was why Francesca had stayed at the General's home after the explosion. She could have made her escape and no one knew the answer but everyone was relieved that Roberto had not been killed. The Argentinian Government was also grateful that he would recover but they were especially glad that they were completely exonerated and there would be absolutely no blame brought upon them.

Letters and telegrams were starting to arrive at the Villa from all over the world when the news came out. Gifts were being sent by people from all walks of life.

They came from peasants who knew what Roberto had done for them and were grateful that he had been spared, and the wealthy from many different parts of the world who flooded the Villa with expensive gifts and baskets of exotic foods. Roberto sent almost everything to the orphanage and to peasants in the village. Reporters had to be turned back as they suddenly swooped down on the Villa. Roberto was big news and now, suddenly, Ramon's picture was also on the front page posing with his machine gun.

Ramon was not too happy about this and everyone wanted to write a story. Diego Sanchez had come to their rescue. The special training he had which included riots and crowd control was being put to good use and he was able to keep things in order. Besides the reporters he kept helicopters out of the area and organized the small important details that the others did not think of.

Terry had phoned and said he was on his way down and had to be cleared by President Gomez because it was getting almost impossible for anyone outside to get to the area. There was one very bad moment before all this came about and it was bound to happen.

Roberto had only been back one week at the Villa and was just starting to feel a little better and more aware of everything. Andre and Shane were with him as he reclined in a big chair under the giant umbrella.

"Jodi-Anne, why haven't I seen Jodi-Anne, is she okay? I hope she didn't go home before the wedding?"

Shane looked helplessly at Andre and Andre stayed very calm, too calm. Roberto looked from one to the other. Shane could not stop the tears that sprang to her eyes and Roberto suddenly had a very bad feeling and knew that something was not right. Andre spoke first.

"There was an accident, Roberto, Jodi was involved in an accident."

"What kind of an accident, what happened to Jodi-Anne—tell me, why has no one said anything?" Roberto hollered out the last two words. He had moved suddenly and Shane had quickly gotten up to put her arms around him. This was exactly what they had wanted to avoid as long as they could. Andre searched for the words that he could use so as not to shock Roberto, but he could not find them.

"Where is Jodi-Anne?" said Roberto, his voice had gotten hoarse as Shane clung to him and cried. Andre looked sadly at Roberto and moved towards him. He put his hand on Roberto's head and said quietly, "she died Roberto; she was buried the day after we retuned from Argentina."

Roberto did not talk and Shane kept her arms around him and cried. Andre prayed over Roberto, his hand still on his head and off in the distance the only sound to be heard was the ocean but this was the one time the soothing sound of the water had no effect on them. Roberto did not move and Shane drew back and wiped her tears. Andre had taken his hand off Roberto's head and he looked down at him. Should they let him grieve or should they call Skye or Ramon? Maybe they should just wait until he was ready to talk. Andre sat beside him and turned to Shane.

"Please Shane, could you ask Rosita to bring a cold drink for Roberto? I'll stay here with him." Shane immediately got up and left and Andre turned to look at

Roberto. He sat very still, there was no expression in his eyes and Andre began to worry.

"Roberto, Roberto," he said softly. He could not hold his hand; that would have helped. He knew Roberto would have squeezed it for comfort but couldn't. "Roberto, don't shut us out," said Andre, "talk, say something."

Roberto was not talking but his mind was working fast. First Beatriz, then Damien, followed by Leandro and now, Jodi-Anne. She was alive when they went to Argentina and buried the day after they returned. It was so hard to believe.

Shane had returned with the drink. She did not elaborate to Rosita and Rosita said she would come outside later with more drinks for all of them.

Shane held the drink with the straw to Roberto's mouth but he turned his face away without looking at them and said quietly; "how did Jodi-Anne die?"

"She was in a Jeep," said Andre, "and it blew up."

Roberto turned his head and looked at Andre. "That is not an accident, why did you say an accident?"

"We didn't want to upset you," said Andre glancing at Shane.

"You didn't want to upset me?" said Roberto slowly. "You didn't want to upset me? I am outraged, it was an act of terrorism; Jodi-Anne was murdered!" Andre did not say anything and Shane held back the tears while quietly sitting beside him.

"Why was she in a Jeep, where did she go? said Roberto, "I do not understand. Get me Juan Gomez on the phone, Lorena, where is Lorena?"

"She went home after the funeral," said Shane sadly.

"Roberto, everything possible is being done," said Andre. "Take it easy and try to relax; you have to get better and this is not good for you." Andre was starting to be concerned.

Roberto was silent for a few moments, then he spoke again.

"Ramon, where is Ramon?"

"He took Camille to school" said Shane. "They will be back in a couple of hours."

Roberto did not talk again. He refused food and drink and just lay there with his eyes closed, his mind racing, and he felt a different pain that now descended upon him to join the others and to haunt him.

Shane had called Skye and told him what had happened and how worried she was and he came by later that day. When he arrived, he spoke very firmly to Roberto while changing his bandages.

"I'm talking to you as a doctor Roberto, not as a brother-in-law. Your burns are healing but you must snap out of this or I will be compelled to return you to the hospital. You must eat and it is imperative that you drink lots of liquids and relax your mind. How are you going to get better? How are we going to get you back on your feet? Damn it Roberto, the Country needs you."

Roberto looked at Skye and nodded. "Okay Skye, okay," he said with a sigh. "Is Ramon back? I must speak to him."

Skye sat down beside Roberto. "Look at me Roberto and listen, please. See Ramon tomorrow, it will be Saturday and there will be no school for Camille. Give your emotions a rest today and see Ramon tomorrow."

Roberto hesitated. "Okay, I will see Ramon tomorrow, tomorrow is fine." He sounded very tired.

Roberto spent some time with Ramon the next day and he did all the talking at first and Ramon said nothing. He sat looking out towards the ocean, his machine gun resting on his knees. Roberto knew that Ramon was not ready to talk and he did not insist. They both sat quietly just taking in the magnificent scenery. After a long silence Ramon did talk finally. "God gives us all this," he said waving his arm from left to right. "Why are we always sad?"

Terry arrived at the airport a couple of days later and was met by Ramon and Lorenzo. On the drive back to the Villa no one talked much and Jodi's name did not come up. As their car drove up, Shane ran outside into Terry's arms.

"It's okay Shane, everything will be okay," he said kissing her cheek.

They went inside and Shane told Terry everything, the shock of almost losing Roberto, and of Jodi's horrible death.

"It's okay," said Terry, "let's not go over this today. Let me see Roberto and we'll just keep everything as light as possible. I can see there is a lot of stress and strain around here at the moment."

"You are so right," said Shane, "come, you must also meet Andre, Roberto's brother. He is with him now."

They went outside towards the back and Andre stood up as they approached. He clasped Terry's hand tightly and smiled. Terry was impressed. "My goodness you look like Roberto, what an amazing resemblance." He went to Roberto and touched his face.

"My favorite brother-in-law, how are you Roberto? You look like a mummy."

"It's good to see you Terry, sorry we can't shake hands."

"Wow, you still look good considering everything that you went through. How did my dowdy little sister catch you?"

"Sit down Terry, you are embarrassing me," said Roberto smiling at him. "Do you realize that you have become the chosen one?"

"The chosen one? Chosen for what, should I be worried? What do you mean?"

"You are the only reporter allowed to come into the area to do the story."

"That's right," said Andre, "all the other journalists were chased out."

"I am getting a hint of favouritism, dear people, am I right?" said Terry.

"Call it what you want," said Roberto, "those are my orders."

"At your service Comandante," said Terry standing up and saluting smartly.

"Sit down Terry," said Roberto with a smile, "we are not joking."

Shane and Andre were delighted. Once again Roberto was able to smile.

"Who's joking," said Terry, "I am going to write such a story that it is going to knock off everything on the front page back home in Toronto. Oh, what a story this will be."

"You'd better let me see it first," said Roberto. Somehow I am a little hesitant about what you are about to write. Please Terry, no sensationalism."

"Who said anything about sensationalism," said Terry trying to look serious. My heading will read something like "Dragon Lady Lures Handsome Comandante To Her Lair."

"Terry," said Shane, "you wouldn't dare."

"Sounds good to me," said Andre laughing.

"Terry" shouted Roberto, "if I have to I will have you put in chains, so help me God."

"Roberto, it is unbelievable that the Dragon Lady has resurfaced after everyone thought she had been killed ten years ago," said Terry. "Her real name I believe was The Contessa Francesca Simone and the last time you saw her was at the Presidential Banquet that you and Shane attended along with Skye and Maria. I understand her bodyguards had followed your car when you left the banquet but your guards new what was happening and they averted a disaster and bombed their car assuming that the Contessa was amongst the ruins. I guess you also assumed that she had a preference for blond, blue-eyed men and seem to target in on Skye at the banquet.

Suddenly, Skye appeared amongst all the laughter and embraced his brother.

"Terry, good to see you. Did I hear my name mentioned and I see you brought laughter with you."

"What can I say dear brother, wherever I go I bring joy and happiness, "said Terry winking at Shane; "I'm just that kind of a guy."

"Skye, tell your brother to behave himself," said Roberto smiling again.

Skye looked at Roberto … "wow, do I see a big change in you Roberto, thank goodness. You want me to tell Terry to behave himself? That would be like telling Ramon to never carry a gun again, ever. Ridiculous, eh." He sat beside Roberto and looked at everyone.
"I have a news bulletin; do I have everyone's attention? Good. Maria just gave birth to a healthy baby boy."

"What?" said Shane jumping up and embracing Skye. Congratulations and good wishes followed and Shane rushed into the Villa to get some champagne. Only Roberto was not able to do so but the happiness and joy was there.

"I didn't phone," said Skye because I wanted to see your faces and I wanted to come over and see Terry."

"How is Maria?" asked Roberto.

"How is she? She's fine, she's ecstatic, we're ecstatic."

"Have you named the little guy?" asked Terry.

"We have, we're naming him Marc Shai," and Skye looked at Roberto and Andre. The sudden emotion that evolved around them could be felt by all.

"Gracias Skye," said Roberto and his eyes had lit up. Andre went one further as his eyes filled with tears. "Si, gracias Skye, we will always treasure this moment for little Marc Shai."

"You're very welcome," said Skye.

"That is so beautiful," said Shane, "Marc Shai Dalinger."

"The Shai stands for Shah," said Roberto, "The Little King."

"I like that," said Skye, "The Little King."

"What a headline this baby would make," said Terry. "Hey, I am an uncle again. When can we take pictures of the little king? When can we see him?"

"Whenever you want," said Skye proudly. "He has lots of dark curly hair and blue eyes, but all babies have blue eyes. He's a handsome little guy."

"Well then, I guess he takes after me," said Terry. You and Maria are so lucky; my genes have passed on to your son."

"Terry, you are too much," said Roberto. "I hope you can stay a while. Have you changed your mind about moving here?"

"First you want to put me in chains, now you want me to live here. No Roberto, I can't but thank you for your generosity, maybe some day. By the way, what do you know about Sierra Castille?"

Roberto looked puzzled. "What is that?"

"You mean who is that," said Terry. "It is a woman, and what a woman."

"A woman?" said Roberto, "I've never heard of her. What do you know of her and why do you ask?"

"Sounds intriguing," said Skye.

"Intriguing is definitely not the appropriate word," said Terry. "From what I have heard, she would make the Dragon Lady look like Alice in Wonderland."

"Where is she from?" asked Roberto.

"I don't have too many details. She is from one of the Latin countries, actually I believe Paraguay. She is what they call Mestizo."

"Mestizo? She would be from a mixed race, white-Indian," said Roberto. "I know in Bolivia they have the Mestizo who make up about thirty percent of the population. She might have migrated to Paraguay. Anyway, who is she and why is she so famous?"

"I really don't want to get into it right now Roberto, if you don't mind. Can we talk about this later? Let's not spoil a beautiful day."

Terry stayed at the Villa for two weeks. He was able to get his front-page story and it was considered a "scoop" for his newspaper. Very laid-back and easygoing, Terry was a favourite of everyone. He spoke to all the gendarmes, bodyguards and even the gardener who seldom appeared and whose English was very limited. He had that special talent that would make a person want to give Terry all kinds of information about themselves and the Dominican. At the dinner table one day, he took Rosita's hand and kissed it announcing to everyone that again he professes his undying love for her.

"Please witness, good people, that once again I propose to our lovely Rosita. If she marries me, she can cook for me forever. This is how much I appreciate her cooking."

"Terry," said Roberto, "we also appreciate her cooking but we do not propose such drastic measures to this lovely lady."

"Drastic measures! Roberto, are you saying being married to me would be drastic? Tsk tsk, you are already married and in no position to talk. Actually my ravishing Rosita would probably prefer me anyway. She can travel the world with me, right Rosita?"

Rosita blushed and laughed. She thoroughly enjoyed Terry's outrageous proposals, which popped up every ten years. "Terry, I think the best thing would be for you to come here when you're hungry, and I will cook for you anything you want."

"Sounds great," said Terry, "let me see, now in a couple of weeks I will be sent to the Middle East to do a story. They are sending me to Iraq for a year. I'll see if I can fly back here on weekends for your cooking, my Rosita. Oh, the perils of life."

"One year," said Shane, "Terry, that means you probably won't be here for little Marc Shai's Christening in a few months."

"I'm really sorry about that Shane," said Terry, "this assignment is crucial for certain people and I have no choice. If I can take time off I will come. Please try to understand Shane and I hope Skye and Maria will understand also."

"Terry, I don't think you have ever ridden any of our horses out here," said Roberto. "If you wish to do so, take a ride with Ramon, it will be quite an experience, I promise you."

"I'd like that Roberto," said Terry, "actually I used to ride years ago with a girlfriend. I can take any horse in the stable?"

"Get Ramon to take out Maharajah," said Roberto. "He is easy to ride and behaves very well."

"Thank you Comandante, I will take you up on that and go look for Ramon," said Terry standing up.

"If you should need riding clothes, take a look in my room Terry," said Roberto.

"Are you kidding Roberto?" said Terry laughing, "you're taller than me and you have shoulders. You're big and strong, I'm pale and interesting but thanks anyway. I have to get going. I must be fair and spread my charm around. See you later."

Roberto shook his head after Terry left. "I would give anything right now to be able to ride with those two, Terry and Ramon. The conversation would be priceless."

Terry found Ramon talking with Lorenzo and Diego. Ramon immediately agreed to ride with Terry and brought out the horse called Maharajah, a magnificent chestnut stallion. They mounted their horses and trotted down the path towards the beach.

Usually the beach would be isolated but since Roberto's incident and Jodi's tragic death, the security was much more evident. President Gomez had insisted on this and had announced that Diego Sanchez be a permanent bodyguard on the premises, much to Roberto's delight.

"Ramon," said Terry, "what do you do for excitement around here when it gets dull?"

"I shoot people," came Ramon's shocking reply.

"Really, and who do you shoot?" said Terry wondering if he really wanted to know.

"Anyone that gets in Ramon's way," he said dryly.

"I hope I never get in your way Ramon," said Terry giving him his best smile.

"I hope so too," said Ramon looking ahead and Terry suddenly stopped smiling and stared.

Ramon looked at him. "This is joke, Terry, you take joke, no?"

"Yeah, yeah Ramon, I take joke. Why am I sweating!"

Ramon looked at Terry and brought his horse to a halt and Terry did the same. "Take off jacket," he said.

"Sure Ramon, anything you say," said Terry starting to remove his jacket.

"Wait," said Ramon, "you don't have to take off jacket because I say so. You afraid of me?"

"Gee Ramon, I don't know. I can't tell when you're joking or serious. I guess it's the gun, it's intimidating."

"Intimi ... what?"

"It's okay, don't worry about it," said Terry as they started to move again. "So Ramon, Roberto's horse is called Allegro, this one is Maharajah, what is your horse called?"

"Ramon's horse."

"Oh, uh huh, of course, that makes sense."

"No one takes Ramon's horse," said Ramon.

"I honestly don't think anyone would consider for a moment taking Ramon's horse."

"Good."

"Ramon?"

"Si?"

"Have you always been like this?"

"Like what?"

"You know, tough."
"Tough? You think I'm tough?"

"That's what they say Ramon."

"Who says?"

"The President of Argentina. He wanted you for his own personal bodyguard. Didn't Roberto tell you?"

Ramon stopped his horse. "Roberto not tell me this."

"Apparently, he was so impressed with how you went after the Contessa that he immediately sent word to President Gomez about how he felt. Maybe Roberto doesn't even know. Maybe I shouldn't have said anything."

Ramon was quiet. He seemed to be thinking.

"Just imagine Ramon, you would live at the Argentina Presidential Palace. It's called Casa Rosada, also known as The Pink House. What do you think of that?"

"I think we go back, I must see Roberto," said Ramon turning his horse around. He did not look happy but then, Ramon never looked happy.

They rode back to the Villa and went inside looking for Roberto.

"He is in the library," said Shane seeing them in the hallway. "You can go in, he's just chatting with Andre."

Andre immediately stood up and pulled out two chairs. "What seems to be the problem?"said Roberto noticing the look on Ramon's face. "Did something happen?"

"Go ahead Ramon," said Terry, "ask him."

"Ask me what?" said Roberto.

"You sending me to Argentina?" said Ramon.

"What for?" asked Robert with surprise.

"To be bodyguard for President," said Ramon. "Is this true Roberto?"

Roberto's mouth dropped. "Where did you hear that?"

"I told him," said Terry, "my Editor back home called and said to get verification about this. Apparently, the President of Argentina had contacted President Juan Gomez and asked for Ramon. I thought you knew?"

Roberto was dumfounded. "I know nothing of this. President Gomez did not say anything." He looked at Ramon who seemed relieved.

"Ramon, I hope you didn't think I would do that," said Roberto. "You are like family, it is unthinkable and besides I could never replace you and wouldn't want to. Andre, get me President Gomez on the phone, now please. I must speak to him and clear up this absurdity."

"Just consider this as very complimentary Ramon," said Terry. Argentina is a big and important Country. I'm not sure what the population is."

"It is roughly thirty-seven and a half million," said Roberto as Andre held the phone for him. Roberto spoke to Juan Gomez and it was true. The Argentinian President had spoken to Gomez about Ramon and Juan Gomez had not even considered telling Roberto and mentioned this to the caller. The Argentinian President said he would wait until Roberto had made some degree of recovery and would contact him at a later date.

"There you have it Ramon, don't even think about it. I know what to tell the gentleman. In the meantime, how was your ride with Terry?"

Ramon nodded and stood up. "Terry is good man, we ride again, si Terry?"

"Wouldn't miss it for the world. Just let me know when Ramon."

There was a knock at the door and Camille looked in. "Papa, I've come to say goodnight."

"Come in Camille, let me see you," said Roberto. "I missed you today."

Camille closed the door and went to her father, sitting on his knee, both arms around his neck. "Are you feeling better today papa?" she asked kissing his face.

"Much better when I see you my little girl," he said wishing he could hold her.

"I pray that you get better fast papa so that we can go riding together," she said putting her face against his.

"Gracias my angel, may God be with you through the night," said Roberto kissing his daughter. "I love you," she said. "And I love you," he said softly.

Camille embraced Andre. "Good night Tio Andre, "I love you," she said as he held her.

"Buenos noches Mantecado, God be with you" he said kissing her. "I love you too."

"Good night Tio Terry, you will be here tomorrow, please?" she said kissing his cheek.

"I'll be here tomorrow, good night, love you baby."

"Good night Ramon," said Camille embracing him. "Thank you for taking me riding, I love you." Ramon held the girl in his arms. "God be with you Camille, see you tomorrow."

Camille left the room and no one spoke for a moment. Everyone felt the impact she had left on them. Roberto broke the silence. "That little girl is so precious to me," he said.

"To all of us," said Andre. "There is something about her."

"She is unbelievable," said Terry, "she has beauty, charm, she is dynamic and only seven years old."

"I worry over her," admitted Roberto, "quite a bit."

"Do not worry," said Ramon suddenly, "I not let anything happen to Camille, I promise this. Must go, buenos noches," and he was gone.

"Terry," said Roberto, "Ramon will be training some new recruits tomorrow afternoon. Why don't you sit in on it and maybe add something a bit different, on a different note to your story for your newspaper."

"I would really like that Roberto. You said tomorrow afternoon?"

"Si, at 3:00 down by the far end of the beach. It's about half an hour from here. Don't walk, it would be better if you take Maharajah. I think you will enjoy it—you'll get a front row show. He's very, how do you say ... agallas, no ... gutsy, that's it, gutsy. Go Terry, then come back and tell me what you think."

"Hmm, now I'm curious," said Terry, "but I'll go and I'd be glad to come back and tell you all about it. You've seen Ramon do this?"

"Si, I have, once. Very entertaining Terry, very."

The next day Terry rode down the beach and reached the area just before 3:00. The sun was not as hot as usual and the gentle breeze seemed to be perfect for what Ramon had in mind. Six new recruits were lined up and Ramon stood before them. Terry stayed seated on his horse and watched.

"All of you familiar with hand grenade?" asked Ramon. The six men nodded. Ramon opened a bag, took one out, removed the pin and threw it towards the men. Three of them threw themselves to the ground, hands over their ears. One of the men standing put his hand up and caught it.

"Pin is out," yelled Ramon and the recruit threw the grenade towards the ocean. It exploded before hitting the water.

"You three," shouted Ramon to the men who had fallen to the ground, "go back to Villa. You," he pointed to the tall young man who had caught the grenade, "name?"

"Samouil," said the recruit.

"How old is Samouil?"

"Nineteen," came back the reply.

"You not afraid of hand grenade?" asked Ramon.

"A little, I need more practice," admitted the recruit.

Ramon looked at him. He had chiselled features, high cheekbones and very dark eyes that were slightly slanted. He appeared to have a definite strain of Indian blood along with the Spanish.

"Good, you are brave and honest," said Ramon. "We give you more practice."

He faced the three men left. "Next," he called out, "tomar como."

"Uh, what's that?" said Terry.

"Hostage taking," said Ramon.

"Oh!"

"Terry, come here," said Ramon.

"I'm only taking notes, remember? Foreign correspondent."

"Now," shouted Ramon, "without horse, rapidamente."

Terry dismounted and walked over to Ramon. He felt like a robot.

"I'm not happy Ramon," said Terry.

"Just listen, you be happy," said Ramon.

"I have trouble listening man. This makes me nervous. Have you ever lost anyone during these manoeuvres?"

"Only one—did not listen."

The movement that suddenly followed was so fast, so typical of Ramon, that Terry did not realize what had happened until it had happened. Ramon's arm was under Terry's neck lifting him off the ground and the other gripping his waist. Terry's glasses had flown off and it was like being held in a circular band of steel as Ramon lowered Terry's feet to the ground.

"This man held hostage," shouted Ramon, "I am unarmed, what do you do?"

"Nothing I hope," said Terry weakly.

"Quiet Terry, okay men, fast, what do you do?"

One of the recruits raised his machine gun.

"Idiota," shouted Ramon, "hostage could get hurt."

"Ya, idiota, maybe even killed," called out Terry nervously.

"Quiet," said Ramon, "you hostage, do not talk, supposed to be scared."

"Hostage is scared Ramon, and choking too," said Terry. "Loosen your grip man, I feel pain. I only came to take notes, remember? Correspondent."

Ramon ignored Terry. "I am unarmed," he called out again, "make move, come forward," and as the recruits moved quickly towards them, Ramon flipped Terry over and landed him on his back. Terry just lay there stunned. He didn't want to move or open his eyes.

"Terry, get up, everything okay," said Ramon, "open eyes, hostage rescued."

"Hostage dead," said Terry, "go away."

"Get up," said Ramon, "over, finished."

"Go to Hell," said Terry not opening his eyes.

It was dinnertime by the time they returned. Ramon helped Terry up the verandah steps and into the Villa. Terry was limping, his hair was disheveled, his glasses on crooked and his jacket torn. Roberto, Shane and Andre were in the dining room and saw Terry limping by held up by Ramon.

"What on earth happened?" called out Roberto as Shane and Andre quickly got up.

"He be okay, I'm just taking him to room," said Ramon, "wants to lie down."

"I'm not okay, he held me hostage," said Terry.
"Let me help," said Andre. "Just think what a story you got for your paper," he said as they took Terry upstairs.

The next day was Saturday and Ramon did not have to take Camille to school. He appeared at the Villa, however, early in the morning and sat in the kitchen with Rosita until the others were up.

"You should come by more often for breakfast Ramon," said Rosita, "you are good company."

"Gracias Rosita, I patrol beach Saturday morning and I do training but today I want to see if Terry okay."

"Let's go inside, I think I hear them in the dining room," said Rosita picking up a plate full of pancakes.

"I bring coffee," said Ramon and followed her. Rosita as usual had placed many delectable dishes on the table and Roberto and Shane had already started with Andre just coming downstairs.

"Buenos dias Ramon," said Roberto, "this is very nice. I hope you will sit and have breakfast with us today."

"Gracias Roberto, no, I am waiting to see Terry, maybe coffee."

"Ramon, you must try Rosita's pancakes, they are to die for," said Shane.

"Speaking of dying," came Terry's voice from the doorway, "I think I've come back to life this morning. Mmm, pancakes, I could smell them coming down the stairs.

Hi Ramon, how is the recruiting coming along?"

"Good," said Ramon, "more today and I wonder if you want to take notes again. Today we go into serious stuff, maybe dangerous, but fun."

"Are you kidding?" said Terry, "do you think I am idiota? Your idea of fun is playing catch with live hand grenades. No, no thank you very much."

"Ramon make joke Terry, you know, funny. I really come to see if you okay. I not mean to throw you like that."

"That's okay Ramon," said Terry piling the pancakes on his plate, "I'm just fine, a few bruises, some shock, great story, but you said the hostage was rescued. What kind of rescue was that?"

"That was not rescue," said Ramon, "I had to stop them. Only Samouil knew what he was doing and I not want you to get hurt—maybe I save your life."

"Oh," said Terry and a thoughtful look came across his face. "Gee Ramon, thanks man, you are all heart and I appreciate that. But, let's just suppose Sami-boy didn't catch the live grenade?" Ramon shrugged his shoulders and drank his coffee.

"May I ask what happened?" asked Roberto looking from Ramon to Terry.

"Not too much dear brother-in-law, Ramon just included me in his training manoeuvres and I was glad to be a part of it."

Shane laughed, "I'll just bet you were," she said.

"How lucky for you, Terry," said Andre.

"Ramon, how about taking a woman hostage today, let's see how brave Senora Shane is," said Terry winking at Roberto.

"Ramon not take woman hostage, especially Senora Shane," he said pouring another coffee and thoroughly enjoying the conversation.

"Oh, that's right," said Terry, "you shoot your female hostages Dragon Lady style."

"Terry," called out Shane, "keep me out of this, we all know you were scared."

"Well you would be too if you had a new recruit aiming his machine gun at you, right Ramon?" said Terry looking at him.

Ramon put down his cup and sighed, "I told you, Terry, I don't let anything happen to you, trust me."

"Trust me, ha," said Terry, "how come you're not eating anything; tough training this morning?"

Ramon paused before answering, then spoke quietly, "Today I teach how you say … unorthodox survival training. Must not eat, will get sick."

Terry stared at Ramon. "You will be sick?" he said, his eyes seemed to open wide.

"Ramon not get sick—recruit get sick. I am not hungry." There was silence for a few moments, then Terry asked curiously, "Would I be allowed to take notes only?"

Ramon shook his head and stirred his coffee. "No one watches when Ramon teaches unorthodox survival training. Not good if you have weak stomach."

Terry stopped eating and stared at Ramon. The silence was deafening.

"Buenos dias," came Camille's voice from the doorway as she entered the room, rubbing her eyes. "I love Saturday morning, I have breakfast with everyone. Oh Ramon, you are here too," and she ran to him and gave him a hug.

"I must leave Camille," he said touching her head and standing up. "Gracias for the coffee, see you later for riding Camille," and he left.

Camille sat beside Shane and chatted with her while Terry tried to compose himself and looked at Roberto.

"Is he for real, did I hear what I think I heard?" he said

"Believe it Terry, he's for real" said Roberto, "different but the real thing. There is no one else like him, and you only know the half of it, the other half is unbelievable."

Terry finished his breakfast quietly, only once muttering under his breath something about losing his sense of humour.

"You'll get it back Terry," laughed Shane, "it probably needs a break away from you but it'll be back."

The following Monday morning, exactly eight weeks after they had been put on, both casts were removed from Roberto's arms. He was beginning to feel normal and started making plans on the way home.

"Don't take on too much right away," Skye had warned. "Shane, make sure he does what we've told him—he still needs extensive therapy on both shoulders."

"I will," said Shane, "but you know Roberto, he'll try to make up for lost time."

When they reached the Villa, Roberto immediately got busy in the library with mail and phone calls. Shane sat outside with Andre under the large umbrella. The sun shone brightly and the birds chatted nearby. Roberto suddenly appeared, a serious look on his face.

"What's happened Roberto?" said Shane as he sat down.

"I just received a call from Juan Gomez. They have in custody two men who they believe may be responsible for planting the bomb in the Jeep that..." He did not finish.

Andre sat up, "that Jodi was in?" he said not wanting to come right out and say the words.

Roberto nodded.

"But Roberto," said Shane, "why would the President be calling you about this, should it not be coming from the police?"

"That's just it Shane," said Roberto shaking his head, "he wants to make sure Ramon doesn't hear about this."

"He might cause a commotion?" asked Andre.

"Si," said Roberto, "he'll take things into his own hands and just start shooting, you know Ramon. I can't say that I blame him, but we want to question these men.

I'm going to leave now and I'm taking Lorenzo with me. I don't know when I'll be back but keep Ramon occupied if you see him. Please, let's keep this a secret."

"What about the newspapers Roberto?" asked Andre.

"The police have already contacted them," said Roberto getting up. "Everything is being looked after. I'm leaving now and I'll see you all later." He kissed Shane and left.

"I worry so much over him Andre," said Shane watching Roberto walk away. "I don't think I'll ever get used to the panic I feel inside when something like this happens."

"Do not worry Shane," said Andre, "Lorenzo is an exceptional young man and he will be with Roberto."

"I know," said Shane, "Lorenzo is marvelous, excellent, but he's not Ramon. I guess we're just used to Ramon."

"Shane, no one is like Ramon, we know this, everyone knows this, it is not fair to Lorenzo to compare him to Ramon."

"You're right Andre," said Shane. "Did you know that Lorenzo was trained by Ramon?

He went though the whole routine with flying colours so that has to say something for him."

"Hmm, and he can still smile," said Andre, "remarkable young man."

"Yes, he does smile quite often, and I like that Andre. However, Ramon says he's going to teach him not to smile—says he'll look tough if he doesn't."

Andre laughed. "How do you teach someone not to smile? I cannot imagine that Shane."

Shane suddenly looked at Andre with a serious expression on her face. "I hope he doesn't do anything drastic Andre. Lorenzo is such a nice person. I think he's about twenty-five years old—he has his whole life ahead of him."

Andre laughed out loud. "Shane, what are you thinking, don't make it sound so morbid."

"I'd rather not say," said Shane looking off into the distance. The sound coming from the ocean was soothing and the heady fragrance of so many blooming flowers permeated the air. Shane closed her eyes and tried to relax.

Chapter Nineteen

Ramon did eventually hear about the arrests but it was too late for him to intervene. The suspects were transferred to an undisclosed area, tried in a private court of law and sentenced to death. Ramon did not talk to anyone for days. He had been unable to finish the job, to destroy Jodi's killers. Roberto gave Ramon strict orders not to train any recruits until he got over "the urge to destroy". He walked around with clenched fists for a week and everyone stayed out of his way except Camille. Terry eventually went back to Toronto and his stories hit the front pages. He was almost immediately transferred out to the Middle East to cover the war in Iraq and would be gone almost a year.

Back in the Dominican, things were beginning to settle down. The danger areas were being cleaned out thanks to the Elite Tactics Emergency Response Units, that had been specially trained by the European agents that Roberto had brought in then also having to pass through Ramon's Unorthodox Survival training. Roberto continued to recuperate and began his extensive therapy at the hospital while Skye and Maria made plans for little Marc Shai's Christening.

General Escobar had placed his youngest son ten year old Ricardo into the same private school in Switzerland as the twins, Frederik and Enrique who immediately formed a close bond with Ricardo.

Roberto wanted to fly to Switzerland but Dr. Valdez thought he should slow down and wait a few more months. Roberto also had in mind to travel to Toronto some time in the next few months. He wanted to see Jodi's parents and Lorena. "There is unfinished business here Shane" he had told her one evening. "Something is undone, I do not feel right and I must see them."

"This brother of mine," said Andre when he heard, "what a heart he has. I am so proud of him."

It was a beautiful Sunday morning in July when Roberto became the Godfather to Skye and Maria's son. He held the baby while the holy water was sprinkled on little Marc Shai Dalinger and Roberto prayed for the miracle child. He gave thanks to the Almighty for these precious moments as he looked down at the beautiful child in his arms. He was completely unaware that at that precise moment General Escobar and his wife Mahala were assassinated in Argentina when the car they were riding in blew up. It was Sunday, July 18, 10:35 A.M.

Almost a year had gone by since the Escobar tragedy. Edouard, the eldest and his two sisters, Christina and Carmen had moved in with relatives. Ricardo wanted to stay in the same school as the twins and also with Roberto, Shane and Camille. He did not want to go back to Argentina and no one forced him to. Roberto wanted to legally adopt him and his lawyers were in the process of drawing up the papers but Ricardo's relatives were reluctant to allow the adoption to go through. Roberto was determined and knew it would take time. He would be patient.

Roberto and Shane sat at the table under the large umbrella. It was a perfect day for swimming as the sun shone brightly and a gentle breeze blew through the palm trees. They could see the children on the beach and their laughter and squeals of delight floated towards them. A short distance away Lorenzo and Ramon patrolled the area and off in the distance the cry of a bird could be heard.

"They look so happy," said Shane heaving a sigh. "I wish they could stay longer with us Roberto, a month will go by so quickly."

"I know, I'm certainly going to miss them when they go back to school. Look Shane" said Roberto sitting up, "how well Ricardo fits into our family."

The twins were teasing Camille and throwing water on her and Ricardo had taken her hand and pulled her behind him protectively.

"Roberto," said Shane sitting up suddenly, "they're holding hands, Ricardo and Camille are holding hands!"

"Si, so they are," said Roberto.

Shane removed her sunglasses, "but Roberto, she's only eight and he's …"

"Eleven," said Roberto, "and what is wrong with that?"

"Aren't they kind of young to be holding hands?" said Shane looking at Roberto with a surprised expression on her face.

Roberto smiled, "not at all, Shane, if I'd known you when you were eight I would have held your hand too."

"Roberto, you would have been fourteen. My family would not have allowed that to happen," said Shane.

Roberto turned and looked at her. She thought of a time long ago, when he had looked at her like that while wearing sunglasses and she could not see his eyes. She could not tell what he was thinking.

"Shane, with no disrespect to your parents, if I knew you when you were eight, and if I wanted to hold your hand, no one on the face of this earth would have been able to stop me."

Shane looked at him. "You're fond of Ricardo aren't you?" she said. Roberto looked out towards the beach.

"Look at them Shane, look at how he is protecting Camille. Already he looks out for her." He stopped and seemed to be thinking, then spoke slowly weighing his words.

"My daughter is very, very precious to me Shane, she looks so much like you. I want only the very best for her, my love, which I'm sure you do too. Ricardo comes from a very proud lineage, I've had his ancestry traced and I've also had a thorough check done on his family background and it is impeccable. This is very important to me Shane."

Shane stared at him. "What are you saying Roberto?"

"This boy is an Escobar which is fine, but I intend to slowly integrate him into our family, our culture, our lives. He will have the same upbringing as Frederik and Enrique and with the highest standard of education possible and I will see to it myself personally that he gets the best military training in existence. Another thing Shane, I have not forgotten something Ricardo's father told me once. It was his wish that his youngest son learn the Basque language. I will honour his request and have Ricardo enter the Ikastolas."

"Ikastolas," said Shane, "what is that?"

Roberto smiled. "These are schools where all the teachings are in the Basque language and I might consider enrolling the twins also. By the time he is eighteen he will be up to my expectation, the perfect specimen. Si, he will be deliberately groomed to my specifications."

Shane stared at Roberto and for a moment she was too stunned to speak. When she did, the tone in her voice sounded incredulous. "The perfect specimen? Roberto, do you know how you sound? You cannot play God and besides, his brother and two sisters might not agree to all of this."

"What is there not to agree to, Shane, Ricardo will have everything, the very best that life can offer. I'm not playing God Shane, I'm only doing what I feel is right for our daughter and for Ricardo also. You can see with your own eyes how he is with us. You heard what he said when they asked him what he wanted. He wants us Shane, and he will have us and we will have him, for the rest of our lives. This is another piece of my dynasty Shane. It started the day I saw you, and it will continue, and my sons will carry on the Castaneda name and tradition and Camille and Ricardo will have the Castaneda blood in their children and their dynasty will be ours, and ours will be theirs. Like the gardenia it will grow more beautiful as time goes by, like you Shane. You are my golden gardenia; you become more beautiful every day. I never have, or ever will, settle for anything ... but the very best."

Shane could not see Roberto's eyes, he still wore the sunglasses but she knew that look would be there, the look she had seen so many times. She gazed out towards the beach. Roberto had already mapped out Ricardo's future, his whole life, his destiny.

The boy was helping Camille build a sand castle. He left her side for a moment and wandered down the beach. Frederik and Enrique were splashing in the water, both excellent swimmers. She loved them all so much, even Ricardo seemed more like a son, and he was polite, intelligent and already showed signs of becoming a very charming young man.

He was returning with something in his hand and gave it to Camille. Shane could hardly believe her eyes—it was a gardenia. She looked at Roberto and he too had seen this. He looked at Shane.

"You see Shane," he said matter-of-factly, "it's like looking at ourselves." He removed his sunglasses and Shane saw that look and she knew there was no stopping him. He spoke quietly. "Just as I said Shane, the boy is ours, we have three sons and a daughter."

They both looked towards the beach again. Ricardo was putting the gardenia in Camille's hair. Roberto's dynasty was alive and thriving and nothing was going to stop it now.

Chapter Twenty

The summer months flew by quickly. The boys were back at school in Switzerland and Roberto was still unsure about sending Camille to Canada or abroad for her education. He preferred to keep her in the Dominican, close to them, and he and Shane decided they would wait another year before making any decisions. In the meantime Ramon, along with Lorenzo would accompany Camille to the school and bring her back and Roberto was satisfied with this arrangement for the time being.

Shane and Roberto flew to Toronto during a weekend to visit the Dalingers and also to see Jodi's family. Ramon had also wanted to see Jodi's parents and personally express his sympathy. They were distressed to learn that Jodi's father had passed away. He had been ill and had not been told about Jodi's death. Roberto was thankful that he was unaware of the tragedy to his daughter or he would never have been able to forgive himself. Lorena cried when she saw Ramon and could not be consoled. Ramon held her then whispered something in her ear and she immediately stopped. She looked at Ramon and said "really?" Ramon nodded and said "really." Lorena wiped away her tears and sat beside her mother, putting her arm around her and she was smiling.

They all ate dinner together and had a very pleasant visit, under the circumstances. By the time they were ready to leave, it seemed evident that Roberto had almost convinced them to move to the Dominican. They rode back to the Dalingers with a feeling of contentment and relief but the sadness was still there. The moment they stepped in the car both Shane and Roberto asked Ramon what it was that he said which made Lorena change so suddenly. "I tell her that Lorenzo say from him special hola and ve con dios, God be with you."

Shane and Roberto exchanged glances. "Ramon, that was so thoughtful of Lorenzo," said Shane.

"He really said that?" said Roberto as his eyebrows shot up.

"Si, he also said do not forget or you answer to me," said Ramon and a surprised look crossed his face. "What do you think he meant by that?"

"I think Ramon," said Roberto grinning "Lorenzo is beginning to sound an awful lot like you. You are teaching him so well."

After spending a few days with Shane's parents they flew back home and immediately got caught up in festivities coming up at the Presidential Palace. Diego Sanchez stood in for Ramon while he was in Toronto and he and Lorenzo looked after security and Camille. Samouil, the new recruit who didn't seem to mind catching live hand grenades in mid-air was nicknamed "Agallas" or "Gutsy". They also discovered he had the uncanny ability to throw himself on a runaway horse, landing upright and not at all fazed. He also had a strong tolerance to pain which they found out one day when his jaw accidentally came in contact with Ramon's elbow and was broken. He refused to stop the manoeuvres until they were completed. Even Ramon was impressed, sort of.

"Ramon," said Roberto after hearing about the incident, "maybe you should let up a little, you know, not come on so strongly."

"I don't think so Roberto, they can take it," said Ramon, "I thinking something."

"What is that?" said Roberto sitting down wondering what Ramon had on his mind.

"We train many men, lots of recruits, si?"

Roberto nodded.

"They come from villages, farms, cities. Everyone wants to come here, work here, be bodyguard. I train maybe, hmm, about twenty-five men every month, si?"

"Si," said Roberto curiously.

"Most are good, young, entusiasta."

"Young and enthusiastic, okay Ramon, I'm following you, continue," said Roberto.

"One recruit is different, like Samouil, one out of six. Maybe next one will be one out of twenty, comprender?"

Roberto was thinking—he looked at Ramon and suddenly realized what he was saying.

"Ramon, are you saying that you want to make up a separate group of hand-chosen men who are specially chosen?"

"That sounds good Roberto, si, that is it. We have one group trained good men, the ETERU." Roberto nodded, The Elite Tactical Emergency Response Unit. Then we have second group, special men also but like Lorenzo, Diego, Samouil, and myself. This group not belong to army, it belong to you and me, to Villa, to hospital, to Senora Shane and Camille. Not big group, small, maybe twenty-five—thirty men. Nowhere in world you find like this. They are the best."

Roberto looked at Ramon for a moment before saying anything. His eyes shone and he seemed to be thinking. "Ramon, you have seen a vision and it is about to transpire. I like your idea, I like it very much. Do we have a name for this group?"

"Da Elegido," said Ramon proudly without hesitating.

"Da Elegido? Da Elegido, select, chosen. I like that Ramon, it is great, you have just given birth to a wonderful idea," and he embraced a very surprised Ramon.

"Given birth?" he said, "what is that you say?"

"Never mind Ramon, the idea is better than wonderful. You have my permission to go ahead with it and let me know what you need to accomplish this. I am so pleased and proud of you. We should have done this a long time ago."

Da Elegido started slowly. Ramon was very particular and took his time. He suggested to Roberto that they dress differently to distinguish them from others and thought black shirts with the words "Da Elegido" written in red in small letters with black headbands would be appropriate. "No one sees them at night," said Ramon. "Must also have better guns."

"They're carrying machine guns Ramon; you have in mind something better?"

"Si," said Ramon, "I find out and let you know."

"You do that, and let me know," said Roberto shaking his head. "You are something else."

"What else?" asked Ramon?

"Never mind, nothing. You're in charge of this operation and you have my permission to go ahead with this project and to do anything you think necessary. I like your idea—God be with you my friend."

"Gracias Roberto," said Ramon, and paused. "Roberto, now you are getting better, we ride again whenever you want, you let me know, si?"

"You mean our midnight rendezvous? I enjoy them immensely. I'm looking forward to our next jaunt and I miss our talks. We learn from each other Ramon and we gain strength from each other, do you not think so?"

Ramon was quiet for a moment and seemed to be thinking. "What are you thinking Ramon, I hope you are not upset" said Roberto looking closely at him.

"No, not upset, just not understand. There are men like ones that kill my parents, my brothers and sisters, then there are men like you. How God make man so different, I not understand this."

Roberto was surprised. He had never heard Ramon mention brothers and sisters, only family, and that was once, only to Roberto several years ago.

"We don't know," he said putting his hand on Ramon's shoulder. "Let's just be thankful for who we are, who we know and what we have."

Ramon nodded. "Buenos noches Roberto," he said and left.

Lorena and her mother arrived in the Dominican on a Sunday morning. Ramon and Lorenzo met them at the airport and brought them directly to the Villa. It was planned that they would stay with Roberto and Shane and later would move into the home that Roberto was having built originally for Ramon and Jodi. It was Ramon's idea that they live there as he felt that he could never feel right in a house that would give him too many sad memories.

Lorena had changed immensely and although she still wore her clothes a little too small or too short, her mannerisms and personality had changed. She was very protective of her mother and held the utmost respect for Roberto and Shane. She was constantly in the kitchen asking Rosita if she could help and Rosita in turn would teach her how to cook amazing meals. Lorenzo's eyes seemed to light up whenever Lorena was in his presence and he seemed more than happy to be responsible for her safety. He was still very shy but both Roberto and Ramon knew that Lorena was something more to him than a pretty blonde teenager. They seemed like opposites, but Lorenzo was attracted to the vivacious Lorena.

"He still smile too much," complained Ramon and Roberto would remind him that he had more reason to smile now that Lorena would be living in the Dominican. Roberto's heart went out to Lorena's mother, a very sweet woman and when he referred to her as Senora Davies, she insisted he call her Sara. Shane took an immense liking to the woman who reminded her of her own mother.

The sun was beginning to sink into the ocean when Lorenzo dismounted from his horse and stood holding the reins. He looked at the horizon then glanced at the girl still sitting on her horse, also looking out towards the ocean. Her long blond hair moved lightly in the breeze, her blue eyes very blue against the smooth tanned skin. She turned and looked at the young man standing beside her.

"Lorenzo, you are an interesting person, did you know that?"

He looked at her and smiled shyly. "You find me interesting?"

"Well yes, you are so shy," she said, "yet you carry a gun, a machine gun at that."

Somehow, I don't connect the two."

"I know how to use it," said Lorenzo quietly. That's all that matters."

Lorena thought for a moment then said, "look at Ramon for instance, he looks tough and mean."

"He is tough and mean," said Lorenzo smiling at her.

"Well there, that's my point, you are not like that."
Lorenzo looked at Lorena still smiling. "No one is like Ramon, that is just him. I am different too in my own way."

"What way is that Lorenzo," she said coyly.

He turned away facing the ocean. "You see me on the outside Lorena, I know I smile a lot but inside, I am not smiling."

"So are you telling me," she said curiously. "that what I see … is not you?"

He sat on the sand and she dismounted and sat beside him. Lorenzo did not answer.

"You don't talk very much," she said pushing back the hair from her face.

"Only if I have something to say," he said staring out across the ocean.

Lorena was quiet for a few minutes then said suddenly, "Lorenzo, do you think I'm pretty?"

"Si," he said still looking out over the ocean.

"Very pretty or so so?" she said looking at him.

"What is so so?" he asked still not looking at her.

"That means not very pretty," she said.

Lorenzo turned and looked at her with a half-smile. "You are not so so, Lorena."

She was starting to get exasperated. "Lorenzo, for heaven's sake, talk, say something, you're driving me nuts." He continued to look at her still smiling. She wanted to hit him and wondered what would happen if she did.

"You are beautiful Lorena," he said suddenly to her amazement. She immediately felt good about herself until he added, "is that what you wanted to hear?"

She was infuriated. She stood up and put out her hand to slap him but he caught her wrist in mid-air. The movement was swift and Lorena felt as if her wrist was being crushed. She was shocked and he immediately released her, standing up and mounted his horse. Lorena was angry. "You're a coward Lorenzo, you find it safer to hide behind your horse?"

Lorenzo looked down at her and smiled—"safer for whom? Come on, we'd better get back." Lorena mounted her horse and turned to him. "I didn't think you were a bully Lorenzo."

Lorenzo was looking ahead, the half smile on his face; I can be a bully Lorena, sometimes."

Chapter Twenty-One

Things were improving greatly in the Dominican. President Juan Gomez had set down rules and with Roberto's army behind him, he had the power of the people who never forgot who Roberto was and what he had done for the Country. They were only too happy to abide by the rules and regulations. Beneficial changes were being made to the lower class that had been neglected for many years. Tourists were beginning to flock to the Country and the import/export business was at its highest level in thirty years. Security and safety was Roberto's responsibility and of the utmost concern to him and President Gomez was extremely pleased with the results. Boutiques were flourishing along with the hotels and restaurants as hoards of tourists began to suddenly appear throughout the year.

Camille continued her schooling in the Dominican at a very private and exclusive school, always accompanied by Ramon and Lorenzo. Roberto continued to visit the orphanage once a week and also found time to visit with Leandro's mother and was very pleased that the boy and two girls were doing well in the private schools. Ricardo attended the academy in Switzerland with Frederik and Enrique and after two years Roberto made plans to have him enrolled in a school in the Basque Country in the northern part of Spain. He then made the discovery that all classes are taught entirely in Basque which meant that the "Ikastola" was out of reach for Ricardo. This had completely skipped Roberto's mind.

Actually, Ricardo should have been enrolled at the very beginning of his education and the boy also was not too happy about being separated from Frederik and Enrique. Shane suggested to Roberto to hire someone to tutor Ricardo in the summer while he vacationed with them. Roberto agreed and made plans for all three boys to take lessons. A tutor was hired, his name was Quinton and Roberto had his background and credentials checked out before he was finally satisfied with the young man. Quinton's background revealed that he was born and raised in the Basque Country and was very nationalistic to the point where he wore the Basque national flag, the Ikurrina strapped across his chest under his clothes.

"Don't you find this a little strange?" said Shane one day.

"Not at all," said Roberto, "he is a Basque Revolutionary and I don't see how this can affect us. He is an excellent teacher—have you noticed how fast the boys are picking up the Basque language?"

"Andre, what do you think?" asked Shane as they sat outside under the large umbrella.

"I think you're both right," said Andre thoughtfully. "He does seem a little extreme when it comes to his Basque background but I've watched him and I agree with Roberto, he is an excellent teacher. He really knows the language from birth and teaches it well, however …" and he paused.

"However what?" said Roberto curiously. What were you going to say?"

"Just an interesting note—Ramon does not like the young man, not at all."

"Ramon doesn't know Quinton, he met him only once," said Roberto, "and they just said hola. How do you know, Andre, that he does not like him?"

"Come on Roberto," said Andre laughing, "you can tell if Ramon dislikes a person. I guess it really isn't fair to Quinton. As you said, Ramon doesn't really know him and I don't know what the problem is."

"Hmm," said Roberto leaning back in his chair and he seemed to be thinking.

"What are you thinking Roberto?" asked Shane.

"I have an idea, but I have to find Ramon," he said standing up. "I wonder where he is at the moment?"

"He's on the beach," said Andre, "the boys are out there and Camille too."

"I can see him from here," said Roberto. "I must speak to him."

"I'll get him for you," said Andre and was up and on his way before Roberto had a chance to say anything. Andre returned in a few moments.

"Ramon is coming, he said he has to get a replacement to watch the kids, Lorenzo is alone, not enough. Those were his exact words," said Andre with a smile.

"What are you up to Roberto?" asked Shane wondering why he would call Ramon away from the beach.

"Just watch and listen," said Roberto, "here he comes now. "Hola Ramon, thank you for coming, please sit down."

Ramon sat down and accepted the cold drink Shane placed in front of him. "I send Samouil out on beach. He and Lorenzo good bodyguards."

"Gracias Ramon, I want your opinion on something," said Roberto. "You are aware that Frederik, Enrique and Ricardo are taking lessons from Quinton to learn the Basque language."

Ramon had suddenly put his drink down, but did not look up. "Si" was his response.
Roberto waited a moment and looked at Shane and Andre. "I was thinking, Ramon, in having Camille also …"

Ramon stood up suddenly and hit the table hard with his fist causing Shane to jump.
"No," he shouted and his eyes looked angry. Andre and Roberto looked at each other, neither one expecting such an explosively negative response.

"Perdon," said Ramon looking at Shane, "I not mean to frighten you. I am sorry." He then turned to Roberto and this time repeated what he said, only this time softly, "no".
"Why?" said Roberto curiously?

Ramon remained standing. "No, she cannot, impossible." He looked at Roberto, "I not let that happen." It was the last sentence that surprised Roberto and also Shane and Andre. Roberto was very quiet and it was evident that Ramon was more upset than angry.

"It's okay Ramon, nothing else, gracias," he said taking off his sunglasses. Ramon did not say anything—he just left. They watched him go down the path and out towards the beach. He said something to Samuel and Samuel left.

"What was that all about?" asked Shane.

"I really don't know," said Roberto. "I wanted to make a point but did not expect that kind of a reaction."

"Roberto," said Andre, "I take it you were going to tell Ramon that you were thinking of adding Camille to his class."

"Si, but I did not expect what happened," said Roberto still looking surprised.

"What I don't understand," said Shane "is what did that sudden outburst have to do with Quinton or Camille?" Roberto said nothing.

The tutoring continued throughout the summer and soon it was time for the boys to go back to Switzerland. The following months went by quickly and soon another year had gone by.

The following years were the same with summer holidays at the Villa and time set aside for tutoring. Marc Shai was already celebrating his seventh birthday, a handsome boy with dark curly hair and light blue eyes. He would spend one weekend a month at the Villa taking riding lessons from Ramon and sometimes from Lorenzo and Samouil.

Ramon's "little army", Da Elegido had grown to seven men. Each one was hand-chosen and had passed the rigid training that Ramon personally put them through and demanded. They were becoming well known throughout the Dominican and other Latin countries were attempting to imitate them. Ramon, however, claimed that his men were the best. Roberto still adored his Shane more than ever and when time allowed they would picnic on the beach, just the two of them, and sometimes ride together under the moonlight. Andre began conducting Sunday sermons at the church where he first became ordained much to the delight of the congregation and Roberto, Shane and Camille along with Lorena and her mother would attend Sunday Mass. Sometimes Skye, Maria and Marc Shai would accompany them and gradually things seemed to normalize in the

Republic. Always, of course, standing at the back of the church would be Ramon, Lorenzo, Samouil, Diego, and three more members of the Da Elegido, proudly wearing their recognizable and now famous black shirts with the red "Da Elegido" lettering and black headbands.

After lunch on Sundays Camille and Ramon would ride out quite a distance past the hospital and sit under the giant trees and talk. Camille had just celebrated her fifteenth birthday and was feeling very grown up indeed. She had known Ramon her entire life and found it very easy to talk to him about anything. It was on one such occasion that she dropped a bombshell in Ramon's lap. They were both sitting under a tree when Camille suddenly took both of Ramon's hands and looked into his eyes. Ramon looked at her questionably. "You want to tell me something Camille?" he asked.

"Yes Ramon, I do," she said as she continued to look deeply into his eyes.

"Speak," said Ramon.

"I love you," she said.

Ramon looked at her strangely.

"I said I love you Ramon, I love you, do you know what I am saying?"

"Si, you tell me you love me. I know, I love you too."

"No Ramon, you don't understand," she said with a sigh, "I love you like a woman loves a man."

He stared at her then said, "why you talk crazy?"

The blazing sun was bright and seemed to be sitting in the middle of the ocean. Orange rays glowed across the rippling waves and the whole sky seemed to light up like fire.

"Do you not want me Ramon?" said Camille looking at him wide-eyed.

"You not talk like that to me Camille, I get angry. Some day you grow up and any man want you."

"I don't want any man Ramon," she said fiercely, "I want you."

Ramon could feel the anger starting up within him. Why was she doing this to him?
Why was she destroying the wonderful relationship they had. She was his best friend's daughter. "No" he shouted, his dark eyes flashing, "what is matter with you, why do you make Ramon angry?"
"Why?" she insisted, "tell me Ramon, does it frighten you to be involved with a Castaneda? Is that too much for you to handle?"

Ramon was shocked at her words. What was happening to this girl he wondered. He remembered a time when he had to lift her onto her pony when she was a toddler and taught her how to ride. He wiped away her tears when she found out she would never see Beatriz again. He was there to pick her up and comfort her when she fell.

"What does that mean Camille, you make no sense. You acting like child, you are child. Do not question Ramon, just listen and obey, okay?"

"I will always obey you Ramon," she said, her beautiful eyes starting to fill with tears, "you know that."

"Then obey me now and do not cry," he said. He knew he would not be able to stand seeing her cry.

"Why Ramon, why, just tell me," she said pleading with her eyes.

He looked at her and touched her cheek gently—it was like velvet. She took his hand and kissed it holding it against her face and he quickly pulled it away.

"You are playing game; Ramon does not like to play game."

"You think this is a game Ramon? I am serious, why don't you want me to love you?"

Ramon did not speak immediately. He looked out towards the ocean and his mind was racing. Why was this happening in his life? Why was Camille talking like this all of a sudden and complicating their lives? Why was he feeling something he had never felt before? Fear, Ramon felt fear and he hated what it was doing to him. He turned and looked at her and when he spoke, his voice was a whisper as he said something that he never thought he would ever say in a lifetime—"I am afraid."

"You are afraid?" she said in amazement, "Ramon, don't tell me this, you are afraid of nothing, everyone knows this. What are you afraid of?"

"You."

"Me? You are afraid of me?"

"Si, you."

"I don't understand Ramon," she said softly. "Now it is you that does not make any sense."

Ramon looked at her. He was struggling with something deep inside him and she had caused it. He was feeling anger but he was feeling something else and she was to blame. What could he be thinking? It was insane, it was impossible, an unthinkable path that had never entered his mind. This was Camille, beautiful innocent Camille, only fifteen years old, he was twenty-two years her senior. She was the only daughter of Roberto Castaneda, Comandante of all the military forces in the Dominican Republic who was also his very best friend.

He suddenly saw the whole picture and it was preposterous. He knew he was treading into extremely dangerous and volatile waters. It was unthinkable, and yet ... he glanced down at her and saw her tears. He meant to only hold her and comfort her as he had on many occasions but when he held her, it seemed different. He could feel himself being drawn to her and his first instinct was to protect her but not as a bodyguard, this time as a man.

He kissed her forehead and suddenly realized she was not eight years old but it was too late. He did not realize he was kissing her lips, ever so gently, almost afraid that she would shatter into a thousand pieces and he would suddenly awaken and find her gone. He stopped and sat back looking at her and what he saw disturbed him immensely—he could see Shane's face before him. She reached out and clung to him and he held her and did not want to let go. He closed his eyes and forced himself to forget everything else. It was Camille who he wanted, yes, it was Camille.

Suddenly, the ecstasy of the moment seemed to be interrupted by a flashing red light and he immediately opened his eyes. It was not a dream, it was real and the red light seemed to be a warning signal deep within his subconscious mind. He looked at Camille, she was Roberto's daughter but it did not matter any more, it was too late for that. He put both hands around her face and drew her to him kissing her passionately and his heart seemed to fly. He knew that he should stop, that it wasn't right and yet it did not seem wrong. Why should he let go of something so amazing that he never knew existed and had just found.

Camille, beautiful young Camille, how could he have known that she could do this to him. Suddenly he stopped abruptly and pushed her away from him.

"Ramon, do not stop," she said putting her arms around him, "I love you."

He pushed her away again roughly. "Get on horse Camille, I take you back." He quickly mounted his horse while Camille just stood still and looked at him.

"Now," yelled Ramon. He did not want to put her on the horse although he could have done so easily. He was afraid to touch her and only wanted to take her back to the Villa and gallop off alone somewhere. He had to get away from her and he had to be alone. She just stood there not understanding why he was treating her like this.

"Camille, now," said Ramon, his tone was angry but his heart was breaking as he forced himself to raise his voice again to her. "Do not make me angry, please Camille, do not make Ramon angry." She looked at him and slowly mounted her horse and wiped the tears on her face with the back of her hand. Ramon looked at her and thought, oh God, this was Camille and she wanted him. Was this really happening? Why was life so cruel?

"Come," he said softly, "we ride back together." He looked at her as they moved on. "Camille, stop crying, you okay?—tell Ramon you okay."

She shook her head and did not look at him and said, "I am not okay."

Nothing else was spoken on the way back but Ramon could still feel the joy that Camille had put in his heart and he was afraid. This was something that he didn't think he could handle and he knew what the consequences would be if he did not put a stop to it immediately.

They had reached the Villa and Camille dismounted and walked towards the steps while Ramon watched and waited. She suddenly turned around and looked at him and as their eyes met, Ramon's heart jumped and he knew that it was too late. It was impossible to end it, already it had started and nothing could stop the inevitable.

Ramon tried to avoid seeing Camille for a week without arousing suspicion. He kept himself busy and arranged for Samouil to take Camille riding on Saturday. They met outside the stable and Camille introduced herself.

"Hola Samouil," she said holding out her hand, "I am Camille."

"Hola Senorita," he said bowing as he took her hand, "I know who you are, Roberto's daughter." He mounted his horse and followed Camille down the narrow path to the beach and brought his horse beside hers as they trotted across the sand. The ocean was just a lull, almost quiet as the waves made a soft splashing sound and the sun had not reached its peak so early in the morning. Samouil was quiet and Camille did not know if this was because he had been told to be quiet or if it was his nature, like Lorenzo. She was soon to find out differently.

"Samouil," she said after they had been riding for about ten minutes, "could I ask your advice on something personal but it is to be kept strictly confidential?"

"Si Senorita," came back from Samouil. He did not seem at all surprised that she would ask that.

Camille drew in a deep breath, "supposing a woman loved a man," and she stopped her sentence and looked at him. Samouil kept looking straight ahead, no expression on his face and Camille wondered if he heard what she said. "Supposing," she repeated, "a woman loves a man." "Si" said Samouil continuing to look straight ahead, "and the man was not convinced," continued Camille. She waited a moment for this to sink in. "Now the woman wants to let him know that she loves him," continued Camille wondering if he was still listening. "You're a man, how does she tell him, how does she convince him, get him to believe that she loves him." She looked at Samouil wondering if she was going to get an answer. He was quiet for a moment and seemed to be thinking, then suddenly stopped his horse. Camille stopped also and looked at him. He was looking at her closely.

"If the woman is yourself, you do not tell him," he said. Camille looked confused.

"Someone who looks like you should not have to tell a man anything." Camille opened her mouth to speak but he put up his hand and continued. "You kiss him."

Camille's eyes widened, "kiss him? Just kiss him? Samouil, how can this tell him how I feel?"

Samouil stared at her for a moment. "Do you not know how to kiss Senorita, I mean really kiss? With your permission …"

"I think I know what you mean," said Camille quickly. She was embarrassed and knew she had made a big mistake by telling Samouil her personal business. How dare he speak to me so suggestively she thought but also realized it was her fault, not Samouil's. She had caused this to happen.

They rode on quietly then suddenly he spoke again. "Does your papa know this?" he asked.

Camille's heart skipped a beat, "does my papa know what?" she said.

"That you are going to throw yourself at a man."

Camille looked shocked. "Samouil, you have no right to say that, I have no intention of doing a thing like that."

"Really!" was his only comment and she regretted having said anything to him.

Another five minutes went by, and Camille was not too happy. Then Samouil spoke again.

"How old are you Camille?" Now she was angry and she stopped her horse and faced him. "Samouil, I don't think that should be any concern of yours."

"Well it is, your safety is my concern. Fourteen perhaps?"

"I'm almost sixteen and it's none of your business," she blurted out.

"Much too young to go around kissing men," he said. "If I were your papa I would spank you."

"Camille was angry. "I wonder what my papa would think if he knew that someone who worked for him was talking like this to his daughter."

Samouil stopped again and looked at her. "Senorita, please be careful, very careful what you say. You are only fifteen years old and maybe I should speak to your parents. You may already be in danger."

Camille stared at him. "I should never have confided in you, in fact I don't think I should ride with you any more. I never had a problem with Ramon or Lorenzo or even Diego. You are insolent and different."

"I've been told that before," said Samouil and he was not bothered in the least bit by her comment as they turned back.

"I think you are a show-off" she said, "you don't even hold the reins when you ride. How do you balance yourself almighty bodyguard?"

"Easy—my gun," he said looking straight ahead. Camille thought for a moment still burning from his comments. "I'll race you back to the Villa brave man, let's go," and she dug her heels into the horse. Samouil knew what she was trying to do. He threw his gun around his neck, grabbed the reins and started to race. She definitely was no match for Samouil who quickly reached the Villa and waited for Camille. Ramon suddenly appeared and looked questionably at Samouil.

"Why you riding like idiot?" he asked. Before Samouil could answer, the sound of horses' hoofs could be heard galloping towards them. Ramon looked up suddenly and angrily grabbed the reins as the horse came near almost knocking him over. He saw who it was and his eyes glared at Camille. She just sat there not knowing what to say as Ramon spoke slowly.

"I tell you many times Camille you not ride like that, you not have experience. I teach you lesson tomorrow," he hesitated then added, "riding lesson. You go inside, I take horse back, go."

Camille dismounted from the horse and looked at Samouil. "I'm sorry Samouil, I didn't mean to get you in trouble." She turned away and went into the Villa as Ramon watched her. He then turned to Samouil and gave a sigh.

"You carry name Da Elegido, sa prestigioso, comprender?"

Samouil knew what Ramon was building up to.

"Si, comprender," he said looking at him.
"When you bodyguard for somebody, you trained to be best in world, okay?"

"Samouil nodded, "okay."

"We have oxido problem, Samouil, you maybe getting rusty, si? Tomorrow morning at 7:00 we go over unorthodox survival—no, we do disciplinary training. Do not eat."

Samouil nodded and Ramon left with Camille's horse.

The ocean was very calm and almost silent. The faint humming sound of the waves was soft, soft like the breeze blowing through the palm trees, soft like the sand that sparkled under the sun, soft like the cry of a bird far off in the distance. Two lone figures sat on the beach, two horses stood nearby. The young girl possessed a rare beauty gifted to her from her mother—porcelain-like skin that did not darken from the sun but glowed radiantly. How it was possible to have skin like that was unbelievable. Her jet black hair hung down to her waist, her features were perfect, her eyes amazing.

The man sitting next to her was deep in thought as he looked out across the ocean. His machine gun rested across his knees, his face darkened from the sun and a vivid scar that started from his hairline ran down one side of his face to his neck. Around his head he wore the black headband of the Da Elegido and dark sunglasses. His hair was long and reached his shoulders. She ran her hand through the sand and watched it run down her slender fingers. The man picked up a hat sitting on her knees and placed it on her head. As she looked up at him, he removed the hat, smoothed back her hair and put it back on. She looked at him and touched the scar on his face and kissed it. He suddenly put his hands on her shoulders and gently pushed her away.

"No, you must not do that," he said, "we might be seen."

"I do not care and neither should you," she said softly.

"I care," he said. "I try stay away from you but is impossible, now I decide."

"What is there to decide Ramon, I will speak to my papa tonight …"

He shook his head, "no Camille, this very difficult, you only fifteen. Is up to me to speak to Roberto. They were silent for a few moments. Only the ocean could be heard but it did not have the usual relaxing effect on the young couple as they sat together feeling the tenseness of their situation.

Finally, Ramon stood up. "I leave now Camille. Your papa to see President Gomez and I must go with him. I take you back to Villa, do not worry." He put out his hand and she took it and stood up. He looked at her and wanted to touch her face and hold her, but he didn't. They mounted their horses and slowly rode back, both of them wondering how the day would end.

The meeting with the President went well and Roberto and Ramon had returned by 9:30 in the evening.

"I must talk to you Roberto," said Ramon as they stopped in front of the Villa.

"I sense this is quite important to you Ramon. Let's take the horses out for a run on the beach."

"Si, very important," said Ramon and they went to get the horses. Roberto was already wearing his riding habit and although very tired, he did not want to refuse Ramon. He got the impression that what he had to say had a sense of urgency and should be put ahead of anything else.

The stars above them shone like diamonds inlaid against a black velvet sky as the ocean hummed softly to all her precious sleeping creatures. It was a night to be remembered in more ways than one.

"What did you have on your mind Ramon?" said Roberto taking a deep breath and feeling his body relax after the long day.

"It is about … about … a woman," said Ramon talking with great difficulty.

"A woman?" Roberto said turning suddenly and looking at him, "I had no idea Ramon.

Is it serious?"

Ramon nodded his head, "very serious."

"Then I am very happy for you my friend, we must go back and celebrate. I will open the best wine that we have. Is the lucky young lady someone I know?"

Ramon stopped and looked at Roberto. His long hair blew slightly in the breeze, his dark eyes looked solemn; he sat very straight and held his head high.

"What is it Ramon, what's wrong?" said Roberto as he sensed something strange.

"Everyone look for someone Roberto, few find what they want."

"I found what I wanted Ramon."

"I know, long time ago."

Roberto looked at Ramon closely. "When did you know that?"

"First day you send me to other house, bodyguard for Senora."

"That was over fifteen years ago Ramon, you knew then?"

"Si Roberto, I knew then."

There was silence for a moment except for the sound of the ocean.

"Have you found what you want Ramon, your partner?"

"Partner? What is this partner; I not like that word for someone I love. Partner, huh, that is for little children when they play, this is not partner, this is … how you say … soul …"

"Soul mate, Ramon, is that the word?"

"Si, soul mate. When you share whole life, not just few years, soul mate, forever like ocean Roberto. Listen to sound, it is forever, ocean never stop, like heart, alive. Not partner, more than friend, she is my heart, my life, I love forever and … and when I breathe, Roberto, when I breathe … it is her."

Roberto had stopped and was looking at Ramon, his face showing great surprise. "I have never heard you say so much and speak so eloquently about anything. Ramon, you surprise me. You have so much hidden inside you that sometimes I think I do not know the real Ramon. So don't keep me in suspense, who is this mysterious woman who has captured the heart of the rough, tough, mean Ramon and turns him into a kitten?"

Ramon looked at Roberto and took a deep breath and said, "Camille."

The two men now faced each other and neither one spoke. The only sound came from the ocean as they sat under the midnight sky just looking at each other for almost a minute, then Ramon spoke again.

"Roberto, I ask your permission for honour of your daughter to be my wife."

Roberto continued to stare at Ramon, then he suddenly sat up straight. "Are you talking about Camille? Are you telling me you want to marry my daughter Camille?"

Ramon looked at Roberto without flinching and said, "si Roberto, that is what I am saying, I want to marry Camille."

Suddenly, Roberto spoke angrily, "If this is a game Ramon, I do not like it."

"No game Roberto," said Ramon, "this serious."

Roberto turned his horse around and motioned for Ramon to follow. He was suddenly very calm as he spoke. "We're going back Ramon, I have to sleep and so do you. We will talk tomorrow, I'm very tired."

Ramon looked at Roberto, a worried expression crossed his face. "You okay Roberto? You feel okay?"

"I'm fine, no more talking, let's just go," and both men rode together along the beach as the darkness enveloped them.

The next morning Roberto was up early. He was careful not to awaken Shane and went downstairs where he found Rosita bustling around in the kitchen. She was surprised to see him.

"You are up early Roberto, you have to go somewhere?"

"No Rosita, I just need some time for myself this morning. I'm going for a walk on the beach."

Rosita glanced quickly at Roberto. "Are you feeling all right, has something happened?"

"I don't know Rosita, I'm not exactly sure," he said pouring a coffee.

"You must have breakfast," she said taking out a plate and opening the oven door.

"No Rosita, coffee is fine for now, gracias. I will see you a little later." He quickly drank the coffee and left leaving Rosita with a puzzled expression on her face.

Roberto went outside and down the path towards the beach. He needed time to think, to digest what Ramon had told him the night before. He sat on the sand looking out towards the ocean and had not realized he had suffered a shock when Ramon had spoken to him and now the numbness had faded and he felt nothing. The sky was cloudless, a very light blue that seemed to come down and meet the ocean in the far distance which was a darker blue today.

Roberto closed his eyes as the sound from the waves seemed to have a tranquilizing effect on him. Camille and Ramon, how can that be he thought thinking about the night before. They are different, too mismatched, she is a child only fifteen, he is thirty-seven years old. This is ridiculous.

He is fascinated with her, that's what it is and she looks up to him as her protector, has always been her protector. He would talk to her, maybe send her away. How could Ramon do this, he trusted him so much.

"Buenos dias," came a voice beside him. Roberto opened his eyes and looked up. Samouil was standing beside him, gun in his hand. "You are alone Senor?"

"Buenos dias Samouil, si, I am alone. What brings you out so early?"

"I came outside and saw you by yourself. You should not be alone, I will stay."

"That's okay Samouil, I do not mind. You look like you are about to shoot someone. May I ask why you are holding your machine gun like that?"

"I always hold my gun like this, I do not carry it on my shoulder like Ramon and Lorenzo unless I ride my horse fast. Ramon always tells me do not carry gun like that but this is my way. I like to be ready for anything. You are not riding your horse this morning Senor?"

"No, I have some thinking to do. Life can be crazy sometimes."

Samouil sat down beside Roberto and took out a pair of sunglasses from his pocket.

"These are extra, Senor, you are not wearing any. Do not think too hard. If problem is not gone in twenty-four hours, take action."

Roberto put on the sunglasses. "Gracias, I left mine at the Villa. What do you mean 'take action'?"

"If problem still exists, then it is serious. However, if it really is a problem, maybe it can be resolved, no?"

Roberto looked at Samouil, "resolved?"

"Si, if problem can be resolved, you can avoid drastic action."

"Drastic action?" repeated Roberto. "Now I know why they call you 'agallas', you are gutsy."

Samouil smiled, "Ramon has a name for everyone."

"Do you like it here Samouil?" asked Roberto taking an immediate liking to him but also picking up sadness.

"Si, of course, but very quiet," he said looking around him.

"Right now it is but we must be prepared for anything," said Roberto looking out across the ocean. Things have settled down tremendously."

"I am ready for anything Senor, I live for danger."

Roberto looked at Samouil. "You remind me very much of myself when I was your age."

"Gracias Senor, it is an honour to be compared to you, I am flattered."
Roberto stood up and took off the sunglasses handing them to Samouil. "Gracias Samouil, I enjoyed our talk but now I must look after my problem."

"If you need my help Senor, anything, I am at your service."

"Gracias Samouil, I will keep that in mind," said Roberto patting his arm and turning towards the Villa, followed by Samouil close behind.

Roberto waited in the library. Ramon would be coming in any minute and he wanted to speak to him again before telling Shane or talking to Camille. His mind was still in a daze, this was his daughter that Ramon was talking about, his precious Camille.

There was a knock at the door.

"Entrar," called out Roberto and Ramon stepped in and closed the door.

"Buenos dias Roberto," said Ramon sitting opposite Roberto. He placed his machine gun across his knees and waited. Roberto gave a sigh, it was not going to be easy.

"Ramon, how long have you felt this way about Camille? I had no idea that this was happening."

"I found out two days ago, Roberto."

"Two days ago?" Roberto was surprised, "you found out two days ago? I do not understand Ramon, why do you say 'found out' and you've known this only two days? Maybe this is an infatuation, please explain this to me."

Ramon moved his chair closer to the desk and leaned forward. "Roberto ..." and that was as far as he got. He was about to ask Roberto what 'infatuation' meant but a knock at the door interrupted them. Roberto looked annoyed—he had asked not to be disturbed.

"Who is it?" he called out.

"It is Andre, Roberto, it is very important."

Roberto immediately stood up. He knew something must have happened; Andre would not have interrupted if it wasn't crucial.

"Come in Andre," said Roberto.

Andre entered and nodded to Ramon but he looked upset.

"Andre, what is it?" said Roberto as a feeling of alarm swept over him.

"We just got a call, there's trouble at the hospital, drug-related and someone has been taken hostage."

Ramon jumped up quickly knocking over the chair, clutching his gun. "Who is hostage?" he said already at the door.

"We don't know," said Andre looking at Roberto and Ramon.

"Quick," said Roberto, "round up your men Ramon and let's go."

Ramon was already going out the door while Roberto took out his gun from the locked cabinet. "Andre, stay with Shane and Lorena and her mom. Don't anyone go near the hospital, I'll call."

Ramon already had Samouil and Lorenzo with him by the time Roberto stepped outside and had left Diego in charge of the Villa. They rode out on their horses, planning to take the back entrance of the hospital. The Jeeps would be a hindrance getting behind the building and they had to move fast. All sorts of things were going through Roberto's mind. Where was Skye, Maria and Marc Shai? Was anyone hurt? Who was being held hostage? Ramon turned to Roberto at the back door of the hospital.

"Lorenzo, Samouil and I going through. Stay here at door inside, do not follow, maybe you get hurt." Roberto wanted to follow but did not want to jeopardize the situation which was already a matter of life or death and he trusted Ramon. Later he would recall these thoughts and remember what he felt. He did not feel helpless, he felt confident and assured.

The three men went cautiously down the deserted hallway crawling on their knees swiftly and silently. No one appeared as Ramon led Lorenzo and Samouil as they had done hundreds of times during practice manoeuvres staying close to the wall and looking into each room as they came to a glass partition.

Two minutes had passed and they had seen no one. Cautiously they approached another window, bent over, their heads below the glass and Ramon slowly raised his head. He saw the hostage-taker holding someone, a machine gun pointed to his head. Ramon gasped, then immediately composed himself. He moved down to the ground and motioned to Lorenzo and Samouil to stay down.

"He holding Marc Shai." Both Lorenzo and Samouil's eyes widened but they were trained to deal with shock and recovered immediately.

"Near back of room," said Ramon, "we've done this hundred times, you know exactly what to do." The two men nodded.

"Now—move and position," and Lorenzo went first, crawling on his hands and knees, quickly and silently like a panther. Ramon followed also on hands and knees then moved in a different direction. Samouil followed Ramon then moved off on his own. They moved with the utmost confidence and skill. The man holding Marc Shai was big and muscular, his arm was under Marc Shai's neck holding him high, his machine gun against the child's head. The boy seemed unusually calm. The man moved to the side of the room and called out in a loud voice:

"I came for drugs, if someone does not get them for me in one minute I will blow his head off."

Lorenzo had silently crawled all the way across the room on his stomach silently, hiding behind desks and chairs and ended up directly behind the man. He counted to three, silently stood up and raised his arm giving the signal for action and immediately hit the man's elbow, the arm that held the machine gun. The movement was swift and the contact was so forceful you could hear the bone crack as the gun flew up in the air firing at the same time.

Almost immediately Ramon snatched Marc Shai and threw him, like a ball to Samouil who was positioned about twelve feet from Ramon. Samouil easily caught the boy and ran out of the room. They still did not know if dynamite was involved. Lorenzo had thrown the man to the ground and Ramon pounced on him like an animal. He was not wired and Ramon looked around the room as he held the man down.

"What are you looking for?" yelled Lorenzo.

"You heard man, drugs, pills, anything," shouted Ramon.

Lorenzo looked puzzled and hesitated for just a moment.

"Pronto," yelled Ramon.

Lorenzo stood up quickly and his eyes darted around the room. A giant-size bottle filled with capsules sat on the counter and he picked it up.

"Open quick," yelled Ramon holding the man down. The man's one elbow was shattered and Ramon held the other arm with one hand and pinched open his victim's jaws with the other.

"Pour," he shouted to Lorenzo and Lorenzo hesitated again and looked at Ramon. He had never seen that look on his face before. He placed the bottle at the man's mouth and Ramon screamed "abra la boca," and Lorenzo started to pour the capsules in. Ramon impatiently grabbed the bottle from Lorenzo and shoved the pills into the man's mouth who was trying to push Ramon off him. He was strong but no match for an angry Ramon and began to choke while slowly losing consciousness.

"You want drugs?" shouted Ramon, "I give you drugs, all the drugs you want." The bottle was half empty and the man's eyes were starting to bulge but Ramon continued forcing the pills into his victim's mouth.

"Ramon, enough, he's had enough," said Lorenzo making the mistake of attempting to take his arm.

"Not enough," said Ramon pushing Lorenzo back with such force he fell backwards hitting his head against a table and temporarily knocking him out. Roberto had rushed in with Samouil and a doctor and they tried to pull Ramon off the unconscious man who had stopped breathing.

"You blow off head of little king? Ramon blows off your head with drugs," he shouted continuing to cram the pills into the man's mouth while the three men tried to pull Ramon off his victim. Lorenzo was trying to get to his feet and the doctor rushed to his side and helped him. Together the four men were able to pull Ramon away from his victim and dragged Ramon out of the hospital and all five men collapsed on the grass out of breath.

"I am okay," said Ramon as they looked at him, "I should have killed him with gun but he wanted drugs so I give him drugs."

Roberto sat on the ground beside him and shook his head. "What were you trying to do Ramon? What in the world was that?"

Ramon adjusted his headband and calmly brushed the dirt off his shirt. "That is part of unorthodox training Da Elegido style." He stood up and looked at Lorenzo and Samouil.

"Good rescue" he said, "you both did good. Lorenzo, you okay?"

"Ya, sure, just great Ramon," he said standing up.

"Good" said Ramon, "see me tomorrow morning at 9:00. I teach you meaning of pronto. Also," and he hesitated, "I teach you how to hate, sometime necessary. Tomorrow morning—9:00, do not eat anything, okay?" Lorenzo nodded. Ramon asked for his gun and looked very cool as he threw it over his shoulder and pushed back his hair. "I go see Marc Shai," he said and walked away.

The doctor watched him go back into the hospital and turned to Roberto. "What specimen of man was that?" he asked in amazement. Roberto just shook his head. "No one asks anymore. He's just the very best in the world at what he does but ... his manner is unorthodox."

Samouil looked at Lorenzo who did not look too happy. "I'll wait for you tomorrow around 10:00 Lorenzo, we'll have breakfast together."

"Don't worry, I've gone through this before," said Lorenzo, "I'll be okay. Come on, let's go see how everybody is doing, I've got a headache, thanks to Ramon."

"What else is new?" said Samouil as the two bodyguards followed Roberto and the doctor back into the building.

"Did Ramon give us a compliment?" said Lorenzo.

"I think so," said Samouil as the door closed behind them.

Maria and Skye had stood by helplessly as the hostage-taker kept Marc Shai with him while he waited for drugs. He had threatened to blow off the child's head if they followed. Now they did not have the words to show their gratitude to Ramon, Lorenzo and Samouil. They were so emotional that all they could do was cling to the three men and thank them over and over again. Roberto held Marc Shai in his arms and the relief and happiness he felt seemed to overwhelm him but he shed no tears, he couldn't.

"We are a family," said Maria through her tears, "we are all like one big family," and Roberto agreed. Skye looked at his son, his face was bruised and there was a bump over one eyebrow the size of an egg but otherwise appeared to be unhurt which seemed to be a miracle considering how fast he had been thrown and caught. He was not at all upset and when someone commented on this he said, "I knew Da Elegido would come for me. Papa, I want to be just like them, I want to be Da Elegido and learn and do what they do."

"We'll see," said Skye touching the boy's face and ruffling his hair.

"I get you Da Elegido shirt and headband Marc Shai, just for you," said Ramon. "You brave little king."

Roberto phoned Shane and quickly gave her only a few details but would tell her everything when they got back. "No one got hurt Shane, everyone is fine and we're leaving now."

"Rosita is making dinner for everyone," said Shane, "bring them all back with you."

Rosita had set up dinner outside near the ocean and they all sat down together including Ramon, Lorenzo and Samouil. Roberto, in all the excitement, had almost forgotten about Camille and Ramon but when he saw them at the table it reminded him and he had to face reality.

Out of respect to Shane and Roberto, Ramon did not sit next to Camille. Roberto wanted to sit with both of them and talk privately. Marc Shai sat between Lorenzo and Samouil and Maria sat with Skye, evidently still shaken but smiling. Everyone seemed relieved and happy chatting about the day's events which could have ended so tragically.

Only Roberto and Ramon seemed a little somber and Camille tried to smile but kept glancing nervously over towards her father and Ramon. No one realized that what had happened at the hospital would become a spectacular event and would hit international headlines throughout the world.

Lorena sat beside Lorenzo and they talked quietly. She had changed immensely. Still very protective of her mother, she felt responsible for her well-being now that her father and sister had both died within weeks of each other. Her taste in clothes was still flashy, too tight and too short. However, Lorenzo did not seem to mind at all. Shane and Roberto convinced Skye and Maria and little Marc Shai to spend the night at the Villa and at about 10:30 the group started to break up.

Roberto called Ramon and Camille to one side and said he wanted to see them in the library. He also asked Shane to stay. After they had closed the door Roberto told Shane what he knew. The look on Shane's face was disbelief.

"Camille, you are only fifteen years old," she said, "I find it hard to believe you would be thinking of marriage so early."

Roberto looked at Shane as his eyebrows shot up. "Shane, the issue here is not so much Camille's age as the fact that these two have strong feelings for each other. I find this to be totally unexpected, unbelievable and unacceptable."

Shane looked into Roberto's eyes for a moment before she spoke, then said, "when two people love each other, really love each other, nothing can keep them apart, neither age, religion, nothing. True love is beautiful and whoever possesses it is truly fortunate."

Camille and Ramon looked at Shane deeply surprised. Roberto's mouth had dropped open as he had not at all expected that kind of reaction from Shane.

"You surprise me Shane, what makes you suddenly become such a vocal expert in …"

"In matters of the heart? she said smiling at him. "You taught me Roberto, you are the most loving, kind and caring man in this world and you taught me well."

Even under his tan the blush on Roberto's face was noticeable. No one had ever seen him blush before and he looked uncomfortable.

"Shane, we are not here to talk about us, we are here to discuss what is happening between our daughter and Ramon. Let's get back on track."

Shane smiled sweetly; "as you wish Roberto."

"Ramon, you know I have much respect and admiration for you. Our friendship goes back many years and we have always been very close." Roberto looked at Ramon and wanted to get across to him how highly he thought of him but what he had revealed to him the night before was out of the question.

"Please do not misunderstand what I am about to say." Roberto hesitated then said with a hint of unbelief in his voice, "you and Camille? All these years there was a special relationship between the two of you, and Shane and I were very thankful for this but when did this change? When did you first tell Camille of your feelings for her?"

"Papa," interrupted Camille, "you do not have the right information. Ramon did not approach me first, it was I who brought this all about. I approached Ramon, I confessed that I love him, I told him I wanted to marry him, he had no idea until I told him this."

Now both Roberto and Shane looked shocked. "You?" said Roberto, "you told Ramon of your feelings?"

"Yes Papa, and he was not too happy, in fact, he got angry but I convinced him, am I not right Ramon?"

Ramon did not talk, he felt uncomfortable and wished he was riding along the beach or tossing hand grenades.

"Is this true Ramon? Is it true what my daughter is saying?"

Ramon looked at Camille—she took his hand and squeezed it and smiled.

"Speak man," said Roberto "did my daughter act in an undisciplined manner? I must know the truth."

"Undisciplined Roberto, no, with heart, si. I love Camille from bottom of heart and she love me. I, Ramon ask with respect, humble respect for your permission Roberto and Senora Shane permission to marry your daughter. I want Camille to be ... my wife. We wait until Camille sixteen and she continue school and I look after her, I always do, nothing new, for rest of our life. I Ramon swear this before you and Senora in presence of God."

Roberto was silent for a moment then spoke. "When Camille is sixteen you will be thirty-eight.

"I aware of that," said Ramon.

"Papa, I am in love with Ramon," said Camille again.

Roberto was quiet for a moment, then spoke. "What about Ricardo?"

"What about Ricardo? said Camille. "I never promised him anything. We never talked about that."

"He must be told Camille," said Shane, "you must speak to him."

"I will maman, I intend to," said Camille tightening her grip on Ramon's hand. Roberto looked at Camille and Ramon, then turned to Shane. They looked at each other for a moment and spoke with their eyes and Shane smiled. Roberto stood up and turned towards Camille and Ramon with outstretched arms. "Welcome to our family Ramon, Que Dios se lo pague."

Ramon and Camille did not hesitate; they were at Roberto's side immediately. "And God bless you Roberto," said Ramon as he embraced Roberto then immediately went to Shane kissing her hand and embracing her.

"Ramon, we are so happy, may God be with you always," she said with tears in her eyes.

"Ve con Dios," Senora Shane, please do not cry Senora." He looked at her, "you always so special to Ramon. I not stand to see you cry."

"They are tears of happiness Ramon, I am so happy." The full impact of what was happening had finally hit Roberto and Shane. Roberto held his daughter in his arms, a feeling of exhilaration had suddenly replaced the doubtful feelings from a moment ago. It was almost a relief. He knew he would not have to worry over his only daughter any more. Ramon had always been there for her and now, always would be. He was the best person, the most trustworthy for his little girl who was not little any more. Roberto also had a fear deep in his heart. He could never forget another young girl, only sixteen, also in love, and it had ended so tragically. He did not want that to happen to his Camille.

"It is late," said Roberto, "tomorrow we will make an announcement to the family and celebrate. Everyone is tired; it was a big day for all of us.

We are grateful to God that Marc Shai's life was spared and we are grateful to God for Camille and Ramon's happiness and extending our family. You are now officially one of us Ramon, God bless you both. Que Dios se lo pague. Let us, just the four of us right now, drink a toast to you both and to our future. This calls for our best champagne," he said getting up with a smile.

"I'll get it," said Shane and they ended the evening with a toast to the future bride and groom and to the future of them all. It was about to become quite a future.

Chapter Twenty-Two

The following day would be a memorable one for everyone. A large barbecue was planned on the beach and tables and chairs were brought in and trucks transporting specially ordered and prepared food for everyone.

Roberto had phoned President Gomez and although it was very short notice he and Isabella would be able to attend later in the day. "It is a special announcement Juan, a surprise, a wonderful surprise. We will tell you when you get here."

A band was flown in and music was played continuously all day. All of the men, the gendarmes and the servants, everyone was included in the celebration, the gendarmes taking turns in patrolling the area and the beach. It was a very tightly knit group and this was evident on how everyone intermingled with each other. Roberto always treated his security forces as special people, almost like family, and they in turn looked up to him and his family with the utmost respect.

Roberto waited for President Gomez and Isabella to arrive, then made the announcement of Camille and Ramon's engagement. The initial reaction of surprise was quickly turned to shouts of ole and the clapping of hands. It almost seemed as if everyone had been waiting for it to happen. Camille and Ramon held hands all evening, Camille smiling and Ramon serious as usual but with a new expression in his eyes. It was obvious to everyone how much they loved each other.

"Ramon," said Andre after congratulating him, "does this mean we get special treatment from you from now on?"

"Very special," said Ramon.

"Like midnight rides on the beach and special talks?" said Andre.

Ramon looked at Camille. "We will always have special talks Andre, maybe not midnight."

"I understand Ramon," said Andre with a smile.

President Gomez and Isabella were very pleased and happy. "I always thought of you as family, Ramon," said the President, "this really does not come as a surprise." He turned to Roberto, "so Roberto, is this your way of making sure Ramon stays with us?" he said winking at Camille. The last I heard the President of Argentina wanted Ramon to be added to his elite group of bodyguards."

"We got that all straightened out Juan, though I don't think the President was too happy," said Roberto.

"Camille," said Isabella, "I understand you will continue with your education after your marriage. I think that is very wise."

"Yes," said Camille, "Ramon insists on it and it's what I want too."

Rosita had come outside, "there is a long-distance call from Terry—he's looking for Ramon."

"Terry?" said Ramon, "he wants speak to me?"

"It looks that way," said Roberto. "You're tied up with the family now, Ramon, there's no escape."

Ramon excused himself and followed Rosita into the library. Terry sounded excited as word had reached him about the daring hostage rescue and he had a number of questions.

"My friends here don't believe that I know you guys but that doesn't matter. Tell me in your own words Ramon how it was done and especially how Agnes caught Marc Shai. They're saying it's like baseball, Dominican style."

"Not Agnes, Terry, Agallas. I tell you everything but first I tell you something else, very important."

"Okay Ramon, shoot, err no, I mean talk."

"I am engaged to Camille."

"Camille who?"

"Only one Camille, Terry, Roberto and Shane's daughter."

"You mean my niece Camille?"

"That's the one Terry, that's right."

"Are you serious man?" came back from Terry.

"You invited to wedding, Terry."

"Wait a minute," said Terry, "are you trying to tell me that you will be my nephew?"

"Hmm, that sound about right," said Ramon. "When you come back for wedding I show you, no, teach you unorthodox training. It makes you very strong, you become different man."

"I don't want to become a different man, I kind of like the old Terry. I've sort of grown fond of him. Anyway Ramon, you're crazy, but if this is true, congratulations. Give me Roberto; frankly I don't believe a word you're saying."

"Gracias Terry, take care of yourself, next time we meet you become Tio Terry, sound funny but we get use to it. I get Roberto for you. Ve con Dios."

Roberto verified the engagement and also gave Terry the information he needed regarding the hostage situation which Ramon had forgotten to tell Terry.

The celebration lasted well into the night. Skye, Maria and Marc Shai stayed at the Villa again that night and left the next day after breakfast. Camille wanted to get in touch with Ricardo but Roberto thought she should see Ricardo and tell him face to face.

"But papa," said Camille, "there was nothing serious between us, I do not owe him an explanation."

Roberto shook his head, "Camille, I think he just took it for granted that the two of you would some day marry. Wait, I think what we should do is have a reunion, a family get-together. I will arrange for Ricardo and your brothers to come back for a holiday, and we will settle everything here, and the sooner the better."

Roberto was able to make arrangements for the three boys to fly down for two weeks and they made preparations at the Villa. Frederik and Enrique were now seventeen years old and Ricardo had just turned eighteen. Shane and Roberto were planning a surprise birthday party for Ricardo and had invited his two sisters Christina and Carmen.

Everyone at the Villa was excited when the boys arrived. It was meant to be a double celebration but things did not turn out exactly as planned. In the beginning the reunion was a happy one but when Camille announced her engagement to Ramon, a shocked expression came over Ricardo's face. The reaction from the twins was delight. They had known Ramon all their lives and to them he had always been family. The transition from bodyguard to brother-in-law was natural for them. Roberto had just assumed that Camille and Ricardo would end up together and Ricardo had also assumed the same thing. Camille's eyes were shining, her happiness was evident and the twins, although happy for their sister, felt sorry for Ricardo. They had grown close to him through the years and they saw how greatly disappointed he was.

Both Frederik and Enrique were tall but Ricardo was taller and quite slim, a handsome boy, but the look on his face showed not just his disappointment but also anger. Shane sat beside him at the table and tried to carry on a conversation. He did not talk very much but when he did it was in a very low tone and only she could hear his words.

"Senora Shane, please do not misunderstand, I hold the utmost respect for you and Senor Roberto, and I always will, but does anyone understand that my heart is broken? Does Camille realize what she has done to me, does she care?"

Shane looked at him, there was anger and hate in his voice and she became concerned. Ricardo made no mention of Ramon as Roberto and Andre tried to spend extra time with Ricardo but the deep hurt that he felt was quite visible.

Early in the evening Camille and Lorena wandered out to the beach where Frederik and Enrique were sitting with Lorenzo and Samouil waiting for Ramon who had been gone all day to the village. He had been asked to accompany two nuns who were going into an unknown area to take food to a family and there might be danger involved in that area. He would be returning to the Villa in the evening.

Roberto looked around for Ricardo and found him in the library looking at the history books. "I'm glad you're here Senor," said Ricardo putting down the book and immediately standing up, "I've made up my mind about something."

"And what is that Ricardo?" asked Roberto motioning to Ricardo to sit down as he sat down also and faced him.

"I've decided to leave the Academy in Switzerland and to continue my education in the Basque Country." He hesitated then added, "with your permission Senor."

Roberto smiled, "I think Quinton has been influential in your decision, am I right Ricardo?"

"Actually, I was thinking about it a year ago but after today, it is what I want. I think you understand how I feel Senor."

"Ricardo, listen to me. You are like a son to us. Shane and I think of you as our own, Frederik and Enrique are very fond of you, you know that, we are family."

"And Camille, is she fond of me Senor? Do I mean anything to her? All these years I thought of her as mine, da prometida." Ricardo hesitated then spoke again. "I have decided to become a member of the Basque Nationalist Party, the Peneuvista."

Roberto pointed to the medallion hanging on a chain from Ricardo's neck with the letters PNV engraved on it.

"This is Peneuvista?" he said looking at Ricardo questioningly.

"Si Senor Roberto. Actually I am already a member," said Ricardo proudly.

"But this, I take it, has nothing to do with your disappointment with Camille; you say you are already a member."

"Si, that is correct Senor, but now I feel that I must get away, as far as possible. My heart is broken Senor, do you understand what I am feeling?"

Roberto touched his arm, "I am sorry Ricardo, I understand your disappointment but I do not like the anger that I detect in your voice. Do not hold it against Camille, this is life and things will happen that we do not like but we must learn to accept. Come, let us join the others—you are like a son to me."

"I cannot accept what has happened, Senor, I feel anger si, and I will never forgive Camille," said Ricardo and suddenly his voice choked but he quickly recovered. "I loved her but I never told her and this was my mistake.

Senor," and he turned angrily towards Roberto, "she is only fifteen, Ramon is much older, how can you allow this? I do not understand."

Roberto gently took Ricardo's arm, "Ricardo" he started to say but he pulled away and angrily left the room. Roberto stood for a moment thinking, he did not like what he had seen and he had a strange premonition that something was about to happen. He finally left the library and went out to the beach. Everyone seemed to be in a jovial mood but Ricardo was nowhere to be seen. Shane came up to him and took his hand.

"Roberto, you look worried about something," she commented, "is anything wrong?"

Roberto shook his head and smiled at her, "nothing to worry about Shane. Where is Camille, did Ramon get back?"

"He did, they're strolling on the beach," said Shane.

"Is anyone with them?" asked Roberto trying to sound nonchalant.

Shane quickly looked at Roberto. She knew by the comment that something wasn't right. "What has happened Roberto? You are not telling me something."

"Everything is fine Shane, don't worry, go sit with Andre. I'll be right back."

Roberto left a very puzzled Shane and started walking down the beach. Suddenly, out of nowhere Samouil came running over and started walking with him.

"No riding tonight Senor Roberto?" he asked.

"Oh Samouil, I was looking for Camille and Ramon, have you seen them?"

"Si Senor, they are farther down, see ahead? Lorenzo and Lorena are with them, also Diego. Look they are sitting down now on the sand."

Samouil was right, Roberto could see them and he heaved a sigh of relief. Samouil looked at him questionably. "What is it Senor, what is bothering you?"

"Everything is fine Samouil, I think I will go back. Why don't you go join them, I will be okay."

Samouil shook his head, "no Senor, your daughter and Lorena have three bodyguards with them. I do not worry and neither should you. I will go back with you Senor, only gendarmes there with the others. I am trained to protect you."

Roberto looked at the young man known to always carry his machine gun in his hands, a serious expression on his face, and he was very impressed.

"Okay Samouil, come on, let's see what the others are up to."

Chapter Twenty-Three

Ricardo left in the morning. No one saw him leave but he had left a note the night before. He felt he owed them that much. He had said goodbye to Frederik and Enrique and made them promise not to reveal when he was leaving and where he would be. He could not bear to say goodbye to Roberto and Shane. Roberto was very disappointed but did not make an issue of it. The encounter in the library the night before still bothered him. He thought Ricardo needed time to cool off and later he would plan to go see him. But first, he ordered a secret investigation done on his whereabouts.

Camille's sixteenth birthday was September 21 and her wedding date was set for November 21. After Camille and Ramon's engagement, everything seemed to settle down at the Villa. Although it came as a surprise to most, it was something seen as most favourable. It was not unusual for Camille and Ramon to be seen together through the years. She had grown up with Ramon always at her side and now, after the initial surprise, it seemed so natural to see them together.

Frederik and Enrique still had almost two weeks left to spend with their family before reporting back to the Academy in Switzerland. Andre was very happy as he sat across from Enrique at the table by the beach. They were having a great conversation and it was a good chance to get caught up with his nephew's life. He had missed so much through the years when everyone thought he had been killed along with the rest of the family and he knew he could never get back what he had lost during those terrible years. He never saw them as small children, wasn't there when they took their first steps, never had pictures taken with them when they we're small. But he was thankful that they had found each other and thankful that he was now involved in their lives.

The twins were now eighteen years old, intelligent, caring young men, handsome and beautiful people like their parents and he was so proud of them. He knew that he would never marry, never have children of his own but Enrique, Frederik and Camille were like his own children and he loved them so much. He looked at Enrique and realized he was talking to him and he had not been listening while deep in his own thoughts. Enrique stopped and looked at him. "Tio Andre, so what do you think?"

Andre smiled and reached out and took Enrique's hand, "I am embarrassed Enrique, I did not hear what you said."

Enrique made a little frown then smiled, "did not hear Tio Andre or was not listening? I can't get angry at you Tio Andre, you are so special to me," and he stood up, reached over and embraced his uncle. "I will just repeat what I said," he said sitting down. "I am considering a career in medicine—I want to be a doctor like Tio Skye. It is important to me what you think about that."

"What do I think?" said Andre, "I am so proud of you, anything you decide will make me proud. Do your parents know?"

"They have a pretty good idea but it was more important to me what you thought Tio Andre and gracias for accepting me for who I am."

Andre looked at Enrique with surprise, "for who you are? What kind of talk is that Enrique?"

"I think papa wanted me to be more like Frederik, you know my papa, he is a military man, but Frederik and I are different Tio Andre, I am me and Frederik is … is … Frederik." Enrique turned and looked out towards the ocean. "I am happy with who I am, Tio Andre, I hope my papa is too."

"Of course he is," said Andre, "his sons and daughter mean everything to him, you know that my sobrino."

"Ah, there you are Gemelo," came a voice from the path and Frederik appeared.

"Buenos dias Tio Andre," he said sitting beside his uncle and putting his arm around his neck. "I hope I'm not intruding on a private conversation Tio Andre."

"Not at all Frederik, I don't think Enrique minds, do you?"

Enrique laughed, "Tio Andre, you must know by now that my brother has a way of convincing people and doing and getting what he wants, in a very nice way, of course."

"Of course," said Andre smiling. He looked at the twins and marveled at how different they were, not just their personalities but also their physical appearance. Frederik's blond hair and light blue eyes were an amazing contrast to Enrique's dark hair and very dark eyes.

"Ah Gemelo, light of my eye, core of my heart, it is a good thing that both of us do not love the same girl. That would be interesting," said Frederik.

"Now where did that come from," said Enrique looking curiously at his brother, "are you trying to tell us something?"

"My, my, my" said Andre, "are we about to enter into the secret and scary life of Frederik Castaneda, the heart-throb, pretty boy?"

Enrique was having a good laugh, "don't stop Tio Andre, I like that, heart-throb, pretty boy, now I have a name for my brother, 'guaperos', si, now I have a name for him."

"Laugh all you want Gemelo," said Frederik grinning, it doesn't bother me. Tio Andre, will you come riding with me? I do not like to ride alone and my brother has never been too fond of sports."

"I would like to Frederik but I will be leaving soon to go to the Cathedral. I am to meet someone there in an hour."

"I'll go with you guaperos," said Enrique grinning, "I do not dislike horseback riding, it's the guns that bother me."

"Go ahead boys, enjoy each other's company. Actually, you won't be alone; you'll find either Lorenzo or Samouil tagging along."

The horses were brought out and just as Andre predicted Samouil appeared out of nowhere.

"This is perfect Samouil, we ride together," said Frederik. "There's something I want to ask you."

The sun was just beginning to sit in the middle of the ocean. Bright red rays were cast across the waters throwing a pink haze across the sky. The three riders slowly trotted across the sand enjoying the view and each other's company.

"Samouil, you're not much older than us are you?" said Frederik glancing at the bodyguard.

"I'm nineteen, I'll be twenty in two months," said Samouil.

"You're only a year older than us," said Enrique, "how can that be?"

Samouil laughed, "do I look that much older?"

"No, don't misunderstand," said Frederik, "I think what my brother means is that you are much more mature. You know what I think Samouil? I think the training you got in Da Elegido has something to do with this. Am I right Samouil?"

Samouil smiled, "si, it teaches you discipline among other things. Not easy but challenging. I like challenge, I like danger, I like excitement. It also teaches you to appreciate being able to exist after Ramon gets through with you. It makes you thankful just to be alive."

Frederik and Enrique stared at Samouil. He was not holding the reins and he held his machine gun against his body.

"Are you taught to ride like that?" asked Frederik.

"No, it's just my preference," said Samouil and they continued down the beach as the sun started to sink into the depths of the darkened ocean. They rode quietly for a while, then Frederik spoke. "I want to join Da Elegido Samouil. What do you think are my chances?"

"Your chances?" said Samouil, "they are excellent. You've already had some training, I'm sure your papa has seen to that. But it's more than that, it is wanting and a desire, in here," and he put his hand over his heart. If you want it badly enough, you can have it."

Enrique laughed, "when my brother wants something badly, nothing can stop him; he always gets what he wants, just goes after it."

"That's good," said Samouil, "see Ramon and talk to him, but it is tough, don't say I didn't warn you. Does your papa know of your desire?"

"No, but it's what I want and it's what I will be, mark my words."

"What about you Enrique, do you have this desire also?" said Samouil.

"No I'm afraid not," said Enrique, "my interests run more towards medicine. God willing, I would like to be a doctor some day like my Tio Skye."

"That is good," said Samouil, "we always need doctors. I think we should be turning back, it is getting dark, your family might be worried."

The next day Frederik sought out Ramon and told him of his hopes of becoming a member of Da Elegido. For some reason Ramon did not encourage Frederik and told him to think about it. When Frederik spoke to Roberto about his desire he was surprised to get the same reaction.

"My son, why don't you consider one of the branches of the armed forces, something under my command?" he said looking at him from across his desk in the library.

"Papa, do you know what you are doing? Do not baby-sit me, I know what I want and stop worrying," said Frederik feeling frustrated.

Roberto was worried, he didn't want to admit it but he remembered only too well what had happened to Leandro. He didn't want to hold a dying son in his arms, he would not be able to live through it. Da Elegido specialized in danger. The insignia on Ramon's jeeps read Policia Intervenciones, Especializada Peligrosas. They specialized in danger only and Roberto was not keen on Frederik joining the group but Frederik was insistent. Finally, Roberto gave in but unknown to his son, he did something that he was not very proud of.

"Ramon, let him train, show him what he must learn but ... be tough but not too tough, I don't want him badly injured. Oh God, what am I saying, I sound terrible, just be convincing Ramon, do you understand what I am trying to do? Let's see if we can change his mind."

Ramon looked at Roberto and gave a big sigh. "This hard for me Roberto, I know him like Enrique and Camille when they little. I not want to hurt him; he is like nephew to me."

"And he is my son and I don't want to see his blood spill on my hands. Please, don't think badly of me Ramon, try to understand, I love him."

Ramon looked at Roberto, "I not think badly Roberto, I too love him, I understand."

Ramon heaved a sigh. "Okay, I do as you say. Life slurps."

"Sucks, Ramon, life sucks," said Roberto.

"I glad you think so too," said Ramon. "Okay, don't worry, it will be done. Don't worry, is our secret, okay?"

Roberto sighed, "gracias Ramon, and remember, be tough but not too tough. I'm hoping he will call it quits and realize it's not for him." He did not want Shane to know what he and Ramon were doing.

President Gomez and Isabella wanted to be involved in the wedding plans and had offered the Presidential Palace for the reception. Camille and Ramon did not want a big wedding and Roberto and Shane tried to keep the guest list under two hundred but Roberto had many friends.

The ceremony would take place in the Catholic Church that Andre had held his sermons before Roberto discovered him and when they found that Andre would be officiating at the ceremony, everyone was overjoyed. Ramon was very touched when Andre spoke to him about bringing in a Rabbi also for the wedding ceremony. Ramon looked at Andre then suddenly pulled him towards him in a strong embrace. "You have given to me the presence of my family's spirit on my wedding day. I will never forget this." Andre smiled until he felt the crush of Ramon's embrace; the man was definitely unaware of his strength.

The day of the wedding arrived and every last detail had been looked after. Roberto was completely satisfied and happy with everything and he spoke to Shane the night before expressing his feelings.

"Shane, I am so happy, yet … that's our little girl getting married tomorrow. Somehow I find it hard to believe."

"I know," said Shane, "I think if they had waited a couple of more years, it would have been easier to accept. I'm so fond of Ramon and I think we've grown to love him but all these years his relationship to us was that of a bodyguard and then he seemed to be like family."

"Exactly," said Roberto, "that's it. "He's been like family through the years but now all of a sudden it's son-in-law. I'm still trying to adjust my thinking to this … my son-in-law?" he said incredulously. "We rode many times on the beach together and had long talks. I never thought of him as a possible son-in-law. We were soldiers together and we faced Carlos the drug king together and we were like close friends and at the same time my little girl was growing up and he protected her for years."

"And he will continue to do so," said Shane putting her hand on his arm. "It was just meant to be, Roberto. Everything in this world is preplanned, I don't think it just happens, don't you think so?"

Roberto looked at Shane, his eyes searching hers for an answer. "Do you think our life was preplanned, Shane? Do you think it didn't just happen?"

"That's what you've always told me about us Roberto, you know, destiny, meant to be, all those wonderful things you said to me."

Roberto drew Shane to him and put his arms around her. "How often I have said my little one that no one has what we have. I'm not talking about yesterday, last year or ten years ago, my beautiful Shane, although they will always be precious to me. I'm talking about now, this very second, this exact moment, I adore you. I love you so much that it overwhelms me and I think to myself how lucky I am because God must love me so much. Shane, he has given me you, my paradise on earth and I am alive to live it." He kissed her ever so gently, his eyes closed and he just held her. This time it was Shane's turn to be overwhelmed. Roberto never failed to surprise her with his deep feelings for her and the tears ran down her cheeks. Roberto drew back and wiped them away.

"I've done it again my little one, I kiss you and you cry. No more tears Shane, tomorrow you will cry when our daughter marries Ramon. Tomorrow will be a big day and the beginning of a new dynasty in our family."

Chapter Twenty-Four

On November 21st Camille Shanelle Castaneda walked down the aisle of Andre's Catholic Church clinging tightly to Roberto's arm as the strains of the wedding march played softly in the background. Her off-the-shoulder white lace and silk gown fitted her slim young body and her veil held back her luxuriant dark hair while white roses and satin ribbons framed her face. She carried a bouquet of white roses. Camille's beauty seemed to be beyond the limit and she looked so much like Shane that Roberto could feel a lump in his throat and with great difficulty he composed himself.

Ramon had wanted his three closest friends to stand up for him at his wedding. Lorenzo was his best man and Samouil and Diego were his ushers. Camille chose two young girls from the orphanage, Amara and Deedee as her bridesmaids and Lorena as her maid of honour. Camille had no close girlfriends. Hers was not a normal life while growing up. Her closest friends were the bodyguards who were with her constantly while she attended school and she was always accompanied by one or two of them who always carried machine guns. Because of this not many schoolmates approached Camille but she did not mind. Ramon was always there and now it seemed only natural that he would be her life mate. Little Marc Shai would be her ring-bearer.

As Camille came down the aisle Ramon turned and looked at her, his eyes not leaving her face until she stood beside him. It was the first time anyone had seen Ramon without his machine gun and black Da Elegido shirt. Lorenzo, Samouil and Diego like Ramon were resplendent in black suits and Andre stood facing them with Rabbi Weinburg at his side. Roberto kissed Camille and went back to sit with Shane. The ceremony was solemn with both Priest and Rabbi officiating and the music was hauntingly beautiful.

Shane, Maria and Rosita cried throughout the ceremony and when they were pronounced husband and wife, everyone witnessed an amazing thing. Ramon turned to his bride and lifted the veil from her face and looked at her. He started to smile and Camille smiled back. No one had ever seen Ramon smile and he just continued looking at Camille and smiling. He kissed his bride and at that moment the sun burst through the stained glass windows casting a warm glow over the couple and the congregation. The Rabbi smiled and looked at Andre and he also smiled and nodded. Something had happened, something that couldn't be explained and everyone in the church had felt it. It was as if a warm hand had touched them and a sudden peacefulness descended upon everyone. It had only lasted a few moments but everyone felt it, like the presence of spirits, like a miracle. It would never be forgotten.

The ceremony had come to an end and everyone stepped outside the church. After the congratulations and picture-taking they all went to the lavish reception being held at the Presidential Palace and it was there where Camille and Ramon surprised everyone with their rendition of the National Dance of the Dominican Republic, The Bachata.

Shane turned to Roberto with a surprised expression on her face, "I didn't know Ramon knew that dance," she said.
"I didn't know Ramon knew how to dance," said Roberto incredulously.

Skye leaned over at the table. "Roberto, it looks like your new son-in-law has a few surprises up his sleeve."

"I thought I knew him," said Roberto.

"I think only Camille knows him and that is all that matters," said Maria matter of factly. All three looked at Maria. "Wow, that is quite a statement coming from my shy little Maria," said Skye. "That did not sound like you."

"Look at them," said Shane, "Maria is right, look at the way she is looking at him."

"Look at the way he's looking at her," said Skye.

"I can't believe that's my little girl up there," said Roberto, his eyes had softened and he looked a little sad.

"Snap out of it Roberto," said Skye, "she'll always be your little girl."

Roberto looked up suddenly. When had he heard those exact words before and then he remembered—Beatriz. Shane quickly took Roberto's hand. "Today is a celebration of our daughter's wedding. Roberto, we are here in happiness, don't let sadness from the past enter our joy. Let's rejoice with Ramon and Camille, this is their day." Roberto kissed her hand and looked into her eyes. "With you by my side, my little one ... and you know the rest, remember?"

"I will always remember Roberto," she said leaning over and kissing him, "always".

"Well, well, well, for an outsider looking in," said Skye, "it would be hard to tell who got married today."

Enrique had approached the table. "Tia Maria, would you please honour me with this dance, with your permission Tio Skye?"

"Of course," said Skye as Maria stood up and took Enrique's hand.

"My nephew is taller than me Roberto," said Skye. "What do they feed them at the Academy?"

"It's his background Skye, his grandfather, his uncles, were all tall," said Roberto. "Who is the girl Frederik is dancing with? I don't think I've seen her before."

"You know your good friends Jose Delacruz and his wife. Isn't he Chief of the Secret Police?" said Skye.

"Si, you are right Skye. Don't tell me that's their daughter Teresa Leone! She's only ... I think ... only fourteen years old," said Roberto. "That's little Teresa? She's changed."

"Roberto, it seems young girls grow up fast in this Country," said Shane, "including our own."

"Hmm," said Roberto thoughtfully, "when did Frederik meet the young lady?"

"If he takes after you Roberto," said Skye, "he probably saw her, walked up to her, introduced himself and asked her to dance with him … no, told her to dance with him whether she wanted to or not."

"Lorenzo had approached the table and had heard the latter part of the conversation.

"Actually, Roberto, I heard what Frederik said. He said I'm going to be part of your life, my name is Frederik and I want to dance with you," and Lorenzo smiled. Shane laughed, "he does sound like you Roberto."

"In that case," said Roberto, I'll have to keep my eye on that boy."

Ramon walked around the table and stood before Shane and bowed. "Shane, you honour me with this dance?" he asked. Shane stood up, she felt strange even though she knew Ramon well. It was only natural that they would dance, but still …

They walked out to the dance floor and started to dance but Shane was very nervous.

"Shane," said Ramon, "you nervous because of me or because everyone watching us?"

"No Ramon, I'm not nervous, I'm all right," said Shane trying to compose herself.

"If you not nervous why you shaking?" he said.

"Ramon, please, you are making it worse for me," said Shane.

"Then I make you laugh," he said with the usual straight face.

"Laugh, you think you can make me laugh Ramon? Then go ahead."

"Okay, remember first day, long time ago, when Damien and I come to big house to stay with you, remember? Roberto sent us."

"I remember Ramon, I would never forget that first day, I was so scared."

"I know. When we sit on grass near you, I see snake on side of your chair."

Shane suddenly looked startled, "a snake?"

"Wait, let me tell you. Damien not see him. If I shoot snake, you be frightened, you frightened anyway. When you get up to go inside, I pick him up and throw him far over fence. Okay? Next day, he come back. Again I throw over fence."

Shane was wide-eyed by now. "Ramon, that is awful, I had no idea."

"Wait, not finished, best part now come. Two more times it comes back, two more times I give him free ride in air." By now Shane was starting to smile and Ramon continued. "Next time I see him Damien feeding it, can you believe? This is why he comes back.

"Oh my goodness," said Shane, "so what did you do?"

"I shoot it, he never come back," said Ramon starting to smile.

"Ramon, you are smiling again. How wonderful to see you smile again."

"And you Shane, not shaking."

"Oh Ramon," said Shane with tears, "you are so awesome," and she kissed his cheek.

"I ask Camille what that means," he said and he kissed her cheek also. Then, he looked at her strangely and something seemed to hit them both for just a second, and it was gone.

They went back to the table and Ramon took Shane's hand and kissed it. "Gracias Shane, I enjoyed our talk and the dance, gracias," and he left.

"I see Ramon is giving out his smiles today," said Roberto, "amazing."

"He's really very sweet Roberto," said Shane happily. "Camille is very lucky."

"Sweet? Ramon sweet? Are we talking about the same Ramon? What has he been telling you Shane? Ramon is anything but sweet. We're talking about your son-in-law, Ramon."

"I know," said Shane, "isn't it awesome?"

President Juan Gomez and Isabella sat at Roberto's table chatting with Skye and Maria when one of the guards quickly came over to the President and whispered something to him. He immediately stood up, his face had become ashen and Roberto saw this and quickly went to his side.

"What is it Juan, what has happened?" he asked with concern.

"My grand-daughter has been kidnapped, we must leave, I am sorry Roberto."

"Philomena? Julio's little girl?" said Roberto aghast.

Juan Gomez nodded.

"I am going too, and so is Da Elegido," said Roberto with determination. He looked around, Samouil was looking at them and Roberto motioned for him to come towards them.

"Quick Samouil, find Ramon and Lorenzo and Diego, there is an emergency, quick."

As they were leaving little Marc Shai ran up to Ramon and clung to his arm. "Espera Tio Ramon, I will go with you."

"No, my little king, run back to your papa," he said but the boy clung to him. There was no time so Ramon lifted the boy and ran back to the table handing him back to a very surprised Skye.

"Hold on to son, we come back," said Ramon ruffling Marc Shai's hair. He reached the others and they were quickly driven to the jailhouse. A suspect was in custody and they had reason to believe that he knew where the child was being held for ransom. As they got out of the car Ramon turned to Roberto. "Give me five minutes with him Roberto. Do not worry, I not kill him."

"Even if you injure him badly, Ramon, he will not be able to talk. Time is precious."

"I know, I know," said Ramon, do not worry, trust me."

Ramon was taken inside and he stepped into the cell. He locked the door behind him, and Ramon looked at the man as the man stared back at him. Ramon glanced at his watch. "Not much time," he said. "Talk, where is child?" The man just shook his head.

"My English not good," said Ramon and he spoke slowly measuring his words. "They teach me word, they say remember ex … ex … ah, si, ex … cru … ci … at … ing, si, that is it, they say I make pain excruciating," he said slowly. "Do … not … make … me … hurt … you."

Outside Roberto waited with the others and he looked at his watch. Three and a half minutes had passed. Suddenly, Ramon came through the door and calmly handed Roberto a piece of paper.

"That is address Roberto and he said he take us there. Very helpful."

Roberto motioned to the men to bring out the prisoner. "He is okay?" said Roberto turning to Ramon.

"Si, I told you he be okay, only crying," said Ramon not looking at him.

"Crying," said Roberto looking suspiciously at Ramon, "why is he crying? What did you do to him?" Ramon shrugged his shoulders and did not say anything.

The child was rescued unharmed and Roberto and his men returned to the wedding reception. Juan Gomez decided to stay with his family after showing his gratitude.

"We will have a celebration party, the kind of which no one has seen when Camille and Ramon return from their honeymoon. Right now, we are so grateful to you Roberto and Da Elegido."

Quite a few of the guests were still at the reception, mostly out of curiosity. They only had bits and pieces of information. Ramon found Camille and she threw her arms around him saying, "I was so worried Ramon."

"Do not worry my Camille, I always tell you, do not worry. Come, we dance," he said putting his arm around her.

"What happened?" she asked as they started to dance.

"I tell you later, everything okay, nobody hurt—almost nobody. Now only think about Camille Rubenstein, Ramon's wife."

"Oh Ramon, you said that so beautifully, 'Camille Rubenstein' she said, her eyes glistening.

"And did you like also, 'Ramon's wife'?" he said tightening his arm around her waist.

"Those are the most beautiful words I have heard ever, Ramon. I love you so much."

"You are very beautiful my Camille, sa precioso."

"Ramon?"

"Si?"

"You have never said I love you."

"You know I do."

"Say it."

"Not here, later."

"Ramon?"
"Hmm?"

"Say it."

"Say what?"

"I love you."

"I know you do."

Camille stopped dancing and looked at Ramon.

Ramon took her hand holding it tightly, "come my Camille, we go back to table. I have talk with you later, you have much to learn."

Camille stared at Ramon. What was he talking about? Why was he treating her like a child? She was his wife. What had happened when they left the reception during the sudden emergency? Ramon pulled out her chair and Camille sat down, Ramon beside her. Lorenzo was smiling as usual and chatting with Lorena. Samouil sat quietly and looked at Ramon then Camille, then back at Ramon. Ramon noticed. Samouil was a very interesting young man. Whoever knew him was aware that he seemed to possess an uncanny extra sense.

"You not dance?" asked Ramon.

"Sometimes," said Samouil.

"I not see you dance tonight," said Ramon, "you not enjoy wedding?"

"Very much Ramon, it is a beautiful wedding. May I have your permission to dance with your wife?"

Ramon looked quickly at Samouil. He liked the young man but did not expect to hear him say that at that exact moment.

"Si, of course, ask her," he said and Samouil immediately stood up. He went to Camille and bowed before her. She stood up, glanced at Ramon as he watched closely, and walked to the dance floor with Samouil.

"What is bothering you Camille?" said Samouil the moment they started to dance.

"It is nothing Samouil, nothing you should be concerned about," she said a little surprised at his candor.

"Camille, I'm going to give you some free advice and I want you to take it."

She looked at Samouil and the first thing that entered her mind was is this a conspiracy?

Is he going to tell her off? How did he know what she and Ramon had talked about? And most of all, who did he think he was to tell her off if that indeed was what he was about to do and at her wedding.

"Continue dancing," he said as she slowed down, "and listen."

By now Camille was beginning to wonder what was going to happen but she nodded. Her wedding reception was turning out to be full of surprises and Samouil continued.

"Camille, you know Ramon better than anyone, better than your father does. Ramon is a very good man but sometimes he shows his eccentric side, you know, does or says something that is hard to believe or understand. But later on, you always find out that he said or did something for a very good reason. Do you follow what I am saying?"

Camille looked up at him, Samouil was very tall and he looked down at her waiting for an answer. She nodded, amazed at the way Samouil was explaining it to her. "When you think about it," he continued, "Ramon is always a few steps ahead of the rest of us. He knows exactly what he is doing at all times. He is one of the most brilliant, ruthless and toughest individuals I have ever known, sort of like a mixture of things but he's also very kind. Put it all together and you have Ramon. What I'm trying to say Camille is trust him and just be patient.

Camille's eyes filled with tears and spilled down her cheeks.

"Stop that Camille or I will be in big trouble," said Samouil looking around. Camille put her arms around his neck and hugged him. "I'm probably putting you at risk for bigger trouble right now Samouil, please forgive me but you are wonderful," she said. "You are opening my eyes to something I could not see. You have done so much for me today how can I ever thank you? Ramon and I will find a special girl for you, someone very special."

"Don't bother," he said as they went back to their table, "I have enough problems right now, I don't need any more. Look at your husband's face. Ramon had stood up as they approached and was looking at Samouil. As Camille sat down Ramon turned to her, concern on his face.

"Camille, you okay, what happened?"

"I'm very okay Ramon, I will tell you later but right now, I love you so much," and she kissed him lightly on the lips.

The reception was lavish, Roberto had seen to that. He wanted the best of everything and had foods imported from all over the world. The celebration lasted well into the night and Roberto had wanted a moment alone with Ramon and he had his chance. Frederik was dancing with Camille and Shane and Skye were on the dance floor. Ramon was alone at their table except for Roberto who sat next to him.

"You do so much for us Roberto, gracias for everything." Roberto smiled, "you were always like family to us Ramon, now you really are. I don't have to tell you how happy and pleased Shane and I are. But, Ramon …"

Ramon had turned and faced Roberto, "si Roberto? You have question?"

Roberto took a deep breath, "Camille is very special to me Ramon, to me and her mother."

"Si Roberto, she is special to me too," said Ramon looking into Roberto's eyes.

"What I'm trying to say Ramon is … she is and always will be my little girl, my only daughter and I love her more than you can imagine. Promise me Ramon, give me your word that you will always look after my daughter and protect her, promise me."

Ramon continued to look deeply into Roberto's eyes as he spoke, "I have always looked after Camille, I have always protected her, you know that Roberto."

"But it is different now Ramon and you know that also. It is not the same."

Ramon did not talk for a moment. He looked away, out towards the dance floor. His eyes rested on Camille. Roberto followed his gaze. She was dancing with Frederik and they were both smiling and talking. She had obviously inherited her great beauty from her mother but there was a child-like quality about her that seemed to still exist in her face and her movement.

"I know Roberto, is different," said Ramon softly, "Camille now my wife." He continued to stare at Camille then turned to Roberto, "I give word, Roberto, I promise she be happy. I always protect her, I will be good husband. Do not worry, I know she very young."

Roberto looked at Ramon and stood up and smiled placing his hand on his shoulder.

Welcome to the family, Ramon. I'd better find Shane; we've only danced once tonight. That's something we both have in common, Ramon. We are both married and happily in love." Ramon nodded and Roberto left to look for Shane.

Ramon sat for a long time deep in thought as the music played romantically in the background then said very softly to himself, "you right, Roberto, you and me, we both have something in common."

It was quite late in the night when Camille and Ramon slipped away to start their honeymoon and Roberto once again smiled happily. His hopes and dreams for the future were all coming true. Everything was turning out as planned and the dynasty that he wanted all his life was building into reality before his eyes.

After the wedding reception Camille had changed into a white outfit that Shane had purchased for her. The white embroidered dress and matching white cashmere cape set off her dark hair and porcelain-like skin. She wore a gold locket around her neck that Ramon had asked her not to open until later that night.

Roberto had clasped his daughter to him. "You know how much we love you Camille," he said as she clung to him with tears in her eyes. Shane embraced her daughter and they both cried a little while Roberto took Ramon's hand and squeezed it hard. As they embraced Roberto said, "from this moment on, Ramon, I shall not worry over my daughter any more. I know that you will always take good care of her. Que Dios se lo pague, ve con Dios."

Camille tearfully embraced her brothers and Andre and they embraced Ramon. The twins were always close to Ramon and their show of affection came naturally. They were glad that he was now really a part of the family.

Chapter Twenty-Five

Camille and Ramon boarded the plane and settled down for the long flight to Rome, Italy. Camille was tired and soon fell asleep, her head resting on Ramon's shoulder, his arm protectively around her. It had been quite a day, almost unreal to Ramon as he thought about the beautiful wedding that Roberto and Shane had given them. President Juan Gomez and Isabella had actually shown up at the airport. They knew Ramon well and were very fond of him and wanted to show their pleasure and acceptance of the union. All had gone well but the only thing Roberto felt uncomfortable about was Ricardo. Roberto knew he would not attend the wedding but thought he would at least send a telegram to show that there was no ill-feeling. They had received numerous telegrams from all over the world, but the absence of one from Ricardo seemed to glare at Roberto and almost put a gloom on the wedding. But Roberto refused to let that spoil Ramon's and Camille's day and he quickly pushed it aside in his mind.

Ramon looked down at his bride and tenderly smoothed back her hair as his lips touched her forehead. She had such a beautiful forehead and once again he marveled at the thought that she was actually his. The stewardess stopped beside them and smiled.

"Senor, is there something I can get for you?" she asked. "Gracias, Senorita, no," said Ramon, "gracias." The stewardess smiled again and left and Ramon put his face against Camille's and closed his eyes. He could feel the tenseness slowly leave his body and he was actually starting to relax, something that he had trained himself not to do. He knew that he would be over-protective but he could not help that. His arm tightened around her and he suddenly felt emotional. She opened her eyes and smiled.

"Ramon, you look as if you are going to cry?"

"No," he said softly looking down at her.

"I thought you were tough, dear Ramon."

"I am," he said sternly, "you not know how tough Ramon is. Now go back to sleep my Camille," and he gently kissed her and tightened his arm around her once again. She closed her eyes and slept, a normal reaction for Camille, after all, the man beside her was Ramon her friend, Ramon her bodyguard, Ramon … her new husband. He would always watch over her and she would always be 'my Camille' to him.

It was very late when they finally reached their hotel and registered. Ramon unlocked the door to their apartment and they stepped inside. He locked the door and quickly went to the window and looked outside.

"Ramon, is something wrong?" said Camille going to his side.

"No, do not worry, everything fine. This is very high, we on eighteenth floor Camille, is that okay?" He turned to look at her. "If you wish we change room."

"I do not mind," she said taking off her cape and kissing him. "As long as I'm with you, I do not mind anything."

Ramon held her and kissed her gently. "We will always be together my Camille—we always been together, si? You want to go out for late dinner or you want we order?"

"I'm really not hungry Ramon." She pushed back her hair, "I am so tired."

"It is okay Camille, we stay." He opened the suitcases and Camille changed into a white satin nightgown as Ramon watched. She was breathtakingly beautiful and he could not take his eyes off her. He started to undress and she stood beside him and put her arms around him.

"Ramon, say you love me," she said, "say it now." He looked at her, wanting to hold her but couldn't. Why was he holding back?

"What kind of question that?" he said.

"Then say it," she insisted.

"Say what?" he said.

"Ramon, I just want to hear you say I love you."

His arms tightened around her, his dark eyes stared deeply into hers and he spoke softly.
"I would rather show you."

"But you won't say it," she said. "Maybe … maybe you don't really love me," and she looked at him teasingly. "How will I ever know?"

He knew how tightly he was holding her, he was aware that she was feeling pain and he felt the love in his heart. It was a deep love for a young girl but not the love for a woman.

"Camille, my Camille," he whispered, "you want Ramon to prove his love to you? You do not know?" He kissed her lightly still holding her in his vise-like grip.

"Then say it," she said looking up at him defiantly, or are you afraid to say it?"

"I see now you not know Ramon," he said quietly. "You very young my Camille, I teach you lesson number one," and he proceeded to kiss her passionately while saying, "I love you my Camille, I love you, I love you," and he continued to kiss her without stopping and repeating the words over and over again. She was like a prisoner in his grip and tried to catch her breath but he did not stop. Why should he stop, she belonged to him, he had always been her guide, her instructor, her teacher for most of her sixteen years and now it was morally legal.

"Ramon, please stop," she finally gasped and Ramon stopped. "I am sorry," she said breathlessly, "I will never doubt you again."

"I know you won't," he said still holding her in his arms. There was something almost unorthodox in his actions like the unusual manoeuvres he portrayed when he trained the men to become Da Elegido but he did not realize it. "Ramon knows you won't, and now my Camille, I will teach you lesson number two."

The sun had filtered through the slats in the blind casting a morning light throughout the room. Camille opened her eyes and turned her head and saw Ramon asleep on his side, one arm around his pillow, his face turned towards her. She looked at her left hand and gave a sigh. It was not a dream, it was true, they were married and she smiled and wanted to touch his face. No, she thought, I will not awaken him—he looked so peaceful, like a little boy. She ran her finger gently down the scar on his face and kissed it then leaned over and kissed his back. It was bare and muscular and she rested her face against it. She had loved him for so long and she tried to think when she had first realized that she was in love with Ramon the man, not Ramon her mentor, her bodyguard, her father's best friend. He did not move and she put the blanket around him and moved closer to her husband. Suddenly she felt his arm go around her and she looked down at him.

"I woke you up Ramon, I'm so sorry," she said as his eyes looked deeply into hers.

"Are you really sorry my Camille," he said softly holding her tight and she smiled. "I been awake long time," he continued, "I look at you while you sleep and I think."

"What were you thinking Ramon," she said closing her eyes and happy just being near him.

"I think ..." and he kissed the top of her head, "I think I see little girl, Roberto and Shane's little girl, and I watch little girl grow up. I take her to school, I teach her to ride horse, I protect her. She is beautiful and I protect her with machine gun. She grow up and I always protect her but ... no one protect me."

Camille looked up at him suddenly and he kissed her forehead and continued. "Nobody protects Ramon's heart. He look at beautiful child grown up and Ramon almost age of her father and heart breaks each time she look at him with beautiful eyes. Ramon hides pain and one day she say 'Ramon, I love you', she wants me and we marry but Ramon is afraid to sleep." He stopped and looked at her. "He thinks he wake up and child-woman is gone and it is only dream."

"Ramon, it is not a dream, I am here beside you, we slept together last night. Oh Ramon, just hold me, never let me go," she said kissing his face.

"I learn new word, my Camille, just for you," he said looking deeply into her eyes. "I practice last week."

"A new word, for me?" she said touching his face, "tell me Ramon, what is it?"

"Big word Camille, unconditional. Ramon gives to his Camille unconditional love, today, tomorrow, always, and especially now, my Camille, my unconditional love."

Suddenly there was a knock at their door and Ramon looked at Camille. She looked surprised and shrugged her shoulders.

"Who is it?" he called out.

"Buon giorno Signor, compliments of the hotel," came back a voice. "Champagne and caviar for the newly-weds."

Ramon's body immediately tensed. They had told no one at the front desk that they were newly-weds. In fact, Roberto had taken great pains to keep the honeymoon away from any publicity and Ramon started to feel uneasy. "Gracias, leave there" he called out, "I pick up."

"Bene, grazie Signor."

By now, Camille was sitting up wide-eyed and wondering what was happening. Ramon put his finger to his lips motioning to Camille not to make a sound. They heard footsteps running to the elevator and the door closed immediately. Ramon stood very still. Why did they run? Why was the elevator waiting? It was obvious the door had closed in a matter of a few seconds. He moved towards the door stealthily like an animal and very slowly opened it. Once again, his eyes darted quickly back and forth as he glanced at the cart that stood by the door and at the same time took in the hallway, the elevators, the doors. No one was around and his eyes shifted back to the cart. A white linen cloth covered the cart and Ramon's sharp eyes traveled down the side and he saw a small black wire hanging from underneath. It was barely discernible. Leaving the door open he quickly went back to Camille and took her hand.

"Do not be frightened," he said, "trust me" and she nodded. They went to the door and very carefully moved past the cart without touching it. Then Ramon quickly picked up Camille in his arms and ran towards the exit kicking open the door. Down the stairs he ran as fast as he could clutching Camille who had wrapped both arms around his neck, her face against his bare chest. "Keep eyes closed," he yelled and continued running and jumping. It came easy to Ramon, it was part of the Da Elegido manoeuvres that he taught the new recruits. The only difference was he knew what was about to happen, this was not a training exercise, it was the real thing and he tried to prepare himself for what was about to follow.

"Keep eyes closed," he yelled and continued running down the flights. They were quite a sight, Camille wearing the white satin nightgown and Ramon wearing pajama bottoms and no top.

They reached the twelfth floor and then it happened. The explosion was very powerful throwing both of them through the air down the flight of stairs to the next landing. The floor was marble, there were no rugs and Camille was immediately knocked unconscious while Ramon lay beside her stunned with pain gripping his body. For about ten seconds there was an uncanny quiet then suddenly there were people running and screaming down the stairs. There was confusion and bedlam all around them and Ramon automatically reached out painfully and took Camille's hand. He looked at her and his heart sank. There was blood running down her face from her head and her arm looked twisted beneath her. He tried to gently move her closer to him, wanting to protect her but feeling helpless. He slowly brought his other arm up to her head to protect her and someone stepped on it and fell and he just lay back still holding her hand, as if it were glued to his and not letting go.

It seemed like a nightmare. He did not know how long they lay there; was it a few minutes, was it five minutes? Suddenly someone bent down and spoke to him.

"Signor, please, do not move her." The voice spoke softly and kindly. Ramon looked up and a police officer was kneeling down beside them, his hand on Ramon's shoulder.

"Do not worry," he said, "I will stay here until the ambulance arrives. You are both injured, try not to move."

It seemed like a miracle; someone must have been praying over them. The people running down the stairs were hysterical and would surely have trampled all over them but the officer was shielding them with his body and was soon joined by another police officer. Ramon was fighting to keep his eyes open as he did not want to lose sight of his Camille. He could not even think of revenge—that would come later. Right now, it was only Camille on his mind and he continued to hold her hand tightly. He must protect her, he promised Roberto and he promised himself. All he could do was pray and hold tightly.

He seemed to drift off then heard voices. "He is strong, he will not let go of her." He opened his eyes and saw the medics standing beside him. One of them knelt down and said "Signor, please, we must put the Signora on the stretcher, you must let go." Ramon looked at him, he had no intention of letting go of Camille and he tightened his grip. The police officer who had found them bent over Ramon. "Signor, I understand how you feel but she must get to the hospital and you also. You are both injured and you are not helping her like this, please, per favore."

"Por favor, llame a un medico," said Ramon hoarsely.

"But I am a doctor, please release her," said the frustrated doctor. It was of no use. He took out a needle and looked at Ramon.

"What you doing?" said Ramon looking angry.
"Le faroun iniezione," he said. "It is okay Signor, just an injection," said the police officer. It took four men to hold Ramon down and give him the injection. They had to pry his hand loose from Camille and shook their heads.

"She must be very special to him," said the police officer and they all agreed.

Chapter Twenty-Six

Ramon awoke in a hospital bed and immediately looked around for Camille. He felt the anger well up inside him and pulled the intravenous off his arm and sat up. A nurse walked in and tried to talk to him but he only shook his head, glared at her and kept asking for Camille. The nurse left quickly and came back with a doctor. He had heard from the others what had happened and told Ramon he would take him to her if he would cooperate. Ramon agreed and they brought in a wheelchair and took him to Camille's room.

When Ramon saw her he tried to stand up but was too dizzy and the doctor moved the wheelchair as close as possible to Camille's bed. Ramon reached for her hand and once again the helpless feeling came over him and he did not like it. She laid motionless, eyes closed and Ramon turned to the doctor with questioning eyes.

"Do not worry Signor, she will be all right. She has a concussion and a broken arm. There are a number of bruises on her legs when she hit the stairs and trample marks on her arms. You have them also. It is a miracle her injuries are not more serious considering the number of frantic people that ran down the stairs, like a stampede. I understand a police officer saved you both or the injuries would have been much worse. We don't know the full extent of your injuries as no x-rays have been taken as yet."

"The police officer, you know his name?" asked Ramon. He remembered the officer that came to their rescue.

"Si," said the doctor," he has made out a report and his name is on it. I can get it for you. But first I would like to hook you up again to the intravenous now that you know the Signora is going to be okay. You must get treatment, you are injured you know."

Ramon shook his head "No, no, cannot leave her, you not understand, I must take care of her," he said. "I stay, when she opens eyes then I promise I do as you say. What your name?"

"I am Dr. Agostini and I will be with you and the Signora most of the time." The doctor admired Ramon, he had never witnessed such devotion and knew that he was suffering with a great deal of pain but Ramon was no ordinary man. He had dealt with pain much worse, much more agonizing during his lifetime. He had been close to death and had refused to die and he was suffering through a forbidden love, a secret love surrounded by storm clouds, frightening, harmful, and so very dangerous. No one would ever know except himself and the pain. Sometimes there was no logic to life or just to live, only to exist.

The doctor looked at Ramon. He had asked him a question but Ramon seemed to be far away. The doctor decided that they would wait for a short time and let Ramon stay a while with Camille.

News traveled fast and Roberto, Shane and Andre boarded the next flight to Italy taking Lorenzo and Samouil with them. They arrived at the hospital and were ushered into Camille's room where they found a haggard-looking Ramon by her bedside holding her hand. Camille had awakened earlier and Ramon was very relieved.

"Ramon," said Roberto, "Dr. Agostini tells me that you have been refusing treatment. You can see for yourself Camille is going to be fine."

The doctor stood beside Roberto. "He will not admit it but we know he is in great pain. He frightened away the last nurse who tried to give him a needle. Talk to him, try to convince him."

Andre had heard the conversation and walked over to them. "Ramon, how are you going to look after Camille if you yourself are not well? They want to take some x-rays; we will go together. Roberto and Shane will stay with Camille and also Lorenzo will stay. We will take Samouil with us—what do you say my fearless friend, or should I now call you valeroso?"

Ramon kissed Camille's hand and tried to stand up but was weak and dizzy. He consented to being wheeled out by Andre as they followed the doctor.

"Samouil," said Ramon as they followed the doctor to the x-ray Department, "what we know about bomb?" Samouil looked at Andre. "You look at me, not Andre," said Ramon with anger. "You know something, talk, and look at me when you talk."

Ramon stood up and had to be lifted to the x-ray table. He was very unhappy and did not like the feeling of being helpless and he had a sudden desire to pick up the table and throw it but he knew that it would not go over too well and besides, it was nailed to the floor. He grimaced in pain and was losing the little patience he had left as Dr. Agostini approached.

"Ramon, let me give you an injection, just for the pain, a relaxer, it will not knock you out."

Ramon shook his head, "no needle, I relax, must know something. Samouil, tell me or no x-ray."

Samouil shook his head, "Ramon, they say you and Camille are lucky to be alive, we will know something soon."

"Soon no good," said Ramon, "NOW." The last word was shouted. Ramon's eyes glared at the nurse as she tried to position him and the scar on his face was very noticeable. The nurse stepped back and looked at Andre and Samouil with frightened eyes. Samouil gave another sigh and walked over to the table and looked down at Ramon.

"Everyone on the eighteenth floor of that hotel was killed instantly and over 250 people injured, some quite badly on the floor above and the floor below. This is a big thing Ramon. It has become a very big criminal investigation by not just the police but the Italian Government has become involved in the search. It is too big for Da Elegido."

"Not too big for Ramon," said an angry Ramon.

"Everyone agrees that the bomb was targeted for you and Camille and the Italian police are waiting to question both of you."

"How they know bomb meant for us? I not talk to anyone."

"Ramon, everyone on your floor was killed and you and Camille were the only ones found alive on the stairs."

Ramon's eyes were wide open. He did not say anything else and allowed the x-rays to be taken without any more fuss. When they left the laboratory, two heavily armed policemen were waiting in the hall and they followed them back to Ramon's room. He was once again hooked up to the I.V. and wondered how long he could just lie there and wait.

The next day Ramon was feeling better and was allowed to go to Camille's room. He was able to move around without the wheelchair and he stayed with Camille and helped her eat breakfast. When they came to take her for another x-ray one of the technicians turned to Ramon and said "do not worry, she will be all right." Ramon looked at him and said "why would I worry?" and the technician hesitated and looked uncomfortable. "Okay, come with us," he said and Ramon followed with Samouil close behind.

The staff at the hospital was beginning to be familiar with Ramon's ways and it was decided that they would all be better off to humour him.

Ramon sat on Camille's bed and held her hand as usual. It seemed almost as if something would happen to her if he let go. It was nothing new, he always held her hand when she was a child and he took her to school while he held his machine gun with the other hand.

"I think the police want to question the both of you today" said Roberto.

"They not have to question Camille," said Ramon, "I not let them."

"There's nothing you can do about it Ramon, they want to help us."

"We'll see," he said then turned to Camille. "Your locket, where is your locket Camille?"

"They took it off me when they brought me in. Open the drawer Ramon, the little table over there" and she pointed to the table. Ramon opened the drawer and took out a box. Inside was her locket and other jewellery she had worn and Ramon took out the locket and handed it to her.

"You open it Ramon, my arm," she said pointing to the cast and Ramon opened it and handed it to her. She read the inscription inside:

> To My Camille
> Only You
> Can Make Me Smile
> Ramon

She looked at Ramon with tears in her beautiful eyes.

"No more tears my Camille," he said putting his arms around her, "now only happiness."

Dr. Agostini walked in at that moment. "I have good news Ramon, the police officer that helped you and Camille will be here in a few moments. He wanted to make sure you were both okay."

Ramon turned to the others, "This person saved our life. We be trampled if he not cover us with body. He is true hero."

"I can't imagine how awful it must have been for you and Camille," said Shane looking very upset. "You were both so helpless and by some miracle this person appeared."

"You said he arrived first on the scene, Ramon?" said Roberto.

"Si, then later I see medic and more police, but people running and falling down stairs when we just lying there," said Ramon shaking his head. "Who does something like this? So many people die."

Just then the young police officer entered the room and looked around smiling. "I am happy to see everyone is okay. My name is Dellini."

Ramon stepped forward and grasped his hand. "Gracias from bottom of my heart. This is Camille, my wife," and the young man bowed and shook her hand.

"You saved our lives, thank you," said Camille with a smile. Ramon went about introducing him to everyone in the room and he shook hands and bowed each time.

"Dellini, I presume this is your surname," said Roberto.

"Si, my first name is Israel but my friends call me Izzy."

Ramon suddenly dropped the glass of water he was holding and it shattered on the floor. All eyes turned to him as he stood there and stared at the officer.

"Ramon, are you all right?" asked Andre with concern. Ramon continued to stare at the young man then spoke; "that is a Jewish name."

"Si," said the officer looking at Ramon curiously.

"But you are not a Jew," said Ramon. It was like a statement.

"No Signor, I am Italian, both my parents are Italian. I was named after my father's closest friend, his name was Israel."

"That was my papa's name," said Ramon quietly.

"My father spoke of him often. They fought together in a war many years ago, he was his best friend. I still remember my father saying he was the bravest, most loyal person with so much integrity and strength like you could not imagine. He said he had a heart like no one else he knew, very kind and absolutely fearless, afraid of nothing."

The room became suddenly quiet. Roberto looked at Ramon who just stood there and Shane looked at the officer, then at Ramon. Camille was looking at Ramon with a worried expression on her face. Finally Roberto spoke. "Izzy, did you by chance know the surname of your papa's friend?"

"Si Signor, I remember it well, my father always talked about him. He would say that he wasn't a tall man, medium height and had many medals for bravery. My father always referred to him as the little king. His last name was Rubenstein, Israel Rubenstein and he had a middle name, let me see if I remember, um, si, it was Ramon."

"Good Lord," said Andre and everyone looked again at Ramon. Ramon had failed to mention his own name when he introduced everyone to Izzy. The officer looked around in bewilderment as Ramon stood very still. Samouil put his hand on Ramon's shoulder—he knew Ramon was traumatized at that very moment and was fighting within himself to keep control of his emotions. Finally he spoke. "That was my papa, you named after my papa. I am his son, Ramon."

The officer stared in amazement, the room was quiet and the sound of a cart being wheeled down the hallway could be heard. "Scusi?" said the officer looking at Ramon in amazement.

"You named after my papa," repeated Ramon, his eyes lighting up. The officer stepped towards Ramon and put out his hand and suddenly they embraced.

"Holy Mother of God," said the policeman, "this is a miracle, you are like my brother, my father must meet you." Ramon did not resist and he looked up. His face was wet with tears.

"You give me new life but you kill my image," he said to the surprised officer.

"Scusi?" he said.

"I suppose to be tough, rough, you know, mean, scary bodyguard. Now I scare nobody, I become second-hand bodyguard, but not your fault, I work on it. I am honoured to know you."

"Ramon, do not worry," said Roberto, "soon you'll be back to scaring us all again, isn't that right Camille?"

"Ramon is really a kitten," said Camille smiling lovingly at her husband.

"This not good," said Ramon, "getting worse."

"It's okay Ramon, we won't tell anyone," said Lorenzo, then added, "unless we have to."

"This is amazing," said the officer. "Out of thousands of law enforcers in the City of Rome, I just happened to be the first to reach the hotel. People were running down the stairs but something seemed to tell me to keep going up so I put my back to the wall and slowly pushed against the crowd going the opposite way. I'm glad I did, Ramon, there was quite a bit of hysteria happening at that moment."

"This calls for a very special celebration," said Roberto, "this moment of happiness means so much not just to Ramon but to all of us." He went up to the young man and they embraced.

"Our President Juan Gomez is giving a special party in honour of our newly-weds and also the fact that their lives have been spared. You are a crucial part of that happening, Izzy. You must come and celebrate with us on that day."

"You come to party, si?" said Ramon eagerly, "you bring wife or girlfriend, maman, papa, you come."

Izzy laughed, "I cannot bring wife or girlfriend, I know what you mean. I have no wife or girlfriend, grazi, but I would like to come, just let me know when. That was not a very good honeymoon Ramon, I am sorry and I apologize on behalf of my Country. We will do our best to find out who is responsible and the guilty party will be punished, you can be sure."

"There is the big question now, not just who but why," said Roberto. "Why would anyone want to do this to Camille and yourself Ramon? So many questions. I believe the police will be asking them soon."

"Scusi Signor, I think I recognize you," said Izzy turning to Roberto. "Are you not Comandante Castaneda of the Dominican Republic?"

"Si, you have a sharp eye young man," said Roberto.

"There has been a great deal of news in our papers recently about the Dominican and your name is always mentioned, quite a few pictures too."

"Pictures?" said Roberto, "why would my picture be shown in the papers recently?"

"I can get the papers for you. And then," he continued turning to Lorenzo and Samouil, "if I am not wrong, I think you belong to the famous Da Elegido, am I right? We know all about you, you are well-known here."

"Si, Ramon, the one with tears in his eyes, he is our profesorado," said Lorenzo smiling.

"Profesorado thinks Lorenzo need more unorthodox disciplinary training when we get back, Samouil, you too," said Ramon.

"I did not say anything Ramon, why punish me?" said Samouil.

"Why you think this is punishment? This good for you, keep you on toe, besides, my image come back, you know, mean, tough. Izzy," he said turning to the officer, "you like to join Da Elegido? I go easy on you, already you have police training, is dangerous but we have fun, just ask Lorenzo and Samouil."

"Si, all kinds of fun," said Lorenzo and Samouil nodded, "si, Ramon is right, we are a ton of fun."

"Grazi Ramon, I admire Da Elegido, everyone does, but my home is here, my family is here but … maybe, I'll see, grazi."

Their stay at the hospital lasted a week and during that time both Camille and Ramon were thoroughly interrogated by the Italian police. Before leaving the hospital Shane and Roberto bought clothes for Camille and Ramon. They had lost everything except what they were wearing when they had fled down the stairs but they thanked God that the two of them had been spared, clothing could be replaced.

The Castanedas and the Rubensteins left on a Saturday morning. They were a very impressive looking group as they left the hospital accompanied by their bodyguards and some of the doctors and nurses had gathered at the front of the building to see them off. A limousine took them to the airport and they boarded the plane and stayed close to each other suddenly feeling the enormity of the horrendous attack. Did it really happen, did all those people die?

Ramon sat beside Camille who was sound asleep, arm in a cast and her head bandaged. Ramon held her other hand and wondered why it had happened, why he had not been able to protect her, his wife.

He looked down at her and he saw a little girl and he blinked his eyes and it was little Camille. He drew in a deep breath and looked at Samouil who was sitting across from him, looking at him. Shane, Roberto and Andre were sitting directly across the aisle with Lorenzo.

"You try to read my mind?" said Ramon when Samouil continued to stare. Samouil kept looking and said, "I don't have to try Ramon, it is a gift."

"A gift?" said Ramon, "good, then I don't have to tell you what I think right now; read my mind."

Samouil did not hesitate. "Tomorrow morning at 7:00, unorthodox disciplinary training, empty stomach." Ramon stared at Samouil then leaned his head against the seat and closed his eyes, "make that survival training."

Chapter Twenty-Seven

Lorenzo and Samouil were becoming like part of the family and this is exactly what Roberto wanted, people around them who were trustworthy and loyal. They arrived back home and Ramon and Camille stayed at the Villa. It was decided that their honeymoon would have to wait and all everyone wanted was to just rest and forget about what had just happened. It was not easy to forget and Ramon was ready for revenge and he wanted it fast. Also the police had suggested that the newlyweds stay close to the Villa during the ongoing investigation because there was a real possibility that they were still in danger. Whoever or whomever was responsible for the attack probably knew by now that it had been unsuccessful and the responsible party might stop at nothing. During all this a telegram had arrived from Terry and some of the gloom seemed to lift as Camille read it out loud.

"Congratulations to my precious sobrina Camille and precious sobrino Ramon on your wedding. Heard your honeymoon hotel lit up the night you stayed there and actually exploded. Ramon, is this part of your unorthodox training? Tsk, Tsk. Seriously, glad you're both okay, God forbid, could have been tragic. Wishing the two of you a lifetime of good health and happiness. Love to the Castanedas and Dalingers and hola to my friends Lorenzo, Agnes, Diego. Passionate kisses to my ravishing Rosita (marry me?). And if I missed anyone, love to them also. Must go, bombs are dropping, Agnes, you'd love it here. Regards, love and anything else you're ready for, Tio Terry.

Ramon tried not to smile but could not help himself. Camille laughed loudly. "Who is Agnes?" she asked.

"That's me," said Samouil shaking his head, "you know, Agallas?" Lorenzo laughed, "don't laugh," said Samouil, "I understand he is looking for nicknames for you and Diego."

"I do not mind at all—Agnes," said Lorenzo and laughed again.

Roberto sat with his arms folded. "I'm so glad the two of you will be okay and we can actually laugh," he said looking at Ramon and Camille.

"I miss Terry," said Shane, "we really need him here. How much longer will he be in Iraq?"

"I believe he has another five or six months," said Andre. "I always pray over him—he is living in danger."

"It's sad to say Andre, but so are we," said Roberto.

"Roberto, can I see you in Library?" asked Ramon.

Roberto looked at Ramon, "sure, can you excuse us please," he said to the others and he went inside, closing the door behind Ramon.

"What is it Ramon, you look serious."

"Si, I am serious Roberto, I get to point," he said sitting down. "You know and I know Ricardo set bomb, I am sure."

Roberto heaved a sigh and sat on the edge of the table. "It did enter my mind Ramon but I didn't want to even think that. However, I don't know of anyone else that would want to do a thing like that to you and Camille. He was pretty upset when he found out about the engagement."

"Do not worry, I find him," said Ramon, "I know what to do."

"Ramon, we don't know for sure, we should just leave it in the capable hands of the Italian police. They are doing the investigation and they will know how to handle this."

Ramon shook his head and stood up. "No Roberto, I do this myself. They almost kill my Camille—I get revenge, do not worry, tomorrow I go."

"You go where, Ramon? We don't know anything yet except twenty-three people were killed in that blast. Do you think the Italian government will let the person or persons responsible get away? Besides, you should be with Camille. She was terribly shaken up by this and she's trying not to show it but I know my daughter and so should you. She needs you now Ramon, stay by her side."

"Samouil and Lorenzo stay with her, I take Diego with me," said Ramon. "I need venganza."

"Right now, you need Camille and she needs you," said Roberto. He stopped suddenly looking puzzled, "You take Diego? Why Diego?"

"Diego from Barcelona, we go to Spain," said Ramon going towards the door. "Do not worry Roberto, soon be over."

Roberto sat looking at the door after Ramon left. He had to find a way to stop him but how?

Ramon had gone upstairs to their room but Camille was not there. Quickly he ran down the stairs and outside wondering if she was on the beach but was beginning to panic. He started to run down the path and suddenly saw her at the large table with Shane and Andre. He was breathless when he reached her having not fully recovered from his injuries but he didn't care.

"Camille, you all right? How you get down those stairs?"

"Tio Andre carried me down," she said with a laugh, "although I told him I was perfectly capable of taking the stairs myself."

"Gracias Andre," said Ramon sitting down next to her. "You have towel around head, you take shower?" he asked.

"Maman washed my hair Ramon; I'm not supposed to get this cast wet."

Ramon removed the towel and commenced to dry Camille's hair gently. "I neglecting my wife, forgive me my Camille."

"I don't think you are neglecting Camille at all," said Shane. "We all help each other all the time."

"Now that's what I like to see," said Andre, "I cannot imagine someone like you Ramon neglecting someone like our Mantecado."

"Gracias Andre," said Ramon, "however, tomorrow I go away." He looked at Camille as she looked up quickly. "Forgive me, I not be gone long," he said pushing back her hair off her face, "we back soon".

"Why Ramon, what has happened?" said Camille with a worried expression, "where are you going?"

Ramon shook his head, "Roberto knows, trust me, do not worry," he said.

Andre stood up and excused himself. He had a bad feeling about something and went into the Villa to look for Roberto. He found him in the library staring into space, tapping a pencil on the desk, deep in thought.

"Roberto, what is happening, where is Ramon off to?" he asked sitting at the desk.

Roberto's face had a worried expression on it. "Andre, I don't know what to do, Ramon is determined that the bomb incident has something to do with Ricardo, and maybe it does. This is too dangerous Andre and I have a bad feeling here. I don't want to risk losing a member of my family and Ramon can be hotheaded. He wants to take matters into his own hands and I've seen that happen before—it's not a pretty picture."

"Roberto, do you actually believe that Ricardo would be capable of something like this? How well did you know the young man?" said Andre trying to fathom the possibility of the situation being so close to home.

Roberto was looking straight ahead, still deep in thought. He turned to Andre and said "I remember asking the boys a question last year, before all of this had come about, and the answers they gave me were most interesting."

"Answers to what?" said Andre still feeling the gloom that had come over him ten minutes ago.

"I asked them separately to give me their honest opinion on bullfighting," said Roberto.

Andre looked surprised, "bullfighting?"

"Si," said Roberto. "Now listen closely to what I am about to say. Enrique said 'Papa, it is cruel and inhuman and should be banned'. Frederik said, 'It is a form of entertainment, should be allowed but do not kill the bull'. Roberto stopped and looked at Andre, "do you follow me so far, my brother?" "Andre nodded, "And what did Ricardo say?"

"He said, 'It is a form of cruelty. I am against cruelty to animals, but humans, that is different'. I asked him what he meant and he said, 'If someone hurts an innocent person, they should be taught a lesson'. I said Ricardo, what do you mean by a lesson and he did not hesitate. He said 'kill, Senor, I would have no difficulty at all in killing someone like that'." Roberto paused then continued, "It's not what he said Andre, although that is bad enough, it's the way he said it. It was chilling and cruel."

Andre was quiet and the sound of the clock seemed loud as it ticked away in the silence. It's odd thought Roberto, he had never noticed the sound before. He looked up at Andre.

"How are we going to convince Ramon to stay out of it while the police do their investigation? Can you help me Andre?" There was a knock at the door and Roberto looked up. "Entrar," he said and Rosita looked in.

"Please excuse interruption Roberto, Andre. Ricardo just phoned now and left message for you Roberto. Did not want to talk, just to tell you he is on his way here to see you, that is all he said."

Roberto looked at Andre then back at Rosita. "Gracias Rosita, that is fine."

After Rosita left Roberto turned to Andre. "Well, that answers our question my brother, now there is no need to convince Ramon not to go but now what?"

"Do you think he is coming armed?" said Andre. "If he is capable of being responsible for what happened in Italy, he would certainly be capable of anything else."

Roberto stood up. "We don't know when he is arriving and with whom if anyone. I don't even want to think like this Andre, we are sentencing the boy before we have proof. I still don't believe he would harm us but I must go outside and alert the guards at the gate. He turned and looked at Andre, "good Lord Andre, I cannot believe this. What is happening? I treated him like my own son—was he that serious about Camille?"

"That's what it's beginning to look like, come on, I'll go with you," said Andre.

"I want everyone out of the Villa except Ricardo and myself," said Roberto.

"I will stay here also," said Andre.

"No, those are my orders Andre," and Roberto's eyes looked stormy. "Take Shane and go out to the beach, please." Andre looked at Roberto for just a moment then reluctantly turned away. The Villa was deserted except for Roberto and Ramon who refused to leave. Roberto knew that Ramon was angry and nothing would make him leave.

Ricardo arrived alone and Roberto met him at the door. They went into the library and sat down while Roberto looked around. Good, he thought, Ramon was nowhere to be seen.

"You and Senora Shane are well I trust?" asked Ricardo politely.

"Si, gracias Ricardo," said Roberto. "You have come here with something on your mind?"

Ricardo hesitated looking at the floor, then he looked up. "I don't want you to think that I am ungrateful to you or the Senora for what you have done for me. I will always treasure the nine years you have given me as part of your family." He hesitated then continued, "I want you to know that I hold nothing against you or Senora Shane. However," and he paused again, "Camille has broken my heart and I cannot leave until I have spoken to her."

"What can you say to Camille, Ricardo, she is already married. Please do not hold a grudge."

Ricardo had turned his eyes towards the window and seemed to be looking at something far away. His next words caused Roberto to shudder.

"I have changed my mind," said Ricardo in a calm voice, "Camille can live but she is about to become a widow and she will marry me. I know this is also your wish Senor, for Camille and me to marry."

Roberto was shocked. "You do not know what you are saying," said Roberto, "do not talk foolishly."

"I know exactly what I am saying," said Ricardo in a steady voice. "At first I had wanted them both to die but they escaped." He turned and looked at Roberto. "I did not plan for those innocent people to become victims but it happened. Camille can live but Ramon must die. It is because of him that this happened; it is not too late for Camille and myself. Please forgive me, all I ever wanted was Camille and this family."

The library door opened and Ramon stepped inside. "Get out Ramon," shouted Roberto just as Ricardo produced a small handgun and pointed it at Ramon. A shot rang out and Ricardo fell to the ground. Roberto carefully placed his gun on the desk and just stood there. Ramon knelt down and looked at Ricardo as Roberto walked over and stood beside them looking down.

"He is dead Roberto, he not kill anymore," said Ramon standing up. "Gracias, you save my life. I never forget this."

Roberto was looking down at Ricardo and he almost seemed too calm. "I killed him Ramon, I could have wounded him but instead I purposely killed him. I aimed at his heart." He turned to Ramon, "I couldn't take a chance, he wanted to kill you and I couldn't let that happen, I had to stop him." Roberto knelt and put his hand over Ricardo's chest. Blood was spurting out of him and onto Roberto's hand.

"What you doing?" cried out Ramon pulling away Roberto's hand.

"Stay out of this Ramon, I've taken his life and I must carry the penalty of his blood on my hands forever as a reminder."

"Reminder for what? You save my life, why you torture yourself?" said Ramon frantically.

"I know," said Roberto calmly, "and I am glad I did but I have taken his and I must pay the price in the eyes of the almighty God." There had been something very sad in Ricardo's last words that Roberto would always carry with him.

"God not want price," screamed Ramon, "don't make me hit you, I not want to hurt you, stop torture, stop it." By now Ramon was screaming and he had put his arm under Roberto's neck pulling him up forcefully but not before Roberto's hands were covered in blood. Lorenzo and Samouil had burst into the room and had taken Roberto outside. Gendarmes were running into the Villa and pandemonium had broken out. Diego had taken Shane, Camille and Rosita outside and when Roberto appeared Shane ran to him sobbing as she clasped him to her.

"He is okay," said Lorenzo, "he is not injured." It was true, Roberto was not injured physically but now he had to deal with the pain that would lay hidden within him, the mental pain. He could feel it resurfacing and wondered why he could not handle the death of a terrorist. He handled fierce fighting in the mountains as a guerrilla leader years ago, why not this? Deep inside he knew why he was punishing himself—he could see before his eyes Beatriz, Damien, Leandro, Jodi-Anne and now, it was Ricardo. These were all individuals that had meant something to him, that he had loved in his own way but must now pay the penalty.

Andre suddenly appeared and went to Roberto's side. He knelt down and spoke to Roberto softly. The others did not hear what was said but gradually Roberto lifted his head and nodded. He stood up and went inside with Shane. They went upstairs and Roberto showered and changed his clothes. He was calm and quiet.

The police arrived and the guns were taken away for inspection and President Juan Gomez made an unexpected gesture. He sent his own personal limousine to pick up Shane and Roberto so that they could stay at one of his homes. The interrogation had not been lengthy and the police knew where Roberto would be during the next couple of weeks if needed. Ramon refused to leave Roberto's side and he and Camille also went along.

Shane, along with Andre, gave orders to completely change the library. They wanted it changed over and renovated by the time they returned. Too many bad memories were connected to that room and Rosita was happy that it was being done. Lorena and her mother, Sarah Davies stayed close to Rosita and helped with the kitchen.

The Italian police were relieved that the bombing massacre had been solved and Izzy had sent a telegram to Roberto which read: "God be with you at this time. There was no other choice, you saved Ramon. You took away Ricardo's pain and possibly prevented further bloodshed and heartbreak. God save you and your loved ones. Izzy."

Roberto handed the telegram to Ramon. Ramon read it and commented, "he make good Da Elegido, si Roberto?"

"Si," said Roberto.

Chapter Twenty-Eight

President Gomez's home was in an isolated area in Dajabon. The size of a small mansion, it was an elegant six bedroom home surrounded by trees and military guards in a very wooded area. Peaceful and quiet, it proved to be exactly what they needed and Roberto proceeded to heal in mind and spirit. Ramon was glad that he could enjoy time away with Camille and still carry his machine gun and Shane was happy because she had Roberto with her every single day.

"I don't know what I would do without you at my side," he said to Shane as they reclined in the garden chairs outside. "I keep getting this fear, this … this …" He looked at Shane, "I just cannot explain it, my God Shane, I love you so much." Shane bent towards him and kissed him on the lips. "I believe you Roberto, you have finally convinced me."

"Finally?" said Roberto, his eyebrows shooting up, "finally?"

Shane laughed, "Roberto, you are so comical."

"No, not that again," he said starting to look serious. "Don't do that again with me Shane, you will be sorry."

Shane was laughing loudly. "Roberto, I just love this side of you."

Camille and Ramon appeared at that moment. "What is happening here?" commented Ramon, "is funny joke?"

"Si Ramon," said Roberto, "your mother-in-law is making a funny joke. She is making fun of me."

"Mother-in-law," laughed Shane, "oh my goodness, that sounds really funny," and she could not stop laughing. Camille had joined in and both women were having a good laugh as Ramon and Roberto looked at each other.

"This is funny?" said Ramon seriously and Roberto shook his head. "Ramon, these women are laughing at us, what do you say we teach them a lesson?"

Ramon nodded, "I know many ways we get venganza, I teach venganza to Da Elegido, but for women, is different. We must wait."

"Wait, why?" said Roberto, "let's teach them both a lesson now."

Ramon shook his head, "I like that Roberto but my wife has cast on arm, Ramon must be fair, give Camille chance to defend herself, what you think?"

Roberto thought for a moment, both women were whispering and laughing and thoroughly enjoying themselves and in a way, Roberto was beginning to feel great joy inside. This was his family and it felt wonderful to be with them this way. Moments like this were rare.

"Okay Ramon, you are right, we must not be unfair but as soon as the cast comes off Camille's arm, we must meet and plan our revenge."

"Si, venganza Roberto, we get venganza. I take out danger part, we just scare them." Roberto glanced at Ramon quickly. "Do not worry, trust me," said Ramon, "no danger, just fun."

They stayed two weeks at the President's mansion before returning home. Juan was disappointed and had hoped they would stay longer but Roberto was eager to get back and check up on happenings at the Villa.

Ricardo's body had been flown to Argentina at the request of his relatives who had wanted him to be buried there. Ricardo's brother Edouard had contacted Roberto by phone and apologized profusely for everything.

"He is our brother," said Edouard, "and although we know he is responsible for all these terrible things, I hope you will understand Senor Castaneda that my sisters and I love him and we always will."

Roberto said he could but the pain was beginning to emerge and he could not talk too long.

"Will you please accept apologies from myself and Christine and Carmen. Senor, we live in such a sad world, I do not know what to say to you, the Senora, to Camille and her brave husband Ramon, except ... ve con Dios Senor."

"There is no need to apologize Edouard," said Roberto, "you have all been through so much. If there is anything I can do for you or Christine or Carmen please let me know, I mean that."

"There is something, Senor," said Edouard, "but I hesitate to ask."

"Please," said Roberto, "you must tell me and I shall be glad to if I can." Roberto was not prepared for what Edouard asked of him.

"The coroner has released Ricardo's body for burial. Would you please come to Argentina for my brother's funeral? I realize what I am asking of you is preposterous."

Roberto was taken aback. He hesitated for a moment with thoughts racing through his head. Was he capable of attending Ricardo's funeral? Was he mentally strong enough to watch the burial of someone he had looked upon as his son for nine years and whose life he had ended?

"Edouard," "si Senor," came Edouard's voice, "I will be there," said Roberto, "please call or wire me all the particulars."

After Roberto hung up the phone he just stood staring at it for a moment. He would go alone, he would not allow Shane to accompany him and he would leave the next day.

He found Shane sitting under the large umbrella on the beach with Camille and Ramon. When he told them what he was planning to do Shane begged Roberto not to go.

"It could be dangerous Roberto, maybe Ricardo has relatives who do not like you for what has happened," implored Shane. "They will all be at the funeral, don't go, please."

"Do not worry Shane, I have made up my mind and I will be careful but I should be there," said Roberto taking her hand and kissing it. "I feel it would be my responsibility. You are so pale Shane, are you all right?" said Roberto looking at her with concern. Shane nodded, "I just wish you wouldn't go."

"Papa, please listen to maman," said Camille, "I too do not like this, do not go please."

"I know you will go," said Ramon, "and I go too. You not go without me."

"Ramon," implored Camille looking anxiously at him and her father, "please no, the both of you, haven't we all had enough of this? How much more can we take? No Ramon, I forbid you and papa, please don't do this to us."

Shane was crying and Roberto took her into his arms. "Only two days Shane, I cannot and will not stay away from you for more than two days. Samouil and Lorenzo will be here for you and Lorena and her mom, and there is Rosita and Andre. You will not be alone," he said wiping the tears from her face.

Camille looked at Ramon and he said, "you know I not let him go without me Camille, please understand," and he kissed both her hands.

The funeral was private attended by only a small group of people made up of relatives only and everything passed without incident. Edouard and his sisters lived in a large home on the outskirts of Buenos Aires and Roberto and Ramon stayed with them.

Back at the Villa Shane sat in the kitchen with Rosita as they drank coffee. "Do not be so sad," said Rosita, "they will be back tomorrow night."

"I feel awful Rosita," said Shane, "I just do not feel right without Roberto. Too much has happened lately, I just do not feel too good."

"Do you not feel well Shane?" asked Rosita with concern, "can I get you something?"

"No, thank you Rosita, I am okay," said Shane, "I … I just don't feel right. I guess I miss Roberto too much."

Rosita smiled, "you are so close to him my dear, do not worry, he'll be back soon."

Shane gave a sigh. She missed Roberto, he had been gone only two days but something else was wrong. She did not say anything to Rosita but she knew something was not right. When she got up she felt a sharp pain in her shoulder but did not let on to Rosita.

"I am going outside for a few moments Rosita, I'll see you later," she said and left the kitchen. Rosita watched her leave and open the Villa door. Suddenly Shane clutched her side and fell and Rosita ran. She reached the door in time to see Shane lying at the bottom of the steps outside. Rosita's screams brought a number of gendarmes to her side. Samouil and Lorenzo were among the first to arrive with Andre running up from the beach. Shane was quickly whisked to the hospital without regaining consciousness accompanied by Lorenzo, Samouil and Andre. Thinking that Shane had injured herself by falling they were shocked to hear that her condition was critical. The doctor told Andre to contact Roberto immediately and Andre looked at the doctor in amazement.

"Is it that serious doctor? He is returning tomorrow evening."

"Immediately," said the doctor, "and if there are any children, contact them also." Dr. Harrington was new at the hospital. He was from England and specialized in Internal Medicine and one of the best in his field.

Andre felt his heart tighten in his chest. He stared at the doctor just as Skye came by quickly.

"It's okay Andre, I've contacted Frederik and Enrique, they will arrive in the morning." His voice was choked, his eyes were red.

"I don't understand," said Andre, "she fell down the steps, what is wrong with her? Did she hit her head?"

"We are not sure," said Skye, "they are taking her into the operating room now. All we know is that she is hemorrhaging internally and we cannot wait."

Rosita held Camille in her arms while they both cried and Maria was in tears while holding Marc Shai on her knee. Lorena and her mother cried quietly in a corner while Lorenzo and Samouil stood by sadly as they all waited.

Chapter Twenty-Nine

Roberto and Ramon flew back immediately and Diego met them at the airport and drove them quickly to the hospital. Roberto did not talk on the plane. He only knew that Shane was quite ill as they did not want to tell him her condition was critical.

He arrived at the hospital, his face ashen, his eyes heavy, and was immediately taken to Shane's room. He stood by her bed and looked down at her lying so still and pale. She was still unconscious and there was the fear that she would not awaken. The doctor spoke to Roberto but Roberto seemed to be in a daze. He did not hear everything but he did pick up some of the words the doctor was saying. It was an ectopic pregnancy, the tube had burst, the Senora had lost a great deal of blood. Transfusions were imperative, a matter of life or death and they were trying to locate someone with the same blood type. The doctor was asking Roberto questions and nothing was registering.

Ramon took Roberto's arm, "doctor asking if anyone has same blood in family," and Roberto shook his head.

He looked at Ramon, his eyes pleading, "Ramon, tell me she's not dying, tell me Ramon, just tell me." Someone pulled a chair up to the side of the bed and Roberto sat down taking Shane's hand, his eyes never leaving her face. Ramon had never seen Roberto so broken up and he did not know what to say. He too was suffering and found it difficult to talk and refused to believe that she was dying. Shane meant much more to him than anyone realized and he took in a deep breath and bowed his head.

Andre had placed a gold crucifix in Shane's hand and he sat on the opposite side near Shane. The doctor came back into the room and stood beside Roberto.

"Do we have your permission Senor to broadcast on national television for a donor? I am impelled to tell you that the Senora will not last more than twenty-four hours if she does not get a transfusion pronto."

If someone had struck a knife in Roberto's heart it could not have been more painful. Publicity was always shunned in any form where his family was concerned but he welcomed anything that could give them hope. Permission was granted and Shane's picture appeared on national television across the Country. In the meantime Roberto stayed by Shane's side with Andre and Ramon. Samouil and Lorenzo stayed by the door while the others prayed in the Chapel down the hallway.

Throughout the night Roberto did not leave Shane's side and his head would slump over once or twice but he never let go of her hand. Only once he spoke in a whisper; "don't leave me Shane, I cannot possibly live without you" and he bent his head again. No one had noticed that Ramon sat numbly by Shane's bedside and did not move.

It was in the early hours of the morning when the news came that a donor had been found. Frederik and Enrique had arrived during the night and had both kissed their unconscious mother and embraced their father, Andre, Camille and Ramon. Roberto was dry-eyed and weak and all he could do was pray and wonder if he was being punished by an angry God. Shane had received the transfusions and everyone waited. If she opened her eyes during the next 24-48 hours, the doctor said she would live, otherwise …

Frederik and Enrique joined Camille in the Chapel and they prayed together. Light was beginning to filter through the blinds and Roberto looked up.

The sun was just beginning to appear against a background of incredible pink and orange with a glorious hue of purple and violet streaking through and it reminded him of their wedding night years ago as he and Shane looked out at the horizon over the mountains. Andre put his hand on his shoulder and Roberto looked up.

"Come Roberto, let us pray together." He went to the other side of the bed and stood opposite Roberto, both arms outstretched, palms up, and began:

"Our Father, who art in Heaven;"

Roberto had lifted his head and was praying with him;

"Hallowed be thy name, thy Kingdom come,"

Ramon came closer to the bed and bowed his head;

"Thy will be done on Earth as it is in Heaven,"

Roberto repeated the words still in a daze;

"Give us this day our daily bread and forgive us our trespasses, as we forgive those who trespass against us,"

Roberto looked at Shane, his hand still holding hers;
"And lead us not into temptation, but deliver us from evil,"

Lorenzo and Samouil had both laid their machine guns on the ground out of respect to the Lord's Prayer, eyes transfixed on Andre;

"For thine is the Kingdom, the power and the glory,"

Suddenly Andre held up his hand, looked at Roberto and smiled and Roberto stopped and just looked as Andre continued;

"Forever … and ever … and ever …"

Roberto stared at Andre in amazement, his eyes lighting up as he said "Amen" and suddenly Roberto's eyes began to glisten and Andre nodded.

"I remember Roberto, praise be to God I remember everything." Roberto felt a tug on his hand and looked down at Shane. Her eyes had opened and she had tightened her grip on Roberto's hand. The joy that Roberto felt from Andre and now all of a sudden he had his dearly beloved Shane back so overwhelmed him that as he bent down and his lips touched her fingers the tears that were absent throughout the years coursed down his cheeks and fell upon her hand. The pain that he had carried within him for years was gone. He could hear music and thought he was hallucinating as the sounds of "A Love So Beautiful" drifted through the air. Shane's voice was barely a whisper as she spoke.

"They're playing our song, Roberto," and she looked at him and smiled weakly.

Someone down the hall had turned on a radio and the song had drifted softly towards them. Roberto put his face against hers and whispered, "will you do me the honour Senora and dance with your husband—our wedding dance?" Roberto was ecstatic yet he also felt humble in the eyes of God but his joy was complete. He kept both arms around his Shane, his face against hers, reluctant to release her even after the song ended. There wasn't a dry eye in the room and finally Roberto sat back and looked lovingly at Shane, then at Andre. God had given back to him his precious Shane and his brother; it was almost too much for him to bear.

Andre kissed Shane's cheek and hand and embraced Roberto. "I will go to the Chapel now Roberto, then we must talk. I have so much to say, so much to get caught up on" and he left. Ramon went to Shane's side and kissed her cheek and hand. He held her for a moment then kissed her forehead and said "Dios gracias, ve con Dios, God bless you Shane." He embraced Roberto and left the room. Samouil and Lorenzo kissed Shane's cheek and hand, embraced Roberto and said they would wait outside.

They picked up their machine guns and left the room leaving Roberto alone with Shane. He looked down at her and could not stop the tears. She smiled weakly, holding his hand.

"My brave, strong Roberto, you are actually crying."

"Si," said Roberto smiling, "and I do not feel the pain any more my little one, the pain is gone. I can now think of Beatriz, Leandro, Damien, Jodi-Anne and even Ricardo, but it doesn't hurt any more Shane, the pain is gone and now I have you and I'll never let you go."

"You also have Andre, Roberto; your brother has come back to you." Her voice was just a whisper.

"What a special day this is my Shane, I guess God loves me after all."

Shane's life had been saved by an unknown donor and the doctor had entered the room to tell Roberto the person wanted to remain anonymous but Roberto could see him if he went down to the lab quickly. Roberto kissed Shane and promised he would return in a few moments. His happiness had given him a surge of energy and strength and he quickly made his way to the lab with Lorenzo. He entered and approached a nurse behind a desk.

"Was someone here a moment ago," said Roberto, "regarding blood transfusions?"

"Si Senor, he just left," said the nurse. Roberto looked down the hall, it was empty and he went back into the hall and pressed the elevator button. It came up immediately and he and Lorenzo got in quickly and went down to the lobby just as they spotted someone going out the front door.

"Quick Lorenzo, stop him, that must be the person," said Roberto knowing in his condition he would not be able to run as fast as Lorenzo. Almost immediately Lorenzo returned holding the arm of the man ... It was Raphael!

Roberto was shocked and just stood still while Lorenzo held on to his arm as they stood in front of him. Roberto could not talk and just stared at Raphael.

"Hola Roberto," said Raphael.

"Raphael? Is it really you?" said Roberto unbelievingly.

"Si Roberto, how are you?"

"You are the donor that saved Shane's life?" said Roberto incredulously.

"I was glad I could do something Roberto," he said.

"Do something! Do something!? You saved my precious Shane's life, Raphael, you gave her life."

Roberto threw his arms around Raphael. Again the tears flowed and Raphael cried with him. Years of heartbreak, sadness, desolation gave way to forgiveness and new found happiness.

Lorenzo swallowed and tried hard to remember what Ramon always drilled into him—"you must look tough Lorenzo, no crying, no smiling, look mean, like this," and he would make a face. It worked, it stopped the tears but did not stop the smile.

"Come Raphael," said Roberto taking his arm, "you must come up and see Shane, this is a very special day."

"No," said Raphael, "I cannot do that."

"Si, you can Raphael, I will not let you go. Don't you see, your love for Shane has given her back to me, she was dying Raphael, do you not realize how grateful I am, what you have done for me, for Shane, for our children? What can I possibly say or do or ..." Lorenzo gently poked Raphael in the back with his machine gun and Raphael said, "you have convinced me Roberto," and he glanced at Lorenzo.

Roberto took Raphael's arm again as they made their way to the elevator. They entered and as the doors closed Raphael turned to Roberto, "you certainly have your men very well trained Roberto, this one is very convincing."

"Lorenzo? Si, you are right Raphael, he is very well trained. He is a member of Da Elegido but he will not shoot—unless I tell him to. It is so good to see you, ah, here we are, what a surprise this will be for Shane."

"Roberto, we must be careful and not shock her," said Raphael as Roberto held onto his arm tightly as they walked down the hall followed closely by Lorenzo still pointing his gun at Raphael. Samouil looked up suspiciously as they approached Shane's room and he entered with them. Camille, Frederik and Enrique stood around Shane's bed while Ramon stood by the window, arms folded.

"Shane, this is the man who saved your life, it is Raphael," said Roberto proudly. Raphael approached Shane hesitantly and looked at her. He made the sign of the cross, bent and kissed her hand and said in a low voice, "can you ever forgive me Shane?" he said looking at her.

"There is nothing to forgive Raphael, nothing. Thank you for saving my life," she said smiling at him. Lorenzo looked at Roberto, "Is it okay if I put the gun down Roberto?"

"Si Lorenzo, by all means, put the gun down, he is not the enemy. Raphael, this is my daughter Camille, my sons Enrique and Frederik. Raphael is an old family friend, we go back many years and of course you know Ramon." Ramon looked at Raphael and did not say anything. There was an awkward moment in the room and Roberto said

"Raphael, Ramon is now my son-in-law, he is Camille's husband."

Raphael looked at Camille and said "you look so much like your mother," then back at Ramon. "I am happy for you Ramon; you have married into a very fine and honourable family. God bless all of you."

Camille smiled, "thank you Senor Raphael and God be with you always. Thank you for saving my maman's life. We will always be grateful to you and I know I speak for my brothers also."

"Raphael," said Roberto, "you met Lorenzo, and the other bodyguard there by the door is Samouil. Come over here Samouil and let Raphael see you." Samouil stood beside Lorenzo and Roberto said "These two young men, along with Ramon are the best bodyguards in the Country, no, correction, in the world.

Samouil here rides horseback without holding the reins. He has trained himself to do this—his balance is extraordinary."

"Is that possible?" asked Raphael with a surprised expression.

"Anything possible," came Ramon's voice from the window, "some things take time but, anything possible."

Raphael nodded, "si, I will remember that Ramon, gracias."

Shane was able to leave the hospital after two weeks. Raphael stayed a few days at the Villa after that at Roberto's insistence and promised to return again. He was surprised and overjoyed when he met Andre and they all agreed that miracles did exist and especially in the Castaneda family. There were more tears as he embraced Rosita, then Roberto and Shane when he was leaving.

"You must keep in touch," said Roberto. "I will know how to find you if you do not."

"Si Roberto, I will," said Raphael. As he turned to leave Ramon suddenly stood before him. He looked at Raphael for a moment with dark flashing eyes. He slowly approached and everyone held their breath. He put out his hand and Raphael took it while a sigh of relief could be heard all around. Suddenly Ramon pulled Raphael to him and held him in a tight embrace. Raphael's mouth dropped open, his eyes surprised.

"I have learned forgive and forget, Raphael. You right, this is very good family, they teach me well." Then he added in a whisper, "gracias, you save Shane's life, gracias."

Andre bowed his head and said, "and now we heal."

Later, after Raphael left everyone gathered outside under the large umbrella. Camille sat close to Ramon and whispered, "I am so proud of you Ramon, you conducted yourself like a perfect gentleman. I always knew you were, now everyone else does too."

"Shh, not too loud my Camille," said Ramon, "I not want them to hear. I must keep image, tough and mean, si?"

"Oh yes, Ramon, very mean," said Camille with a straight face.

Ramon looked at her, "I not scare you any more my Camille?" Camille laughed, "any more? Ramon, you never frightened me, even before we married, why would I be afraid of you now? You are beginning to sound like my papa when he talks to maman. Oh Ramon, you do not frighten me at all, and I love you so much," she said kissing his cheek.

Ramon frowned, "then my Camille, I must skip lesson number two and we go to lesson number three. This we call Drastic Lesson."

Camille looked at Ramon as he took her hand and brought it up to his lips. "And suppose Ramon I do not want to skip lesson number two?" she said with a teasing smile.

"You trust me my Camille, you not need lesson number two, trust me," he said kissing her forehead, "better we skip one lesson—Ramon put you in advance class."

Chapter Thirty

Shane's recovery was quick under Roberto's loving care. He hovered over her and was teased constantly by everyone but he did not mind. He had his Shane and that meant everything to him. As soon as Shane's doctor gave his permission, Roberto and Shane would go riding together, early in the morning, carrying a lunch packed by Rosita. Off they would go just as the sun was coming up and as they rode along the white sands, Roberto would look lovingly at Shane.

The early morning breeze blew through her hair and her eyes sparkled and shone. Her incredible skin glowed in the early morning light and she wore a white riding outfit that Roberto had bought for her. A gardenia was pinned to her top and as she turned and smiled at him he was suddenly smitten with the woman beside him. He leaned over and held the reins stopping her horse as she looked at him questionably. Roberto dismounted and slowly lifted Shane and held her.

"Do you have any idea Senora what you do to my heart when you look at me like that?" he said carrying her towards a cluster of palm trees. He laid her gently on the ground and kissed her then took the gardenia off her top and pinned it in her hair. "I love you Shane," he said looking into her eyes, "I love you so much that sometimes I think … I think …" He stopped and sighed as he lay beside her, his arm around her and he touched her face tenderly. "I sometimes wish I didn't love you so much my darling, too much of anything is not good. You have put a hold on me Shane, something comes over me when I look at you and I have this sudden desire to kidnap you again and take you away from all this, just you and me my darling. Am I beginning to sound strange, I hope I am not frightening you—do you believe me when I say that I love you so very very much?"

Shane looked at him tenderly, her hand caressed his cheek and her fingers ran across his lips. He kissed her fingers and she put her arms around his neck. "Of course I believe you Roberto, you've told me so many times and I love to hear you say it. Now let me tell you something Roberto. I loved you when we got married years ago but today the love I feel for you is timeless, never ending, eternal, it has no beginning or end." She then kissed him gently and Roberto just looked at her, his eyes stayed open.

"What is it Roberto," she said, "why are you looking at me like that?"

Roberto kept looking at her, then he said "you did it again, Shane, this power that you have over me, I don't know what it is, I can't think clearly when you do that." He stood up quickly, "what do you say we have some breakfast Shane and then I might be better company. Some coffee might help me to fight off this obsession I have with you."

"Okay Roberto," she said as he walked towards the horses, "but then, it might make it worse." He turned around and suddenly looked at her and she smiled at him. He kept looking then said quietly, "Shane, are we going to have breakfast or aren't we?"

Shane looked down, "I'm sorry Roberto, I promise to behave."

Roberto untied the picnic basket from his saddle that Rosita had packed and returned to sit beside Shane. He spread out the cloth and unpacked the basket. "This is exactly what I like Shane, the sun, the ocean, the breeze," and he looked at her, "and you all to myself."

Shane laughed, "Roberto, you know you will always have me all to yourself no matter where we are, but let's think seriously about something."

"This is not serious?" he said with a twinkle in his eye.

"President Gomez is giving a party" she continued, "do you remember he had mentioned this when Ramon and Camille were married? He called the other day and I spoke with him."

Roberto looked up, "no one told me he had called, why was I not advised?"

"You were sleeping," said Shane with a smile, "and he did not want you disturbed. He wanted to know how I was and if two weeks this Saturday sounded all right, and for me to ask you and now I am asking you, my husband."

Roberto handed Shane a sandwich and set out the coffee. "Your husband says this sounds great. What a celebration this will be Shane, we must all attend. What is the latest on Terry, is he still in the Middle East?"

"Good news on Terry," said Shane. "Ramon heard from him and he is arriving next Monday."

"Ramon heard from him? said Roberto with surprise, "all of a sudden his affection for Ramon and Camille has come before us?"

"I guess so," laughed Shane, "I think Terry was impressed and acquired a new respect for Ramon since taking part in his training manoeuvers. Maybe he's thinking of joining Da Elegido."

"I'd really like to see that," said Roberto laughing, "remind me to mention it to Ramon when we get back."

Roberto did mention it to Ramon when they returned and Ramon said he would be glad to put Terry into the next unorthodox training session. "Will make him glad he is alive" was his comment. "Make him strong man."

The day of the big party arrived. Shane and Roberto arrived late with Ramon and Camille. Ramon had been unable to find some important papers and they had been held up but were finally on their way. The Presidential Palace was brightly lit up and they could hear music. They rushed to the door and entered. Suddenly the music stopped and everyone called out "SURPRISE!" It was a surprise wedding anniversary for Roberto and Shane—20 years. Roberto and Shane stood stunned as everyone crowded around them with congratulations.

Juan Gomez and Isabella led the way while Camille and Ramon stood proudly beside them. They were followed by Enrique, Frederik, Skye, Maria, Marc Shai, Andre, Terry, yes, Terry made it in time, Rosita, Lorena, her mom Sara Davies, Lorenzo, Samouil, Diego, Shane's mom and dad Jim and Harriet Dalinger, numerous gendarmes that had stayed near the Villa for years, Izzy the Italian police officer with his father Gino Dellini, and countless other close friends of Roberto and Shane. Then the music started up again and they were playing Roberto and Shane's wedding song. Roberto looked at Shane and took her hand.

They went out on the dance floor and started dancing to "A Love So Beautiful," and it was.

As they danced Shane said "Roberto, look around you," "I'd rather look at you Shane," he said holding her close and looking into her eyes. "Roberto, the dynasty you always talked about, dreamed about, it's around you, it's a reality. Look my darling, it has actually happened."

Roberto looked up, Terry was laughing and talking with Skye, Maria was talking with Camille and with Mr. and Mrs., Dalinger, Lorenzo was sitting and laughing with Lorena and her mom. Marc Shai sat on Samouil's shoulders, Ramon was in deep conversation with Izzy and his dad. Andre sat with Diego, Enrique and Frederik and all four were talking and laughing. It was truly a day for celebrating.

Yes, Roberto was surrounded by his loved ones, his friends and the dynasty that he yearned for, and best of all, he had Shane in his arms. He looked down at her and smiled.

The music had stopped, their song had come to an end and he just stood there holding her close to him. Suddenly he felt a hand on his arm and looked up. Enrique stood before them smiling.

"Papa, may I have your permission to dance the next dance with the most beautiful woman here?" Roberto stepped aside and smiled as Enrique took his mother's hand and put his arm around her waist, his dark eyes looking at her lovingly and the music had started up again.

"Oh papa, did you hear," he said as Roberto turned to walk away, "we will be having a new neighbor in Monte Cristi. She's moving here tomorrow from Paraguay." He kissed Shane's forehead; "Frederik says next to maman, she is the most beautiful woman he has ever seen. I must meet her papa, her name is Sierra Castille."

Roberto stood still for a moment and frowned. This could mean trouble but maybe he was just jumping to conclusions. But then again, Enrique did say, "a new neighbour," and this sounded disturbingly too close to his family. He refused to let this spoil the evening and looked around. He saw Juan and Isabella

Gomez and joined them and soon it was forgotten as the three of them got into a deep discussion about the politics of the country.

Shane was happy just to be with Enrique as they danced and talked, unaware that someone was watching them closely.

Ramon sat at a nearby table, a drink in his hand and his eyes focused on Shane. He could not deny the feelings inside him. For twenty years he had loved this woman but did not realize how much. He knew it was something that would never stop and this was the only time he felt fear because he knew that he might not be able to control it. He had to be careful but did not know how long he could live like that. The Castanedas were his family whom he loved and respected and he did not want to spoil anything. He would never hurt Camille whom he also loved dearly, but it was different, very different. With Shane it was more than a sexual desire it was a love that he had never experienced before which made him feel whole again and forgiving of all the awful things that had happened to him. She made him believe that the world was not imperfect and that life was worth living. He glanced at Shane again, "dear God" he prayed, "please give me strength to not love her so much." Even he did not know that in the next few months something would happen that would be so alarming and unexpected that it would horrify him and almost cost him his life. It would turn Shane into a survivor to live in shock and mistrust and if revealed, would be devastating to everyone especially Roberto and Camille.

The evening went well and after the music and dancing speeches were given followed by toasts and remembering the last 20 years. There was sadness and also warmth and happiness that could be seen and felt amongst them as they partied throughout the night.

At one point Roberto took Shane's hand and guided her to a window away from the crowd. "I want you all to myself," he said putting his arm around her waist and drawing her to him as she rested her head on his shoulder. They were alone except for each other and this was all they had ever needed. They could hear their song, "A Love So Beautiful," playing softly in the background and Roberto tightened his arm around her, his lips touching the top of her head as they gazed at the magnificent scene before them.

Once again Mother Nature did not disappoint them. She had dressed the sky in black velvet and adorned her with exquisite diamond stars. A strong breeze had come in from the ocean and rustled through the palms while a full moon glowed brilliantly as it looked down at the waters below. It was the same moon that shone through the heavens eons ago, the same stars, the same ocean. It would continue for Roberto and Shane and it would continue for their loved ones. It would put away the yesterdays and bring to them the tomorrows filled with love, laughter and always the tears.

Yes, the tears would be there because nothing stays perfect forever except … Roberto and Shane's love.

978-0-595-44906-4
0-595-44906-9

41-7590888

Printed in the United States
96738LV00003B/70-111/A